# Chasing the Killer

Rebecca Lange

Published by Rebecca Lange, 2023.

CHASING THE KILLER

**First edition. October 31, 2023.**

Copyright © 2023 Rebecca Lange.

ISBN: 978-1957089379

Written by Rebecca Lange.

# Table of Contents

For lovers of diet spice: enough tension to swoon, not enough to scandalize.

First edition. October 31, 2023.

Second edition. December, 2025.

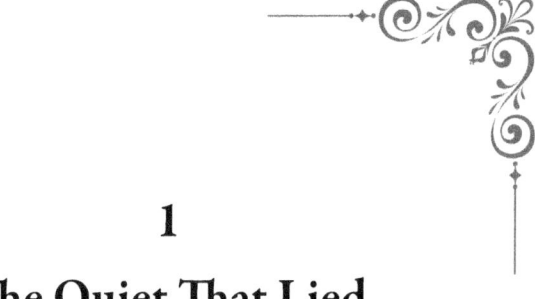

# 1

# The Quiet That Lied

It was quiet when Hope stepped through the vast front doors of the mansion. Too quiet. Not the gentle hush of a late evening nor the serene stillness of a well-ordered home. This was a hollow, unnatural silence that pressed against her ears. Where were the servants?

She knew her father was away at a medical convention, preparing to present the new treatment and several medications he had created. Her grandmother had accompanied him, of course. But the rest of the household? The staff? The people who kept the estate breathing and moving? They would never abandon their posts, not all at once, not without reason.

Her instincts had not lied to her. A sense of dread had been clawing at her all evening, and now it wrapped itself fully around her. Something was wrong. Terribly wrong. A cold, crawling sensation climbed her spine, as though the air itself carried malice.

Hope shivered and stepped farther inside, groping along the wall for a lamp. Why in the world had they left the entrance hall in complete darkness? The servants always lit the sconces before dusk. Even if the family was away, they maintained them, for safety, for propriety, for normalcy. But nothing felt normal tonight.

Her thoughts drifted back to the ball she had fled only an hour before. To Eric. To the look of irritation sharpening his features when she tried to explain her unease. She was growing tired—bone-tired—of his controlling nature. Lately, it seemed to tighten around her like a vise. Every decision questioned, every instinct dismissed.

She had confided in him quietly, telling him of the overwhelming feeling that something dreadful was about to happen, that she had to return home. Instead of concern, he had scolded her.

He reminded her, loudly, that the ball was essential to his budding career as a lawyer, that influential families were in attendance, and that as his fiancée, her duty was to remain at his side.

Hope had lifted her chin and insisted she would follow her intuition. She would leave.

And he, his voice edged with a coldness she was coming to recognize far too often, had informed her he would not allow it.

Hope scoffed under her breath, the memory still burning hot in her chest. Eric had practically caged her at the ball. Every time she tried to excuse herself, he dragged her into yet another conversation with his clients or fellow lawyers, discussions that had nothing to do with her and in which she had no interest whatsoever. He didn't even glance at her to see if she wished to be included. She was simply... an accessory. A prop on his arm.

And her arm, he kept a firm grip on it. His fingers curled possessively around her elbow, tightening whenever she shifted, making it impossible for her to slip away without causing a scene. To anyone watching, it might have seemed gentlemanly. To her, it felt like a restraint.

As the night dragged on, that dreadful feeling inside her swelled until it was almost suffocating. Her pulse quickened. Her skin prickled. She had to get home. Now. At last, Hope mustered a polite smile and murmured something about needing to use the washroom.

Eric had finally released her arm, but not without a stern warning not to be long. The moment she rounded the corner and disappeared from view, she sprinted. She locked the washroom door behind her, shoved open the window, and climbed out into the crisp night air. Her dress snagged on the sill, ripping in several places as she tumbled onto the grass below. Dirt smeared across the delicate fabric, but she hardly noticed. None of it mattered. All she cared about was getting home. Getting there before whatever was coming arrived first.

Hope shook her head now, fury mingling with unease. She was utterly appalled by Eric's behavior, by the entitlement in his voice, the way he had spoken to her as though she were a stubborn child rather than his future wife. Who did he think he was? He did not own her. He never would.

After rummaging through several drawers in the old walnut cabinet, an heirloom that had belonged to her father's grandfather, Hope finally found a half-empty box of matches.

Her hands trembled as she struck one against the side. The flame flared to life, wavering in the draft of the silent hall. She lit the kerosene lamp on the table beside the cabinet, and warm light spilled outward, pushing back only a fraction of the oppressive darkness.

The faint ticking of the grandfather clock echoed through the entrance hall, each second piercing the quiet like a warning. Beyond that... nothing. No footsteps. No voices. Not even the distant clatter of cookware from the kitchen. The silence felt wrong, unnatural. Almost hostile.

"Mama?" Hope called, her voice tentative, swallowed quickly by the cavernous space. She stepped farther in, shrugging off her coat. She had just lifted it toward the hook when a faint sound drifted to her ears. A moan. A whisper. Closer than she expected.

Hope snapped her head up, lifting the lamp higher. Shadows gathered thickly beneath the staircase, and one seemed unnervingly still. She moved toward it quickly, her pulse pounding in her ears. The moment the lamplight hit the figure on the floor, Hope's breath ripped out in a horrified gasp. Her mother lay crumpled on the polished wood, blood streaking from the corner of her mouth. Her eyes were closed, her complexion ghostly pale. Only the faint, agonized moans slipping from her lips proved she was still alive.

"Mama!" Hope dropped to her knees beside her, setting the lamp carefully on the floor so she could take her mother's cold, trembling hand. Tears burned her eyes, but she forced them back. Her mother needed clarity, strength, not hysteria.

"Mama, what happened? Where are all the servants?"

Her mother's eyelids fluttered. Speaking was clearly painful, every breath shallow, every word a battle.

"Hope... what made you come home so early?" she whispered.

"I—I had a feeling. Something pressed me to come home. I couldn't stay at the ball."

But as Hope looked at her mother's wounded body, she felt the blood drain from her face. The truth struck her with brutal clarity. Her mother was dying. Blood wasn't just at her lips. It pooled beneath her back, dark and spreading. Her mother drew in a ragged breath.

"Someone... came into the house. I was... shot. Three times. In the back. I think I fell over the banister." Her gaze drifted toward the stairs before unfocusing again. "I was unconscious... I don't know how long."

Hope pressed a trembling hand to her mouth. Panic surged in her chest like a tidal wave, but she forced herself to breathe slowly. Her mother needed calm. She needed hope, even if Hope herself felt none.

"Who did this? Where are the servants?" she asked.

"I don't know," her mother breathed, barely audible.

"I need to fetch Doc Baker. He'll know what to do." Hope started to rise, but her mother's grip tightened weakly around her hand.

"No. Don't leave me," she gasped, then broke into a violent, choking cough. Blood splattered across her sleeve.

Hope stared in horror. "Mama... oh, Mama..."

Her mother's breathing was uneven now, every inhale a desperate grasp for air. Hope glanced around helplessly, as though the walls might answer her or offer aid. When she finally found her voice again, it came out thin and cracking.

"Did... did the intruder take anything?"

Her mother nodded faintly. "I think so. He went into my study. Took something from the desk. My diary... I had it with me when I fell. When I woke... it was gone."

Hope swallowed hard. "How do you know he entered the study?"

"When I came to... I saw his shadow. He was still there. He didn't just flee. He was searching for something. Something important." She coughed again, weaker this time, blood staining her lips. Hope squeezed her mother's hand, trying not to break as she watched her strength fade with each passing breath.

When the coughing fit finally subsided, her mother's eyes found hers, glazed, yet filled with fierce love.

"I love you, Hope," she murmured. "Always listen to your heart. Don't let anyone... control you."

Hope's brow furrowed. "Who would try to control me?" The fear in her voice trembled like a string pulled too taut. Her mother swallowed with difficulty.

"You'll find answers... when you find my diary. I need you to—" But the sentence broke off. Her mother's head slipped to the side. Her chest stilled.

Hope froze. For one suspended moment, her mind refused to understand. Refused to accept. Then grief slammed into her, sharp enough to steal her breath. A raw, broken sob tore from her throat as she folded over her mother's still body, clutching her tightly.

"I love you, Mom," she cried, gasping between sobs. "Please... please don't leave me..." Her heart felt as though it were shattering, piece by piece, under the weight of loss. So consumed was she by grief that she didn't hear the door open. Didn't hear it close. Didn't hear the footsteps approaching. But she felt the hand, firm, steady, rest on her shoulder.

"Hope," Doctor Baker said gently, his voice threaded with sorrow, "let me take a look at your mother."

Hope shook her head, tears streaming down her face.

"It's too late," she whispered hoarsely. "Mama is dead."

The physician gently eased Hope aside so he could tend to the lifeless form on the floor. Hope allowed it, though her fingers clung to her mother's gown for a moment before she released it. Tears still streamed down her cheeks, blurring her vision, until movement to her right caught her eye. *Mia.* Her young maid stood trembling near the base of the stairs, her hands pressed to her mouth as silent sobs shook her shoulders. In the lamplight, her face was blotched red, her eyes wide with horror.

"Mia," Hope whispered, reaching out. The maid hurried to her, falling to her knees beside her mistress. Hope took the girl's hand, squeezing it tightly. "Where is everyone? Did you see what happened?"

Mia shook her head, tears spilling freely.

"No, miss. I—I didn't see it happen." Her voice broke as she brushed at her cheeks with her sleeve. "Mr. Pratt dismissed most of the staff for today and tomorrow, told them to go home and spend the time with their families. Those of us without family close by were ordered to remain in the servants' quarters. He said Mrs. Spencer wished to be left alone, on account of some... bad news she'd received. And that Master Spencer himself had given instructions she was not to be disturbed."

She inhaled shakily, though her attempt to control her sobs failed. Hope felt her grief twist with unease. Mia's voice dropped to a frightened whisper.

"I was going to obey, but then I heard gunshots. Loud ones. From downstairs. I asked Mr. Pratt if I could go see if Mrs. Spencer was all right, but he told me not to worry. He said the shots had come from outside." She shook her head violently. "I knew that wasn't true. I knew they came from inside the house."

Hope's breath hitched, her fingers tightening around Mia's.

"When I insisted," Mia continued, "Mr. Pratt said he would check himself. But..." She swallowed hard. "But I never saw him leave the servant quarters. Not once."

A chill slid down Hope's spine.

"My heart wouldn't let me sit still," Mia whispered. "So, I disobeyed. I crept out. And that's when I found your mother... l-like this." A sob tore through her. "I ran as fast as I could to fetch Doc Baker. I'm so sorry, Miss Hope. I'm so sorry I was too late!" She broke completely then, collapsing against Hope in wracking sobs.

Hope, though drowning in her own grief, wrapped her arms around the young maid and held her firmly. She stroked Mia's hair, soothing her as best she could, even as her own tears continued to fall.

"You did your best, Mia," she whispered, her voice raw but steady. "None of this is your fault. My mother's death is not on you." She pulled the trembling girl tighter against her. "Thank you for trying to save her. Thank you for going for help. You were brave, braver than you know."

Mia cried harder, clinging to her, and Hope closed her eyes, fiercely holding on to the one small piece of humanity left in the room.

Doc Baker gave Hope's shoulder a gentle squeeze before turning to Mia.

"Fetch a blanket," he said quietly. "We need to cover her."

Mia nodded through her tears and hurried off, her footsteps echoing through the hollow silence of the house. Hope remained where she was, sinking onto the bottom step of the staircase as though her legs could no longer hold her. She folded her hands in her lap, but they trembled uncontrollably. Tears still streamed down her cheeks, dripping onto her torn dress without her noticing. None of what Mia had said made sense.

*Bad news?* What bad news could her mother possibly have received that would require total isolation? Had a relative passed away? Had something happened at her father's convention? No, her mother would have told her. She always told her. And why would her father instruct the butler, of all people, to keep everyone away from her mother? That wasn't how their household worked. Her father trusted the staff implicitly. He never issued odd, overly strict commands like that. The questions swirled in Hope's mind, heavy and suffocating.

*Why had Mr. Pratt insisted the gunshots came from outside? Why had he refused to let Mia check on her mother? Why claim he would investigate, only to remain in the servant quarters the entire time?* Hope pressed a hand to her mouth. The bitter taste of fear filled her lungs. Her mother was dead. Her gentle, loving, fiercely intelligent mother, gone. Shot in the back. Attacked from behind by a coward.

Hope's breath hitched as another wave of grief crashed over her, stealing what little strength she had left. She wrapped her arms around herself, rocking slightly, as though it might ease the pain splitting her chest.

Mia returned, clutching a folded blanket to her chest, her shoulders shaking. She set the lantern aside and handed the blanket to Doc Baker. The physician lifted it with solemn care, then draped it over Hope's mother, covering her still form from the world. Hope swallowed a sob at the sight.

"Mia," Doc Baker said gently, "find some of the male servants. I need them to help transport Mrs. Spencer's body to my clinic as soon as possible. We must examine her properly." His voice was steady, but grief lingered at the edges. Mia nodded, wiping her cheeks with her sleeve before hurrying out again.

Hope watched her go, then stared at the still, blanketed shape on the floor, her mother's shape, and felt something shift deep inside her. Grief, yes. But something else. Something sharper. Something awakening.

The physician had just gathered his bag and was preparing to leave when the front door opened again. Cold air swept into the hall, and Hope's father stepped inside, her grandmother close behind him. Their footsteps faltered as they took in the scene, the lamplight, the physician, the blanket-covered body on the floor. Confusion flickered across their features. Yet not a trace of alarm.

Not a flicker of fear. Not even grief.

"What is going on here?" Winston Spencer demanded, his voice loud, impatient, almost annoyed. Doc Baker stepped forward at once.

"Mr. Spencer... your wife has passed away. I am deeply sorry."

Hope didn't look at her father. She couldn't. She couldn't bear to see how little the news would likely affect him. Instead, she turned when she heard brisk footsteps approaching. Her grandmother crossed the room with purpose and stopped directly in front of her.

"Hope Georgiana Spencer," the older woman snapped, her voice sharp as ice. "Look at your dress. Absolutely ruined. Why can't you show more care for the fine things you are given?"

Doc Baker stared at her grandmother in disbelief. Hope rose slowly, the movement stiff and controlled. Her face was expressionless, her eyes hollow. She was used to this coldness, this relentless criticism, but the physician felt the weight of it like a blow. No warmth. No sympathy. Not even a question about her welfare.

"Really, Grandmother?" Hope asked quietly, though her voice trembled with restrained fury. "That is the first thing you choose to notice?" She could feel old lessons clawing at her, be polite, be meek, do not raise your voice. But something inside her cracked. Her mother's blood still stained her hands. Her mother's body still lay on the cold tile floor. She drew a long, steadying breath.

"These stains," she said, lifting her dress slightly, "are from my mother's blood. She was murdered tonight."

Her grandmother scoffed. "There are more than stains, Hope. You tore several holes in it. And truly, even if tragedy had not struck, you always manage to ruin your beautiful dresses. Your father spends a fortune on you, and this is how you show gratitude? I am ashamed—"

"Yes, I know, Grandmother," Hope cut in sharply, no longer able to hold back. "You are ashamed of me. You always have been. But while you lecture me about fabric, your daughter-in-law's body is lying right there." She pointed to the blanket-covered form on the floor. "Does that matter to you at all?" Her heart pounded wildly. She could hardly breathe. Still, the words poured out, years of hurt, disappointment, and suffocated emotion finally breaking free.

"I'm aware you never cared for Mama or for me," Hope continued, her voice trembling with pain, "and that you pride yourself on being cold and unimpressed by tragedy. But even someone like you should have the decency to show a shred of compassion tonight." She met her grandmother's eyes, bright with anger, grief, and betrayal. The older woman opened her mouth to retort, but Winston stepped between them.

"Let's everyone calm down," he said, raising a hand. "Hope has just experienced something... traumatic. Her emotions are understandably heightened."

"That does not excuse rudeness," his mother snapped. "Nor destroying an expensive gown."

Doc Baker exhaled slowly, fighting the urge to speak up. He had not interacted with the Spencers often, but tonight the truth settled heavily in his chest: there was no warmth in this home. No tenderness. Hope, he realized, had just lost the only person who had loved her without condition. And her father still had not even looked at her.

"Mother, it is just a dress," Winston barked, irritation finally flaring. His sharp tone startled his mother enough that she turned in a huff and stormed up the stairs.

At that moment, the butler and several servants emerged. They moved quietly, mechanically, lifting the covered body and carrying it toward the door. They passed Hope without so much as a glance, no word of comfort, no expression of sympathy. She stood frozen, unable to move, unable to breathe.

Doc Baker watched this with a tightening jaw. Then he made a decision. Once the servants had stepped outside, he crossed the room to Hope. Without saying a word, he pulled the trembling young woman into his arms. She stiffened in surprise, her hands hovering awkwardly at her sides. Kindness was so foreign here, she scarcely knew how to respond.

After a heartbeat, she leaned into him, slowly at first, then fully, as grief overwhelmed her. Soft, broken sobs shook her slender frame. Doc Baker held her firmly, one hand at her back, offering the comfort she should have received from her own family.

"You're not alone, Hope," he murmured quietly. "Not as long as I'm here." And for the first time that night, Hope allowed herself to believe it.

Hope did not speak another word to her grandmother or her father after Doc Baker departed. She could not. Grief clogged her throat, fury churned beneath her ribs, and disappointment pressed against her chest like a crushing weight. Instead, she slipped away unnoticed, though *unnoticed* hardly applied in a household where no one bothered to look at her, and made her way up the sweeping staircase to her room.

Her footsteps felt heavy, each one echoing in the hollow silence of the mansion. A home that should have been filled with frantic concern remained eerily calm, as though nothing of consequence had happened. As though death were simply another inconvenience to be tidied up by morning. She closed the door behind her and leaned against it, exhaling shakily. Tears burned behind her eyes, but she was too numb to release them.

She knew her father's side of the family lacked warmth. She had grown up under their rigid expectations and clipped tones. But her grandmother's reaction tonight had been frigid even by Spencer standards. It was as if her mother's death held no significance whatsoever, as if her daughter-in-law had been nothing more than a replaceable inconvenience.

*Is this what life and death mean to them? Is this the value of a human life in the Spencer household?* A cold shiver ran down Hope's spine. She wished, more than ever, that she knew her mother's family, anyone who could anchor her, who could tell her who her mother truly was before she had become Mrs. Spencer. But she had no names. No histories. Not even a place to begin. Only her father's single, unyielding narrative: *They abandoned her. They disowned her the moment she married me. That is all you need to know.*

Hope had been ten years old when he had first told her that, eight years ago now. It had been one of the few times she had dared to ask about her mother's childhood, about the people who had raised her. But the subject had been shut down instantly. Brutally. No one in the household was permitted to speak of the family her mother came from. The servants were instructed to remain silent. Even her mother had seemed afraid to defy her husband on the matter.

Hope remembered the times she had tried to ask again. Quiet questions. Whispers of curiosity. Small pieces of longing she had hoped her mother might answer. Her mother had tried, tried to speak, tried to share, but the moment her father discovered their conversations, his fury had been swift and punishing. For days afterward, Hope had been kept separate from her mother, forbidden to even approach her. Kept away as though she were a danger, not a daughter searching for truth.

The memory ached now, throbbing like a bruise reopening.

Hope sank onto the edge of her bed, her hands buried in the torn, bloodstained fabric of her gown. Her heart felt as though it were splitting between fresh grief and old wounds.

*What else had her father kept from her? And why?* Tonight, everything she had once accepted as truth began to unravel, and Hope realized that her mother's death might be only the beginning of a much darker mystery.

Hope pushed herself up from the bed and crossed the room in slow, deliberate steps. She stopped at the window, resting her hand against the cold glass as she stared into the moonlit darkness outside.

*Don't let anyone control you.* Her mother's final words rang through her mind with startling clarity, sharper now than when they had been spoken through blood and fading breath. Hope inhaled sharply, her eyes widening as realization dawned. Was that the reason her mother had said those words? Had they been far more than a gentle reminder, had they been a warning? Had her father controlled her mother the same way he controlled everyone else? Had he used the one thing her mother cherished most, their bond, Hope's love, to bend her to his will?

Memories flickered through Hope's mind like shards of broken glass. Times when her mother had tried to speak about her past. Times when her father had intervened. Times when Hope had been kept away for days afterward, her mother's eyes hollow with guilt and fear. Had that been punishment? Manipulation? Or something far worse? The thought turned her stomach, leaving her cold and breathless.

She pressed her forehead to the glass and closed her eyes for a moment, trying to steady her racing pulse. She wanted, desperately, to follow that dark trail of thoughts, to examine every painful possibility until she uncovered the truth. But speculation could only take her so far. Guessing would solve nothing. And with her mother gone, the last thing she needed was to drown in half-formed fears. She needed answers. Real answers. Answers that would break through the lies that had wrapped themselves around her life for years. And she would find them. No matter what it cost her.

# 2
# A Daughter's Oath

Hope was exhausted, utterly drained in body and spirit. She had attempted to fall asleep more times than she could count, but every time her eyes closed, images from the night before flashed behind them, her mother's blood, her grandmother's coldness, her father's indifference, Mia's terror. Rest was impossible. Her thoughts circled endlessly, tightening around her chest like a vise. Finally, with a shaky exhale, she pushed the blankets aside.

*Maybe fresh air will help.* Anything to clear her mind, even for a moment. She reached for her coat draped over the chair beside her vanity, but something beyond the window caught her eye, a flicker of motion. Hoofbeats muffled by the damp morning earth. Hope stepped closer.

A rider approached the estate, passing through the tall wrought-iron gate. The horse was a sheriff's mount. She recognized the distinct saddle and the gleaming badge pinned to the man's coat even from a distance. Her pulse quickened. The sheriff. He was here. Which meant he had come to speak with her father about her mother's murder. Which meant he might already have questions, or answers. Answers Hope needed more desperately than air.

Her heart pounding, she spun away from the window. Fresh air forgotten. Grief forgotten. Fear forgotten. Only one thought remained: *I must hear what they say.*

She tore open her bedroom door, her skirts sweeping behind her as she flew down the hallway. The mansion's silence felt heavier this morning, almost suffocating, but she didn't let herself slow. She descended the staircase two steps at a time, gripping the banister to steady herself as she rounded the corner. Her father's study door was just ahead, closed, as always, when things were not meant for her ears. But today, she refused to let that stop her. Hope lifted her chin, braced herself, and hurried toward the door, determined to get answers. No matter what waited on the other side.

"Hope, what are you doing here?" her father demanded the moment she opened the study door. Irritation creased his brow, as though she were an inconvenience rather than a grieving daughter. She ignored him entirely.

"Sheriff Craig," Hope said, stepping fully into the room, "do you bring any news? Have you found any evidence, anything at all, that will help us solve my mother's murder?" She spoke quickly, breathlessly, her whole body leaning toward him with desperate expectation. But the sheriff flicked a brief glance toward her father before answering.

"We can't yet say whether she was murdered," he replied carefully.

Hope stared at him, stunned into silence. Had he truly said that? Even Winston Spencer shook his head at such an absurd statement.

"You're joking, right?" Hope snapped, shock igniting instantly into anger. "She was shot in the back three times. In what world is that *not* murder? You're not about to suggest she died of natural causes, are you?" She took a breath, attempting to steady the tremor in her voice, but the fury boiling inside her would not be contained.

"Stop treating us like fools and start doing your job," she continued sharply. "Unless, of course, you'd prefer the entire town to know you're incompetent at even the simplest tasks. Or are you perhaps a coward?"

"Hope!" her father barked, his tone sharp with warning. He shot her a reproachful look, more performative than sincere. She could tell he agreed with her but wanted to preserve appearances.

Hope returned her gaze to the sheriff. His face had reddened, jaw tight, clearly fighting the urge to retort. But Winston Spencer was not a man he dared offend.

"Now," Hope pressed, "what evidence have you found so far?"

Sheriff Craig exhaled, bracing himself. "I'm afraid there is no helpful evidence, Miss Spencer. Whoever planned this knew exactly what he was doing. He left nothing behind."

Hope narrowed her eyes. "So, what's the plan, then? What will you do about it?"

"I've sent telegrams to all surrounding towns and districts," he replied. "Sheriffs have been instructed to keep an eye out for a fugitive. But..." His shoulders lifted slightly. "We know nothing about him. There isn't much they can do."

Hope stared at him in disbelief. "That's it? Have you even checked the house? My mother's room? The grounds? Did you consider the possibility that the killer dropped something, anything?"

The sheriff glared at her. "I know how to do my job," he snapped. "And I'm telling you—we have nothing to go on. Whoever killed your mother was experienced. Besides the telegrams, there isn't anything else we can do."

Hope's breath caught. "You're not going out there to find him? To look for him?"

"It would be a waste of time," he said through gritted teeth. Perhaps he meant to calm her. Instead, her outrage detonated.

"A waste of time?" she shouted, slamming her palm onto her father's desk. "My mother was murdered in cold blood by a coward who shot her in the back, and you can't be bothered to investigate? You're just going to let him walk free?"

"Hope," her father snapped, irritation sharpening his voice. "Watch your tone. Remember your manners. You're becoming hysterical."

She scoffed. "My mother was killed last night, Father, and the sheriff just admitted he can't be bothered to pursue her murderer, and you expect me to be calm? I believe I have every right to be hysterical."

"That's not what he said," Winston replied dismissively.

"Yes, it is," she shot back. "Calling it a 'waste of time' means exactly that."

"There is nothing we can do," he insisted.

"Of course there is!" she countered. "If the sheriff won't do his job, hire someone else. Contact the marshal headquarters. Have them investigate."

"They won't solve it either."

Her eyes flashed. "So, you don't care either?"

"I care," her father snapped. "But there is nothing we can do."

"I don't believe that," Hope said, her voice trembling with restrained fury. She looked ready to strangle both men with her bare hands.

"Listen," Winston said, attempting to regain control, "let's worry about the investigation after the funeral tomorrow."

Hope gasped. "Tomorrow? Already? Why the rush? Why is no one willing to investigate and get answers?"

"I have a business trip the day after tomorrow," he said simply. "I'll be gone several days. It's best to handle the funeral before I leave."

Hope bit her lip hard and shook her head slowly. Her father had never been close to her, but this, this was beyond anything she could endure. She stepped closer, her voice shaking with emotion.

"Father, we may not have much of a relationship, but I loved my mother. She was the only person in this house who cared for me. You are a wealthy man. It would take little effort for you to ensure this is thoroughly investigated." Her blue eyes locked onto his. "I'm asking you, begging you, to try."

Before he could respond, a knock sounded at the door. Eric Westerwald stepped inside, his presence immediately tightening Hope's jaw. She spared him only a fleeting glance before returning her focus to her father.

Winston sighed. "I'm sorry, Hope, but my business is in a difficult place right now. I don't have extra money for private investigators or U.S. marshals."

Hope's voice dropped dangerously low. "Your business is more important than your murdered wife?"

"That isn't fair," Eric snapped, stepping forward as though assuming authority. His disapproving glare was sharp. "Your father is grieving in his own way."

"Is he?" Hope asked, coldly. "Do you call it grieving when a man prioritizes profit over justice for the woman he supposedly loved?"

"That is enough," Eric clipped, his tone scolding, patronizing. "You're being disrespectful."

Hope let out a humorless laugh. "How did I not see it? I'm surrounded by heartless men. Not one of you has asked how I'm doing. Not one of you has offered comfort. I want answers, and if none of you will do what needs to be done, then I will investigate."

"Don't be ridiculous," Eric scoffed. "You're making a fool of yourself. You're a woman with no experience. If the sheriff can't solve this, you certainly won't."

"I beg to differ," Hope said icily. "Simply by making an effort, I'm already doing more than the sheriff."

"I won't allow it," Eric snapped. Hope froze. Her voice turned to steel.

"Excuse me?"

"I said I won't allow it," he repeated loudly. "You are my fiancée and will be my wife soon. I expect perfect obedience from my wife. You answer to me. You're not of age yet, and you depend on me financially. I forbid you from doing something so foolish. My reputation is at stake, and I will not have my future wife gallivanting around playing sheriff."

Hope's expression didn't waver. Her voice cut through the room like a blade.

"You know what, Eric? You and I are done." She tore the engagement ring from her finger and threw it at his feet. "I will not be controlled by you, or anyone else. You expect perfect obedience? Good luck finding someone willing to give you that. I never will."

Eric stared at her, stunned. Outrage quickly replaced shock.

"I don't accept this. We are still engaged."

Hope scoffed. "I don't care what you accept. We're done. You care only about your reputation, your image, and my father's wealth. You parade me around like a trophy, but I mean nothing to you. You're selfish, arrogant, and now you think you can control me? Absolutely not."

Her father shot to his feet. "Hope, calm yourself. Your behavior is outrageous. I won't have you speaking to your fiancé like that. If you cannot control your temper, I will send you to a boarding school where obedience is drilled into you."

Her breath caught, but he wasn't finished.

"You will not play investigator. I forbid it. This is not how we raised you. Yes, you're hurting, but that does not give you the right to be disrespectful. Remember who you're talking to. I intend for you to inherit everything, but only if you are married. I chose Eric as your husband. You will marry him. You do not get a say."

Hope's voice was low, trembling. "I don't get a say in who I marry?"

"That is correct," her father said coldly. "You will accept the decisions made for you."

*Don't let anyone control you.* Her mother's dying words surged back like a storm. Hope drew a slow breath, her mind racing. *Choose your battles, Hope,* her mother had often said. *Don't push him too far.* But she also knew she couldn't stay silent. Not now. Not ever. At last, Hope raised her head. Her voice was calm, eerily calm.

"I don't want anything from you, Father. Not your money. Not the mansion. None of it. Give it to your other children." She cast a cold, sweeping glance at all three men. "I'm done." And with that, she turned and strode out of the room, slamming the door behind her.

Eric took a step to follow, but Winston grabbed his arm.

"She's just upset," he muttered. "Deeply saddened by her mother's passing. That's all. She'll calm down. She'll come around. She always does. She would never disobey us on purpose."

But neither man noticed the small, cold truth hanging in the air: Hope Spencer had just reached her breaking point. And she was never coming back from it.

Hope stormed into her bedroom and slammed the door behind her with enough force to rattle the hinges. She barely made it three steps before her strength gave out. She collapsed onto the bed, burying her face in the coverlet as a fresh wave of tears surged, hot, furious, blinding. Tears of rage. Tears of grief. Tears for everything she had just endured. Her whole body trembled. Every word spoken in that study replayed in her mind, her father's cold indifference, the sheriff's dismissive shrug, Eric's arrogant demands. Their voices blended into a single, suffocating reminder of just how alone she was now.

Her mother had been the only person who truly saw her, who loved her without conditions or expectations. And now she was gone. A sob escaped Hope's throat, muffled against the bed linens. She squeezed her eyes shut, fists clenching so tightly her nails bit into her palms.

"I will find out who did this," she whispered hoarsely. "I will find him. And whoever is behind it, I will uncover the truth." She pushed herself upright, her breath shaky but her resolve hardening with every word. "I'm going to get justice for you, Mama. I swear it."

The room was quiet, the silence almost reverent, as though even the walls were listening. Hope wiped her tears and inhaled slowly, letting the fire inside her settle into something sharper. Clearer.

A blade instead of a flame. She didn't trust her father—not anymore. Not after everything she had seen and heard. Not after years of secrets and silence. A man who rushed a funeral, refused an investigation, and placed business above his wife's death was capable of far more than neglect. No, she didn't think he was innocent. But suspicion was not enough. She needed proof. Real, undeniable proof.

Hope stood from the bed, her chin lifting with new purpose. She would not be silenced. She would not be controlled. She would not give up, not until every lie was exposed. And she knew exactly where she would start. *Her mother's diary.*

The funeral was agonizing for Hope. She stood beside her mother's casket, feeling as though the world had narrowed, to a single point of pain in her chest. Only two people, Doc Baker and Reverend Shaw, showed her any genuine compassion. They remained close by, offering quiet words, steady hands, and the kind of presence that made breathing a little easier. Everyone else had come out of obligation, not love.

Her father stood stiffly near the front, his expression unreadable, as if he were attending a business meeting rather than burying his wife. Her grandmother remained as frosty as ever, lips pursed in disapproval, behaving more like she had been inconvenienced, than bereaved. A few extended relatives drifted about, murmuring polite phrases, but none of them looked truly saddened. None had tears in their eyes. None reached for Hope or asked how she was bearing such a crushing loss. And not one of her stepsiblings bothered to attend at all.

Hope had felt lonely before, but this was something darker. Something heavier. For the first time, loneliness felt like hopelessness, like a shadow settling inside her ribs. Her mother had been her best friend. Her safe place. Her fiercest protector. Georgiana Faith Spencer had always seemed so gentle, so composed, so graceful, but when it came to Hope, she had been a lioness. A shield. A source of warmth in a house built of ice. And now she was gone.

Hope stood apart from her family throughout the service. She did not cling to her father's side. She did not seek her grandmother's approval. She avoided the relatives who offered stiff, mechanical condolences. And when the funeral luncheon began, she refused to attend altogether.

She had no desire to sit in a room filled with false sympathy and insincere politeness. She knew the truth. She was the only one who genuinely mourned her mother.

Her grandmother was still offended by the confrontation two nights earlier, and her father avoided looking at her unless absolutely necessary. His indifference was a fresh wound layered atop the old ones.

Then there was her 'fiancé'. Eric, who now tried to soften his voice, offer gentle touches, and pretend he was the attentive suitor he had once been, back when he wanted to impress her, back when she believed he was kind. But Hope saw through it now. She recognized the calculated sweetness, the forced tenderness meant to coax her back into compliance. She did not fall for it. Not anymore. Not ever again.

She kept her distance from all of them, choosing instead to sit beside her mother's grave long after the others had left, letting the silence wrap around her. Because in that silence, she felt closer to her mother than she had during the entire funeral. And in that silence, one truth returned with growing force: She would get justice. She would uncover the truth. She would not let her mother's death be forgotten or dismissed. Not while she still had breath.

Her father left for his business trip the following day. Hope didn't bother to see him off, let alone wish him farewell. He walked past her room without a word, without a glance, only the sound of his polished boots echoing down the hall and the slam of the front door marking his departure.

Her grandmother left shortly after. She announced, rather loudly, that she would be spending several weeks visiting one of Hope's uncles. She packed hurriedly, made no attempt to check on Hope, and swept out of the house with her usual frostbitten dignity. Hope doubted she would spare a single thought for her granddaughter.

Hope watched both departures from the upstairs landing, unseen and unheard. And for once... she didn't mind. In fact, she preferred it. Her father and grandmother had a way of making the mansion colder simply by existing in it. Their presence amplified her loneliness, made every room feel heavier, every breath more hollow. When they were home, she felt like a stranger living under her own roof, tiptoeing around their indifference and expectations.

When they were gone, the silence felt different. Still painful. Still echoing with grief. But not suffocating. Not oppressive. Not laced with disapproval and scrutiny. Hope stood in the empty hallway, listening as the last carriage wheels faded into the distance. For the first time since her mother's death, she exhaled without feeling as though her chest might crack open.

Yes, she was alone. But she had always been alone with them here. Now, at least, she could think. She could breathe. She could begin to plan. And she would finally have the space to chase the answers everyone else was determined to bury.

It was early afternoon when Hope finally gathered the courage, and determination, to begin searching the house. The oppressive stillness of the mansion wrapped around her like a warning, but she pushed it aside. She was certain now that Sheriff Craig had lied. He had not looked for evidence. He had not examined the scene. He had not even cared. So, she would.

Hope moved slowly along the upstairs banister, her fingers brushing the polished wood as she scanned every inch for anything out of place. A smudge. A misplaced object. A sign of struggle, anything. Her heart thudded heavily in her chest with each step. She descended the stairs and approached the spot where she had found her mother. The memory hit her like a punch to the stomach, but she forced herself to look closely at the floorboards, the walls, the banister. Nothing obvious remained.

Holding her breath, she made her way to her mother's study next. The room smelled faintly of lavender and old parchment, a scent she had always associated with comfort and conversation. Now it felt haunted. Hope circled the study multiple times, checking beneath furniture, behind curtains, and along the edges of the rug. It wasn't until her third inspection that something caught her eye. A sliver of white between the desk and the closet.

Hope dropped to her knees and reached for it. The paper was wedged tightly, but after a moment of tugging, she managed to free it. She unfolded it and felt her stomach flip. A ferry ticket.

San Francisco → Oakland. She stared at it in disbelief. If the killer had dropped this, then he had a plan. A clear plan. And he was heading toward the mainland. But for what purpose? Where would he go next?

Hope tucked the ticket into the hidden pocket of her dress and resumed her search. She walked toward the windows, examining the frames and locks, then paused to look outside. A few birds hopped across the garden path, pecking at the ground. Then she saw it. Another slip of paper, lodged in a small bush directly below the main window. Her pulse spiked.

She hurried downstairs, nearly tripping over her skirts in her haste. The wind had begun to pick up, rustling the leaves as she dashed across the porch. She reached the bush just in time to snatch the paper before the wind could carry it away. Hope unfolded it with trembling fingers. A letter, short, hastily penned, addressed to someone named *Mr. Anthony Whitmer*. Her breath caught as she read:

Anthony,

*I booked the ferry for you. Once you are in Oakland, you will take the train to Sacramento and travel from there to Winnemucca, Elko, and several other stops until you reach Cheyenne in Wyoming. Cheyenne is only a small town, but there is another woman who has knowledge of our plans, and we need to take care of her as soon as possible.*

*Meet me at the saloon in Elko, so we can discuss your next assignment in more detail.*

Lester

Hope's heart pounded so hard she thought it might burst. Another woman. Knowledge of their plans. *Assignment.* Murder. Her mother's death was not an isolated crime. It was part of something much, much bigger. And Hope had just uncovered the first thread.

*Lester.* Hope stared at the name written at the bottom of the letter, her mind racing. Who was Lester? And more importantly, who was the woman they intended to murder next? A cold shiver ran down her spine. Hope's breath hitched, but only for a moment. Something inside her hardened. Right then, right there, she made up her mind. She would go after her mother's killer herself.

She knew the risk. She knew the danger. But she also knew that no one else would lift a finger. Her father wouldn't. The sheriff refused. Eric wouldn't even allow her to leave the house, let alone travel alone. Hope clenched the letter tighter in her fist. If justice was going to happen, she would have to pursue it.

She hurried back into the house, climbed the stairs two at a time, and slipped into her room. With a trembling but determined hand, she spread the ticket and the letter across her writing desk and reached for paper and ink. She began making a list, items she would need, disguises she would use, money she had to gather, and the route she would follow.

Once the list was complete, she stood before her wardrobe and pulled open the doors. A cascade of elegant, expensive dresses stared back at her, silk and taffeta, lace and ribbon, things she had never asked for, never wanted. She touched one with the tip of her fingers, then exhaled sharply. They would all go.

She rang for her maid. When Mia appeared, Hope instructed her to pack nearly all the fine gowns worn only once—and return them to the dressmaker. Along with the dresses, Hope wrote a firmly worded letter requesting full reimbursement in cash. Mia blinked at the request but obediently gathered the clothing, her arms full of silk and satin as she left to deliver the parcels.

The moment the girl was gone, Hope darted into the hallway and slipped into her half-brothers' old rooms. Dust coated most surfaces. Neither boy had visited in years. She rummaged through their closets, searching for trousers, shirts, jackets, anything rugged or plain enough to disguise her. If she traveled as herself, the killer, or anyone sent to watch her, would spot her easily. If she traveled as a young man, she might pass unnoticed.

Hope stuffed several articles of clothing into her carpet bag, choosing garments that could be layered, altered, or worn for weeks on end. She packed as lightly as she dared, but with enough essentials to last the journey.

Returning to her room, she laid everything out across her bed. Her heartbeat thudded with a mix of fear and adrenaline. It was unfortunate that the letter gave no date for the killer's departure, but the ferry ticket told her enough. The murderer had left San Francisco the day after her mother was killed.

Hope unfolded the letter again, studying every detail. At the bottom, in a different hand, sharper, more slanted, someone had scribbled a list of hotel names. Her pulse raced. The killer must have written those names himself. Hotels he planned to stay in along the way. Landmarks to track him. It was a trail. A dangerous one, but a trail nonetheless.

Hope pressed a hand to her heart, steadying herself. Whatever it took, she would follow it.

And she would not stop until she found him.

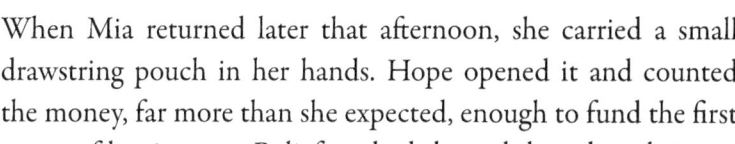

When Mia returned later that afternoon, she carried a small drawstring pouch in her hands. Hope opened it and counted the money, far more than she expected, enough to fund the first stages of her journey. Relief washed through her, though it was quickly replaced by renewed determination. Every coin would have to be used wisely.

"Thank you, Mia," she said softly, squeezing the maid's hand. The girl nodded, unaware of the magnitude of what Hope was about to do.

Once Mia left the room, Hope sat at her desk and spread out her findings. The original letter lay before her, weighted at the corners by inkwells to keep it flat. She didn't trust anyone, not even the marshals, to simply hand it back after reviewing it. Evidence tended to disappear in cases involving powerful men, and her father had influence, whether he chose to use it or not.

So, Hope took a fresh sheet of paper and carefully copied the entire letter, line for line. She made sure the handwriting looked natural enough to pass as a second copy, then folded it neatly and left it in the center of her desk. At least she would have something to fall back on if the marshals kept, or 'lost' the original. She also scribbled down the ferry ticket information: the departure point, the date, the destination. Everything she might possibly need if someone tried to claim she had misread or misunderstood the details.

As she finished writing, her stomach tightened with nerves. She didn't know how the U.S. Marshal headquarters would respond. Would they take her seriously? Would they help? Or would they dismiss her the same way the sheriff had? Still, she had to try.

Hope straightened, folded the letter, tucked it securely into her bodice, and walked downstairs without hesitation. She found the butler polishing silverware in the kitchen corridor and cleared her throat.

"Mr. Pratt," she said, her voice steady and polite, masking the storm inside her, "please arrange for a carriage at once. I need to go into town."

The man blinked in surprise but bowed stiffly.

"Of course, Miss Spencer. I will see to it immediately."

Within minutes, Hope stood in the entry hall, purse hidden beneath her cloak, determination hardening her expression. She was going to the U.S. Marshal headquarters. She was going to present her evidence. And she was going to fight, no matter who tried to stop her.

# 3

# When the Law
# Refused to Listen

On the way to the U.S. Marshal headquarters, Hope couldn't help questioning herself. Was this truly a good idea? Would they take her seriously, or would she be dismissed once again, this time by federal officers instead of a lazy sheriff? But deep down, she already knew the answer. She had to try.

She needed to know, without a shadow of doubt, that she had done everything in her power before throwing herself into the dangerous journey ahead. She was terrified of what her plan required, frightened of stepping into a world where killers lurked and conspiracies stretched across state lines. But she had no choice now. She knew too much. And she knew they planned to kill another woman. She could not sit idle and let someone else die, not when she held a piece of the truth in her hand.

As soon as the carriage pulled up in front of the U.S. Marshal headquarters, Hope leaned forward.

"Please wait for me," she instructed the driver. "I won't be long." Then she hurried inside. The headquarters bustled with activity, deputies, marshals, and clerks moving about with purpose. Hope straightened her shoulders and approached the front desk, rehearsing every detail in her mind. She explained the letter she had found, the ferry ticket, the sheriff's suspicious behavior, and the fact that another woman's life might be in danger.

They listened. They didn't laugh at her. But their expressions told her everything. They did not believe her. Hope felt anger surge through her, hot and bright, but she did not argue. She did not beg. If even federal marshals refused to listen, then she would not waste her breath pleading with them. They didn't even ask to see the evidence she had brought. That was answer enough.

When she stepped back outside, the cool air struck her like a slap. Hope clenched her jaw and climbed into the carriage with renewed determination.

"Stop at the ferry station before we return," she said. The driver nodded, and they set off.

At the station, she inquired about the next ferry departure, pretending to be a curious traveler. The attendant flipped through his schedule book before confirming, "Next boat leaves at six o'clock tomorrow morning, miss."

Hope thanked him and returned to the carriage. Once seated, she leaned forward again and spoke softly but firmly to the driver.

"Please be at my house tomorrow morning at five."

The man tipped his hat. "Of course, Miss Spencer."

Hope settled back against the cushions as the carriage rolled toward her father's estate. Her heart pounded with fear, but beneath it, something stronger pulsed. Resolve. Purpose. And the certainty that she was done relying on anyone else to save her mother, or the next victim. The journey would begin at dawn. And she would be ready.

When Hope returned to her room, there wasn't much she could do except wait. She laid out her clothing, simple, practical garments she could layer or alter if her disguise required it and double-checked the hidden pockets she had sewn into her reticule. The small compartments would keep her money safe, even if someone rifled through her belongings. She paced the room restlessly, glancing at the clock every few minutes.

She planned to gather provisions for the journey later, once the servants retired to their quarters and no one would question why she was packing food and water. Her plan was nearly complete. All she needed now was time.

She was about to go downstairs for supper when the door opened quietly and Mia stepped inside.

"Miss Spencer," the maid said softly, "Doc Baker and Reverend Shaw are here to see you."

Hope blinked in surprise. She hadn't expected visitors, certainly not them. For a moment, she simply stared, her breath catching with a mixture of astonishment and warmth. Doc Baker and Reverend Shaw had been her mother's closest friends, the only two people her mother trusted without reservation. They had been steady figures in Hope's life as well, kind, compassionate, and protective in ways her own family had never been. And during the last few days, Doc Baker had offered more comfort than her father had shown her in eighteen years. Hope's throat tightened.

"Thank you, Mia," she said at last. "I will come downstairs shortly. Please ask them to wait in the parlor."

The young maid nodded and slipped out. Hope turned back toward her mirror, smoothing her hair with trembling fingers as she took a deep breath. Her heart thudded nervously. Should she tell them?

Part of her longed to share her plan, to finally have someone listen, someone care. If anyone in the world might understand why she had to leave, it would be Doc Baker and Reverend Shaw. They had loved her mother too. They would want justice. They would want the truth exposed. But another, more cautious voice whispered warnings. What if they disapproved? What if they insisted, she stayed? What if they told her father, or worse, tried to stop her themselves?

Hope swallowed hard. She needed someone to know... someone who might help her if she never returned. Yet she couldn't risk losing her only chance to follow the trail. Her hands tightened around the edge of her vanity table. What should she do? With another deep, steadying breath, Hope turned toward the door. Whatever happened next, she would have to choose her words carefully.

Doc Baker and Reverend Shaw rose to their feet the moment Hope entered the parlor. Both men offered her warm, gentle smiles, smiles meant to comfort, but Hope could not bring herself to return them. Her face felt too tight, her heart too raw. Still, she stepped forward and shook their hands.

"Reverend Shaw, Doc Baker," she said politely, though her voice carried the exhaustion of the past days. "How kind of you to call. Is there a reason for your visit?" She sank gracefully onto the settee, folding her hands in her lap. Despite their age, both old enough to be her father, she had always felt a sense of genuine friendship with them, something she had never known with her own family. Reverend Shaw sat beside her and gently took her hand between his.

"Hope," he began, his voice full of compassion, "we simply wanted to make sure you are all right. The last few days have been challenging, and now, with your father gone and leaving you here alone—"

Hope let out a short, bitter scoff.

"Father has never been here for me. Not truly. He and Grandmother have been cold and distant for as long as I can remember. His departure the day after my mother's funeral hardly surprises me."

The two men exchanged a somber look and nodded in understanding. Doc Baker leaned forward in his chair, clasping his hands as though trying to steady himself.

"I've spoken to Sheriff Craig multiple times," the physician said quietly. "I've tried to get him to do something, anything. But he insists there is nothing he can do."

Hope shook her head. "Thank you for trying. But he made it perfectly clear to me that he has no intention of investigating. He wouldn't even consider the evidence of foul play."

"There has to be something we can do," Doc Baker said, frustration heavy in his tone. His kind eyes flicked toward her anxiously. Hope shrugged, though the tension in her shoulders revealed how much she had already considered this.

"I went to the U.S. Marshal headquarters today," she admitted. "They listened, but..." She inhaled sharply. "They didn't believe me. Not really. They didn't say it outright, but I could see it in the way they looked at me."

Reverend Shaw's eyebrows rose. Doc Baker's mouth tightened.

"But I did find something," Hope continued, her voice gaining strength. "In my mother's study. Something that gives me a place to start."

The room went still. Both men stared at her in stunned silence.

"You... found something?" Reverend Shaw asked slowly, as if he needed to be sure he had heard correctly. Hope nodded once, firm, controlled.

"Are you going to tell your father?" he asked gently. Hope's expression hardened instantly. Her eyes steeled with resolve.

"No," she said, her voice quiet but fierce. "I will not tell him." She drew a deep breath. "Because I am going after the killer myself."

The words hung in the air like a crack of thunder. Doc Baker's face paled. Reverend Shaw looked as though the wind had been knocked from him. Both men stared at her, not with disbelief in her ability, but with fear for her safety. Hope held their gaze, unflinching. Her decision had been made. And nothing would turn her from it now.

At last, Reverend Shaw found his voice.

"Hope," he said gently, concern heavy in his tone, "we understand your grief. Losing your mother like this is devastating. But you must not do anything irrational or dangerous without thinking it through."

Hope lifted her chin, defiance sparking in her eyes.

"I *have* thought this through. Repeatedly. I made a plan. I made lists. I'm fully aware of the risks, and I'm going," she said firmly. "You won't stop me." She swallowed hard, her voice softening into something wounded.

"Mom told me, before she died, that I'd find answers once I found her diary. The killer took it. I don't know why or what she wrote, but she clearly left something there that she wanted me to know."

The men exchanged a quick, troubled glance.

"We can't let you go alone," Doc Baker said quietly. "Your mother made us promise, long ago, that if anything ever happened to her, we would keep an eye on you. Protect you."

Hope's breath hitched. "She told you that?" Her voice wavered between shock and anguish. "Did she... did she think something would happen to her? Are you keeping something from me?"

Both men shook their heads emphatically.

"No," Reverend Shaw assured her. "Your mother shared many things with us over the years, but she never spoke openly about what happened inside your home. We knew she was unhappy, but she wouldn't say why." His shoulders sagged. "She only asked us to look after you if she could not."

"And that is what we're doing," Doc Baker added. "By telling you not to go, we're fulfilling her request."

Hope scoffed, her expression turning steely.

"Well, now you've done your duty. But it isn't going to stop me."

Doc Baker closed his eyes briefly, gathering patience. He knew the Spencer stubbornness, and Hope had inherited every ounce of her mother's resolve.

"I will go with you," Reverend Shaw said abruptly. Hope blinked at him, stunned.

"No, you won't. You can't just leave town. You have a congregation. People depend on you."

"San Francisco has other reverends," he replied calmly. "My congregation will manage without me for a few weeks."

"I don't want you to come," Hope snapped, her voice sharper than she intended. "This is dangerous. I will not have you killed because of me."

Doc Baker leaned forward, exasperation etched across his face.

"Do you hear yourself, Hope? You refuse his help because it's dangerous, yet you, an eighteen-year-old young woman, plan to travel across the country and confront a murderer alone?"

"That's correct," Hope said flatly. "At least that way, I risk only my own life. Not someone else's."

"I won't allow that," Reverend Shaw said, his tone suddenly firm, firmer than she had ever heard from him.

Hope glared. "You don't get a say, Reverend Shaw."

He raised an eyebrow. "Let me make this very clear, Hope Spencer: I will not let you do this alone. You may choose to accept my presence... or I will simply follow you. And trust me, you cannot prevent me from joining you."

Hope stared at him, jaw clenched, breath tight with frustration. She had never seen him so unyielding, so determined. It infuriated her.

"I'm leaving tomorrow morning at five," she said, giving him a pointed, challenging look.

"I'll be here," he answered smoothly, without the slightest hesitation. Hope threw her hands up.

"Why are you so stubborn?"

"Because," he replied, entirely unimpressed by her glare, "I am dealing with a very headstrong young lady, one who needs protection, whether she likes it or not."

Doc Baker coughed to hide a grin. Hope scowled. She exhaled dramatically.

"Fine."

"So, what's your plan?"

She reluctantly explained everything, her findings, the ferry ticket, the letter, the hotel names scribbled at the bottom. The men listened intently, nodding.

"I'm also hoping to find answers about my mother's family," Hope added. "I've been thinking a lot these last days... and I realized something. Father never let Mama and me be alone for long. Someone was always around. And somehow, he always knew when we discussed something he didn't like."

Reverend Shaw frowned. "So, you know nothing about your mother's side of the family?"

Hope shook her head. "Nothing. Not their names, not their ages, not where they live, nothing. All I know is her maiden name: Stewart. I tried to find more in my father's study, but he keeps everything locked. There's nothing there about her relatives. It's maddening."

Doc Baker nodded sympathetically.

"Your mother rarely spoke about them."

Hope's eyes snapped toward him.

"Did she say anything? Anything at all?" Then her expression shifted as realization bloomed. "Maybe... maybe she didn't talk to protect them. To keep them safe from my father."

Reverend Shaw's eyes widened. "You think your father is dangerous?"

Hope didn't hesitate. "Yes. I do."

The room froze. She continued, her voice urgent, trembling with conviction.

"I don't know him well, not really, but I believe he had something to do with my mother's death. Maybe not directly, but somehow. He loved her once... or I think he did... but things changed. Something happened. He's involved in something criminal. I can feel it. And Mama must have uncovered it." Her voice fractured.

"Tell me, what kind of husband reacts like that when his wife is murdered? He arranged the funeral before speaking to the sheriff. He refused any investigation. He didn't even comfort me. That is not normal. Even if they were on the verge of divorce."

Doc Baker and Reverend Shaw exchanged horrified looks.

"And the letter I found," Hope added, her voice dropping, "makes everything clear. There's another woman, someone in Cheyenne, who knows something too. They want to kill her as well."

The two men gasped.

"And the marshals didn't take that seriously?" Reverend Shaw asked, outraged. Hope shook her head bitterly.

"Maybe because I'm young. Or because I'm a woman. I even offered to show them the letter. They didn't want to see it."

"For heaven's sake," Doc Baker muttered. "That's outrageous."

"I know," Hope said, clenching her fists. "Sheriff Craig was just as bad. He insisted he had searched for evidence, but I found both pieces of evidence in less than an hour. Either he lied, or he is completely incompetent."

The two men coughed into their hands, barely hiding their agreement, and faint amusement at her bluntness. Reverend Shaw cleared his throat.

"Are you planning to travel straight to Wyoming?"

Hope shook her head firmly. "No. I need to catch up to the killer first. We know almost nothing about the woman in Cheyenne. We don't know what she discovered or why they want her dead. And I doubt she would know the name Anthony Whitmer. That seems to be a false identity." She looked at both men, fear and determination entwined in her gaze. "We follow the trail. We follow the killer. And we find the truth, whatever it costs."

When the household finally grew still and the last lamp upstairs was extinguished, Hope slipped from her room and padded quietly down the hallway. The house felt different at night, emptier, colder, but she moved with purpose.

She entered the kitchen, careful not to disturb a single pan or creaking floorboard. Once inside, she lit only a small lantern, just enough light to see by. Her heart pounded with each soft footstep, but she forced herself to remain calm. Every sound felt magnified in the silence, the ticking of the clock, the distant rustle of wind outside, even her own breathing.

Hope opened the pantry and began gathering provisions. With quick, practiced movements, she packed as much food as she could reasonably carry without weighing herself down: dried fruit, biscuits, jerky, bread wrapped in cloth, and a tin of tea leaves. She added a few apples and a block of cheese from the cold cellar, knowing they would last only a short while but would sustain her through the first day.

She tied the bundle tightly, hiding the food at the bottom of her carpet bag beneath her spare clothing. Hunger was the least of her worries, but she needed to be prepared. Even with the money from the dresses, uncertainty pressed heavily on her. The farther she traveled, the more expensive supplies would become. She couldn't afford to make mistakes, not now.

# 4

# Dawn Will Find Her
# Gone

Before returning upstairs, she hurried to her mother's study one last time. The air in the room still carried faint traces of her mother's lavender perfume, gentle, comforting, heartbreaking. Hope's fingers trembled as she searched through the desk drawers again. And then she found it. Tucked beneath a stack of letters was a plain envelope, sealed but unmarked. Curious, she opened it and nearly lost her breath. Several hundred dollars lay inside. Hope's hand flew to her mouth as emotion washed over her. Her mother had hidden this. Saved it. Prepared it, for something.

Perhaps for an escape. Perhaps for Hope. Perhaps for a day when she might need it most. Hope swallowed hard, tears burning her eyes.

"Thank you, Mama," she whispered.

She tucked the envelope safely into the deepest pocket of her reticule. Her father would never miss it. He possessed so much wealth that a few hundred dollars would not even cause him to blink. And this money... this money felt like her mother's final help. A last act of protection. Her mother had intended it for something important.

Now, Hope would use it to find justice. She closed the study drawer softly, took one last look around the room, then slipped back into the hallway, her bag a little heavier, her resolve a great deal stronger. Tomorrow, her journey would begin,

It was a strange, almost surreal feeling to step out of her father's house the next morning. The sky was still pale gray, caught between night and dawn, and the air carried the chill of the early hours. Hope paused at the edge of the porch, gripping the strap of her carpetbag tightly. She didn't know if she would ever return.

The mansion behind her looked cold and unwelcoming, as it always had. And yet, for eighteen years, it had been the only home she knew. Now she was walking away from it, possibly forever. She might die chasing a murderer. She might discover truths she had never imagined. She might even find her mother's family and realize they weren't the monsters her father had portrayed. Anything could happen.

A tremor passed through her, fear, anticipation, and the strange, liberating sense of stepping into a life that was finally her own. Reverend Shaw stood near the carriage, waiting. His coat collar was turned up against the wind, his hat pulled low over his brow. The moment he saw her, he straightened and offered a nod, not overly cheerful, not overly solemn, but steady. Reliable.

Part of Hope was grateful for his presence. She had never traveled farther than the neighboring towns, and the thought of crossing half the country alone left her breathless with nerves. Having someone she trusted, someone who had loved her mother, made her feel less isolated. But another part of her simmered with frustration. She didn't want anyone else in harm's way because of her choices. She didn't want to be responsible for another death. The thought alone tightened her chest.

Still, Reverend Shaw stood firm, resolute as ever. And Hope knew by now that no amount of arguing would sway him. She let out a quiet sigh and descended the last step of the porch.

"Good morning," he said gently, though shadows of worry flickered in his eyes. Hope nodded, her jaw set with stubborn resolve.

"Good morning," she replied, her voice carrying both gratitude and lingering irritation. The Reverend opened the carriage door for her.

"Ready?" he asked. Hope swallowed hard, then stepped inside.

"As I'll ever be."

They traveled through the day and well into the evening, arriving in Winnemucca just as lanterns were being lit along the streets. Dust clung to their clothing, and fatigue settled deep in their bones. Both Hope and Reverend Shaw were too tired to speak much. They collected their room keys from the clerk, exchanged a weary good night, and retired to their separate rooms.

Hope awoke early the next morning, long before dawn had fully broken. Sleep had not come easily, and now it refused to return. She stood by the small hotel window and watched townsfolk pass, miners heading to work, ranch hands hauling supplies, travelers lingering for coaches. Any one of them could be Anthony Whitmer.

The thought tightened her chest. The stagecoach to Elko wasn't leaving until noon, giving them several hours to explore, but without knowing what Anthony looked like, asking questions felt impossible. She might pass him on the street and never know. Or worse, he might pass her.

When they reached Elko hours later, Hope and Reverend Shaw decided to separate. He crossed the street to the post office to send a telegram updating Doc Baker, while Hope headed straight for the hotel. Her pulse thrummed with adrenaline.

Inside, she rang the bell at the front desk and waited. After a moment, the head porter appeared, a polished-looking man with a neat mustache and sharp eyes.

"How may I help you, Miss?" he asked politely. Hope cleared her throat and summoned her most innocent expression.

"I'm here to meet my uncle, Mr. Anthony Whitmer. Would you be so kind as to show me to his room?"

The porter shook his head. "Mr. Whitmer left this morning, I'm afraid."

"Oh no!" Hope gasped dramatically, pressing a hand to her heart. "I was afraid of that. I missed the stagecoach yesterday and had to travel today. My mother said she would send him word I was coming, but I suppose the message didn't reach him." She infused just enough sadness into her voice to be convincing. When she met the porter's eyes, his expression softened at once.

"I was hoping to surprise him," she continued. "I haven't seen him in two years. Do you know where he's headed next? I wanted to see him off before he leaves for the East Coast."

The porter brightened, relieved to be of use.

"He mentioned renting a horse and riding to Snowville today. It's a long ride, likely the whole day."

Hope widened her eyes in admiration.

"Do you know when the next stagecoach leaves for Snowville?"

"I believe tomorrow morning, ma'am."

"Thank you." Hope offered her most dazzling smile. "You've been very helpful."

His cheeks flushed at the praise.

"Well," she added lightly, "since my uncle has already left, I'll need a room for the night. Would it be possible to have the room he stayed in? In case he forgot something important." Her tone was sweet, polite, and perfectly calculated. The porter melted.

"Certainly, young lady." He scribbled down her information, accepted her payment, and handed her the key.

"I am much obliged," she said warmly, turning, only to nearly collide with Reverend Shaw, who had been standing just behind her. He wore a wide grin. Heat crept up Hope's neck.

"Well, Miss Spencer," he said, folding his arms, "I am thoroughly impressed. You certainly know how to play these games. That was remarkable acting, and very convincing lying."

She lifted her chin with playful pride.

"I do what I can. At least we know we're following the right trail. And I secured his room, which means we can search for anything he might've left behind."

Reverend Shaw nodded, though the sparkle of amusement remained in his eyes.

"I suppose I'd better get a room as well." He winked, an unexpected gesture that made her cheeks burn even hotter. He stepped aside as if to pass her, but then his gaze snapped upward, over her head. His expression shifted instantly, alert, assessing, cautious. Before she could ask what was wrong, he reached out and pulled her sharply into his arms.

"What are—!" Her words died as his lips pressed against hers.

Hope froze. Shock exploded through her, white-hot and paralyzing. Her heart thundered against her ribs, her breath catching painfully in her throat. She had been distracted, glancing toward the lobby entrance, and had no time to react before she found herself wrapped in the reverend's arms, his kiss quick, forceful, and undeniably intense. Heat flooded her face. She knew she must be crimson. But her shock ran deeper than embarrassment. Reverend Shaw, gentle, solemn, respectable Reverend Shaw, had just kissed her. Deliberately. And Hope couldn't yet begin to make sense of it.

As soon as Hope's brain caught up with reality again, instinct took over. She shoved at Reverend Shaw's chest with both hands, but he didn't budge. Outraged, she began hitting him in earnest, fists striking wherever they landed. Still, he refused to release her. Only when he finally relaxed his grip did she stagger back, fully prepared to bite his head off. But before she could utter a word, he clamped a firm hand over her mouth and dragged her with him out of the entrance hall.

"Mmmph—!" Hope tried to pry his fingers away, kicking at his boots, but it was no use. He half-guided, half-carried her down the corridor with surprising speed and strength until they reached her newly assigned room. He snatched the key from her hand, unlocked the door, and all but pushed her inside before shutting it behind them. Only then did he remove his hand from her mouth.

"How dare you?" she exploded immediately. "Who do you think you are? Why would you kiss me? You're a reverend, a reverend and old enough to be my father! Is that why you insisted on coming with me? Not because you wanted to protect me, but because you—because you—" Words failed her. Outrage did not.

"What made you think it was acceptable to pull me into your arms and kiss me like that? I did not consent, and I certainly hope I've never given you the impression I harbor any romantic feelings toward you!" Her voice vibrated with fury. Her blue eyes sparkled dangerously, like bright shards of ice, and she began pacing the room in rapid strides, clearly trying to calm herself but far too agitated to succeed.

Reverend Shaw stood against the closed door, a faint grin lingering on his lips, one that only intensified her anger. She spun toward him, ready to unleash another tirade, when he gently pressed a finger to her lips.

"Hope," he said, attempting a serious expression. "You must at least give me the chance to explain. Yes, that was bold. Yes, it was inappropriate. But I had a good reason."

"A good reason?" she repeated, incredulous. "You're right, it was inappropriate. Extremely."

"I saw someone come in behind you," he said calmly, "someone who should not see you."

"And kissing me was the only way you could think to hide me?" Hope demanded, still blazing with indignation. Her temper had been lit like a fuse, and his boldness had thrown fuel on it.

"I didn't have time to pull you aside," he replied. "Sheriff Craig had just walked in. He was looking right at us. And not only did I have to hide you from him, but he must not see me here either."

Hope blinked, her mouth parting slightly. Her anger faltered, but only a fraction.

"That is not an excuse," she insisted. "Our reputations could have been completely ruined if he had seen us. You were reckless. Completely out of line. And you took advantage of the moment." The death glare she leveled at him would have made braver men wilt. Instead, he had the audacity to grin again.

Hope opened her mouth to continue her scolding, but a sudden knock at the door startled her into silence. Her breath caught as she whipped around, stepping aside automatically. Reverend Shaw's expression sharpened. With a calmness she found infuriating, he moved to the door and opened it, just enough to see who was on the other side. What happened next would change everything.

A sheriff and a deputy stood on the other side of the door. Reverend Shaw's posture stiffened, but his expression remained composed. Frozen behind him, Hope felt her stomach plummet. This was exactly the kind of scandal she feared.

"May I help you, gentlemen?" Reverend Shaw asked politely, stepping just far enough into the doorway to block their view of Hope. Several hotel guests hovered behind the lawmen at a distance, whispering and watching with a mix of curiosity and judgment. Hope's pulse pounded in her ears. The sheriff's eyes narrowed. It was clear he wasn't here by chance.

"Several guests reported," the sheriff said coolly, "that you grabbed and kissed a young woman against her will, then forced her into this room."

Reverend Shaw didn't flinch, but Hope caught the tension in his jaw.

"We need to determine whether she's safe," the sheriff continued. "May we come in and check?"

The hallway had grown eerily quiet. A few gasps rippled through the onlookers. The deputy shifted, one hand resting near his holster, as though expecting trouble. Hope's heart slammed against her ribs. If they came inside, they would see her. And if Sheriff Craig was still nearby, he would recognize her immediately. She and the reverend would both be ruined, their reputations shredded, and worse, her investigation and disguise would be compromised.

She was suddenly, painfully aware of how close Reverend Shaw had pulled her earlier. Anyone who had witnessed it might genuinely believe she had been dragged in unwillingly. This was bad. Very, very bad.

Hope swallowed hard and met Reverend Shaw's eyes. He subtly shifted one foot backward, a silent signal to stay behind him, stay quiet, stay hidden. The sheriff's gaze sharpened. Time seemed to slow. And in that suspended moment, Hope realized she and the reverend were one wrong word away from disaster.

Before Reverend Shaw could open his mouth to defend himself, Hope surged forward and slipped past him, planting herself squarely in the doorway. She flashed a sweet, utterly disarming smile that made the sheriff blink in confusion.

"I'm afraid that was my fault, Sheriff," she said brightly, her tone sugary enough to rot teeth. "My husband was simply trying to stop me from saying something I might regret."

A ripple of surprise passed through the watching crowd. Hope forged on, lowering her voice as though confessing something terribly embarrassing.

"You see... a young man harassed me on the street earlier and followed me into the hotel." She pressed a hand delicately to her chest. "I put him in his place, of course, but I have a dreadful temper. When I get angry, I... well... say things that are not very ladylike."

A few nearby guests chuckled, visibly relaxing.

"My husband here was just trying to prevent me from causing a scene and exposing my potty mouth," Hope continued, casting her eyes downward as if mortified by her own lack of decorum.

The chuckles grew. Several guests exchanged amused glances before drifting back to their rooms, satisfied with the explanation. Only the sheriff lingered.

"This man is your husband?" he asked, lifting an eyebrow pointedly toward Reverend Shaw. His tone made it clear he had noticed the age difference and found it questionable. Hope swallowed, then forced a confident nod.

"I know the age difference seems significant," she said airily, "but he isn't as old as he looks."

Reverend Shaw stifled a cough that suspiciously resembled a laugh.

"My temper and sass have probably added a few gray hairs that weren't there before," Hope added, giving him a sassy sideways glance. Reverend Shaw bowed his head in exaggerated suffering, earning a few more snickers from the hallway.

Hope rolled her eyes dramatically, doubling down on her story. It was so sincere, so convincingly exasperated, that the sheriff finally cracked a grin.

"Well," he said, clearing his throat, "it appears everything is in order, then." He tipped his hat. "Sorry for the disturbance."

"Not at all," Hope said sweetly. "Thank you for checking."

Satisfied at last, the sheriff excused himself, and the deputy followed. Their footsteps faded down the hallway. Only when they were gone did Hope exhale, her knees suddenly weak. They had escaped disaster, but barely.

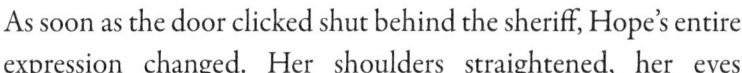

As soon as the door clicked shut behind the sheriff, Hope's entire expression changed. Her shoulders straightened, her eyes hardened, and she turned to face Reverend Shaw with a look that could have melted steel.

"You owe me, Reverend Shaw," she said curtly. His mouth twitched into a grin.

"Why did you say I was your husband?" He asked it lightly, but amusement shone in his eyes.

Hope's cheeks were still bright red, a hue that only deepened under his gaze.

"How else could I explain the kiss without getting you arrested?" she snapped. "I wanted to say you were my father, but I am fairly certain a father doesn't kiss his daughter on the lips, and if he does, he deserves to be in jail."

He cleared his throat and rubbed the back of his neck, looking both ashamed and impressed by her quick thinking.

"You do realize," he said slowly, "that by telling them I'm your husband, we now have to share this room."

Hope's eyes widened. Her cheeks, already hot, flared into an outright inferno.

"No, we do not," she hissed. "The porter wasn't around to hear that. And if anyone asks, you can tell them I threw you out because you snore." Her fierce determination made him chuckle, right up until she continued with a sentence that wiped the humor clean from his face. "And I hope you know that after what just happened, we will be splitting ways. I will not keep you as my travel companion."

His jaw dropped. He stared at her, stunned.

"Hope," he began carefully, "I told you before we left that I would not let you travel alone."

"And I told you," she said sharply, cutting him off, "that I didn't want you to come in the first place. The way you treated me just now shows a complete lack of respect. You never would have crossed such boundaries if my mother were still alive and with me." Her voice shook, not with fear, but with betrayal.

"I can't trust you. Not anymore. You overstepped, and you know it. You may return to San Francisco immediately."

"Hope—"

"I've made up my mind," she said firmly. "Please leave my room." She crossed the room, grabbed the door handle, opened it wide, and gave him a pointed tilt of her head toward the hallway.

Reverend Shaw looked genuinely flabbergasted. Until the day before they'd left San Francisco, he had barely known she possessed a temper. And he certainly hadn't known she was such a spitfire, fierce, sharp-tongued, and utterly unbending when she felt wronged.

"I see you need time to calm down," he said at last, striving for patience, "but I am still not letting you travel alone."

Hope shot him one final, withering glare, one that could have felled an ox, then shut the door in his face.

Hope spent the next hour searching every inch of Whitmer's room, rifling through drawers, checking beneath the bed, feeling along the seams of the mattress, and examining every corner where a careless traveler might have dropped something. But Whitmer had been careful. Too careful. There was nothing. Not a receipt. Not a scrap of paper. Not even a stray thread.

Her anxiety knotted tighter with every passing minute, and the lingering tension with Reverend Shaw only made the pressure in her chest worse. She couldn't stay here with him breathing down her neck, insisting on protecting her. She needed distance. She needed time to think. And she needed to leave before he made good on his promise to shadow her. She couldn't wait until morning.

Hope sprang into action. She gathered her bags, adjusted her hat, and hurried downstairs, forcing herself to remain composed despite the panic threatening to claw its way up her throat. The same porter from earlier stood at the front desk, polishing a stack of room keys. He looked up with a welcoming smile that quickly shifted to concern when he saw her face.

"Forgive me," Hope said breathlessly, letting her voice tremble just enough. "Is there another hotel nearby? A young man has been following me... since Winnemucca. He just arrived in town. I saw him. He terrifies me."

The porter blinked, startled. "A young man? Miss, if he's dangerous, we should alert the sheriff—"

She shook her head violently. "I—I don't know if he's dangerous. He's just always there. Watching me. Showing up wherever I go." Her voice hitched. She lowered her gaze, pressing her hand to her trembling lips. "My uncle, Marshal Whitmer, was supposed to protect me, but he left sooner than I expected. I can't wait until morning. I need to get away before the man finds me."

It wasn't real fear, but her acting was flawless. Her eyes welled with tears, and the porter's expression softened immediately.

"Oh, Miss..." he murmured sympathetically. Hope chanced a glance toward the entrance and froze. Sheriff Craig had just walked in.

# 5

# Arrow on the Open Plain

Her heart nearly stopped. She began to shake deliberately, but convincingly.

"That's him," she whispered urgently, tilting her head toward the door. "He's here. He can't see me. Please..."

The porter's face hardened with protective resolve.

"Come with me," he whispered. He stepped quickly from behind the counter and ushered her through a narrow side door into a small office. Hope slipped inside, and he shut the door firmly behind them. Only when they were alone did he turn to face her.

"The next hotel is in Halleck," he said quietly. "It's a few hours' ride from here." Hope let out a shaky breath. "Is it easy to find?"

"Yes," he assured her. "Just follow the road east. It leads straight there. And you can't miss it. The U.S. Army has a camp nearby. You'll see their flags long before the buildings."

Relief washed through her like a warm tide.

"Thank you," she whispered. "Thank you so much. Please... please promise me you won't tell anyone where I've gone."

The porter nodded solemnly. "I won't tell a soul."

Hope squeezed his hand gratefully. Her escape route was set. And this time... she would travel on her terms.

Hope hurried across the street, her heart pounding, and made her way to the nearest livery stable. The groom on duty looked up, startled by the urgency in her voice as she requested two horses. Traveling on foot, or with her luggage slung over one weary mare, would slow her far too much. Two horses would give her flexibility, speed, and a way to carry her belongings without drawing attention.

She was profoundly grateful for the countless riding lessons she'd received throughout her childhood. At the time, she had thought them merely another expectation of proper Spencer upbringing. Now, she understood they were a lifeline.

She quickly secured her bags to the second horse, tying the straps with practiced efficiency. Then she mounted the first, swinging into the saddle with an ease born of years in the riding arena. With a quiet nudge of her heel, she urged the horse forward, guiding both animals out of town and onto the quiet road leading toward Snowville.

She hadn't traveled far when she pulled off beside a thick cluster of trees and dense bushes, the perfect hiding spot. She dismounted, looped the reins around a low branch, and slipped behind the foliage. It was time to disappear.

Moving quickly, she shed her dress, folding it tightly and packing it into one of the saddlebags before the chill of the morning air could bite too deeply into her skin. Then she reached into the bag for her half-brother's clothes: trousers, braces, a plain shirt, a worn vest. The fabric hung loosely on her slender frame, but that was ideal. She tucked the excess neatly, cinched the belts tight, and rolled the pant legs until they sat properly in her boots.

Next came her hair. She twisted it up, pinned it brutally tight against her scalp, then pulled the wide-brimmed cowboy hat low over her face until her features were cast in shadow. Her reflection in the small metal mirror she carried startled her. She didn't look like Hope Spencer anymore. She looked like a slight, wiry young cowboy, travel-worn, unremarkable, someone who could blend into any crowd. Perfect.

To hide the delicate curve of her neck, she tied a dark neckerchief beneath her chin, pulling it high. Gloves concealed her small hands, further masking her femininity. Every inch of her had to say *boy*, not *girl*.

Finally, she checked her weapons. No gun, but she had a sharp knife strapped to her boot. And the bow and arrows she'd packed, though elegant and clearly crafted by a skilled artisan, were reliable. She had been practicing archery since childhood, one of her mother's favorite pastimes—and Hope's skill had become exceptional.

She ran a hand along the polished wood of the bow. It would have to be enough. Taking a deep breath, she returned to the horses and mounted again, her disguise complete. The sun climbed slowly behind her as she rode. Hope Spencer was gone. In her place rode a determined young traveler, someone no one would look twice at. Someone capable of following a killer across a continent.

The ride itself was dull and uneventful. Rolling grasslands stretched endlessly in every direction, broken only by the occasional cluster of shrubs or wandering antelope. Hope tried to stay alert, but the monotony made her grateful when a distant shape finally appeared on the horizon. A town—Halleck. And near it, the unmistakable flutter of flags: the Stars and Stripes, and nearby, the bold colors of the U.S. Army. She exhaled in relief. Civilization. Safety. Or at least... a place to rest.

It was still several miles away, though, and her horses needed a break. Hope guided them toward a lone cottonwood tree standing atop a small hill. From there, she could see miles of sunlit prairie stretching in every direction, rippling gold and green. And a herd of buffalo, hundreds of them, grazing peacefully not far away.

Hope dismounted, her legs stiff from the long ride. She pulled the canteen from her saddlebag and took a long, refreshing drink, her gaze drifting back to the magnificent herd. Calves trotted near their mothers. Bulls snorted at one another. The ground vibrated faintly beneath their heavy steps. It was serene. Too serene. She had just slung the canteen back over the saddle when thunder cracked across the prairie. Gunfire.

Several sharp, violent shots shattered the silence, startling Hope so badly she gasped aloud. A flurry of crows burst from the trees, cawing their alarm into the sky. Hope spun toward the herd. A group of men, six, maybe seven, were advancing slowly on the buffalo, rifles raised. They fired methodically, dropping animal after animal where they stood. Hope's stomach lurched.

Why? Why were they killing them? Not for food, not in such numbers, not indiscriminately. More shots rang out. Bulls roared in panic, or pain. Calves scattered, terrified. Dust rose in choking clouds as the animals stampeded to escape the slaughter. A bullet struck the ground near Hope, kicking up dirt. Her horses shied nervously.

She ducked instinctively behind the ridge of the hill and peered over the edge. Her breath caught in her throat. Just below her, lying motionless in the grass, were two calves, still small, barely weaned, and their mother. Blood darkened the soil beneath them.

A sob tore from Hope's chest before she could stop it. Her heart cracked open. Her hands trembled with grief and rage. She scrambled down the small hill, dropping to her knees beside the lifeless calves. Their fur was still warm. Tears filled her eyes, burning, blinding, as she pressed a shaking hand to her mouth. This wasn't hunting. This was murder. A massacre.

She surged to her feet, boiling fury inside her. Waving her arms frantically, she shouted at the distant men.

"STOP! STOP IT! LEAVE THEM ALONE!" Her voice was loud, raw with rage, but the men were too far away. Too focused on their slaughter. They didn't even glance in her direction. Hope turned back toward the prairie and realized it was worse than she'd thought.

Dozens, maybe fifty, buffalo lay fallen across the field, their massive bodies crumpled in the tall grass. The ground was littered with the sprawling tragedy of it. Hope felt sick. The senseless killing, the waste, the cruelty, tore at something deep inside her.

Before she could gather her wits, a new sound rose behind her. The thunder of many hooves. Fast. Close. And then, howls. Wild, fierce, echoing cries that sent chills racing down her spine. Indians. Dozens of them. Racing straight toward her.

Hope whipped around, her breath freezing in her throat. A large group of warriors thundered straight toward her, bareback riders painted for battle, their horses, swift and sure, their voices rising in fierce, echoing cries that made the earth tremble beneath her feet. Terror surged through her so violently she nearly stumbled. Her heart slammed against her ribs, but instinct and desperation propelled her up the hill. She scrambled to her horse, grabbed the reins with shaking hands, and hauled herself into the saddle.

"Go!" she gasped, kicking the horse sharply. The animal leapt forward, hooves pounding as it tore across the prairie toward the distant army camp. The second horse, tied to the saddle of the one Hope rode, followed just as fast. Hope leaned low over the horse's neck, urging both animals on, but the warriors were gaining.

Arrows sliced through the air, whistling past her ears. One struck the ground inches from her horse's hooves, spraying dirt. Another zipped past her shoulder so close she felt the rush of wind against her cheek. Panic clawed up her throat. *They can't think I did this. They can't. They can't.*

She tried to push the horse harder, but it was already running at full speed, its breath coming in ragged bursts. The army camp was still too far away, a blur of flags and wooden gates in the distance.

A shadow passed over her. Then pain exploded through her arm. An arrow struck just below her shoulder, burying itself deep in her flesh. Hope cried out, a strangled, guttural sound, as white-hot agony shot down her arm and across her chest. The force nearly knocked her from the saddle. She swayed, her vision wobbling. Stay on the horse. Stay on. Stay—

Her fingers clenched weakly around the reins as she fought to remain upright. The world blurred, sunlight streaking into sharp lines, the ground tilting wildly beneath her. Somehow, she kept the horse moving forward.

She was only yards from the army camp gate when her strength finally faltered. Her breath came in shallow, panicked gasps, every inhale seared with pain. Her sight dimmed, colors washing out to gray. She barely registered the thunder of hooves behind her, different now from the ones chasing her. Shouted orders. The crack of gunfire. Soldiers. Galloping out of the gate, rifles raised, driving the warriors back across the prairie.

Hope tried to look at them, tried to stay upright, but her body was failing. Two riders veered toward her, shouting something she couldn't make out through the ringing in her ears. Everything was foggy... blurred... slipping away. Her horse slowed, sensing her slackening weight. The pain in her arm pulsed, sharp, overwhelming, and then her knees buckled in the saddle. The world tilted.

A soldier reached out. But Hope's vision went black before he could reach her. She slid sideways from the horse, the ground rushing up to meet her, and everything dissolved into darkness.

Captain Jeremy Sheffield and Second Lieutenant Peter Williams spurred their horses forward the moment they saw the lone rider staggering toward the fort. The young cowboy, at least, that was what he appeared to be at first glance, was slumped in the saddle, barely holding on. An arrow jutted from his upper arm, blood staining his shirt and dripping down his side. The captain exchanged a quick look with his lieutenant.

"He's going down," Williams said sharply, already angling his horse to intercept.

"Move!" Captain Sheffield barked.

They reached the rider just as the cowboy's body sagged sideways. The horse, confused and frightened, slowed to a stop. Sheffield leapt from his mount before it had fully halted, boots hitting the ground hard as he lunged forward. He caught the falling figure in his arms a split second before the young man hit the dirt.

But the moment the body settled against him, something felt wrong. Too light. Too slight. Too... fragile. The cowboy's wide-brimmed hat slipped off during the fall, tumbling to the ground and landing upside down near their boots. Captain Sheffield froze. A cascade of long, pale-blonde hair spilled free, sliding over his arm like silk. His breath caught.

"My word." He looked up at Lieutenant Williams, shock written plainly across his face. "This isn't a cowboy," he said, his voice barely above a whisper. "It's a young woman."

Williams leaned closer, eyes widening in disbelief. The disguise had been convincing, the hat, the loose clothing, the neckerchief, but up close there was no mistaking it. Her face, though ashen and contorted with pain, was delicate. Feminine. And she couldn't have been more than eighteen or nineteen.

Sheffield swallowed hard. "What in blazes is she doing out here alone?" His voice tightened with disbelief and concern. He shifted her carefully in his arms, mindful not to jostle the arrow embedded in her upper arm. Her head lolled against his shoulder, her skin cold and clammy.

"Why is she dressed like this?" Williams murmured, still stunned. "And alone in the middle of buffalo country? This is soldiers' ground, dangerous even for us."

Captain Sheffield didn't answer at once. His jaw clenched as he adjusted his grip, lifting her as though she weighed nothing at all.

"I don't know," he said at last, eyes narrowing. "But we're going to find out." He gathered her more securely against his chest and strode toward the fort gates. "Bring her horses," he ordered. "I am going to take her to the infirmary before she loses any more blood."

The wind whipped around them, carrying the faint scent of dust and prairie grass, while the woman in his arms drifted deeper into unconsciousness, unaware that her desperate escape had delivered her into the care of soldiers now determined to save her life... and uncover her secrets.

When Hope finally opened her eyes, for a moment she couldn't remember who she was, where she was, or why her body felt so heavy. Everything was hazy, floating in a thick fog of pain and exhaustion. She blinked, her gaze drifting upward. A wooden ceiling. Soft lamplight. The faint scent of antiseptic herbs and clean linens. She was lying in a bed.

Confusion flared. She pushed herself up instinctively, and pain exploded through her arm so violently she cried out, collapsing back against the pillow with a sharp gasp. Cold sweat prickled across her skin. The arrow. Memory slammed into her like a runaway stagecoach, buffalo, gunshots, Indians, the frantic ride toward the army camp, the agony in her arm, the world tilting into blackness.

Hope swallowed hard and forced herself to look at her injury. Her sleeve had been carefully cut away, and a neat bandage wrapped her upper arm where the arrow had pierced her. Someone had tended her wound, cleaned it, treated it, wrapped it. A jolt of vulnerability ran through her at the realization that someone had undressed her, but relief quickly followed when she saw they had been respectful, cutting only the damaged sleeve.

She shifted cautiously, trying to ease the throbbing in her arm, when the door creaked open. A nurse stepped inside, a middle-aged woman with kind eyes and a calm, reassuring presence. She smiled warmly.

"I'm glad you're awake," she said softly. "How are you feeling?"

Hope's voice was barely above a whisper.

"I... I'm not entirely certain."

"That's to be expected after what you went through." The nurse stepped closer, adjusting the blanket around her. "You're in the infirmary here in Halleck. There's no town doctor, but the army camp has one. He operated on you when they brought you in."

Before Hope could respond, the door opened again. Two soldiers entered, one older, with silver hair and wise eyes, the other young, tall, and strikingly handsome. Both wore expressions of concern rather than intimidation. The older man nodded courteously.

"I'm Dr. Lewis. You're very fortunate, young lady. Angels must have been working overtime on your behalf."

Hope managed a weak, grateful smile. The two men pulled up chairs and sat beside her bed. Hope nearly groaned. Clearly, they were here for answers. The younger soldier cleared his throat. His voice was deep, steady, and unexpectedly gentle.

"I'm Captain Jeremy Sheffield," he said. "Doctor Lewis is right. You're lucky. Several more arrows were fired at you, but only one struck."

Hope's stomach twisted. The image of the buffalo calves flashed through her mind. Tears stung her eyes.

"Why?" she whispered, her voice thick with emotion. "Why were those men killing the buffalo? They were slaughtering them for no reason." She blinked back the tears angrily. "It was senseless. Cruel."

Dr. Lewis and Captain Sheffield exchanged a glance, long, careful, and telling. Sheffield inhaled slowly.

"They're hired by the railroad," he said. "Clearing the area for future tracks."

Hope's expression sharpened instantly. A spark of fury burned behind her blue eyes as understanding settled in.

"That is not the reason," she said firmly. "The government wants the remaining free tribes forced into reservations. They're wiping out the buffalo to starve the tribes, to destroy their livelihood." Her jaw clenched. "Killing their game is the easiest way to push them off their land."

Both men stared at her, surprised, perhaps even stunned. Most women Hope's age didn't speak like that. Many men didn't either.

Hope noticed their expressions but said nothing. Her governess had educated her far more thoroughly than her father ever intended. And once she grew older and saw how deeply involved her father was in politics, how loudly he voiced his opinions, she demanded her own education in political matters. Her father, of course, despised the idea. He didn't believe women needed opinions. He believed women existed to listen, obey, and remain ignorant of anything of substance.

Which only made Hope more determined to learn.

# 6

# Snowville Shadows and Stable Flames

Captain Sheffield leaned back slightly, his chair creaking beneath him as he studied her with renewed focus. His eyes narrowed, not with suspicion, but with a thoughtful curiosity, as though he were quietly discarding every assumption he had made the moment he'd first seen her disguised as a young cowboy collapsing at the fort gates.

"I see," he said at last, his voice low and measured. There was no skepticism in it now, only respect. "You're... very well informed."

Hope held his gaze, her expression steady despite the lingering pain throbbing through her arm.

"I had to be," she said softly. "No one else ever wanted me to know the truth."

Something shifted in his posture at that. He leaned forward again, forearms resting on his knees, the faint lines of command and responsibility etched into his face deepening with thought.

"Most people," he said carefully, "prefer comfort over truth. Especially when the truth threatens power."

Hope's lips curved in a sad, knowing smile.

73

"I wasn't afforded much comfort growing up." Her fingers curled into the blanket at her side. "But I learned early that ignorance is just another form of control."

Captain Sheffield exhaled slowly, as though her words had struck something personal. He had seen obedience drilled into soldiers, fear used as leverage, silence demanded as loyalty. But hearing such clarity from someone so young, and so wounded, caught him off guard.

"You're not wrong," he said quietly. "And you're braver than most for refusing to stay blind."

Hope didn't respond immediately. Instead, she turned her gaze toward the small window, where afternoon light filtered in, pale and uncertain.

"I didn't choose bravery," she murmured. "I chose survival."

When she looked back at him, there was no plea in her eyes, only resolve. Captain Sheffield straightened, something firm and unspoken settling between them. Whatever had brought this young woman to his fort, bleeding and disguised and hunted, he knew one thing with certainty now: She was not someone to underestimate.

Captain Sheffield hesitated before answering her, his jaw tightening subtly. Hope understood the pause. As officers of the U.S. Army, they could not openly criticize government policy, not even when they agreed with her.

At last, he murmured, "You are not wrong."

Hope swallowed. "Then why were the Indians attacking me? I was no threat to them. Did they think I was part of the buffalo massacre?" Her blue eyes widened, raw and earnest, the concern behind them impossible to miss.

"Most likely," Captain Sheffield replied. "They killed two of the men who were shooting the herd. With you being nearby, and dressed as you were, they may have assumed you were with those hunters."

"I see..." she whispered. A tremor ran through her. She would never blame the tribes for defending what was theirs, but being mistaken for one of their enemies chilled her to the bone.

Sheffield studied her for a long moment. Then, with curiosity rather than accusation, he asked, "Why are you dressed like a man?"

Hope's cheeks flamed. "I thought it would be safer, since I'm traveling alone."

"Traveling alone?" His brows rose. "A young lady has no business being out here without an escort. This is the Wild West. What happened earlier is a perfect example of why people call it that. Why are you traveling alone?"

"I have my reasons," she murmured, her gaze dropping to the blanket. She couldn't bear his piercing, assessing stare, not when she felt so exposed. His voice softened, though it remained firm.

"Would you be willing to share those reasons with us?"

She shook her head. "You wouldn't believe me. And if you did, you'd think I was mad."

"I'm already thinking that," he replied with a teasing smirk. She looked up sharply. He winked.

"What's your name?"

"Hope. Hope Spencer."

"Well, Miss Spencer," he said, flashing a smile that could charm stone, "it's a pleasure to make your acquaintance. But I still want to know what brought you all the way out here."

She sighed heavily. "It's... a very long story."

"That's all right," Captain Sheffield said with a shrug. "We have plenty of time. There's not much excitement out here apart from stampedes, skirmishes, and the occasional arrow."

Dr. Lewis snorted under his breath. Hope stared at the captain, weighing her options. Would telling him help, or only make things worse? He seemed capable, intelligent... and maddeningly persistent. And infuriatingly handsome. His gaze remained steady on her face, patient and strangely reassuring.

"I promise," he said quietly, "we will listen with the intent to help, not to judge."

Heat crept up Hope's neck and into her cheeks. He wasn't the first man to look at her intently, but he was the first who made her feel... *seen.*

"I told the U.S. Marshals in San Francisco," she said sharply, trying to regain her composure, "and they didn't believe me. So why would you?"

"You came here from San Francisco alone?" Dr. Lewis exclaimed, eyes widening.

"Not exactly," she muttered. "I left my travel companion in Elko."

"And why would you do that?" the physician pressed.

Hope's lips tightened. "Let's just say... I no longer wished to travel with him."

The men exchanged a knowing look, one that made her grit her teeth. She didn't owe them her life story, but Captain Sheffield was relentless.

"And why," he asked again, "are you out here?"

Hope's irritation flared. This man was impossible. Persistent. Infuriating. And unfortunately, correct. He would not leave her alone until she answered. She rolled her eyes, inhaled deeply... and suddenly everything poured out of her. Every detail. Every suspicion. Every piece of evidence she had collected. By the time she finished, both men sat frozen, their expressions a mixture of disbelief and dawning horror.

"I knew you wouldn't believe me," she snapped before either could speak.

"Whoa, no one said that," Captain Sheffield replied quickly, hands raised in surrender. Dr. Lewis nodded in agreement.

"But you think I shouldn't have left San Francisco," she said flatly. They hesitated. That hesitation was answer enough.

"Yes," the captain admitted. "We do think that. This is a dangerous land, and your mission..." He paused, visibly struggling. "Miss Spencer, it's dangerous for soldiers, let alone a petite young woman."

"What was I supposed to do?" Her voice shook, not with fear, but with determination. "The sheriff back home refused to investigate. My father didn't care. And the U.S. Marshals dismissed me." Her eyes brightened with fierce resolve. "I won't let my mother's murder go unpunished."

Their smiles were soft, admiring, though Captain Sheffield quickly hid his, behind a cough. Before either man could respond, the nurse stepped back into the room.

"Miss Spencer," she said gently, "a gentleman is waiting outside to see you. Shall I allow him in?"

"What's his name?" Hope asked, unease trickling down her spine.

"Reverend Shaw."

Hope's breath caught. *Of all the people she didn't want to see...*

Hope sighed softly. How in the world had he found her so quickly? The porter had promised he wouldn't tell a soul. But there was no escaping Reverend Shaw now. Resigned, she nodded to the nurse. It wasn't long before he stepped into the room. Hope nearly gasped.

Reverend Shaw's eyes locked onto her instantly, deep, searching, far too perceptive. But it wasn't his piercing stare that stole her breath. It was... him. His full beard was gone, replaced by a dark, scruffy shadow that made him look younger, almost rugged. And where had the silver streaks gone from his hair? His dark brown waves looked richer, fuller, almost vibrant. Had he lost weight in the last two days? Or was it simply the lack of facial hair that revealed a stronger jawline? What on earth had possessed him to transform himself? And why did it unsettle her so terribly?

Dr. Lewis and Captain Sheffield rose to greet him. Reverend Shaw returned the gesture politely, but his gaze was drawn back to Hope with startling intensity, as if he had come all this way for her and only her. He stepped to her bedside.

"Hope," he said, his voice low, warm, and far too gentle for someone she'd expected to scold her. She braced herself, chin lifted, spine straight, ready for a lecture. But none came. "Why did you just leave?" he asked instead. "Do you know how worried I was?"

Hope blinked, caught off guard. She searched his face for irritation or frustration but found only genuine concern. And that... that completely disarmed her.

"I told you I wouldn't travel with you any longer," she countered, attempting irritation but landing somewhere closer to bewildered defensiveness. "I don't see why you're surprised." Her cheeks burned hotter. She tried to look anywhere but at him, yet she felt his gaze like a hand beneath her chin, urging her to meet his eyes. "How did you even find me so fast?" she demanded. "I specifically asked the porter not to tell anyone where I went. He swore he wouldn't."

Reverend Shaw exhaled heavily.

"He didn't," he said quietly. "When you disappeared and the porter refused to tell me anything, I went to the livery. They told me a young woman, who matched your description, rented two horses. They also mentioned where you said you were heading."

Hope lowered her eyes, guilt trickling down her spine. At least the porter hadn't betrayed her trust. But she could still feel Reverend Shaw's stare, steady, penetrating, impossible to ignore.

"When I arrived in Halleck and asked around," he continued, "I was told you'd been brought here. To the infirmary." His voice dropped, strained. "Hope... what happened to you?"

She couldn't answer. Instead, she turned to Captain Sheffield with a silent plea.

*Please. Explain. I can't.*

He nodded. "Miss Spencer was fleeing from attacking Indians," he said evenly. "She was struck by an arrow before we reached her."

Reverend Shaw inhaled sharply. Hope didn't dare meet his eyes. She closed hers, bracing for anger, chastisement, perhaps a lecture on recklessness and foolishness. But when she finally looked at him, there was none of that. Only fear. And relief. And a depth of worry that made her chest tighten painfully. After a long moment, he tore his gaze from her and turned to the physician.

"How long before she can travel?"

Dr. Lewis folded his hands. "She won't be able to ride for at least a week, possibly longer. If she takes the stagecoach instead, she should be well enough to travel in two days."

"The stagecoach only stops here once a month," Captain Sheffield added, "and the next one is due in two days, just as the doctor said."

Reverend Shaw nodded slowly, absorbing every word.

"Then that's what we'll do," he said.

"But make sure she sees another physician as soon as possible," Dr. Lewis added firmly. "The wound must be checked. If it becomes infected—" He stopped short. Hope rolled her eyes faintly.

"I'm sitting right here, you know."

Reverend Shaw didn't even blink.

"Good," he said calmly. "Then you heard the physician."

Hope's cheeks flared again, part annoyance, part something far more dangerous. Something she wasn't ready to name.

Hope was restless throughout the night. Every time she closed her eyes, her thoughts refused to be quiet. They spun, tangled, and inevitably settled on the one man she wished they wouldn't.

*What is happening to me?* She rolled onto her other side with a frustrated sigh. Her arm throbbed, but it wasn't the pain keeping her awake. It was the confusing, ridiculous, thoroughly inconvenient flutter in her chest every time she thought of Reverend Shaw.

A man old enough to be her father. A reverend, for heaven's sake. A man she had been furious with only a day earlier after that sudden, ill-timed kiss. And yet... one shave, one startling transformation of his appearance, and suddenly her pulse behaved like a runaway filly whenever he so much as looked at her. This made no sense.

She pressed her uninjured hand to her forehead. None whatsoever. She *should* still be angry about the kiss. She *should* be scolding him in her thoughts, lecturing him, listing every reason he was insufferably overprotective and interfering. Instead, her traitorous mind kept drifting back to his face, the strong line of his jaw revealed by the missing beard, the warmth and intensity in his eyes, the gentleness in his voice when he'd spoken her name. Each time the memory surfaced, her heart thudded so loudly she feared the nurse in the next room might hear it.

Surely this was the medication, she reasoned wildly. It *had* to be the medication, Dr. Lewis had given her something for the pain. Perhaps it was stronger than he realized. Perhaps it was making her think, and feel, things she normally wouldn't. Yes. That had to be it. There was no rational explanation for why a young woman who had sworn she would never travel with him again was now lying awake, cheeks warm, wondering what his smile might look like if she apologized... or what it would feel like if he ever kissed her again, properly, without panic or pretense. Hope groaned and dragged the blanket over her head.

"Oh, this is absurd," she muttered silently. *I'm not thinking about that. I refuse to think about that.* But she did. And her heart continued to race. And the night remained stubbornly sleepless.

Reverend Shaw visited her the very next morning, so early the sun had barely pushed its way over the distant hills. Hope had just shifted upright against her pillows when the door creaked open. The moment he stepped inside, her heart lurched, not a gentle flutter this time, but a full, traitorous leap that sent warmth rushing up her neck.

*Get a hold of yourself, Hope,* she scolded silently, closing her eyes for a brief breath. It did very little good. His presence filled the small infirmary room instantly, quiet, steady, and disarmingly confident. He pulled a chair close to her bed and sat, leaning forward slightly, elbows resting on his knees. His eyes, soft yet searching, held hers with an intensity that made her stomach twist.

"Hope," he said quietly, "will you promise me something?"

She swallowed, bracing herself.

"Please... don't ever just run off like that again. It drove me mad not knowing where you were."

The honesty in his voice unsettled her more than anger ever could. She drew in a deep breath, forcing her pulse to steady, then met his gaze head-on.

"Will you promise," she countered, "not to overstep boundaries again and kiss me without permission?"

His lips twitched, as if he were fighting back a very dangerous smile.

"I already told you I had no choice."

"We always have a choice, Reverend Shaw."

He leaned back slightly and exhaled. "Sheriff Craig was walking toward us. If I'd pulled you aside suddenly, it would have drawn attention. He wasn't there by accident. I'm convinced he was looking for you. The way he stared..." He shook his head. "If he'd gotten close enough to see your face, everything would have fallen apart."

Hope folded her arms and arched a brow.

"So, your brilliant solution was to kiss me?"

"Yes."

The simple, unwavering answer sent a jolt straight through her. He continued before she could respond.

"By leaning in, I gave him something else to stare at. He turned back toward the exit. That's when I let you go, but I covered your mouth because, well, I knew you were about to explode."

"Darn right I was," she muttered. This time, he didn't hide the grin. The sight of it made her chest feel uncomfortably warm.

"I didn't intend to make you uncomfortable," he added more softly. "I had a single second to decide. And that's... why it happened."

Hope studied him closely, searching for arrogance or deceit. She found neither, only sincerity, plain and disarming. Somehow, that irritated her even more. Before she could respond, he nodded toward the door.

"Dr. Lewis said you're allowed to get up now, carefully. There's not much to see here in Halleck, but if you feel well enough, we might take a walk. Fresh air could do you some good."

A walk. With him. Wonderful. Terrifying. Heat crept into her cheeks. Why did her confidence evaporate every time he offered one of those warm smiles? Her heart thudded so loudly she was certain he could hear it, surely the whole infirmary could. Still, he waited patiently for her answer, his hand extended. Not touching her. Not pressuring her. Simply offered. She swallowed.

"Sure," she managed quietly. "Let's... go for a walk."

His smile broadened, rich with something that made her pulse skip. He stood and reached for her hand to help her rise. The moment their palms touched, a spark shot up her arm so suddenly she nearly gasped. She prayed he couldn't feel her trembling.

Just then, the nurse entered, pausing as she took in the sight of their joined hands. She gave them a knowing nod before returning to her work. Hope, mortified, flustered, and unbearably aware of the reverend still holding her hand, decided fresh air might indeed be necessary. Very necessary.

They walked side by side in a quiet, almost fragile silence. The morning sun was already scorching, pressing down with the dry heat that seemed native to every inch of Nevada. Hope scrunched her nose. She had never liked heat, never liked the way it clung to her skin and stole her breath. It made her appreciate the cool coastal breezes of San Francisco more than ever.

When they reached a small stream trickling between boulders, Reverend Shaw gestured for her to sit. They settled on warm rocks overlooking the water. For a few blissful seconds, the steady rush of the stream drowned out Hope's thoughts. Then she felt it. That unmistakable, unnerving sensation of being watched. She shifted, resisting the urge to fidget.

*Why does he keep staring at me?* Every time she glanced sideways, he looked away just a moment too slowly, caught somewhere between admiration and curiosity. Heat flared in her cheeks again. She scrambled for something, anything, to break the awkward, rising tension. Before she could speak, he suddenly sprang to his feet.

Hope jumped. "Reverend Shaw—?" But she didn't get to finish. In one swift movement, he scooped her into his arms, lifting her clean off the rock. Hope let out a breathless gasp, her hands instinctively clutching his shoulders as he carried her several steps back.

"What are you—Reverend Shaw, put me down this instant!" Her face burned hotter than the desert sun, though she wasn't certain whether it was fear or something far more dangerous that made her heart hammer. He didn't release her. Instead, he angled his body protectively around hers and nodded toward the rock where she'd been sitting moments before.

"Look," he murmured. Hope followed his gaze and gasped again, this time in horror. A large scorpion crouched exactly where her hand had been, its tail curled, pincers poised. A violent shudder rippled down her spine.

"Oh." It was all she could manage. "Thank you," she whispered at last, thoroughly shaken. She kept her eyes fixed on the creature rather than on the reverend, because he still held her effortlessly against his chest, and acknowledging *that* felt far more dangerous than the scorpion.

"My pleasure," he replied softly, a quiet smile tugging at his lips.

He didn't set her down until the scorpion finally scuttled away into the brush. Only then did he lower her gently to her feet. Hope's legs wobbled embarrassingly, and she prayed he hadn't noticed. She felt pale and breathless, and not solely from the near encounter.

"I think," she murmured, struggling to regain her composure, "I've had enough of the outdoors for today."

"I understand perfectly," he said with a warm, reassuring smile that sent another flutter racing through her stomach. "I despise those creatures myself." He offered her his arm for support. For a heartbeat, Hope hesitated. Then, cheeks still flushed, she placed her hand in the crook of his arm and allowed him to guide her back toward the infirmary, her pulse thrumming far louder than the stream behind them.

They reached Snowville late the following afternoon. By then, Hope was drained, physically aching, mentally stretched thin. Her arm throbbed with every sway of the stagecoach, and her nerves were frayed after the long, dusty ride. But nothing prepared her for Snowville itself.

The *town*, if it could even be called that, consisted of a saloon, a livery, a small post office, and a general store. No hotel. No boarding house. Not even a shabby inn. Just a saloon.

Hope's stomach dropped. The very idea of sleeping above a saloon, filled with drunk men, foul language, and questionable cleanliness, made her want to turn around and walk back to California. But they had no choice.

Inside, the saloon was dim, thick with pipe smoke and the sharp bite of cheap whiskey. Men sat at scattered tables, some laughing, some scowling, all of them staring when Hope entered. Even with her hat and loose-fitting shirt, she felt painfully exposed. For the first time since leaving San Francisco, she truly understood how vulnerable she was out here.

Reverend Shaw seemed to sense it instantly. He shifted closer, his shoulder brushing hers, until he stood like a solid wall between her and the nearest table of rough-looking cowhands. His posture was calm, controlled, but unmistakably protective. It helped. A little. They ordered supper, and Hope positioned herself with her back to the door, hoping not to draw attention. She tried to focus on her food, but her skin prickled with unease. The murmur of voices, the heavy boots passing behind her, every sound made her heart jolt.

They had just finished eating when someone at a nearby table shoved back his chair and yelled toward the entryway, "Hey, Whitmer! Over here!"

Hope froze. Her fork slipped from her hand and clattered against her plate. Slowly, unwillingly, she turned. And then she saw him. A man entered, a monster of a man, with a long, gruesome scar running from his cheek down his neck. Greasy hair jutted from beneath a hat that had seen far better days.

When he grinned, his mouth revealed rotting teeth that made her stomach twist. He looked exactly like the kind of man who could kill without losing a moment's sleep.

But it was the *other* man, the one who had called out to him, who stole the breath from her lungs. Hope felt the blood drain from her face. Her vision blurred around the edges. No. Impossible. And yet the memory struck her with the force of a hammer—

*A warm September evening. A walk in the park. Her mother's hand in hers. A carriage pulling up beside them. A man lunging out, grabbing at her mother. Hope hurling herself between them.*

*A brutal fist gripping her hair. Her head slamming into the carriage door. Voices shouting.*

*Her mother screaming her name. Darkness.*

Hope's breath hitched. Her pulse erupted. Her hands trembled violently. It was him. The man across the saloon. The man who had once tried to kidnap her mother. She shot to her feet, nearly knocking over the table, but her knees buckled. Reverend Shaw caught her immediately, his arm firm around her, steadying her shaking frame.

"Hope, what is it?" His voice was low and urgent. His brown eyes were filled with concern.

"I need to get out of here," she whispered, her throat tight. "Now. He'll see me, he'll recognize me."

Reverend Shaw's expression sharpened instantly. Understanding, and something fierce, flashed in his eyes.

"I can't stay," she whispered, trembling. "Please... please, we have to leave." Her entire body shook, from fear, from memory, from the shock of confronting a ghost she'd thought she'd buried.

Reverend Shaw didn't hesitate. He slid an arm beneath her knees and lifted her. Hope's breath caught, because he held her as though she were precious, breakable, something he would defend with his life.

"Lean your head against my shoulder," he murmured close to her ear, his voice low and protective. "Turn away from the room. No one will see your face."

Hope nodded, pressing her cheek against the warmth of his shoulder. His scent, clean soap, leather, and something warm and unmistakably masculine, wrapped around her, grounding her, steadying her racing heart.

He carried her out of the saloon without hesitation, shielding her completely from view, every step radiating certainty and strength. For the first time since the nightmare memory resurfaced, she drew a shaky breath that didn't break.

Outside, the cool night air hit them like a splash of water, but Hope barely felt it. Her pulse thundered in her ears as Reverend Shaw tightened his hold just enough to keep her steady. His eyes swept the empty street, searching for somewhere, anywhere, safe enough to disappear into. But the tiny town of Snowville offered very little. The general store was dark. The post office shuttered. The saloon behind them held the danger they were trying to escape. The only building with a lantern still lit was the livery stable.

"Over there," he murmured. Without waiting for her response, he guided her swiftly toward it. The smell of hay and horses greeted them as they slipped inside. Rows of stalls lined the walls, and somewhere in the back a horse snorted softly. The stable manager, a burly man with kind eyes, looked up in surprise.

"Well, howdy! Didn't expect company this late. You lookin' to hire out some horses?"

Reverend Shaw shook his head, his arm still protectively around Hope as he positioned himself between her and the rest of the stable.

"No. My—" He stumbled for a moment, then finished, "...my companion ain't doin' so good. We just need a quiet place."

The man's expression softened immediately. He stepped closer, his gaze shifting to Hope's pale face and trembling hands.

"Ma'am, you all right?"

Hope swallowed, but no words came. Reverend Shaw answered for her.

"She's had a shock," he said, his voice low and steady. "A bad one."

The man nodded sympathetically.

"Well, reckon you came to the right place. Ain't nobody gonna bother you in here." He hesitated, then frowned slightly. "But if she's truly ailin'... you want me to fetch the doctor?"

Reverend Shaw lifted his brows in surprise.

"You... have a doctor here?" It wasn't judgment, it was genuine disbelief. Hope had seen posters advertising Snowville as little more than a whistle-stop. A town this small shouldn't have more than a barber and a blacksmith.

The stableman grinned, puffing up just a little with hometown pride.

"Sure do. Doc Foster. Mighty good man. Knows his herbs better'n most city quacks. I'll fetch him right quick." Before either Hope or Reverend Shaw could protest, the man was already heading for the back door, calling over his shoulder, "Won't be but a minute!"

The door swung shut, leaving Hope and Reverend Shaw standing in the quiet dimness of the stable, lantern light flickering softly across their faces. Her breath trembled. His hand was still on her arm, steady, warm, grounding, yet he made no move to pull away. In the stillness, with only the rustle of hay and the distant howl of wind outside, Hope realized just how close she had come to collapsing in that saloon.

She turned her face up toward him, her voice barely a whisper.

"Thank you... for getting me out."

His gaze softened, deepened. His thumb brushed ever so slightly against her sleeve.

"I'd never let anything happen to you, Hope."

Her heart missed a beat. The stable suddenly felt far too quiet. Far too intimate. Far too dangerous. And yet... she didn't step away.

Reverend Shaw turned fully toward Hope. She sat hunched on a straw bale, her shoulders trembling, her face as pale as moonlight. No matter how fiercely she blinked, tears kept rising, spilling over despite her efforts to hold them back. He squatted in front of her without hesitation.

"Hope," he said softly, urgently. "What is going on?"

His voice alone nearly undid her. She pressed a hand to her forehead, but the tears came anyway, hot, relentless, born of fear and shock. She forced the words out between shallow breaths, recounting every detail of the memory that had slammed into her: the carriage, the sudden attack, the man's face, the brutal blow to her head, the panic, the pain, the screams. She spoke quickly, almost frantically, as though reliving it all over again. Reverend Shaw's face drained of color.

"And you are absolutely certain," he asked slowly, "that he was the man who tried to kidnap your mother?"

Hope nodded, her hands shaking. "I... I didn't remember it until now. Or maybe I did, but only in flashes I thought weren't real." She swallowed hard. "But when I saw him... it all came back. Every bit of it."

Reverend Shaw inhaled sharply, an audible, disbelieving sound. Then something shifted in his expression. The concern remained, but beneath it burned something fiercer. Protective. Dangerous. The look of a man who would willingly face an entire saloon full of outlaws if it meant keeping her safe.

"Listen to me," he said firmly, placing a steadying hand on her knee. "I'm going to see if this town has a sheriff, or anyone in authority who can be trusted. I need to know who these men are and whether we're in danger here."

Her fingers tightened in her lap. "Please... just be careful."

He touched her cheek gently, brushing away a tear that escaped despite her attempt to hide it.

"I will," he murmured. "But you must stay here. Stay in the stable. Don't step outside. Don't go near the saloon. Don't let anyone see your face."

Hope nodded, trembling.

"I'll be back shortly," he promised. He stood, but not before giving her one last searching look, as if memorizing her face in case danger lurked closer than either of them realized. Then he turned and strode out of the stable into the dim twilight.

Hope watched him disappear through the wooden door. The moment it swung shut behind him, her breath faltered. She closed her eyes, fighting to steady her racing thoughts and the pounding of her heart, half from terror, half from the realization of just how much she had come to rely on him. The quiet of the stable pressed in, around her. She hugged her arms to her chest and whispered into the dimness, "Please... come back safe."

"So, it was you, Hope Spencer," a low, venomous voice snarled behind her. Hope's blood turned to ice. She spun around, and her heart plummeted. Both men from the saloon stood in the doorway of the livery. Whitmer's hulking figure blocked the moonlight behind him. Lester stepped forward, his smile a horrible twist of malice.

"Do you want me to get her, Lester?" Whitmer asked, almost bored. Lester shook his head, eyes glinting.

"No need," he said with a slow, predatory grin. "I'll take care of her."

Hope stumbled backward, her pulse thundering as she searched desperately for something, anything, to defend herself.

"Why did you kill my mother?" she shouted at Whitmer, her voice cracking with grief and fury. He didn't even glance her way. He simply turned and walked off into the shadows, as if the question were beneath him. As if the life he had stolen meant nothing.

"Why were you trying to kidnap her?" Hope cried, this time aimed at Lester. He was smiling. A sick, gleeful smile that made Hope's stomach churn. She shifted her stance, her injured arm throbbing. Her eyes darted around the stable, bridles, buckets, tools, bales of straw. None of it seemed enough against a murderer.

Lester took a step forward. Hope took one back. He took another. She retreated farther, her heart pounding so loudly she could barely hear his footsteps. He saw the fear in her eyes. He enjoyed it. Suddenly, he lunged.

Hope reacted on pure instinct. Her hand shot out and grabbed a bridle hanging on a hook. As he closed in, she swung the heavy metal bit with all the strength she had left. It connected with his skull in a sickening crack. Lester howled, stumbling back, clutching the side of his head.

Hope didn't wait. She backed away, panting, and her gaze landed on a shovel leaning against a support beam. She seized it just as he regained his balance. His eyes were filled with murderous rage now, no smirking, no taunting. Just cold, lethal intent. He charged.

Hope lifted the shovel with both arms, pain blazing through her wounded shoulder, and swung.

The impact sent him crashing backward onto the dirt floor. But the effort tore her stitches wide open. White-hot agony seared through her arm. She dropped the shovel and collapsed to her knees, clutching her sleeve as warm blood soaked through the fabric. Her breath came in ragged gasps.

Lester staggered to his feet, blood streaming down his face. His fury transformed him into something animalistic. Terrifying. Hope braced herself for another attack. But he didn't come toward her. Instead, he slipped a packet of matches from his pocket.

"No," Hope whispered, realizing what he intended. He struck several matches at once, the flames flickering wildly in the dim barn light, then tossed them into the dry straw near her. Fire erupted instantly. The blaze leapt upward, hungry, ferocious, licking along the floorboards and jumping from bale to bale. Horses screamed and thrashed in their stalls.

Hope couldn't see Lester anymore through the smoke and fire, but she heard his footsteps retreating. She coughed violently as smoke filled her lungs. She had to get out. She had to save the horses. Despite the agony tearing through her arm, she forced herself up and stumbled toward the stalls. She fumbled with latches, throwing each door open. Panicked horses barreled past her, nearly knocking her down in their desperate escape.

The fire spread faster than she could move. Hope grabbed the shovel again, beating at the flames, but it was useless. The inferno grew with every second. Her eyes watered. She coughed harder, her lungs burning. Her vision blurred. Still, she reached the last stall, yanked the latch open, and watched the terrified animal bolt through the smoke. The flames roared behind her now.

She turned toward the exit, stumbling through the thick haze. Her foot snagged on the bridle lying in the straw. She crashed forward, hitting the ground so hard the breath was knocked from her lungs. Her strength was fading fast. The fire surged closer. Heat seared her face. She clawed at the ground, trying to push herself up, but her injured arm gave out beneath her.

Just as consciousness began to slip away, two strong arms scooped her up. Someone shouted something, but she couldn't make out the words. She saw shapes rushing in, men beating at the flames with blankets, throwing water, shouting orders. The world tilted. Dimmed. And dissolved into darkness. Hope let go. And everything went black.

# 7

# In Her Shaking Hands

When Hope opened her eyes, the world returned in soft, blurry fragments. A ceiling she didn't recognize. Lantern light glowing warmly against pale wooden walls. The faint scent of antiseptic herbs. Somewhere nearby, hushed voices murmured, and the distant clatter of boots echoed against a wooden floor. It took her a moment to realize she was in some kind of infirmary. Her arm ached, but it was wrapped neatly in fresh bandages. Someone had re-stitched the torn wound. Someone had saved her.

Before she could shift or sit up, several figures stepped closer to her bed.

"Hope," Reverend Shaw murmured, his voice gentle as a breeze. His face appeared above her, eyes warm and filled with such raw concern she felt it like a touch. "How are you feeling?"

Hope tried to smile, but it dissolved into a cough. He immediately lifted a cup to her lips, helping her sip water.

"I think... I'm all right," she whispered. "What happened to the stable?"

"We managed to save most of it," he assured her. "And the horses."

Her breath shuddered. "Did Whitmer and Lester escape?" Worry flared in her eyes, bright and urgent.

"Whitmer escaped," Reverend Shaw said with a frown. "But Lester didn't get far. Soldiers arrived in time to arrest him. He's locked up now." He squeezed her hand gently, grounding her. "You're safe."

A young soldier stepped forward, straightening his uniform.

"Miss Spencer, we received a telegram from Captain Sheffield," he said. "He informed us of your situation. Since our unit was closest to Snowville, we came as quickly as we could." His expression softened slightly. "We apprehended the man who trapped you in the stable and set the fire. He sustained some... significant head injuries." His lips twitched, almost approvingly. "Can you tell us what happened?"

Hope nodded weakly and explained everything, the attack, her desperate blows with the bridle and shovel, the fire, freeing the horses, her attempt to escape. When she described striking Lester hard enough to knock him down, two soldiers at the back let out low whistles, clearly impressed.

Reverend Shaw and the lead soldier exhaled in relief.

"So, he didn't physically harm you?" the soldier asked.

"No," Hope said. "He tried. But he didn't."

The soldier nodded. "How is he connected to your mother's death?"

Hope inhaled deeply, steadying herself.

"He was one of the men who tried to kidnap my mother last year. And... he signed the letter ordering Whitmer to kill her."

Anger flashed across the soldier's features.

"Thank you," he said firmly. "We'll transfer him to the nearest sheriff and ensure he remains in custody."

Hope nodded. The group saluted lightly and filed out, everyone except Reverend Shaw, leaving the room quiet once more. He remained seated beside her bed. Leaning forward, he studied her with a mixture of guilt and fierce protectiveness.

"Hope," he said quietly, "I'm so sorry I left you alone in the stable. I shouldn't have gone."

She shook her head, her eyes softening.

"What happened wasn't your fault. Neither of us knew he'd seen me at the saloon. Or that he followed us." She took a shallow breath. "And... if I'd had my way, I would have been traveling alone anyway."

He looked down, absorbing her words, then nodded with solemn understanding.

"We should get some rest," he murmured. "It's well past midnight." He yawned, rubbed the back of his neck, then settled deeper into the chair beside her bed as if fully intending to stay. Hope blinked, startled, and instantly blushed.

"Aren't you going to sleep at the saloon?"

He shook his head, lifting his gaze to hers. There was quiet steel in his eyes.

"After what happened tonight," he said, his voice hardening, "I'm not leaving you again."

"But—"

He raised a hand, silencing her gently.

"Don't argue with me, Hope." His jaw tightened, his voice raw with emotion. "When I came back and saw flames pouring from the stable windows... I thought my heart had stopped." His eyes darkened. "I am not making that mistake again." The fierce determination in his expression stole her breath.

Her cheeks burned, but beneath the embarrassment, warmth bloomed in her chest, quiet, fierce, undeniable. Though she turned her face away to hide the rising blush, some vulnerable, aching part of her was profoundly relieved that he wasn't leaving her alone. Not tonight. Maybe not ever.

Hope let out a long, weary sigh as she and Reverend Shaw stood outside the small Snowville post building, waiting for the stagecoach. The morning air was crisp, but it did nothing to ease the tightness in her chest.

"There's no way of knowing where Whitmer went," she murmured, her voice barely above a whisper. "We know his destination, yes, but he could have taken any road, any trail. He could be anywhere by now."

Reverend Shaw stood beside her, his hat pulled low over his brow, arms folded as if containing his own frustration. He nodded slowly.

"That's true," he admitted. "But he could also be lying low for a short while. And honestly?" He glanced down at her. "I'm hoping that's exactly what he does."

Hope blinked, surprised. "Why?"

"Because it gives us a chance," he said quietly. "To get ahead of him. To reach Wyoming first. Sergeant Ride told me that when the soldiers checked his room at the saloon, the window was wide open. Whitmer must have seen them coming and realized he had no time."

Hope shivered, not from the cold. The image struck her vividly: the window flung open, curtains snapping in the night wind, an empty room where a killer had stood only moments before. The thought sent a chill straight through her.

"He saw the soldiers," she echoed. "He knew he was in trouble."

Reverend Shaw nodded. "Exactly. Which means his escape was rushed. He won't have planned his next steps as carefully as he usually does."

Hope wrapped her arms around herself. Even with Reverend Shaw at her side, unease coiled beneath her skin. She couldn't stop replaying the moment she'd seen Anthony Whitmer in the saloon. How her body had gone cold, how her knees had weakened, how fear had seized her in a way she hadn't known was possible.

"I never wanted to see his face again," she whispered. "Not ever. And now that I have..." Her voice faltered. "I don't think I'll ever forget it."

"You won't face this alone, Hope," Reverend Shaw said gently. She dared a glance up at him. The warmth in his eyes was unexpected, steady, reassuring, almost achingly gentle. For a fleeting moment, she felt a sense of safety she hadn't known in days... maybe weeks. His presence wrapped around her like a shield. The distant clatter of wheels broke the silence. The stagecoach was approaching. Hope straightened, drawing in a slow breath as she watched it crest the hill.

"Wyoming," she whispered. "I suppose that's where everything leads now."

Reverend Shaw stepped just a little closer, close enough that she could feel the quiet strength radiating from him.

"And no matter what waits for us there," he said softly, "we'll face it together."

Her heart skipped, not from fear this time, but from something far more confusing. And far more dangerous.

They had been traveling for nearly the entire day. The heat, the dust, the constant jostling of the stagecoach, all of it blurred together until the moment the driver leaned back and shouted that they were only a few miles from their destination. Relief had barely begun to loosen the knot in Hope's chest when gunfire cracked through the air.

Hope jerked upright as the stagecoach lurched violently. She leaned out the window just in time to see the driver tumble from his seat, then the second man fell after him, both bodies hitting the ground with lifeless thuds. A scream lodged in her throat. Each man had been shot in the side of the head.

Before she could fully comprehend the horror, Reverend Shaw grabbed her and hauled her down, dragging her out of sight as more gunshots tore through the coach. Splinters rained down like shrapnel. Through the shattered slats, she saw them, two riders galloping toward the stagecoach, guns raised.

Hope's breath caught, but she forced her trembling hands to reach for her bow and arrows. Before she could notch the first shaft, bullets slammed into the coach again. Reverend Shaw jerked forward with a sharp cry and collapsed back against the seat.

"Reverend—!" Hope's voice broke. Then she saw the blood. A dark crimson bloom spread rapidly beneath his shoulder, far too close to his heart. "No..." The word escaped as a broken whisper.

She squeezed her eyes shut for a single heartbeat, forcing panic down, then snapped them open again. He was sweating, his breath coming in ragged, uneven gasps. The riders slowed as Hope loosed two arrows in rapid succession. One man screamed as her arrow found flesh. The attackers veered off, retreating just enough to regroup at a distance.

"Hope..." Reverend Shaw gasped. "Rip my shirt. Take my knife. Get the bullet out."

Her eyes flew wide. "I—I can't. We need a doctor. We need—"

"We're in the middle of nowhere." His breath shuddered as pain crumpled his expression. "If we wait, the wound will fester. Please... Hope."

With trembling hands, she tore his shirt open. The moment she saw the torn, bloody flesh, her vision rippled. Tears sprang into her eyes.

"I can't do this," she cried, panic rising like a tide. "I'm not a doctor. I could kill you. This is why I told you not to come. You could die because of me!"

"Hope." His voice was weak but steady. "Look at me."

When she didn't, his hand, shaking but determined, lifted her chin. His gaze locked with hers. Calm. Steady. Full of trust.

"It's not your fault," he whispered. "None of this is your fault. You didn't force me to come. I chose to. And I trust you. I know you can do this."

Gunfire echoed again, farther away now. Whoever remained was fleeing. She had seconds, maybe less. Her gaze darted wildly around the coach.

"Something... something clean..." Her fingers brushed the underskirt in her bag. She pulled it out, hands trembling violently.

"Just do it, Hope," he murmured through clenched teeth. "Don't look at me. Just... do it."

She whispered a desperate prayer and made the cut. Reverend Shaw gasped, his hand spasming against the seat, but he didn't pull away. Hope forced herself not to look at his face. Not even once. Her stomach churned. Twice the bullet slipped from her grip. Twice she had to cut deeper. Each time he moaned, and each sound carved into her heart.

Finally, the bullet clattered onto the floor. Hope exhaled shakily. With trembling hands, she tore long strips from the underskirt and layered them over the wound. As she wrapped the bandages around his torso, her fingers brushed his warm skin. Her cheeks burned. She refused to look at him, refused to acknowledge the panic and the other, far more dangerous feeling fluttering beneath her ribs. When she finished the final knot and dared glance up, he gave her a weak but grateful smile.

"Thank you," he whispered.

Before she could answer, hoofbeats and wagon wheels approached. Hope peered out the shattered window.

"A buckboard," she breathed. Reverend Shaw nodded painfully. "Help me get a shirt on before they see this."

She dug out a clean shirt from his bag. When she leaned in to help him into it, her breath caught. His chest, solid, warm, undeniably masculine, was inches from her. Too close. Far too close. Her fingers brushed his skin as she guided his arm into the sleeve, and her heart raced so quickly she feared he might hear it.

She fastened each button with excruciating care, but the more she focused on the task, the more aware she became of his nearness... the heat of his breath... the way his dark eyes never left her face. By the time she reached the top button, her cheeks were blazing. Then his hand brushed her chin again, tilting her face upward. Her breath stalled.

He leaned in—closer. Hope jerked back, pulse pounding, nearly stumbling as she scrambled away. She was trembling, and she hated how her body betrayed her. The buckboard rolled to a stop, saving her from further humiliation. Two men peered through the broken door.

"Are you two all right?" one asked.

Hope forced a steady breath. "For the most part. He's been shot. I removed the bullet, but a doctor should look at it."

They introduced themselves as Brother Jacob Middleton and Brother Jeremiah Matthews, kind, warm, smiling despite the grim circumstances. They helped Reverend Shaw down and gathered their bags. When they mentioned they belonged to the Church of Jesus Christ of Latter-day Saints, Hope listened with polite curiosity, though her fingers fidgeted with the hem of her sleeve. Her thoughts kept drifting back, to the blood, the gunshots... and Reverend Shaw's near kiss. When they asked what had brought her so far from San Francisco, she answered honestly. Their expressions turned grave.

"Does that mean the stagecoach attack was personal?" Brother Jeremiah asked. The implication struck her like a blow. Reverend Shaw had nearly died because someone was hunting her. Her knees buckled. She gasped for air. Immediately, all three men stepped toward her. Reverend Shaw took her hand firmly.

"Breathe, Hope," he murmured. "Slowly. That's it."

She steadied. Mostly. But when Brother Jacob gently asked whether she had found her mother after the attack, something inside her cracked. Hope couldn't speak. Her throat tightened painfully. She nodded once, tears filling her eyes.

Needing air, she whispered, "Excuse me," and fled toward the lake. There, she collapsed to her knees, scrubbing the blood from her hands as tears spilled over uncontrollably. She tried, tried so hard, to swallow it down, to choke it back. But days of fear, grief, anger, and exhaustion ripped free, and sobs tore from her chest.

She didn't hear him approach. Not until his warm hand gently closed over hers. Hope startled as Reverend Shaw pulled her up, then into his arms. Her cheek pressed to his chest, her tears dampening his shirt. She cried until the sobs faded into shivers. He held her through all of it. When she finally stepped back, flushing with embarrassment, he didn't comment. He only offered a soft, reassuring smile.

"Let's go," he said gently. "Brother Jacob and Brother Jeremiah will take us to their settlement. It's close."

Hope nodded, wiping her eyes with the back of her hand. But before she turned away, she risked one glance back at him. And the look he gave her, tender, protective, unguarded, made her heart flip in a way she could no longer deny. Her journey had grown far more complicated than danger alone. And she wasn't sure which frightened her more.

It was a beautiful, small Christian settlement, quiet, orderly, peaceful, but Hope noticed instantly that there was no hotel, no saloon, no boarding house. Only neat little homes, a schoolroom, a church, and fields stretching beyond.

"Welcome to Saint Charles," Brother Jacob said as he helped Hope down from the buckboard.

Before she had fully steadied herself, a woman approached, warm eyes, a welcoming smile, the gentle confidence of someone accustomed to caring for everyone around her. Brother Jacob pulled her aside and whispered a brief explanation of what little they knew about Hope and Reverend Shaw. The woman didn't hesitate. She stepped forward, reached for Hope's hands, and pulled her into a firm, motherly embrace.

"Oh, honey..." Her voice was soft and full of compassion. "I'm so sorry you've had to go through so much heartache."

Hope's throat tightened. Her eyes burned again.

"Why don't you join us for supper?" the woman offered cheerfully. Hope immediately glanced toward Reverend Shaw, then shook her head quickly. "Oh no, that's a very kind offer, but we don't want to impose."

"Nonsense." The woman waved the concern away. "We would love to have you. And of course, you'll stay with us until you leave. You and your husband can sleep in our guest room."

Hope gasped, turning crimson so fast she nearly swayed. Her husband? Her burning gaze darted to Reverend Shaw, who was most definitely enjoying her mortification, then back to the woman. How could she possibly assume...? And why did no one seem to notice the age difference? Though, to be fair... Reverend Shaw did look younger now. Suspiciously younger. Was that why he shaved and dyed his hair? No. Absolutely not. She shut that thought down immediately.

"He is not my husband," she said quickly, voice small and mortified. "We're not married."

"Oh!" The woman's smile didn't budge. "Engaged, then?"

Hope wished a hole would open beneath her feet and swallow her whole.

"No. Not engaged. Not courting. Not anything. He is the reverend from home, and he insisted on traveling with me so I wouldn't go alone."

"What a shame," the woman sighed dreamily. "You two make such a beautiful couple."

Hope's cheeks turned into a wildfire. Reverend Shaw coughed to hide a laugh. Brother Jacob cleared his throat loudly.

"Abigail, leave the girl alone," he scolded gently. "You're embarrassing her."

Abigail grimaced, immediately apologizing.

"I'm sorry, dear. Come now, let's get you settled." She turned to Reverend Shaw. "We'll have our daughters stay in the guest room with Hope, and you can have their room."

"You are very kind, Mrs. Middleton," Hope said, still recovering.

"Oh, none of that. Call me Abigail," she insisted with a warm smile. "You'll be here for a while."

Hope blinked. "...A while?"

Abigail tilted her head. "Didn't Brother Jacob tell you? The next stagecoach won't come through until the end of the month."

Hope's jaw dropped. "That's... nearly four weeks! We can't possibly stay that long. We must keep going."

"You can't," Abigail said simply. "There's nothing to be done. And we are happy to have you."

"But—"

Reverend Shaw cleared his throat.

"Perhaps it's good for us to take a little break." His voice was calm, soothing. "Hope, you've been injured twice in just a few days. You need to rest. We both do."

Hope shook her head violently.

"But they don't know us! And Whitmer is out there somewhere. What if he brings danger to this settlement? These people have families!" Her breath quickened, chest rising and falling too fast. Reverend Shaw stepped forward, concern etched into every line of his face.

"Hope—"

"No!" Her voice broke, raw. "You were nearly killed already. I will not drag innocent families into the path of a murderer. I should never have told you, my plan. I should have left San Francisco alone."

Abigail, Brother Jacob, and Brother Jeremiah all froze. Even with limited details, they understood now, this girl was unraveling.

"You need to calm down," Reverend Shaw said softly. "We're both tired. Both hurt. Staying won't harm anyone."

"I'm not staying." Hope backed away, breath coming faster. "You stay here. Heal. I'll go on foot. I won't risk anyone else's life."

They could all see it. She was slipping into shock. Brother Jeremiah rushed off for help. Abigail stepped forward, trying to soothe her, but Hope recoiled.

"Hope, sweetheart, look at me," Abigail urged gently. Hope's eyes remained fixed on the ground, haunted, frantic.

"Thank you for your hospitality," Hope whispered, backing away. "But I can't stay. I must find my mother's killer. It's my responsibility. I won't draw anyone else into danger." She turned to flee—straight into Brother Jacob's arms. He caught her instantly, holding her firmly but gently as she struggled.

"Let go of me!" Hope cried. "You have a family. You shouldn't worry about me. I'll be fine. Please, let me go!"

Abigail reached for her cheeks, trying to lift her face.

"Sweet girl," she whispered, "you were led here for a reason. Stop fighting us."

"No, I wasn't," Hope insisted, voice breaking. "I'll bring danger to you. I nearly had Reverend Shaw killed. I won't do that to anyone else."

Reverend Shaw stepped in, his expression fierce and protectively tender. He reached for her chin, carefully, gently, and tilted her face up until her blue eyes met his.

"You didn't do anything to me, Hope," he said softly. "Whitmer didn't shoot me because of you. And even if he had, none of this is your fault."

Tears welled again. She swallowed hard.

"You went after him," he continued, "not for revenge, but to prevent another woman's death. Your courage is why we left San Francisco. And you need to hear this: you were not safe there anymore. Leaving was wise, not foolish."

She shook her head faintly. "But I shouldn't have let you come..."

"I wanted to come," he said firmly. "I chose this. Because you needed protection, and because Doc Baker and I agreed that, with your father failing in his duty, it fell to us to step in."

Hope closed her eyes. A tear slid down her cheek.

"It isn't your job to protect me," she whispered. "My father never did."

Abigail gasped softly. "Your father never stood up for his own daughter?"

Hope shook her head slowly, finally meeting the older woman's eyes.

"He never hugged me. Never comforted me. Never encouraged me. It was always my mom." Her voice wavered. "The first time a man held me was the night my mother died. Doc Baker held me because my father didn't care."

Reverend Shaw's eyes darkened with grief and understanding.

"He didn't do it out of pity," he murmured. "He did it because he loved your mother, and he knew you needed what your father denied you."

Hope exhaled shakily. "Father never allowed any man to get close to me, except the man he chose as my husband. And Eric—Eric was possessive, not affectionate. To be honest, I'm still shocked he didn't stop Doc Baker from hugging me that night."

Abigail placed a comforting hand on her shoulder, her expression warm and steady.

"Well," she said gently, "you're safe now. And until the next coach comes, you're staying with us. We'll take care of you."

Brother Jeremiah returned, and with him came an older man with silver-streaked hair, sharp eyes, and a calming presence. He carried a worn leather satchel and moved with the quiet authority of someone long accustomed to tending the sick.

"This is Dr. Taylor," Brother Jeremiah announced gently. Hope drew a steadying breath. Her panic had ebbed, though her limbs still trembled faintly. Dr. Taylor studied her for a moment, his gaze kind yet assessing, before nodding toward the Middleton home.

"Let's get you both somewhere warm," he said in a low, reassuring voice. "I'll look after you properly."

They walked together to the Middletons' home. Abigail hurried ahead to prepare the guest room, fluffing pillows and lighting a small oil lamp, while Brother Jacob ushered them inside. Dr. Taylor set his satchel beside the bed and motioned for Hope to sit.

"Miss Spencer first," he said gently. Hope hesitated, embarrassed to be the center of concern again, but Reverend Shaw gave her a small nod of encouragement. She sat on the edge of the bed as the doctor knelt beside her and carefully unwound the makeshift bandages. He worked with practiced hands, efficient, gentle, no wasted movements. Hope flinched once or twice, but he murmured reassurance with each adjustment. Abigail stayed close by.

"You did well to come here," he told her. "The arm is healing, but you're exhausted, child."

Hope swallowed hard. "I'm... better now. I'm sorry about earlier."

"No need for apologies," Abigail replied, giving her hand a warm squeeze. Dr. Taylor nodded, his tone warm but firm.

"You've suffered more shock than most grown men could withstand. Your body is simply telling you it needs rest." He cleaned the wound with warm herbal water, applied a soothing ointment, and wrapped her arm with fresh cloth. Then he handed her a small cup filled with pale tea that smelled faintly of chamomile and mint.

"This will settle your nerves and help you sleep later," he said. "Take it slowly."

Hope obeyed, grateful for the warmth spreading through her chest after the first sip. Once he was satisfied with her condition, Dr. Taylor turned to Reverend Shaw.

"Your turn, Reverend."

Reverend Shaw gave Hope a reassuring half-smile before shifting forward so the doctor could access his shoulder. Dr. Taylor carefully removed the bandages, examining the stitches and the wound.

"My word..." the doctor murmured, impressed. He glanced between the Reverend and Hope. "Miss Spencer, did you remove the bullet yourself?"

Hope looked down. "Yes... but I didn't want to. I was terrified I'd make it worse."

"Well," Dr. Taylor said with clear admiration, "you did a remarkably clean job for someone without medical training. Very neat cuts. And this," he tapped the white cloth Hope had used, "is clean material. You helped prevent infection."

A flush of relief warmed her face.

"She's extraordinarily capable," Reverend Shaw said quietly, watching Hope with an expression that made her heart flutter. Dr. Taylor cleaned the wound more thoroughly, stitched the cuts, applied ointment, and wrapped Reverend Shaw's chest and shoulder with practiced efficiency.

"With proper rest, good food, and the teas I'll prepare, your wounds should heal quickly," he said. "You're both strong, but don't rush this. Bodies recover best when minds are calm." He packed away his tools and gave Hope a final, reassuring smile. "You're safe here, Miss Spencer. Truly."

Hope exhaled slowly, feeling, for the first time in days, a fragile thread of safety weaving itself around her.

# 8

# Safe Within These Walls

When everyone had gathered in the sitting room, Abigail's sharp, assessing eyes moved from Hope to Reverend Shaw and back again. She crossed her arms.

"What happened to you two?" she demanded. Reverend Shaw cleared his throat and sat a little straighter.

"Hope was attacked by a group of Indians. They shot at her with arrows. One struck her arm."

"Goodness gracious!" Abigail exclaimed, eyes widening. "Why on earth would they shoot at a girl? Did they injure you as well, Reverend?"

He shook his head. "No. I wasn't with Hope when that happened." His eyebrow lifted pointedly in her direction. "She... snuck off on her own."

Hope stared at the floor, cheeks burning with embarrassment.

"And why would you do that?" Abigail scolded, planting her hands on her hips and fixing Hope with a motherly, but unmistakably firm, glare.

"Because he kissed me," Hope blurted before she could stop herself. Silence fell like a dropped skillet. Abigail turned her head slowly, very slowly, toward Reverend Shaw. Her eyes narrowed into a look that suggested he was about to receive a lecture that would make fire and brimstone seem gentle. The Reverend coughed and fixed his gaze on the ceiling. Abigail drew in a deep breath and released it in a long, measured sigh.

"Well," she said dryly, "that sounds like a complicated situation we'll discuss later... after our children have gone to bed." She sent Hope a playful wink, which only made the girl turn an even deeper shade of red. "Now then," Abigail continued, redirecting her stern attention back to the man, "what injury have *you* received?"

"Our stagecoach was attacked earlier," he explained. "A bullet hit me here." He touched his chest lightly. "Hope was able to remove it."

Abigail's jaw dropped. "My word. I think the two of you ought to stay right here and not go anywhere else. If you keep up this pattern, you'll get yourselves killed within a week."

Brother Jacob chuckled under his breath, shaking his head.

"All right now," he said warmly, stepping in before Abigail's worries could multiply. "Let's have some supper. I'm sure you're both famished."

Relief washed over Hope. Supper sounded like heaven, warm food, a quiet place to sit, and perhaps a moment where she wasn't recounting near-death experiences or explaining unexpected kisses. She glanced at Reverend Shaw. He gave her a small, apologetic smile that made her heart flutter and her stomach twist with nerves she refused to name.

Together, they followed the Middletons toward the kitchen, drawn by the comforting aroma of fresh bread and simmering stew.

The food was delicious, simple, hearty, and wonderfully filling, and Hope could hardly believe how peaceful the Middleton household felt. Even more astonishing was how well-behaved the family's eight children were. Their ages ranged from nineteen all the way down to four, and yet the supper table had been calm, cheerful, and full of gentle chatter.

The oldest son, Samuel, was a striking young man with warm hazel eyes and a boyish smile. Hope caught him glancing at her now and then, and though it made her shy, she found him kind. His friendliness carried none of the arrogance she had endured growing up among society men.

Esther and Elizabeth, the seventeen- and sixteen-year-old sisters, sat on either side of Hope as though they had claimed her at once. Within minutes, they were chattering away as if they had known her their entire lives. Their enthusiasm was infectious, and Hope felt herself smiling more than she had in days. She would be sharing the guest room with them during her stay, and the thought was surprisingly comforting.

After supper, Abigail shooed the younger children off to get ready for bed. Esther and Elizabeth whisked the dishes into the kitchen. Hope began to rise to follow them, eager for something to do, but Abigail stopped her with a warm but firm hand on her shoulder.

"Oh no, sweetheart. You are our guest. Go find a nice spot by the fire and relax."

Hope hesitated, but the sincerity in Abigail's smile left her little room to refuse. Brother Jacob and Samuel headed outside to tend to the animals, leaving the house quiet except for the crackle of the hearth.

Reverend Shaw joined her in the sitting room and lowered himself into the chair beside her. For a few long minutes, he said nothing, he simply watched her. Hope shifted. Then shifted again. Her cheeks warmed under his steady, unreadable gaze, and finally she sprang to her feet.

"I—I think I should help with the dishes," she muttered, escaping into the kitchen before he could protest.

Esther and Elizabeth looked up the moment she entered and welcomed her with bright smiles. The sisters were naturally cheerful, chatty, and full of curiosity. Hope found herself relaxing again, until Elizabeth leaned closer with a conspiratorial grin.

"I heard Dr. Taylor talking with Reverend Shaw," she whispered. "He said you removed the bullet from his chest. Did you have to take his shirt off for that? I bet he looks just as manly as I imagine. Tell me, does he?"

"Lizzie!" Esther gasped, whipping her sister with a scandalized glare.

Hope froze, mortified. Her face lit up like a lantern. Elizabeth's grin widened with mischievous delight, her eyes sparkling. Under different circumstances, Hope might have been amused. But given the whirlwind of conflicting feelings she had toward the reverend, not to mention her own frazzled confusion, Elizabeth's blunt remark struck far too close to home. Before Hope could manage even a stammered response, a sharp voice cut through the kitchen.

"Elizabeth Cathleen Middleton."

All three young women jolted and turned. Abigail stood in the doorway, arms folded, her expression stern enough to drain the color from Elizabeth's cheeks.

"That remark was beyond inappropriate, young lady. You will not speak that way again. Is that understood?"

Elizabeth nodded so fast her braids bounced. Hope, still burning, wished she could dissolve into the floorboards. Abigail spared her a sympathetic glance, blessedly choosing not to address her embarrassment, and then pointed toward the sitting room.

"Go on back, dear. We'll be in shortly."

Hope returned reluctantly, half hoping the reverend had stepped outside. But Brother Jacob and Samuel were already back, seated with him near the hearth. Abigail and her daughters joined moments later, Abigail settled beside her husband with her knitting. Esther and Elizabeth flanked Hope again, no doubt hoping to hear the rest of the adventure they had only overheard in fragments.

"I'm curious about the things you mentioned earlier," Brother Jacob said gently, only to receive a nudge from Abigail. He cleared his throat. "I'd like to hear the whole story. But if you'd prefer the younger ones leave the room, just say so."

The three older children groaned at once, protesting, but one look from Abigail silenced them instantly. Reverend Shaw glanced at Hope.

"I'm willing to share what we've experienced, if Hope is comfortable with that."

Every eye turned to her. Hope rolled her own dramatically, earning muffled giggles from Esther and Elizabeth.

"Of course I'm not comfortable," she muttered. "But we already told part of it, so... we might as well." She shot the reverend a pointed side-glare, just to make sure he understood she blamed him for her current mortification.

And just like that, the evening unfolded into warmth and laughter. The family gasped in horror at parts of the story, clucked in sympathy at others, and teased one another—and Hope and the reverend—whenever the opportunity arose. Even Reverend Shaw relaxed, chuckling at moments Hope never would have expected.

By the time the fire had burned low, Hope felt something she hadn't felt since her mother died: Safe. Welcomed. Almost... home. She couldn't quite believe how completely the Middleton family had wrapped her into their circle. It felt as though she had known them forever. The tightness in her chest eased, just a little.

She felt deeply grateful when she finally lay down in the soft guest bed. Esther and Elizabeth whispered across their shared mattress, moonlight pouring through the window and casting a pale silver glow over the room. Everyone was tired, but sleep did not come immediately, least of all for Hope, whose mind still spun with the events of the day.

"I think Sam has taken a fancy to you," Elizabeth giggled suddenly, breaking the quiet. Hope froze. A moonbeam fell squarely across her face, making it impossible to hide the instant blaze of red that rushed into her cheeks.

"Lizzie!" Esther hissed, though she was smiling.

"It's true," Elizabeth insisted. "There aren't many girls here old enough to marry. And you are very beautiful, Hope. Just wait, half the older boys in our settlement will be lining up to court you."

Hope groaned and pulled the blanket higher.

"Reverend Shaw is very handsome," Elizabeth added in an admiring whisper, quiet enough that their mother wouldn't hear from across the house, but loud enough to make Hope want to disappear beneath the quilt entirely.

Esther rolled over to face her. "Were you really outraged when he kissed you?" she asked softly. "Or... was it your first kiss?"

Hope sputtered, unable to form even a half-coherent reply. Before she could gather herself, Elizabeth shot upright in her bed, braids bouncing.

"Are you in love with Reverend Shaw?"

Hope nearly fainted. Her heart stuttered. Her entire body felt hot enough to set the room ablaze. How in the world did these girls feel comfortable asking such questions already?

"Elizabeth!" Esther swatted her sister's arm. "You mustn't always be so forward."

But Elizabeth barely noticed the rebuke. Her eyes stayed fixed on Hope, bright with mischief and curiosity. After several painful seconds, Hope finally found her voice, albeit a strangled version of it.

"What—what makes you think something like that?" she demanded, pressing her hands to her burning cheeks. "Why would you think I could have romantic feelings for my *reverend*?"

Elizabeth began ticking items off on her fingers.

"Well, for starters, he's very handsome. And secondly, he clearly adores you."

"He does *not* adore me," Hope protested, though even she heard the weakness in her denial. "He... he simply feels obligated to look after me. He was a close friend of my mother's and now believes he must continue to protect me. He told me that himself." She added quickly, "And he is old enough to be my father."

Elizabeth made an indignant face. "He doesn't look that old."

Hope sighed. "That's because he shaved his beard not long ago. It makes him look more youthful."

Esther's tone softened. "Hope... I don't think you're right about his motives."

Hope's stomach fluttered, unhelpfully. "What do you mean?"

"He doesn't strike me as a man who protects someone because he *feels obligated*. And the way he looks at you..." Esther paused, giving Hope a knowing, older-sister glance. "It's not obligation."

Hope felt as though the air had been knocked from her lungs. Her chest tightened. Her heart thudded faster than she liked. She shook her head vigorously, as if she could scatter their words out of existence.

"All right, you two," she said with forced playfulness, though her voice trembled. "This conversation is making me very uncomfortable. It's late. We should go to sleep."

The sisters exchanged a look, then nodded and settled beneath their blankets. Silence returned to the room. But Hope's thoughts refused to quiet. The question she had tried to bury now echoed loudly in the dark house: *Was she in love with Reverend Shaw?* She pressed a hand to her racing heart, horrified by the flutter deep within her chest, and even more horrified by the truth she was afraid to admit. Because something was happening to her. Something she didn't understand. Something she wasn't sure she could control.

When Hope woke the following morning, sunlight was already streaming gently through the curtains. Elizabeth and Esther's side of the bed was empty. The girls must have risen long before dawn. She stretched cautiously, mindful of her arm, and then dressed for the day.

The moment she stepped out of the guest room and into the hallway, the scent of fresh bread and something sweet baking, cinnamon, perhaps, filled the air. Hope followed it toward the kitchen, where Abigail stood at the table kneading dough. The woman looked up at once and beamed.

"Good morning, Hope. Did you sleep well?"

Hope nodded. "Yes, very well. I'm sorry I slept so long."

Abigail waved a flour-dusted hand, brushing the apology aside.

"You hush with that apologizing. You've had too much stress, too little food, far too little sleep, and heaven help you, more danger than any young woman ought to face in a lifetime. Rest is exactly what your body needs." She reached for a small jar on the shelf.

"Later, I'll help you put more of Dr. Taylor's ointment on that arm. He said it should ease the discomfort and help the wound close faster."

"Thank you, Abigail," Hope murmured, touched by her kindness. "Where is everyone this morning?"

"Our younger children are in school. Jacob and Samuel are working the fields, and I believe Reverend Shaw went out for a walk shortly after sunrise. The girls are in the garden behind the house, tending the vegetables."

Hope straightened, a little. "May I do something to help? I don't want to be idle."

But Abigail was already shaking her head before Hope finished speaking.

"Not until I decide your arm can handle it. You need rest, not chores. Dr. Taylor said you must avoid straining the muscle, at least for your first week here."

"But—"

Abigail lifted one eyebrow, the gesture so motherly and authoritative that Hope almost smiled.

"Hope Spencer," she said in mock sternness, "you'll do as you're told, young lady. We aren't risking another injury or letting that wound get infected, not under my roof."

Hope smirked, unable to keep the teasing sparkle out of her eyes.

"Yes, ma'am."

Abigail's stern expression melted into a grin.

"Much better. Now, you may go outside if you like, but I'd better not find you pulling weeds or hauling water with the girls. Enjoy the sunshine. Walk a little. Breathe in the fresh air." She paused, then added with a chuckle, "And if you run into Sonny, our youngest, well, he's a good-hearted rascal, but don't let him goad you into anything wild. That child has more energy than a herd of colts."

Hope laughed softly. For the first time in days, her chest didn't feel quite so tight. She thanked Abigail again, and with her arm cradled protectively against her, stepped out toward the back of the house, toward the garden, the girls, and perhaps even toward Reverend Shaw... though she was far less willing to admit that last thought.

"Good morning, Hope!" Esther called cheerfully from the garden and hurried over, brushing soil from her skirt. "Have you had breakfast yet?"

Hope shook her head, but before she could say a word, Esther gasped, spun on her heel, and ran straight for the house.

"I'll get you something!"

Hope blinked. She didn't even have time to protest. Elizabeth approached next with her usual bright energy, and Sonny barreled toward Hope at full speed.

"Hey, Hope!" he shouted, launching himself forward, only to be yanked back by Elizabeth.

"Careful, Sonny!" she scolded. "Hope's arm is hurt. You must be gentle."

Sonny's big blue eyes lifted solemnly to Hope as he plopped down beside her on the steps.

"Does it still hurt?"

"A little," Hope admitted. "Mostly when I move it too much."

"I'm sorry."

Hope smiled warmly at him. "That's all right. It will heal."

Abigail and Esther stepped out of the house moments later, Esther carrying a steaming bowl. Abigail shook her head remorsefully.

"I am so sorry, Hope. I should have asked earlier if you wanted breakfast."

"Please don't apologize," Hope insisted. "You have a large family to care for."

"Still," Abigail murmured, pressing the bowl of porridge into Hope's hands, "you are our guest. I ought to remember my manners."

She turned to her daughters. "You two, back to your chores. Once you're finished, you may show Hope around."

"Yes, Mama," they chorused, disappearing into the garden. Sonny remained faithfully glued to Hope's side. When she finished her meal, he hopped to his feet.

"Do you want to come with me?" he asked, eyes sparkling with excitement.

"What are you doing?" Hope asked, hiding a grin.

"I'm fishing!" he announced proudly. "I haven't caught anything yet, but I will."

She laughed softly. "I'd love to join you. I've never gone fishing before."

His mouth fell open in shock. "Never?"

She shook her head. Without hesitation, he grabbed her hand and tugged her along toward the lake. Hope listened as he chattered enthusiastically, demonstrating how to hold the fishing pole, how to wait, how to jiggle the line. His excitement was both earnest and utterly charming. They sat side by side on the grassy bank, but before long, Sonny's attention drifted. He abandoned his line and began hopping around behind her.

Hope was lost in her thoughts when a low growl snapped her attention sharply to the side. She turned—and froze. Sonny was only steps away from a large raccoon. Hope's stomach flipped. She knew raccoons could be aggressive when cornered, but this one... this one wasn't behaving normally. It wasn't running away or baring its teeth. It sat eerily still, white foam clinging to its snout. Alarm shot through her.

"Sonny," she said quietly but urgently as she rose. "Come to me. Don't touch the animal."

"But it's so cute," Sonny protested, reaching out. "I just want to pet it."

He was one step away. Hope didn't hesitate. She sprinted forward, grabbed him around the waist, and yanked him back. Sonny yelped as she hauled him away and took off running toward the house, dragging him behind her. The raccoon's growl deepened. Hope prayed it wasn't following, but she didn't dare look back. Inside the house, with the door slammed safely shut, Hope gasped for breath. Sonny wriggled, whining.

"You ruined everything!" he complained, reaching for the doorknob. Hope intercepted his hand. His face crumpled into the beginnings of a tantrum, but when Abigail rushed in, he halted immediately and settled for a dramatic pout.

"What happened?" Esther demanded as she and Elizabeth hurried in, alarm written across their faces.

"Hope didn't let me touch the animal," Sonny muttered miserably. "She just grabbed me and pulled me away."

"Something was wrong with the raccoon," Hope said quickly. "It didn't act frightened or aggressive. It just sat there. And there was foam around its mouth."

All three Middleton women gasped.

"I don't know exactly what was wrong with it," Hope continued, "but it growled like it meant business. I just... had a strong feeling I needed to get him away."

"Esther," Abigail said sharply, her face already pale, "go to the fields. Tell your father and the other men. They need to kill it before it bites someone."

Esther nodded and bolted out the door. Abigail knelt and pulled Sonny into her arms.

"Son, what Hope did was right, and very brave. Do you remember what happened to Brother Jonas's dog?"

Sonny's eyes widened. He nodded slowly.

"That dog was bitten by a sick raccoon," Abigail said softly. "It turned rabid and had to be put down before it hurt anyone."

Sonny swallowed. "Would the raccoon have attacked me?"

Abigail nodded gravely. "It might have."

Sonny turned wide eyes toward Hope.

"I'm sorry I got mad at you... and thank you." He shuffled closer and wrapped his arms tightly around her. Hope's throat tightened.

"Elizabeth, take Sonny upstairs," Abigail instructed. Elizabeth nodded and guided her little brother away. The moment they were gone, Abigail pulled Hope into a firm embrace.

"Thank you," she whispered, her voice thick. "Thank you for saving my little boy."

Hope blinked. "I—I don't understand."

Abigail guided her to the sofa and sat beside her.

"Hope, that raccoon had rabies. We don't know why it happens, but every animal that catches it turns violent. It's fatal. Several of our neighbors have lost dogs because of it."

Hope gasped. "Has... has it ever killed a person?"

Abigail's eyes dimmed. "Yes. The Tuckers lost their eight-year-old daughter last year. Their dog bit her after being infected. It was... a terrible passing."

Tears burned Hope's eyes. Her heart ached for a child she had never met, and for the family left behind. Abigail wrapped an arm around her shoulders.

"You listened to your instincts and saved Sonny's life, Hope. If that raccoon had bitten him, he would have died."

"Is that why you sent for Brother Jacob?" Hope asked quietly.

"Yes," Abigail replied. "When anyone sees a sick animal, our men must put it down. It protects the entire community."

Hope nodded, unable to speak for a moment. Her heart still raced at the thought of what might have been. She whispered a silent prayer of gratitude, first for Sonny, then for the instincts that had pushed her into action just in time.

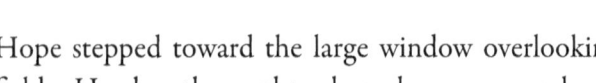

Hope stepped toward the large window overlooking the back fields. Her breath caught when she saw several men striding across the land with rifles in hand. Brother Jacob led the group, Samuel right beside him, their expressions grim and determined.

Hope's heartbeat quickened. She wasn't a woman who wished death on any creature, least of all one that was suffering, but she knew this was necessary. The raccoon was gravely ill, beyond saving, and the community couldn't risk another child, or anyone, being harmed. Putting it down was an act of mercy, not cruelty.

She pressed a hand to her chest as the men fanned out, searching the brush and tree line. It felt like an eternity before a series of sharp gunshots cracked through the afternoon air. Hope's shoulders sagged in relief. It was done. The threat was gone. Abigail, who had heard the shots as well, nodded grimly.

"Good. Now everyone can breathe a little easier."

Sonny, who had been hovering restlessly near the back door, perked up.

"Can I go back outside now?"

"No." Abigail pointed a stern finger at him. "You, and everyone else, are staying indoors until I say otherwise. I won't have anyone out there while the men are handling things."

Sonny pouted, but even he understood the seriousness of the situation. When the older children returned from school later that afternoon, their laughter and chatter filled the house at once. It didn't take long, however, for Abigail's patience to wear thin. The restless energy of eight children cooped up indoors was enough to test the resolve of a saint. Finally, Abigail clapped her hands sharply.

"That's enough running and noise. Everyone outside, to the fields. Your father and brother need help preparing for the fall harvest, and I need a quiet house before I lose my mind."

A chorus of groans followed, but no one dared argue. Esther and Elizabeth exchanged knowing glances as they ushered their younger siblings out the door. Hope watched them go, touched by the rhythm of this remarkable family, protective, united, and quick to pull together in a crisis. And for the first time since leaving San Francisco, she realized she felt... safe. Not because danger wasn't still lurking somewhere in the world, it certainly was, but because she was surrounded by people who genuinely cared.

Hope found herself growing anxious as supper time approached. The questions Esther and Elizabeth had asked her the night before still spun through her mind, circling, tightening, fluttering, until her pulse raced and her stomach felt like a nest of restless butterflies. She had never felt this confused before. Never.

Her engagement to Eric had been her father's arrangement, not her choice. And though she had once admired Eric's charm and handsome features, she had never truly loved him. His controlling disposition had smothered her fragile admiration quickly, leaving only discomfort... and later, resentment.

Compared to that cold, clipped memory, what she felt now, this warmth, this nervous trembling, this unbearable awareness, was entirely foreign. And that terrified her.

What was she supposed to make of these feelings? Why did her breath catch every time she thought of him? Why was she dreading, and longing for, the moment she saw Reverend Shaw again? The knowledge that Esther and Elizabeth would be watching her like hawks only tightened the knot in her stomach.

When the front door opened, Hope panicked and ducked behind the large cupboard, feeling wholly ridiculous yet unable to stop herself. She pressed a hand to her racing heart as Reverend Shaw stepped inside. Her breath hitched.

His sleeves were rolled up, revealing strong, sun-browned forearms. His shirt clung to his broad chest and shoulders from working outside, outlining muscles she had absolutely no business noticing. Heat rushed up her neck. She jerked her gaze away and practically threw herself into an armchair.

*He is old enough to be your father,* she scolded herself. *And he's a reverend. A reverend.*

Who would return to San Francisco as soon as he was healed. Before she could sink deeper into her spiraling thoughts, Sonny barreled into the room and onto her lap, nearly knocking the air from her lungs.

"Read this to me!" he demanded, thrusting a book toward her. Then a little softer: "Please?"

"*A Christmas Carol?*" Hope raised an eyebrow, smiling gently. "Sonny, sweetheart, it's August."

He nodded solemnly. "It's my favorite."

Hope couldn't deny him, not with those earnest blue eyes, so she began reading. She grew so absorbed in the story that she didn't notice Reverend Shaw move behind her until his deep voice sounded close to her ear.

"Good book?"

Hope jolted violently, nearly dropping it. Sonny snatched the book before it hit the floor.

"Reverend Shaw!" Sonny scolded with surprising indignation. "It isn't nice to sneak up on people. You scared Hope."

"I did?" the reverend asked, sounding far too innocent. Sonny nodded gravely. "How should I make it up to her?"

Hope wished, bitterly, that the floorboards would swallow her whole. Sonny scratched his chin thoughtfully.

"Well... when Daddy scares Mommy, he gives her a kiss and apologizes."

Hope's heart stopped. Her breath vanished. Her face burst into flames. She darted a desperate glance toward the doorway, and nearly whimpered. Esther and Elizabeth stood there, both biting their lips to contain laughter. Brother Jacob walked in behind them, grinning so broadly she wondered if his face hurt. Surely this wasn't happening. Hope dropped to her knees in front of Sonny, cupping his face so she wouldn't have to look at anyone else.

"Your mommy and daddy are married," she whispered urgently. "It's fine for married people to kiss. Reverend Shaw and I are not..." She swallowed. "...married."

Sonny held her cheeks between his little hands.

"But isn't it okay to kiss someone when you love them, even if you aren't married?"

Her stomach plummeted to her boots. Why—why was nobody rescuing her?

"Sometimes," she croaked, praying this moment would end.

"And don't you love Reverend Shaw?" Sonny asked, refusing to release her face. Hope very nearly blacked out. Behind her, she heard a poorly muffled snort, Elizabeth, absolutely. Possibly Esther too.

"We... are friends," Hope managed.

"And friends love each other," Sonny concluded happily. She wished the heavens would send a lightning bolt straight through the roof.

"Are we friends, Sonny?" she asked quickly, desperate to redirect the conversation before she burst into flames. He nodded.

"Does that mean I can kiss you?" she teased lightly, leaning in with a playful smile.

He turned pink. "Not on the mouth."

"No, not on the mouth," she promised, pressing a gentle kiss to his cheek. Satisfied, Sonny beamed, then ruined everything.

"Now you can kiss Reverend Shaw!"

Hope's eyes flew open in horror. Thankfully, mercifully, Abigail swept into the room like divine intervention.

"That's quite enough, Sonny," she declared firmly. "We do not tell other people to kiss. Go wash up for supper."

Sonny scampered off. Hope straightened, refusing to look at Reverend Shaw. Her cheeks burned so hot she wondered if she might melt the carpet beneath her feet.

"And you," Abigail continued sharply, turning to her husband and daughters with hands planted on her hips like a general reprimanding her troops, "should be ashamed of yourselves. Standing there watching Sonny make poor Hope completely uncomfortable. You should have stepped in the moment that boy opened his mouth."

Jacob had the nerve to smirk sheepishly. Esther and Elizabeth, mortified, apologized in unison before retreating into the kitchen with their heads ducked like scolded hens. Abigail exhaled through her nose and marched straight to Hope. She cupped Hope's cheek, then pulled her into a warm, motherly embrace.

"Thank you," Hope whispered into her shoulder, her voice barely audible.

"Anytime, honey," Abigail murmured, hugging her tighter. "If Sonny, or anyone in this household, ever puts you on the spot again, you come to me."

Hope nodded gratefully and stepped back, believing the storm was over. It was not. Abigail turned like a striking hawk, straight toward Reverend Shaw.

"And *you*, Reverend Shaw," she scolded, pointing a firm finger at him, "ought to be ashamed as well. Why didn't you rescue her? Don't just stand there with that cheeky grin, I saw it. Instead of helping the girl, you watched her turn beet red like she'd swallowed a stove ember."

Hope dropped her gaze quickly, but not before a small, wicked smirk curved her lips. Abigail putting him in his place felt... entirely too satisfying. Thinking she was free to escape before her blush returned, Hope slipped toward the hallway leading to the guest room. She didn't make it far.

A hand clasped her arm, not roughly, but firmly enough to stop her. She gasped softly, whirling, and found Reverend Shaw beside her. His expression was unreadable... except for the unmistakable flicker in his eyes.

Without a word, he guided her out the back door and onto the porch, away from prying eyes.

# 9

# Between His Arms
# and the Abyss

"What has gotten into you?" Hope demanded, though her voice betrayed her racing pulse. He stepped just close enough to crowd her space, lowering his head until his eyes locked with hers.

"I saw that smirk," he said quietly, the low timbre of his voice rippling straight through her. "You enjoyed Abigail scolding me a little too much, young lady."

"Oh, did I?" she returned sweetly, lifting her chin. "I don't recall you coming to my rescue when Sonny put me on the spot. I'd say the scolding was well deserved. Abigail was the only one in this household who defended me."

His lips curved, slow and dangerous.

"That smirk was pure sass, Hope," he murmured. "And I believe you're in need of a lesson." He clasped her wrist gently and tugged her closer. Her breath hitched, a soft, involuntary sound she hoped he hadn't heard. His nearness made her lightheaded. The warmth of his body, the scent of clean soap and sun, wrapped around her like a spell.

"Let go," she whispered, though she wasn't sure she meant it. Before he could respond, Abigail's voice rang from inside the house.

"Supper is ready!"

The reverend leaned in, far too close, and brushed his lips near her ear. She felt his breath against the sensitive skin beneath it.

"You are one lucky girl," he murmured, his voice vibrating through her. "I suspect Abigail has a sixth sense. Otherwise..." He didn't finish the sentence. He didn't need to. Hope's pulse thundered in her ears. She mustered every ounce of bravado she didn't feel.

"I think she simply knows when someone is overstepping boundaries."

He drew back just enough to meet her gaze, eyes bright, amused, and smoldering.

"Oh, I assure you, Hope," he said softly, "I'm very aware of the boundaries." The slow grin that followed told her he was also very willing to test them.

The following two weeks passed more quickly than Hope would have believed possible. Rain fell almost every day, drumming softly against the windows and turning the fields into puddles. The gloomy weather only strengthened Abigail's resolve that Hope and Reverend Shaw must rest, heal, and recover properly. She insisted on early bedtimes, warm teas, and quiet afternoons.

Dr. Taylor stopped by daily, his calm voice and steady hands bringing reassurance. Hope's arm was healing well, and though

Reverend Shaw still winced when he lifted his left arm a certain way, he was nearly back to full strength. Watching him regain his vigor stirred something warm and unfamiliar in Hope's stomach, a flutter she tried her best to ignore.

One morning, as Hope braided her hair, Esther burst into the room with a brighter grin than the sun outside.

"Are you ready for our End of Summer dance tomorrow evening?" she asked, eyes sparkling.

Hope blinked.

"I... don't know," she admitted. "But it does sound like a big deal around here."

"Oh, it is!" Esther declared enthusiastically. "It's one of our favorite events of the entire year."

"Will everyone come?" Hope asked.

Esther shook her head. "Children stay home. It's for everyone fifteen and older."

Hope nodded slowly, but her expression fell.

"I don't even have a dress for such an occasion."

Esther's grin turned mischievous. "Are you sure about that?"

Before Hope could respond, Esther clasped her arm and tugged her gently down the hall to the guest room. Lying across Hope's side of the bed was a dark green dress, simple, elegant, and beautifully made. Hope froze, her mouth falling open.

"I... I can't take one of your dresses."

"It's not one of ours," Esther replied proudly. "Grandma made it for you."

Hope stared at the dress, stunned into silence.

"Why would she do that?" she finally whispered. "She doesn't even know me."

"Grandma heard about everything you've been through," Esther said softly. "She has a soft spot for girls brave enough to stand up for themselves."

"I must pay her, then," Hope said immediately, instinctively reaching for her reticule.

"No, that's quite all right," Abigail said as she stepped into the room, Elizabeth close behind her. "Mom wouldn't take a cent for it."

"But your family has already done so much for me," Hope whispered, overwhelmed. Abigail didn't respond right away. Instead, she crossed the room, placed her hands gently on Hope's shoulders, and pulled her into a warm, steady embrace.

"You were led to us for a reason," she murmured against Hope's hair. "And you slipped right into our hearts the moment you arrived. God knew you needed a safe place... and I think He knew we needed you, too."

Hope swallowed hard, blinking rapidly as emotion stung her eyes. She clutched the fabric of Abigail's apron, feeling, for the first time since her mother's death, something achingly familiar. Family. Home. Belonging.

Hope, Esther, and Elizabeth looked radiant as they stepped into the large gathering hall. The walls were strung with lanterns, their warm glow reflecting off the polished wooden floors. Hope's dark green dress fit her beautifully, the soft fabric flowing gracefully as she walked. Abigail had styled her blonde hair with care, pinning it up so that only a few delicate curls framed her face, softening her features and drawing attention to her bright blue eyes.

Abigail stepped beside the girls, smiling as she watched her son Samuel and Reverend Shaw from across the room. It was painfully obvious, almost laughably so, that both men were utterly captivated by Hope. Samuel looked as though he had forgotten how to breathe. Reverend Shaw... well, he looked like a man fighting every instinct not to stride across the room and claim her arm.

The community leader welcomed everyone, and moments later several men lifted their instruments. Brother Jacob tucked the fiddle beneath his chin and began to play a lively waltz, filling the air with cheerful warmth.

Reverend Shaw didn't give anyone else a chance. Before Samuel, or even Esther, could blink, he crossed the room with purposeful strides. Hope's heart skittered in her chest as he stopped before her and bowed slightly.

"May I have this dance?" he asked, flashing a smile so devastating she felt her breath catch. It wasn't the polite smile of a clergyman, it was the smile of a man who had made up his mind.

Hope's instinct was to decline. Run. Hide. But she had no polite excuse. And worse... she wanted to dance with him. The heat blooming in her cheeks made that painfully clear. She nodded.

He took her hand gently, and even that light touch sent a spark racing up her arm. He guided her onto the dance floor with effortless confidence, and as the music swelled, she realized something else entirely: Reverend Shaw was an exquisite dancer. He moved with surprising grace. His hold was firm yet protective. When he drew her into his arms, every nerve in her body came alive.

"You look breathtaking tonight, Hope," he murmured. Her heart thudded. She kept her gaze lowered, unable to meet his eyes.

"Should you be saying such a thing as a clergyman?" she whispered, trying, and failing, to sound stern.

"I am also a man," he replied softly, "and men are not blind."

Hope swallowed hard. His tone, low, warm, confident, was unraveling her one careful thread at a time.

"It isn't right for you to say things like that," she insisted. "I—"

She faltered when his fingers brushed her chin, tilting her face upward. She didn't dare breathe. Their faces were inches apart now. He reached up and gently swept a curl behind her ear.

"There is nothing wrong with showing affection," he murmured. His touch seared her skin. Heat flooded her cheeks. She stepped back at once, her voice trembling with a mixture of outrage and something she refused to name.

"You are being inappropriate, Reverend," she said sharply. "I've asked you, not once, but several times#, to respect boundaries. Yet you continue to push them."

A slow grin curved his lips, infuriatingly confident. And pleased. Far too pleased. He pulled her closer and spun her gracefully beneath his arm, making her gasp. When he caught her again, he leaned down, his lips brushing close to her ear.

"You can pretend all you want, Hope," he whispered, "but I know you feel this. You're just as attracted to me as I am to you."

She jerked back, eyes wide. "Stop trying to confuse me. This isn't right. You're—you're old enough to be my father. There is nothing—"

"Why," he interrupted gently, "do you keep returning to that excuse? Many older men have married younger women. It is hardly scandalous."

She stiffened, her outrage flaring anew.

"If you cannot respect my wishes," she hissed, "then you are not the man I believed you to be."

His expression softened. The teasing vanished.

"Hope," he whispered, eyes earnest now, "I truly care about you."

Her breath caught. "I know," she said quietly. "And that is all right. But let's leave it there." She held his gaze, hoping he could see the plea in her eyes, because it was real. She already cared too deeply, and she did not trust her own heart. He studied her, for a long moment. Then he sighed... and nodded. But even as they continued the waltz, Hope felt it in her bones. This wasn't over. Not even close.

When the musicians paused to rest, Esther looped her arm through Hope's and suggested they take a short walk along the lakeshore. The night had grown colder, but the moon glowed bright and full, casting silver ripples across the dark water. They stayed close to the lantern-lit gathering hall, yet even so, the shadows fell deeper away from the music and laughter.

Esther had just turned toward Hope, her lips parting as if to ask a question, when the crunch of footsteps on gravel made them both look up. Three older boys emerged from the darkness.

"Well now, Esther," one of them drawled, stepping forward as if he had every right. "Who's that you got with ya?"

Hope froze. Something in his eyes, an oily mix of hunger and entitlement, made her stomach twist. He wasn't smiling. He was smirking. And he looked at her as though she were a prize to be claimed.

"Go away, Jared," Esther said sharply, though Hope could feel her trembling beside her. "You know you're not supposed to come near me again."

Hope's eyes widened. *Again?*

Jared's grin deepened. "Calm down. I ain't here on your account." Then his gaze slid to Hope. "I'm here for the pretty one." He reached out and brushed the back of his knuckles along Hope's cheek. She recoiled instantly and slapped his hand away. His smirk didn't falter, if anything, he looked amused.

"Another wildcat," he said, grin curling. "Just how I like 'em."

Before either girl could react, Jared lunged forward. His arms clamped around Hope's waist, strong and unyielding, and he dragged her backward toward the water. Her boots skidded on the damp grass.

"Let go of me!" Hope snapped, twisting violently, but his grip only tightened. He smelled of whiskey and sweat, too close, too strong. Panic flared hot in her chest. Esther rushed forward, but the other two boys stepped into her path, blocking her.

"Move!" Esther cried, her voice cracking. The boys only chuckled. Jared kept hauling Hope toward the dark shoreline. The cold water shimmered dangerously close now, only a few paces away. Hope's heart hammered against her ribs as she dug her heels into the earth, fighting with everything she had to break free. The night air seemed to thicken around her. She knew one thing with absolute certainty: if Jared pulled her into the water, or out of the light, she would be in terrible danger.

Hope tried to scream for help, but Jared clamped a hand over her mouth so tightly her jaw ached. Her cry died in her throat as he dragged her the last few steps toward the shoreline. Then, without warning, he hurled her into the lake.

Hope plunged beneath the icy water, the shock stealing her breath. She burst back to the surface, gasping, hair plastered across her cheeks. Her dress soaked through instantly, weighing her down as she fought to stay upright. But Jared was already beside her. He seized her arm, iron fingers biting into her skin, and hauled her with him as he swam along the shoreline. Hope clawed at his wrist, twisted, kicked, anything to break free, but he was too strong. Panic clawed up her throat.

The farther he pulled her, the darker it grew. The lantern glow from the dance faded behind a curtain of reeds and low, tangled bushes. The water here was murkier, stiller, and far more isolated.

"Let—go—of—me," she tried to scream, but barely managed half a syllable. Every time she opened her mouth to cry out, Jared shoved her head underwater again. Cold darkness closed over her, muffling her terror. She thrashed, lungs burning, only to be yanked back up long enough to gulp a frantic breath before he forced her under again. Fear blinded her senses. Her injured arm screamed with pain at every struggle.

Hope surfaced once more, gasping wildly, her vision blurring. She twisted desperately, reaching for the reeds, the bank, anything, but Jared dragged her farther into the shadowed water, his grip relentless. Her pulse roared in her ears. No one could see them here. And no one could hear her.

The two boys shoved Esther so hard she hit the ground with a thud. The breath knocked from her lungs. By the time she scrambled back up, they were already sprinting away into the darkness, Jared and Hope completely gone. Panic exploded in her chest.

"HELP! HELP!" she shrieked, her voice cracking as she bolted toward the sound of music and laughter. Her skirts tangled around her legs, but she didn't stop, not until she burst, breathless, into the lantern-lit square where the dance was still in full swing. Her father saw her first.

"Esther?" Brother Jacob rushed toward her, Samuel and Reverend Shaw only a heartbeat behind him. "What's the matter, child? Where is Hope?"

The moment she saw her father's face, the last of her composure shattered. She threw herself into his arms, sobbing so hard she could barely form words.

"J—Jared... Jared and his friends were waiting for us," she choked, trembling violently. "He grabbed Hope. He dragged her away, and his friends held me back. I couldn't stop them. I tried, Daddy, I tried—"

Brother Jacob stiffened, his expression turning deadly serious. Samuel's fists clenched until his knuckles went white. Reverend Shaw's face drained of color, leaving only fierce determination behind.

"Where?" Reverend Shaw demanded, his voice tight. "Where did he take her?"

Esther lifted a shaking hand and pointed toward the dark stretch of land behind the houses.

"He pulled her toward the lake," she sobbed. "I saw him. He went that way."

Reverend Shaw didn't wait for another word. He was already running, Samuel on his heels and Brother Jacob right beside them, all three sprinting toward the shadowed path leading down to the water, lanterns swinging wildly as they raced into the darkness.

Jared slammed Hope's body hard into the muddy bank, the breath jolting painfully from her lungs. Before she could recover, his filthy hand clamped over her mouth and his weight pinned her into the cold mud. His lips crushed against hers, violent, suffocating, uninvited. Hope thrashed, kicking wildly, but he was stronger, fueled by sickening intent.

When she managed to wrench her head to the side to breathe, he seized her again and forced her underwater. Freezing water filled her ears and nose, the world going dark as she struggled. Panic seized her. She surfaced with a gasp, just in time for him to shove her under again. He was going to drown her. Or worse.

When he finally dragged her back up, he pinned her as before, hands fumbling aggressively at the buttons of her dress. Hope slapped him as hard as she could across the face. He jerked back with a snarl, but the moment of space was all she needed. Her hand shot into the mud behind her. She grabbed a fistful, thick, wet, gritty, and flung it straight into his open mouth and eyes. Jared gagged violently, coughing and sputtering, clawing at his burning eyes.

Hope scrambled back, sucking in air, then kicked him with every ounce of strength she had. Her boot slammed into his chest, sending him stumbling backward into the black water. She lurched to her feet, only to be yanked back down when Jared's hand clamped around her ankle. Hope shrieked, trying to rip her leg free. Then angry barking exploded through the night. Brother Jeremiah's dogs.

A growling pack burst through the reeds. Two lunged straight for Jared. With a panicked roar, he released Hope and vanished beneath the surface of the lake, disappearing into darkness. Hope crumpled where she stood, collapsing into the mud. Her entire body shook violently, breath coming in small, broken gasps. She hugged her knees and rocked, terror overwhelming her. Tears spilled freely, raw, uncontrollable sobs. Someone whistled in the distance, but the dogs didn't leave her side. They formed a protective circle around her, growling into the night.

A hand touched her shoulder. Hope screamed, pure, piercing terror.

"Hope, it's me. It's me." Reverend Shaw's voice was soft and urgent. It took several seconds for the words to register. When she finally looked up, she saw his face, etched with worry, eyes dark with fear for her. Her sobbing intensified, breaking into helpless, shaking cries. "Oh, Hope..." he breathed, drawing her gently into his arms.

She didn't resist. She couldn't. She clung to him, trembling uncontrollably, burying her face against his chest as if trying to disappear into the safety he offered. He held her firmly with his good arm, one hand cradling the back of her head while she cried and cried. Brother Jeremiah arrived just as Brother Jacob and Samuel raced toward them, breathless and frantic.

"Did you see what happened?" Brother Jacob demanded. Brother Jeremiah's jaw clenched.

"No. But I heard her scream. When I came out, I saw Jared hurl her into the lake." His voice shook with fury. "I ran back for my dogs and sent them after him." He glanced down at the animals still guarding Hope. "Good boys," he murmured, rubbing their heads with pride.

Hope didn't lift her face from Reverend Shaw's chest. She was still shivering violently. Shock, fear, and icy cold wrapping around her like iron bands. Reverend Shaw noticed. He tugged off his jacket with one hand and wrapped it around her trembling shoulders before pulling her back against him. Brother Jacob clasped Brother Jeremiah's hand.

"Thank you for looking out for her."

"Anytime," Brother Jeremiah replied grimly. "Those boys have gone too far. They harass every girl in this settlement. It was only a matter of time before something like this happened."

Samuel stared out at the dark water, fists clenched at his sides.

"If I find Jared," he muttered, "I'll drag him to the sheriff myself."

Reverend Shaw's arm tightened protectively around Hope, his jaw rigid with barely contained fury.

"He will answer for this," he said quietly. The intensity in his voice made every man present believe it.

# 10

# A Price on Her Head

As soon as they slipped through the church's back door, the men guided Hope down the dim hallway and into a small classroom. The room smelled faintly of chalk and lamp oil, calm, familiar scents that stood in sharp contrast to the terror she had just endured. Reverend Shaw helped her sit, keeping his hand steady on her shoulder until she was settled.

Within moments, Esther and Abigail rushed in, Elizabeth close behind. Abigail went straight to Hope and wrapped her in her arms, pulling her into the kind of motherly embrace Hope had been starved for since childhood. Hope wasn't crying anymore, but her pallor was alarming. Her eyes looked hollow, wide, dazed, and filled with fear she was struggling desperately to suppress.

"Hope," Abigail whispered, brushing a damp strand of hair from her cheek. "Esther told us what happened, but darling... do you want to talk about it?"

Hope shook her head immediately. Talking about it would make the nightmare real all over again. She couldn't bear that, not yet. Reverend Shaw lowered himself into a squat in front of her, bringing his face level with hers. She lifted her eyes to his for the briefest moment, and the sight of his gentle concern nearly broke her resolve. Everyone in the room saw it, saw how hard she was fighting not to fall apart again.

"Did he hurt you?" he asked softly. Hope pressed her trembling lips together and looked away. She didn't answer. Abigail knelt beside her, her voice warm and steady as she smoothed Hope's wet hair back.

"Honey... please tell us what happened. Don't keep the fear bottled inside. You don't have to give every detail, just enough so we know how to help you."

Hope swallowed hard. Her hands twisted in her lap before she finally whispered, her voice thin and strained, "He... he kept pushing me under the water. Every time I tried to scream, he forced my head down again." She squeezed her eyes shut. "I thought... I thought I was going to drown."

A collective gasp filled the room.

"Oh, sweetheart," Abigail breathed, gathering her into another tight embrace. "You're safe now. You hear me? Safe."

Reverend Shaw placed a hand lightly on Hope's knee, not possessive, not intrusive, just a quiet, grounding touch.

"You're here with us," he said softly. "And nothing will ever happen to you while we're near."

Hope let out a shaky breath, her defenses finally beginning to lower as comfort surrounded her from every direction.

Hope barely spoke for the rest of the evening. Even when she finally slipped beneath the covers, her mind refused to find peace. She lay stiff and silent until Esther settled into bed beside her. Only then did Hope's whisper break the quiet.

"How can he call himself a Christian when he targets women like that?"

Esther let out a long, weary sigh. "We don't believe he's religious at all, neither he nor his friends. They only claimed to be when they arrived a few months ago. They built a cabin on the edge of the settlement but refused every offer of help. They keep to themselves, hunt just enough to survive, and nothing more. And sometimes..." She hesitated. "Sometimes they disappear for weeks."

Elizabeth, already propped up on her elbows, nodded.

"Dad and Sam tried welcoming them when they first arrived. Jared met them with pure hostility. Their place was filthy too, with no respect for anything or anyone. Nobody here had a good feeling about them, but we still tried to show charity." She shook her head. "It didn't matter."

Esther turned onto her side, her eyes shadowed with old fear.

"Jared did to me what he did to you today, grabbed me, tried dragging me off, wouldn't let me go. Brother Jeremiah and Bishop Walker warned him that if he ever attacked one of us again, he'd be forced to leave. They said if he refused, they would bring in lawmen."

Elizabeth huffed softly. "And what did Jared do? He vanished. Hid until things cooled down, then came back like nothing had happened."

Hope's stomach twisted uneasily. "So... he'll hide again after tonight?"

"Most likely," Esther said bitterly. "He always runs when he thinks he might face consequences."

Elizabeth reached over and gently squeezed Hope's hand.

"But don't be afraid, Hope. He won't get away with this. The men here are fiercely protective, of every woman, not just their own families. When Brother Jeremiah saw you struggling, something in him snapped, and he sent his dogs immediately. And now every man in Saint Charles will be watching for Jared's return."

Esther nodded. "We're convinced Jared is hiding from the law, and his two friends as well. No decent young man joins a tiny family settlement unless he's running from something. That's why everyone keeps an eye on them."

Hope swallowed hard and stared up at the wooden ceiling, trying to let their words soothe her. Knowing the community was alert helped... but the memory of the lake and Jared's hands still clung to her like a shroud.

The next morning, Hope woke with the faint, disorienting sense that something terrible had happened... and the equally sharp certainty that it had. The memory lingered like a bruise beneath the surface, tender and impossible to ignore. She dressed slowly, carefully schooling her expression into calm, before stepping out of the guest room. She would not unravel again. Not here. Not when these people had given her so much kindness. Still, the unease clung to her.

She noticed it almost immediately, though no one drew attention to it. Brother Jacob lingered near the doorway when she crossed the yard. Samuel appeared whenever she stepped outside, always busy with some task that somehow placed him within eyesight of her. Reverend Shaw was never far either, his presence quiet but constant, as if he were standing guard without ever making it feel like confinement.

Beyond them, other men moved along the outer edges of the settlement. Some carried rifles. Others walked with purposeful strides, scanning the tree line, the shoreline, the narrow paths that led away from Saint Charles. There was no alarm, no shouting, no fear openly displayed, only calm vigilance, steady and unspoken. No one told her she was being protected. They simply did it.

The realization tightened her throat. After so long feeling alone, hunted, and exposed, silent solidarity wrapped around her like a shield. These men did not watch her as though she were fragile or broken. They watched the world instead, standing between her and whatever danger might still lurk beyond the fields.

Hope paused at the edge of the yard, breathing in the clean morning air. The knot in her chest eased, just slightly. She felt something unfamiliar but desperately needed. Safety. Not complete. Not guaranteed. But enough. And for now, it was enough to let her take another step forward.

---

"Hope," Abigail said gently one morning, wiping her hands on her apron, "would you like to help me in the kitchen today?"

Hope hesitated, her cheeks warmed.

"I would love that... but I must admit, I know nothing about making food. We had servants." Her voice trailed off, embarrassed by the truth. Abigail's smile was warm and reassuring.

"Don't you worry, honey. Everyone starts somewhere. You'll learn to cook in no time, I promise."

And so began a new rhythm to Hope's days. She and Abigail spent long stretches of time together in the kitchen, kneading dough, chopping vegetables, stirring stews, and laughing over Hope's first clumsy attempts at everything. The atmosphere was patient, safe, and strangely familiar. It reminded Hope of the quiet afternoons she had once spent with her mother, watching her embroider or helping her prepare tea.

Abigail had a gift for teaching. There was no scolding, no judgment, only encouragement and gentle correction. Before long, Hope discovered she enjoyed the work. She liked the warmth of the hearth, the scent of fresh bread, the satisfaction of producing something with her own hands. Each day, she felt a little more capable, a little more confident.

But even with this new comfort, the attack from Jared lingered like a shadow over her thoughts. She never spoke about it, not to Abigail, not to Esther, not even to Reverend Shaw. Yet the fear clung to her. She avoided stepping outside alone. And when she had to leave the house, she made certain someone walked with her, even if it was just little Sonny.

The settlement tried to return to normal. Several days after the dance, the community planned a cheerful family picnic at Bear Lake. Esther and Elizabeth were eager to go, and Brother Jacob's family invited Hope more than once. But Hope declined with a soft smile, claiming she needed a quiet day to herself. No one pressed her.

The men of Saint Charles had been keeping a close watch on the outer roads since the night of the attack. Not long after, they discovered that Jared and his friends had abandoned their cabin entirely. It stood empty, no supplies, no clothing, no personal belongings. They had vanished. The knowledge eased the community's nerves, though the men continued to check the surrounding area regularly. Life slowly settled back into its familiar rhythms. Everyone was beginning to relax again. Everyone... except Hope. A knot of unease still lived in her chest. One she wasn't sure would disappear anytime soon.

Hope relished the quiet. For the first time since arriving in Saint Charles, the entire house was hers. Everyone had gone to the picnic. The home was peaceful, sunlight drifting through the windows, the gentle ticking of the clock, the comforting smell of bread she had helped bake that morning. She spent the late morning resting and reading by the fire, letting herself enjoy the rare stillness.

By early afternoon, a warm, hopeful spark settled in her chest. She wanted to do something kind in return for everything the Middleton family had given her. So, she slipped into the kitchen, rolled up her sleeves, and went through Abigail's pantry. A hearty vegetable soup... she could do that. A pie? Well, she might manage.

She followed every step Abigail had taught her, tasting carefully, adjusting a pinch here and there. When the soup came together beautifully and the pie browned to a perfect golden crust, Hope felt a swell of pride. It was the most normal, peaceful moment she'd felt in weeks.

She ladled a little soup into a spoon, testing whether it needed more salt. That was when arms circled around her from behind. One banded around her waist, tight and unyielding. The other clamped across her upper chest, locking her body against a hard, unfamiliar torso. Hope froze, her entire body turning to ice. A hot breath brushed her ear.

"Did ya reckon you weren't gonna see me again, Hope Spencer?" The voice was a low, hateful snarl. Jared. Hope's stomach plummeted.

"Let me go," she hissed, trying to wrench free, but his grip only tightened.

"Real shame..." he murmured, leaning in to breathe her in, his lips ghosting along her neck. Hope's gut twisted violently. "...that a gal as pretty as you's gotta be sent back to San Francisco."

Her pulse hammered. "What are you talking about?"

"Oh... you ain't heard?" His smile was pure venom. She felt it scrape against her skin. "Your pa's put out a call, an' a mighty fine reward, for whoever brings his little girl home. Guess stayin' outta the big towns kept you hid." His chuckle slithered down her spine. "'Til now."

"I didn't avoid anything. I'm trying to—"

"Sure, sure, I know." He sighed, mocking her to her face. "Out chasin' your mama's murderer, are ya? Poor, brave little lamb." His voice sharpened like a spur. "A girl like you? You ain't built for the kind of men behind this."

Her blood chilled. "Behind what?"

He didn't answer. Instead, his arms crushed tighter around her ribs, forcing the breath from her lungs.

"C'mon. Let's find us a cozier spot. And quit the act. I know damn well you ain't got nobody with you." He began dragging her backward, his grip bruising. Hope grabbed desperately at the counter, nails scraping across the wood. Every muscle strained. When she lost her footing, he yanked her hard, pulling her out of the kitchen. Her fingers brushed something, cold steel. A knife.

She curled her hand around it, keeping it hidden.

"I got a soft spot for little wildcats," Jared murmured at her ear, lips grazing her neck as he forced her forward. "Your ma had that same fire."

Hope froze mid-struggle. Her heart slammed painfully against her ribs.

"What did you just say?"

"Could be I met your mama," he drawled, "'bout the time I swung by your place the night she died."

"You," her voice cracked with disbelief and rage. "...you killed her?"

"Reckon I helped her along to the grave," he said with a mean little chuckle. "Slipped a couple extra bullets into her back. Real sweet lady. Screamed just the same as you."

A white-hot fury roared through Hope's veins. She shoved against him with every bit of strength she had. Jared only laughed and tightened his arms, lifting her slightly as he pushed her toward the sofa.

"And now—"

Hope drove the knife into his leg. Jared screamed, an animalistic cry, and stumbled backward. Blood seeped rapidly through his pants. But the pain only made him vicious. His face twisted, eyes burning with hate.

"You oughta clear outta here while you still can," he snapped. "Whitmer's on the trail right now. He'll torch this place clean off the map if they shelter you. Folks' here'll die unless you turn yourself in." He lunged. Hope reacted without thinking. She shoved him with everything she had.

He stumbled... tripped backward... and crashed headfirst against the sharp edge of the table. His body crumpled to the floor. Still.

Hope dropped the knife. A sob tore from her chest as she backed away, trembling violently. Her lungs couldn't catch breath. Her arms shook. Panic clawed at her throat. Fear. Pain. Rage. Grief. It all flooded her at once, crushing her until she sank to her knees. He had killed her mother.

He would have killed her. And now this settlement, this kind family, was in danger because of her.

Hope covered her face with her hands and cried, her sobs wracking her entire body. She hadn't been wrong. She should have left the moment she arrived. She had never been more certain of anything.

As she stood there, struggling to pull air back into her lungs, Hope felt her sobs slowly ebb, until a hand closed around her arm. She screamed. Terror seized her whole body. She spun around wildly, shoving, swinging, certain Jared had already regained consciousness and come back for her. Her fists flew, but her wrists were caught in a firm grip.

"Hey—hey, it's me. It's me, Hope. Reverend Shaw." His voice was gentle, low, steady. He pulled her straight into his chest, wrapping both arms around her trembling body. Hope sagged against him, her breath shaking, her heart still racing at a painful pace. She pressed her forehead against the fabric of his shirt, her body instinctively leaning into his warmth... the only safe place right now.

"It's all right. I've got you," he murmured into her hair. His hand came up to cradle the back of her head, anchoring her as she fought to steady her trembling. After several long minutes, her sobs finally slowed. Hope pulled back just enough to look up at him, still clutching his shirt with one hand.

"How... how can you be here?" Her voice cracked. "I thought you were at the picnic."

"We were," he said, concern tightening his features. "Esther caught sight of Jared sneaking around your place. She told Abigail, and Brother Jacob flagged Sam and me. We rode back as fast as we could. Brother Jeremiah brought his dogs."

Hope swallowed as loud barking echoed outside, fierce, frantic, purposeful. The back door opened, and Brother Jacob, Sam, and Brother Jeremiah came in, hauling a bound and unconscious Jared between them. His hands and feet were tied, rope wrapped tightly around his chest and arms. They dragged him back out, moments later, the dogs guarding him closely. Only then did Hope truly exhale, shaky, uneven, but relieved.

Reverend Shaw guided her to the sofa and sat beside her, taking her hand gently. She didn't pull away. She didn't have the strength to. Brother Jacob and Brother Jeremiah returned and sat across from her, their expressions grave.

"Hope," Brother Jacob said quietly, "please tell us everything."

She nodded, though her voice trembled as she recounted what had happened. The attack. The threats. Jared's confession about her mother. The horrifying revelation of her father's bounty. The warning about Whitmer. When she finished, the room was silent.

"My father made me a target for bounty hunters," she whispered. "I thought Jared only wanted the money, but he's more involved in all of this than I realized."

The men exchanged troubled looks.

"What will happen to him now?" she asked softly. Brother Jacob offered her a steady, reassuring smile.

"He's tied up and locked in a secured shed. Sam and Brother Jeremiah's dogs are keeping watch. Once the others return from the picnic, the men will rotate through the night. Tomorrow, we'll take him to Camp Conner in Soda Springs."

"But will they believe you?" Hope asked, her fears tumbling over one another. "No one else heard his confession."

"Captain Sheffield sent out warnings," Reverend Shaw reminded her gently, squeezing her hand. "After Halleck. And the officer in Elko sent word as well. They know a murderer is on the loose. Jared won't be dismissed."

"But he only told me," Hope insisted, shaking her head. "There were no witnesses."

"He assaulted you, twice," Brother Jeremiah said firmly. "He's attacked girls in our settlement before. The army won't shrug this off. He'll be held until the proper authorities take him."

Hope drew a shaky breath.

"But Jared said Whitmer is on his way here. I don't know when he'll arrive, but... we can't stay. I can't endanger you all."

"Don't you worry about that," Brother Jeremiah said at once. "No one is getting to you. And no one is burning down our settlement. We'll guard every acre if we must."

But Hope's face crumpled with crushing guilt.

"I should never have left San Francisco," she whispered. "None of this would have happened. I brought danger right to your doorstep."

Reverend Shaw reached for her hand again, but this time, she jerked away.

"This isn't your fault," he said earnestly. "Your father didn't know you'd come here. Whitmer and Lester saw you. That's the only reason you're being targeted now. You are not to blame."

"Will you stop saying that?" Her voice rose, trembling but fierce. She shot to her feet, tears burning her eyes. "I *am* to blame!" she cried. "I was angry and grieving and reckless. You warned me not to do something impulsive, and I did anyway. I don't even know if the woman in that letter is still alive. I don't know if I've risked everything for nothing!" Her breath broke on a sob. No one spoke. No one moved. And before anyone could reach her, she turned and fled down the hallway, slamming the guest room door behind her.

The silence she left behind was heavy, worried, aching, and filled with the kind of fear only love... or something dangerously close to it... could stir.

The rest of the family returned from the picnic in high spirits, laughing and chatting, until they were met at the door by

Brother Jacob and Samuel. The mood shifted instantly. Word spread through the house within moments.

Abigail clutched her chest and closed her eyes in relief, while the older children exchanged wide-eyed looks of gratitude and disbelief. When they learned Jared had been caught, and that he would finally be taken away to face the punishment he so richly deserved, an unmistakable wave of relief swept through the household.

Shoulders sagged. Tension melted. Even the younger children sensed the change, quieting as they glanced at their parents for reassurance.

Abigail pulled Hope into a fierce hug the moment she saw her, whispering a trembling, "Thank the Lord you're safe," into her hair. Esther and Elizabeth crowded close as well, their expressions a mixture of outrage, protectiveness, and deep, heartfelt relief.

The entire household felt lighter, safer, knowing the danger had been contained, at least for now. And yet, every grateful glance they shared made one thing painfully clear: just how close they had all come to losing Hope... and how deeply she had already become part of them.

# 11

# When Safety Feels
# Like a Sin

Hope was unusually quiet when she returned to the sitting room a short while later. Jared's attack, his vile confession, his threat, the sickening closeness of danger, lingered in her bones like a chill she could not shake. She tried to hide it, but Reverend Shaw saw straight through her. The worry in his eyes followed her every movement. Abigail bustled into the kitchen to begin supper, but scarcely a moment later, she let out a startled gasp.

"Oh, my goodness, did one of the neighbors bring us soup and pie?"

Everyone exchanged questioning glances. Hope's head snapped up.

"I—I made it," she admitted softly. All eyes turned to her. Heat rushed into her cheeks at once. Abigail's face bloomed into a radiant smile as she crossed the room and swept Hope into her arms.

"It might not be warm anymore," Hope murmured shyly.

"It smells heavenly," Abigail replied. Then she clapped her hands once. "All of you, go wash up. Supper is ready!"

As the others drifted toward the washbasin, Reverend Shaw lingered behind. He stepped closer to Hope, arms folded casually, the corner of his mouth curved in unmistakable mischief.

"You made supper?" he asked, his voice low and teasing. Hope narrowed her eyes.

"Is that so surprising to you?"

"Well," he drawled, "you did grow up with servants."

"And that disqualifies me from knowing how to cook?"

"I didn't say that."

"If you're worried it tastes awful, or that I accidentally poisoned it," she said with exaggerated calm, "you're welcome to skip the meal entirely. No one will force you to eat my dangerously incompetent cooking."

His brows shot up, caught between laughter and disbelief. Before he could retort, Abigail popped her head back into the room.

"Supper is ready!"

Hope lifted her chin. "Reverend Shaw wishes to skip supper because I made it."

Abigail stared at him for a beat, then burst into laughter at his horrified expression. Before Hope could escape, Reverend Shaw's hand closed around her wrist, and in one smooth motion, he hoisted her over his shoulder as though she weighed nothing.

Hope yelped. "Reverend Shaw! What are you doing?" Her voice echoed as he carried her straight toward the yard.

"Your sass is entirely out of control, young lady," he said matter-of-factly. "A bath in the lake might restore your humility."

Hope kicked her legs, careful not to hurt him.

"No! No, please don't. I made supper for everyone. Doesn't that cancel the sass?"

He stopped—but did not set her down.

"I spent hours in that kitchen," she continued dramatically, "chopping vegetables, stirring soup, baking a pie. Do you really think such honest labor deserves cruel and unusual punishment?"

His shoulders shook as he stifled a laugh. Still, he didn't release her, so Hope pressed on, adopting a tone of exaggerated tragedy.

"Do you think the Middleton family will forgive you for tossing the poor girl, who worked tirelessly to feed them, into the lake?"

That did it. He finally lowered her from his shoulder, but no farther than necessary. His hands stayed where they landed, strong and warm around her waist, steadying her. Suddenly she was standing inches from him, close enough to feel the heat of his breath brush her cheek, close enough that her heart forgot its proper rhythm entirely. His voice dropped, low and dangerous, curling down her spine like warm smoke.

"You're lucky I'm starving," he murmured, eyes narrowing with playful threat. "Otherwise, your guilt-tripping wouldn't have saved you. Don't think for a second I wouldn't have followed through." The way he looked at her then, amused, intense, protectively unrestrained, nearly robbed her of speech. Hope swallowed hard, her pulse drumming wildly.

"Of course, Reverend Shaw," she managed, though her voice came out breathier than she intended. "I would never doubt you."

"Good," he said softly, his gaze dipping to her lips for the briefest heartbeat before returning to her eyes. He leaned in just a fraction, enough to send every nerve sparking. "Keep that in mind, young lady."

Her breath caught, truly caught, as though the air itself had tightened around them. Then Abigail's call rang out again, slicing through the moment like a bucket of cold water. Hope stepped back at once, flustered, cheeks burning with warmth she couldn't pretend was embarrassment alone. Reverend Shaw let his hands fall away slowly, but the smirk lingering at the corner of his mouth remained. It lingered like a promise she wasn't sure she wanted to avoid... and absolutely wasn't ready to unravel.

Despite the playful banter earlier with Reverend Shaw, Hope remained withdrawn for the rest of the evening. She barely touched her supper, pushing pieces of bread around her plate until even Sonny noticed. Worried glances followed one after another, first from Reverend Shaw, then Abigail, then Brother Jacob, each of them sensing something was wrong, yet nobody was able to coax a word from her. Hope offered only tight smiles and quiet nods, keeping everyone at a careful distance. She had folded in on herself completely, like a flower closing at dusk.

By the time the family retired for the night, an uneasy stillness had settled over her. She lay in bed, staring at the wooden ceiling beams as sleep refused to come. Her mind replayed every terrifying word Jared had spoken.

*Whitmer is coming. Whitmer is close. And he will burn down the entire settlement to get to you.* These kind, generous people had taken her in without hesitation. They had fed her, clothed her, protected her. She could not repay them with destruction.

Her heart hammered as she turned onto her side, watching the soft rise and fall of Esther's and Elizabeth's steady breathing. When she was certain they were both deeply asleep, she slipped quietly from the bed. Her arm still ached, but she ignored it. There was no room left for fear now, only resolve.

She dressed quickly in the moonlit darkness, pulling on her skirts and boots as silently as she could. She reached for the small wooden table, took a sheet of paper, and, hands trembling, began to write. Not to the Middletons. Not to Reverend Shaw. But to Anthony Whitmer. Her breath shook as she formed each word, forcing her hand to remain steady.

When she finished, she folded the letter and tucked it into her pocket. The moon was bright that night, spilling enough silver light across the room for her to see clearly. She gathered a few necessities, some clothes, her bow and arrows, her knife, and stepped toward the window.

Hope hesitated only a moment, her throat tightening. Leaving like this, without saying goodbye, without giving them the chance to stop her, hurt almost as much as everything else she had endured. But staying meant danger. Staying meant harm to people who did not deserve any part of her nightmare.

She pushed the window open slowly, wincing as it creaked just slightly. Then she climbed out into the cool night air, lowering herself carefully to the ground. She pulled the window shut behind her. And without looking back at the warm, safe home that had sheltered her these past weeks, Hope slipped into the darkness—alone.

Hope took a slow, steady breath, though the effort did little to calm her racing heart. The night air was sharp and cold, biting at her skin the moment she stepped away from the Middleton home. Shadows stretched long across the settlement, shifting with every flicker of moonlight. She wrapped her arms around herself, not entirely from the chill. Being alone out here, after everything that had happened, terrified her. But she forced her feet forward. She had made her choice.

All she needed was a place to hide for a day or two, somewhere far enough from the settlement that no one would be in danger, yet close enough that she could plan her next move. Somehow, she had to reach Cheyenne. Somehow, she had to finish this before Whitmer reached anyone else.

She followed the dirt road toward the forest, each step crunching softly beneath her boots. Every rustle made her flinch. Every distant hoot of an owl sent her pulse leaping. The darkness beneath the trees was thick and suffocating, but she refused to turn back. When she reached the abandoned cabin Jared and his friends had lived in, the very sight of it made her shudder. She stood frozen for a moment. If Whitmer came looking for her, this would be the first place he checked. That was exactly what she needed.

Her hands trembled as she stepped inside the empty structure. Moonlight trickled through broken slats in the walls. The place smelled of rot and damp wood. She found a nail beside the door frame, and fixed her note to it, pressing firmly until the paper caught and held. A message for Whitmer. A lure. A safeguard for the Middletons. Whatever it needed to be. Her breath hitched again as she stepped back outside. The forest loomed ahead, dark, silent, waiting.

Despite the terror creeping up her spine, she hurried deeper into the woods. She remembered a walk around Bear Lake with Esther a few days earlier, how they had spotted a small cabin tucked behind a cluster of pines, perched on a hill with a view of the water. It had seemed charming then.

Now, it felt like her only refuge.

The moon was bright tonight, a cold silver lantern guiding her steps. Hope bent down, snatched up a fallen branch, and brushed away her footprints as she went, sweeping each mark from the earth. If Whitmer followed... she would not lead him straight to the people who had shown her nothing but kindness.

With the forest swallowing her whole, Hope tightened her grip on the branch, lifted her chin, and walked toward the hidden cabin, alone, shaking, but determined.

Hope did not feel safe, not for a single moment. Every rustle made her whip around. Her breath caught in her throat. Every snap of a twig sent her pulse racing. Shadows seemed to lunge at her between the trees, and more than once she imagined yellow eyes watching her from the darkness. The fear of wolves or mountain lions prowling nearby was enough to keep her half-running for most of the walk.

By the time she reached the lonely cabin on the hill, she was trembling with exhaustion and thirst. She stopped several yards from the door, forcing herself to listen carefully. Nothing. Only the wind whispering through pine needles. Then—water. A faint splashing sound, like a trickling stream.

She followed it until she reached a tiny spring bubbling out from beneath a boulder. Relief washed through her. She knelt, pulled her canteen from her bag, and filled it. The first few sips burned down her parched throat. She filled it again.

The moment she rose to her feet, a long, mournful howl cut through the air. Hope nearly dropped the canteen. Her heart leaped into her throat as another wolf answered from somewhere deeper in the woods. They sounded close, too close. Panic jolted her into motion. She grabbed her bags, bow, and arrows and hurried back toward the cabin, stumbling over the uneven ground. She rushed inside, slammed the door shut, and locked it, pressing her back against the wood as she listened to her own frantic breathing.

The cabin was filthy. Moonlight spilled through a cracked window, revealing thick dust, sagging spiderwebs, and a thin mattress that looked as though no one had slept on it in years. The smell of mildew clung to the air. Hope staggered to the bed and sat down, then folded over herself as sobs finally broke free. She felt more alone than she ever had in her life.

Leaving San Francisco had seemed like the only path forward, but tonight she wished nothing more than to undo the past few weeks. If she had stayed, she would never have met Whitmer or Lester or Jared. She would still be safe in her room, sewing or reading, pretending the world wasn't dangerous. But she would also be trapped under her father's thumb. Married off to Eric. Used, controlled, silenced, just as her mother had been.

Hope wiped at her tears with shaking hands. She knew, deep down, painfully deep, that Reverend Shaw had been right.

Staying at home would not have saved her. Not from Whitmer. Not from Eric. Not from the life they intended to force upon her. And she knew something else, too. If she had stayed silent about the letter... if she had ignored the warning about another woman being hunted... she would never have been able to live with herself.

Still, anger welled inside her, hot and helpless. Why had she been thrown into such a hopeless storm? Why did everything she did seem to lead someone else into danger? Why did guilt cling to her even when her heart insisted, she was doing what she must? Her chest tightened until she could hardly breathe. She missed her mother desperately. And, painfully, she wished Reverend Shaw were here. His calm voice. His steady presence. The way he grounded her with a single look. She longed for him to take her hands and tell her everything would be all right.

But he needed time to heal. And she could not let him be hurt again because of her. Curling onto the mattress, clutching her bow to her chest, Hope closed her eyes. The darkness pressed in around her, the forest whispering outside, but she forced herself to stay quiet... to breathe... to survive the night. She would face whatever came next alone.

"Hope is gone," Esther burst out, breathless, as she and Elizabeth rushed into the sitting room.

Reverend Shaw shot to his feet so quickly his chair scraped harshly across the floor. Brother Jacob rose as well, alarm tightening every line of his face. Abigail froze mid-step, turning slowly toward her daughters as though she hadn't heard correctly.

"What do you mean, gone?" Abigail whispered, her voice already trembling. "Esther... what are you saying?" The color drained from her cheeks. Esther shook her head, wringing her hands.

"She wasn't in her bed when we woke up. She was there last night, we saw her, but this morning the blanket was pulled back, and she was gone."

Elizabeth stepped forward, her face pale.

"Some of her things are missing too. Her bow and arrows... her knife. A few of her clothes." Her voice cracked. "And, the window was closed, but it was unlatched."

Reverend Shaw's expression hardened to stone, fear and fury clashing in his eyes. He moved toward the hallway at once, striding with grim purpose.

"Show me."

Abigail pressed her hand to her mouth, shaken. "Oh, my word... What was she thinking? Why would she leave in the middle of the night?"

Esther exchanged a helpless glance with her sister.

"She was... quiet yesterday. More than usual. After the attack... and then Jared's threat..." Her voice wavered. "I should have stayed awake. I should have checked on her."

Reverend Shaw reappeared in the doorway moments later, his breath shallow, his jaw tight with barely contained panic.

"She's gone," he confirmed, his voice low and grim. "And she left on foot."

Abigail gasped, clutching her apron. Elizabeth's eyes filled with tears.

"We have to find her."

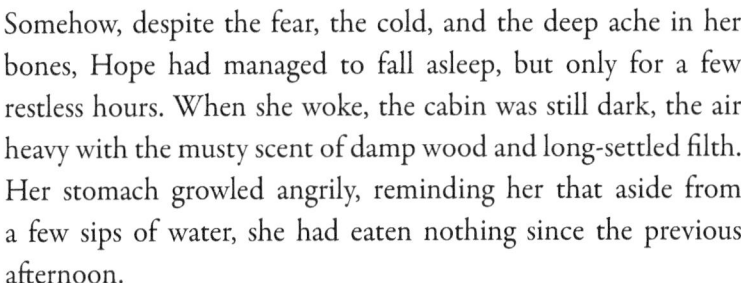

Somehow, despite the fear, the cold, and the deep ache in her bones, Hope had managed to fall asleep, but only for a few restless hours. When she woke, the cabin was still dark, the air heavy with the musty scent of damp wood and long-settled filth. Her stomach growled angrily, reminding her that aside from a few sips of water, she had eaten nothing since the previous afternoon.

Her heart sank. Once again, she realized, painfully, that she had acted in haste, allowing terror and guilt to drive her more than reason. She wrapped her arms around herself, shivering as she took stock of her situation. She had a bow and arrows... but no matches. No flint. No way to start a fire. Even if she managed to hunt for something, and that alone felt doubtful, she wouldn't be able to cook it.

The thought made her stomach twist. She couldn't skin an animal. She had never cleaned a fish or plucked a chicken. She would starve long before she mastered any of that. Forcing herself not to panic again, Hope searched the cabin, opening every cupboard and drawer. Dust. Moldy rags. Empty shelves. Of course there was no food. Her shoulders slumped. She wouldn't last long like this. Staying here meant waiting for starvation... or for Whitmer to find her first. She stepped outside.

Dawn hadn't fully broken yet. A faint gray light laced the treetops, creeping across the mountains like a timid whisper. The air was still and biting cold, her breath puffing in pale clouds. Every rustle in the forest made her flinch. But there was no point in staying. Tightening her grip on her bow, Hope started walking in the direction she believed she needed to go, toward Wyoming, toward Cheyenne, toward whatever destiny lay ahead. And away from the people she feared she had already placed in danger... simply by staying.

"Why would she just take off like that? We finally got through to her... I thought we had." Reverend Shaw dragged a hand through his hair, attempting to look composed, but the fear etched into his features betrayed him. His voice trembled, just enough to be heard. Abigail's eyes darted between the men.

"Did she perhaps believe what Jared told her?" she asked quietly. "About Whitmer coming here to burn down the settlement if she stayed?"

The realization struck them like a blow. None of them had truly considered it, at least not fully. Reverend Shaw's face drained of color.

"Of course," he whispered. "Of course she would believe that." His jaw tightened, the muscles in his neck flexing as guilt flickered across his eyes. "She thinks everyone gets hurt because of her. She must have believed she was protecting us." His voice roughened. "She ran off alone because she was afraid... and because we didn't reassure her enough."

Brother Jacob stepped forward and laid a steadying hand on the reverend's shoulder.

"We'll find her," he said firmly. "Brother Jeremiah's dogs are excellent trackers. And she left on foot, there's only so far she could have gone."

Reverend Shaw nodded, though the worry never left his eyes.

"Sam," Brother Jacob called sharply, "go gather every able-bodied man. Tell them to bring guns, lanterns, and anything else we might need."

"Are we taking horses?" Samuel asked. His father shook his head.

"No. She'd hear us coming and either bolt, or hide, just to avoid us. Tell the men we'll meet at the abandoned cabin those boys lived in. If Hope left any kind of clue behind, that's where we'll find it."

Samuel was already halfway out the door before his father finished speaking. Abigail pulled her shawl tighter around her shoulders, her voice thick with worry.

"Please bring her back safely."

"We will," Reverend Shaw said, his tone low, fierce, and unyielding. "I won't lose her." He turned toward the door, his stride purposeful, fear burned away and replaced by iron resolve. The search for Hope had begun.

---

Hope hadn't gone more than a few hundred yards when a sudden rustling in the bushes beside her made her freeze mid-step. She tightened her grip on her bow, pulse leaping. The sound grew louder, something small but fast, darting through the underbrush. She backed away instinctively. Eyes locked on the quivering leaves... and failed to notice the uneven ground behind her. A skunk burst from the bushes onto the narrow path.

Hope gasped and stumbled backward. Her foot dropped straight into a shallow ditch hidden by tall grass. Her ankle twisted violently beneath her with a sickening jolt, and her balance vanished.

She tumbled down a short slope, rolling through dirt and brittle brush. Branches scraped her arms, snagged her skirt, and knocked the breath from her lungs until her fall ended abruptly in a dense thicket.

For a long moment, Hope lay still, staring up at the pale morning sky while her heart hammered wildly in her chest. Pain pulsed through her ankle, hot, sharp, relentless, but the rest of her body seemed intact. Scratched. Shaken. Bruised. But... not broken. She let out a trembling breath and brushed dirt from her hair and face, hands shaking as she tried to steady herself. Just one more reminder, she thought miserably, of how utterly unprepared she was to survive on her own.

# 12

# When the Wolves
# Broke In

"Have you found anything?" Reverend Shaw asked, his voice tight with worry. One by one, the men around him shook their heads. They had searched the abandoned cabin, the clearing, and the surrounding trees, but there was no trace of Hope, no footprints, no discarded belongings, nothing to point them in the right direction.

"Wait, there's a note," Sam Middleton called out. He had spotted a small piece of paper tacked beside the doorframe and quickly pulled it free, dust clinging to its edges. He handed it to Reverend Shaw, who unfolded it with trembling fingers.

*Anthony Whitmer,*

*I've left the settlement. Please leave the people living there alone. They don't know where I went, and they have nothing to do with it.*

*Hope*

Reverend Shaw swallowed hard. A muscle in his jaw tightened. So, Abigail had been right all along. Hope truly believed Whitmer was coming for the settlement. She had been frightened enough to flee into the wilderness alone, wounded, with no supplies, no protection. The thought made his stomach turn.

"She thinks Whitmer is coming here," he muttered, shaking his head. "She thinks she's protecting us by running off."

Brother Jacob stepped closer.

"Whitmer wouldn't be reckless enough to attack a settlement," he said firmly. "Not one full of armed men and families ready to defend themselves. Murderers hide. They don't walk straight into a firing line."

Reverend Shaw nodded, but his expression remained grim.

"Hope doesn't understand that," he said quietly. "She's thinking with her heart, not her head. She's so determined to carry this burden alone..." His fingers curled around the note, crushing the paper as frustration and fear warred in his chest. "Why can't she accept the protection she's been given? Why does she think her life matters so little?"

Sam placed a steady hand on his shoulder.

"Because she's scared," he said gently. "And she's used to no one protecting her."

Reverend Shaw lifted his gaze toward the dark line of the forest, his eyes hardening with resolve.

"Then we'll find her," he said. "Before Whitmer does. And before she gets herself killed."

The men nodded grimly and turned toward the trees, lanterns raised, the search beginning in earnest.

Tears sprang into her eyes as she hauled herself upright again. The moment she put weight on her foot, white-hot pain shot up her leg. Her ankle was far more injured than she had realized. Every instinct screamed at her to sit down, to rest, to breathe, but she didn't have that luxury. Not with Whitmer out there. Not with danger closing in from every direction.

Rain clouds rolled over the mountains, heavy and dark, and a chill crept through the forest. She needed shelter, soon. Somewhere to hide. Somewhere to think. Gritting her teeth, Hope searched until she found a sturdy fallen branch. Using it as a makeshift crutch, she dragged herself back onto the path.

Every step was agony. Even with the branch steadying her, pain throbbed through her ankle until nausea rose in her throat. Time stretched into slow, grueling hours without rest, her breaths turning short and ragged. Her boot tightened painfully as her ankle continued to swell. Just when she thought she couldn't force herself forward another step, she saw it through the trees, a cabin. Worn. Crooked. Half-hidden. But unmistakably a cabin. Relief hit her so hard she nearly sobbed.

She unslung her canteen, took a careful sip of the lukewarm water, nearly gone now, and lowered it again.

A deep, vicious growl rumbled behind her. Hope's heart stopped. She turned, and ice flooded her veins. A pack of wolves stood on the slope above her. Eight of them. Large. Lean. Starving-looking. Their eyes glowed faintly in the dim light. They weren't curious. They were hunting. She tightened the canteen strap across her chest, slung her bags securely so they wouldn't slip, and without daring to look back again, began limping toward the cabin as fast as her injured foot would allow.

Branches slapped her face. Rocks nearly sent her tumbling. The stick bit into her palm. Behind her, the wolves broke into a run, she heard paws tearing through brush, harsh panting closing the distance. Pain ripped through her ankle, but she pushed harder, dragging herself the final yards. She reached the cabin, wrenched the door open, and stumbled inside.

Before she could turn fully, bodies slammed against the door. Hope cried out and threw her weight into the wood, her shoulder shaking violently as claws scraped and snarls vibrated through the thin boards. Her strength faltered. Her feet slid on the filthy floor. Then, *click*. The lock caught.

Hope collapsed where she stood, gasping for air, her entire body trembling. Tears blurred her vision, but she forced herself to stay alert. The danger wasn't over, not yet. The wolves continued to hurl themselves against the door, snapping and growling, determined to get inside. She wiped her face with the back of her shaking hand and scanned the room.

The cabin was a wreck, rotting beams, broken furniture, filth ground into the floorboards. Cold wind whistled through holes in the roof, setting the shadows shifting. She dragged herself across the room, ignoring the screaming pain in her ankle, desperate for something, anything, to reinforce the door. Nothing. Until she reached the corner near the fireplace. Beneath a half-collapsed cupboard sat a wooden box filled with firewood.

Hope limped to it, seized the edge, and heaved with everything she had left. Inch by inch, she scraped it across the floor, groaning as pain lanced through her foot. By the time she wedged the box against the door, the wolves' growls had deepened, louder, angrier. They rammed the door again, rattling the frame. Hope pressed her back against the wall, breathing hard. She was safe, for now. But she was injured. Alone. Trapped. And the night was only beginning.

Hope staggered backward, her breath sharp and uneven. Her heart pounded so hard it felt as though it might crack her ribs. She scanned the tiny, decrepit cabin for somewhere, anywhere, safe to rest, but there was little to be found. Only a warped bed frame with a thin, discolored mattress that looked as though it hadn't been cleaned in years.

She grimaced. Under any other circumstance, she would never have gone near it. But her ankle throbbed with blinding pain, and her body trembled from exhaustion and terror. She couldn't remain standing.

Moving carefully, she lowered herself onto the gritty mattress, forcing herself not to think about the stains or the sour, musty smell clinging to it. She eased off her boot with a hiss of pain. Her ankle was grotesquely swollen now, the skin stretched tight and angry, glowing red even in the pale moonlight filtering through the broken roof. If only she had something, anything, to cool it. Ice. Water. Cloth. Herbs. But the cabin was barren. No food. No blankets. No supplies. Every shelf stood empty. Even the fireplace held nothing but cold soot. Her canteen still hung around her neck, pitifully light when she lifted it. Barely enough water for a single sip.

Then she heard it. Movement above her. Slow. Deliberate. The unmistakable thud of paws. Hope froze as several wolves climbed onto the sagging roof, their weight creaking the beams as they paced and snuffled along the edges, searching for a way in. A heartbeat later, rotten wood splintered. A board gave way and crashed onto the floor, scattering debris across the cabin.

Hope screamed and scrambled backward, pain ripping through her ankle as she clutched the mattress to keep from falling. The opening wasn't large enough for them to squeeze through, but she could see them. Dark snouts pushed into the gap, teeth flashing, breath steaming in the cold air as they scented her. She clapped a hand over her mouth, terrified even her breathing might draw them in. Her thoughts unraveled. Completely.

Why did disaster keep finding her? Why did every place she sought for safety turn into another nightmare? Exhaustion and fear churned together until her vision blurred. With trembling hands, she brushed dirt from the mattress and dragged her bag beneath her head as a makeshift pillow. Pitiful comfort, but it was all she had. Cold seeped into her bones. There was nothing to shield her from it. No blanket. No coat. Not even a scrap of cloth to block the wind that howled through the holes in the roof.

Then the sky split open. Thunder boomed like cannon fire, rattling the fragile cabin. A moment later, rain poured through the broken ceiling, icy droplets striking her skin like needles. She curled tighter, trying to shield herself, but there was no escape. Water streamed down the walls, soaked her hair, seeped into her clothes.

That was it. Hope pressed her face into her bag and finally let go. Real, wrenching sobs tore from her chest, grief and terror she had held back for days. She cried for the fear, the loneliness, for her mother, for Reverend Shaw, for the Middletons... and for the crushing guilt of believing she had brought danger to them all.

Her body shook until she could barely breathe. Outside, the wolves continued to growl and pace. Inside, Hope curled into the smallest shape she could manage, drenched, freezing, heartbroken... and utterly alone.

"The dogs are getting restless," Brother Jeremiah murmured, watching his hounds rush back and forth, noses glued to the ground, tails stiff with agitation. "They keep circling the cabin and the clearing. I think Hope stayed here last night... but she must have left at first light."

A heavy silence settled over the men. Reverend Shaw's jaw tightened as he studied the tracks leading away from the abandoned cabin. The ground was still soft from the night's moisture, and faint boot prints marked the direction she had gone, but the wind was already sweeping dust across them, erasing her trail inch by inch.

One of the searchers glanced up at the sky and swore under his breath.

"Should we stop here for the day or keep after her? That storm looks ready to tear the mountains in half."

Thick, dark clouds rolled over the ridge, bruised purple and gunmetal gray, gathering speed as they swallowed the light.

"We keep going," Reverend Shaw said immediately.

"We keep going," Brother Jacob echoed at the same moment, his voice firm and unyielding.

The other men exchanged glances, then nodded as one. No one doubted the urgency. The tension in the air was sharp enough to taste, fear for the girl they were searching for, and fear of what... or who... might already be hunting her.

Brother Jeremiah whistled sharply, calling the dogs back. They came reluctantly, circling his boots, panting and whining, anxious to continue.

"They'll find her," Brother Jacob said quietly, gripping Reverend Shaw's shoulder. "But with that storm rolling in, we'd best move fast."

Reverend Shaw barely heard him. His eyes were fixed on the horizon, on the path Hope had taken.

"Hold on, Hope," he whispered under his breath. "We're coming."

Hope jolted awake with a scream lodged in her throat as something slammed violently through the window. A thick tree branch burst past the shattered frame, spraying splinters across the room. The storm outside had grown vicious, rain hammered the cabin in relentless sheets, and the wind shrieked through the trees like a living creature.

Her pulse thundered as she pushed herself upright. The entire wall shuddered with each gust, and the broken window rattled dangerously, jagged shards of glass clinging weakly to the warped frame. Her breath caught. It wouldn't take much, one strong gust, one falling branch, and the rest of the window would collapse entirely. Then nothing would stand between her and the wolves pacing outside.

Hope's gaze flicked to the dark shapes barely visible through the storm. Their growls rose and fell with the wind, low and hungry. Every so often, a muzzle pressed between the glass shards before jerking back, stung by the sharp edges. That glass, those jagged teeth of the window, was the only thing stopping the animals from forcing their way inside. But the frame was splintering. The storm was worsening.

Fresh terror seized her chest. If another branch struck the house... if the wind twisted the frame just enough... if one wolf pushed too hard... they would get in. Hope scrambled off the filthy mattress, nearly collapsing as pain flared through her injured ankle. She stumbled backward toward the far corner of the cabin, her hands shaking so violently she could barely think.

"Please... please hold," she whispered to the trembling window frame, her voice raw and thin.

Lightning flashed, flooding the cabin with harsh white light. For one terrible second, everything stood stark and clear, the broken branch sprawled across the floor, the glass shards clinging stubbornly to the frame, the wolves hurling themselves against the door, their bodies slamming into the wood, the roof sagging beneath rain and clawing paws. And her—small, cold, alone, trapped with no way out.

Thunder cracked overhead, shaking the cabin to its foundations. Hope wrapped her arms around herself, fighting the rising panic. She needed to think. She needed to survive until morning.

But one more blow to the window might make that impossible.

"The dogs have found her scent, and look, there are footprints." Brother Jeremiah crouched beside the narrow path, rain dripping from the brim of his hat as he examined the ground. The rest of the search party gathered around him, lanterns flickering against the storm-dark sky.

"It appears she was startled by something," he continued, brushing his fingers lightly over the disturbed earth. "Her tracks veer sharply off the path. See how the dirt's gouged out here? She must've stumbled, probably tripped over something and rolled down the mountainside a few feet."

Reverend Shaw stepped closer, his breath catching as he peered over the edge. Jeremiah pointed to the flattened patches of rain-soaked brush below.

"She climbed back up," Jeremiah added. "But her prints are uneven now, broken apart, deeper in places. That means she was limping. She's hurt."

Reverend Shaw's jaw tightened. Brother Jacob scanned the misty tree line with narrowed eyes as the rain poured harder, pattering against their hats and shoulders, muffling every distant sound. The men began calling her name, repeatedly, voices echoing through the forest. No answer came back. Only the wind... and the low rumble of distant thunder.

"If she's injured," Brother Jacob said grimly, "we're running out of time. Wolves, mountain lions, any predator would find her easy prey in this weather. Especially if she can't run." The worry etched into his face cut through the storm itself. But Reverend Shaw's expression, pale, rigid, burning with fear, was even more devastating. He looked like a man holding himself together by sheer force of will.

"We'll find her," he said, though his voice shook beneath the fierce determination. His gaze dropped again to the broken footprints leading deeper into the wilderness. "We have to."

Brother Jeremiah signaled to the dogs. They barked sharply and pressed their noses to the soaked earth.

"They're ready," he said. "And she can't be far ahead."

The men exchanged a tense, resolute look, then pushed forward after the hounds, lanterns bobbing as they disappeared into the storm.

Hope jolted upright just as another violent crash shook the cabin. This time she saw it, the massive tree beside the window finally gave way under the storm's fury, smashing through the remaining frame and sending splinters flying across the room. Her breath hitched. A wolf, a huge, gray, snarling beast, slipped through the jagged opening, its eyes glowing in the dim, storm-lit room. More claws scraped against the wood outside.

Hope's pulse pounded in her ears. She scrambled back, desperate, reaching for anything that might help her defend herself. She knew the truth: her chances of surviving eight wolves while trapped in a broken cabin were next to nothing.

Her trembling hands closed around her canteen. She yanked it upward, trying to use it as a weight, but the wolf lunged before she could swing. Its jaws clamped onto the metal and leather strap. Hope choked as the strap snapped tight around her throat. She gasped, clawing at it with one hand while swinging her bag wildly with the other, striking the wolf repeatedly. A second wolf leapt through the shattered window, snarling, fangs bared.

The first wolf tugged harder, dragging her halfway across the filthy mattress, the strap biting deep into her neck. Spots burst across her vision as her airway constricted. Desperate, she grabbed her bow and slammed it toward the second wolf. It snapped its jaws around the wood, ripped it clean from her hands, and flung it aside like kindling.

She could barely breathe now. Her fingers wedged between the strap and her throat, but the wolf kept pulling, trying to drag her off the bed entirely. Hope's vision blurred. Panic clawed at her chest, cold, crushing, suffocating. Then—barking. Fierce. Furious. Close.

One of Brother Jeremiah's dogs burst through the shattered window in a blur of fur and muscle, slamming into the second wolf and knocking it sideways. They crashed across the floor, snarling and biting. More barking erupted outside. And then, gunshots. Sharp. Immediate. Deafening.

Someone slammed against the door, trying to force it open through the barricade she'd shoved there earlier. Hope tried to suck in air past the constricting strap, tears streaming down her face. The cabin exploded into chaos, wolves, dogs, gunfire, and someone shouting her name. But she could barely hear any of it over the desperate, ragged rasp of her own breath as she fought to stay conscious... and stay alive.

The leather band snapped with a violent crack, and Hope was hurled backward, slamming into the wall so hard her teeth rattled. For a single heartbeat, she could breathe again, but the wolf was already on her. It lunged, landing above her with a heavy thud, its snarling jaws inches from her face. Hot breath and thick strands of slobber splattered her cheek as its lips peeled back, revealing rows of yellow, deadly teeth. Its growl vibrated through her chest, a low warning of the inevitable.

Hope sucked in a broken gasp, her throat raw from choking. Panic clawed at her lungs, but instinct surged stronger. Her hand shot out blindly, fumbling across the filthy floorboards until her fingers closed around one of her arrows. The wolf lunged. Hope didn't think. She drove the arrow upward with every ounce of strength left in her trembling body. A sickening thud. A furious yelp.

Then, silence.

The wolf's eyes widened in shock before it staggered backward, the arrow buried deep in its chest. For a breathless moment, it swayed, blood bubbling around the wound, then it collapsed in a heavy heap beside her. Dead.

Hope lay frozen, panting, tears streaming down her cheeks. Her hands shook so violently she nearly dropped the arrow. She stared at the unmoving wolf, unable to believe what she had just done. She had pierced its heart. She had survived. But the victory was short-lived. Snarling still echoed outside. Another body slammed against the door. And Hope knew, the danger wasn't over.

Hope felt like she was suffocating. She dragged in air in broken gasps, but each attempt to breathe only made her chest constrict tighter. Panic clawed up her throat, choking off her sobs until she could barely force a sound out at all. The dog and the second wolf were locked in a vicious, snarling blur of teeth and fur, crashing across the cabin floor. They slammed into the bed, making the entire frame jolt beneath her. Hope cried out and covered her head with her arms. Another gunshot split the air, sharp, deafening.

The wolf's weight vanished. The snarls went silent. Hope lifted her head just as Reverend Shaw reached for her hand. The moment her eyes met his, the last of her strength crumbled. She threw herself into his arms, clutching him with desperate force. He lifted her off the ground without hesitation, holding her tightly against his chest.

That was all it took. Her sobs erupted, shaking her so hard she could barely remain upright. She gasped for air between cries, her fingers curling into the fabric of his coat as though he were the only solid thing left in her world. Reverend Shaw pressed his cheek against her hair, stroking the back of her head with one steady hand. His voice was low, soothing, and achingly gentle.

"Shh... it's all right. You're safe now. Breathe with me, sweetheart. Slow breaths. That's it. We're here. You're safe."

It took time, long, agonizing minutes, before her breathing finally steadied. While she clung to him, the men dragged the wolves outside, secured the broken door as best they could, and coaxed a fire to life in the hearth to warm the chilled cabin.

When her sobs quieted, Reverend Shaw eased her back onto the bed, though he remained seated beside her, refusing to put any space between them. Brother Jacob stepped forward first, pulling her into a firm, fatherly embrace. Brother Jeremiah followed, brushing her hair back from her damp cheeks with surprising tenderness.

When the men finally settled into place, their eyes remained fixed on her, concern etched deep into their features. Hope immediately dropped her gaze to her lap, ashamed of how broken she felt.

Reverend Shaw wouldn't allow it. He gently placed two fingers beneath her chin and guided her gaze back to his.

"Why did you take off, Hope?" His voice was soft, but an ache beneath it tightened her chest. "Why didn't you stay where you were safe, where we could protect you?"

Her eyes filled again, though she fought the tears stubbornly.

"Jared threatened me," she whispered. "He said Whitmer was on his way to the settlement... and that he'd burn everything if I stayed." The guilt she had been carrying for hours crashed over her anew. She pulled her hand away from Reverend Shaw's and wrapped her arms around herself.

"I didn't want anyone to get hurt because of me," she said, her voice trembling. "None of you deserve to become targets just because I am one." She swallowed hard and looked away. "I know I walked straight into danger. I know it was foolish. But leaving felt like the only way to protect all of you."

Reverend Shaw reached for her again, his expression torn between frustration, relief, and something deeper, something that made Hope's breath hitch. Something she didn't want to think about.

"Why did you follow me?" Hope's voice cracked under the weight of the question. "Why did you risk your lives for me? I'm nothing to you. We aren't blood related. I'm practically still a stranger. If my own father doesn't care enough about me to keep me safe..." Her voice faltered. "Why would any of you?"

She looked from Reverend Shaw to Brother Jacob to Brother Jeremiah, her confusion and heartbreak laid bare. None of it made sense to her. Strangers shouldn't care more than family, yet here she sat, surrounded by men who had chased through a storm, hunted through the mountains, and faced down predators... all because of her.

"Oh, Hope..." Brother Jacob reached for her hand and drew her gently into a warm, fatherly embrace. She felt his steady heartbeat against her cheek, and it nearly shattered her all over again.

Brother Jeremiah cleared his throat softly.

"You are not 'nothing' to us," he said firmly. "And you are certainly no stranger. I know this way of living, this kind of community, might be foreign to you. Especially after how your father treated you. But love isn't limited to blood." He squeezed her hand reassuringly. "And I'm not talking about romance. I'm talking about human decency. Compassion. The kind of love families choose."

Hope blinked up at him, confused... but listening.

"Let me tell you something Abigail's family taught my wife," Brother Jeremiah continued quietly, the firelight flickering across his solemn face. "Because her past... is not so different from what you've been through."

Reverend Shaw's eyes sharpened with concern as Jeremiah spoke.

"My wife grew up in a home full of fear," he said. "Her father was controlling, cruel, and when no one was looking, violent. One day, when she was fifteen, she witnessed him beat her mother to death."

Hope gasped softly, covering her mouth.

"She ran to the sheriff," Jeremiah continued, "but her father was influential. Persuasive. No one believed her. Her mother's body was later found in a river, and he blamed two robbers passing through town. They were hanged for a crime he committed."

"That is horrible," Reverend Shaw murmured, shaking his head. Brother Jeremiah nodded, his eyes dark.

"It was a terrible injustice. When my wife continued to speak the truth, her father beat her, locked her away, trying to break her spirit. She eventually escaped and fled... but no one helped her. No one believed her."

Hope's heart ached. She wasn't sure whether she wanted to cry or scream.

"It was Abigail's parents who took her in," Jeremiah said. "Her father tracked her down, demanded she return home, threatened the family... but Abigail's parents stood between them. Abigail's father, an attorney, took him to court. He hired investigators. Dug up years of evidence her father had buried. In the end, justice caught up to him. He was sentenced to life in prison."

Hope's eyes were wide, locked onto his.

"And Abigail's parents?" she whispered. "They adopted her?"

He smiled gently. "Yes. They gave her the home she'd never had. And when she once asked them, just as you asked us, why they would do something so extraordinary for her, Abigail's father told her something she has repeated her entire life."

Brother Jacob slid an arm around Hope's shoulders and finished the story himself, his voice soft but steady.

"'It isn't blood that teaches us who to love. It's the heart. Blood might make a family, but the heart recognizes its own. Sometimes we meet someone and feel an instant bond we can't explain, because our hearts remember them, even if our minds don't. The heart speaks to the heart, and that's what binds people together.'"

Hope drew in a trembling breath as tears filled her eyes. She tried to pull away to hide her reaction, but Brother Jacob tugged her right back into his arms and held her solidly against him.

"We love you, Hope," he said, his voice thick with emotion. "Yes, we've only known you a short while, but you came into our lives like a whirlwind. You belong with us. You're part of our community. Part of our family. And family, real family, doesn't leave each other behind."

Brother Jeremiah nodded firmly. Reverend Shaw's gaze softened, the raw worry in his eyes turning into something deeper, something that almost frightened Hope. But she felt it, and she understood something with startling clarity. She was not alone after all.

Despite all the comforting words and the many arms that had wrapped around her, Hope was freezing. A tremor she couldn't control worked its way through her, and a faint dizziness blurred her vision at the edges. She hadn't eaten properly in nearly three days, her canteen was almost empty, and every ragged breath reminded her of just how weak she truly felt.

But she didn't want to admit any of that, not after everything these men had done for her. Not after the trouble she had brought upon them. So, when the room fell quiet for a moment, she pushed herself off the bed, determined to get closer to the fire. It was a mistake.

The moment her injured foot touched the ground, pain shot through her like a white-hot knife. Her ankle felt twice its normal size, tight, throbbing, burning. She bit hard into the inside of her cheek to keep from crying out, but tears flooded her eyes anyway. Still, she limped stubbornly toward the hearth, dragging her foot behind her, refusing to crumble in front of them. She didn't get far.

Reverend Shaw was beside her before she even realized he had moved. In one smooth motion, he swept her off her feet and into his arms. Hope let out a startled gasp, her fingers instinctively clutching his shoulders as he carried her across the room. He set her gently onto a stool directly in front of the fire, positioning her so the warmth of the flames washed over her chilled skin.

Startlement gave way to relief. She managed a small, grateful smile, though her cheeks flushed beneath the intensity of his gaze.

"Hope..." His voice was low, firm, and uncomfortably perceptive. "Have you eaten anything since leaving the settlement?"

She hesitated. The truth sat heavy in her stomach, well, it would have, if there had been anything there. She felt his eyes on her, steady and unyielding, as though he could read every lie she considered offering. Slowly, she shook her head.

Before she could attempt an explanation, Brother Jacob, Brother Jeremiah, Sam, and even one of the other men reached into their packs and pockets, pulling out bits of food, jerky, bread, dried apples, anything they had. They pressed it into her hands until she could hold no more. Reverend Shaw crouched in front of her, uncorked a canteen, and lifted it to her lips with a gentleness that made her throat tighten.

"Drink," he said softly. Hope obeyed. The water felt like life itself. Each swallow eased the pounding in her head, loosening the tight coil of fear lodging in her chest. Warmth from the fire spread through her frozen limbs, thawing her inch by inch. The dizziness faded just enough for her senses to return. The men spoke quietly behind her, but all Hope could hear was the steady rhythm of Reverend Shaw's breathing, still close, still constant. He hadn't stepped away. He was watching her with careful attention, far more protectively than a mere clergyman should.

Hope lowered her eyes, her heartbeat quickening in a way that had nothing to do with fear or hunger. She was safe and she was warm. Something she was truly grateful for.

The group left at first light the following morning. Hope's ankle was still swollen, angry red, and throbbing with even the slightest movement, and the weight of her boot alone made her wince. But instead of admitting she needed help, she squared her shoulders, planted her stick firmly in the ground, and glared at Reverend Shaw as if sheer stubbornness could override pain.

"Hope, I can see from a mile away you can't use that foot," he said, exasperation already tightening his jaw. "And frankly, you shouldn't even want to."

"I can walk slowly," she insisted.

His irritation sharpened. "You can hurt yourself a lot more if you don't stop being so darn stubborn."

"You men came all this way to rescue me," she said. "I don't think you, or anyone, should have to carry me. It was my own fault I got injured."

"From what you told us, you were startled by a skunk." He gave her a pointed look. "Getting hurt isn't your fault. It happens. And it'll take us twice as long to get home if we let you walk."

She lifted her chin, eyes flashing. "You don't have to wait for me. You can go ahead, and I'll follow at my own pace." With a firm grip on her stick, she began limping toward the path. Behind her, Reverend Shaw stared after her in disbelief while Brother Jacob and Brother Jeremiah tried, and failed, to hide their amusement.

"Hope Spencer," Reverend Shaw called sharply, "if you think we're leaving you behind after rescuing you from a pack of wolves, you are mistaken. You are wasting everyone's time."

Hope spun around. "Brother Jacob and Brother Jeremiah and the others can go ahead. I don't want to hold them back. But why would I be wasting *your* time? It's not like you have anywhere to be."

Brother Jeremiah coughed loudly to hide his grin. Reverend Shaw shot him a glare.

"Abigail would give us a piece of her mind if we returned home without you," Brother Jacob added, "and found out we allowed you to walk in this condition."

Hope sighed, suddenly looking smaller, frustrated more with herself than with them.

"Perhaps I can walk until it becomes too hard?" she offered. "I'll let you know when that happens."

She turned pleading eyes toward Brother Jacob, but Reverend Shaw cut in before he could respond.

"I've had enough of this nonsense." He strode toward her with determined steps. Before Hope even had time to gasp, he bent and hoisted her over his shoulder.

"Put me down!" she yelped, pounding uselessly against his back. "I don't want you to carry me!"

"And I'm done arguing with you," he replied coolly. "You need to stop letting your pride get in the way and admit you need help."

"This isn't pride! I just don't want to be a burden!"

"How thoughtful of you," he said dryly, not even pretending to hide the sarcasm.

"You don't believe me?" The hurt slipped into her voice before she could stop it. That did something to him. He let out a quiet sigh, set her carefully down on a tree trunk beside the path, and squatted so they were eye level. His anger softened into something gentler, steadier.

"I believe you don't want to be a burden," he said quietly. "I know you're not trying to be difficult. But I also think... after everything your father and Eric did, controlling you, silencing you, forbidding you to investigate anything, you're trying to prove them wrong."

Hope's throat tightened.

"You're making decisions based on emotion to show you can do what they said you couldn't," he continued. "You want to prove you don't need anyone. But in doing so, you're forgetting your own safety, and the safety of those who care about you."

She swallowed hard, unable to look away.

"You need to think about the people who care about you," he said softly. "And I don't just mean the Middleton family. Or Brother Jeremiah. Or me." His expression warmed, gentle and firm at once.

"What if you find your mother's family? Don't you think they would be devastated to lose you? Your grandparents, aunts, cousins, people who may not even know you exist yet. Would it be fair for them to lose your mother... and then lose you too?"

Hope lowered her eyes, shame flooding her. Everything he said was true. She had let fear and anger lead her. She had walked straight into danger, more than once, and placed others at risk with her. Her mother had begged her not to let anyone control her. But Hope realized now she wasn't meant to let her own emotions control her either.

After a long moment, she looked up and met Reverend Shaw's gaze, warm, steady, and unwavering.

"Forgive me," she whispered. "You're right. I wasn't thinking about anyone else. I didn't want my father's control over me to win... so I pushed too far the other way."

His smile was gentle. Proud. He reached out and squeezed her hand, his thumb brushing her knuckles in a way that sent a quiet flutter through her chest.

"We're not trying to protect you because we think you're incapable," he murmured. "No one could face this alone, Hope.

It's all right to accept help." He hesitated, then added softly, "Maybe... maybe your mother could have been saved too, if she had let others step in. If she hadn't felt she had to face everything alone."

# 13

# No Gentle Lessons

When Hope stepped out of the house several days later, Reverend Shaw was waiting near the porch, arms folded loosely, posture relaxed, but his eyes sharpened the moment they landed on her. Her foot, thanks to Abigail's relentless care, was nearly healed. She moved without limping now, though she still favored it slightly.

"Where is everyone?" she asked.

"Abigail took Sonny and the older girls to visit a neighbor." His gaze remained fixed on her. She felt it like a warm hand against her cheek. A faint blush rose, and from the way his lips twitched, he noticed. "After everything that's happened since we arrived..." He paused, then continued, voice low and decisive, "I've decided you need to learn how to shoot a gun."

Hope stared at him, first stunned, then incredulous.

"You know how to use a weapon?" she asked at last. She tried to keep the sass out of her voice, but judging by the spark in his eyes, she failed spectacularly. "Is that part of the training for becoming a reverend?"

"Yes," he answered dryly, "right after the course on dealing with sassy young women."

Her cheeks heated instantly, but she refused to flinch, lifting her chin instead. He grinned, thoroughly amused.

"For your information," he added, "I grew up on a ranch."

"I didn't know that. Was my mother aware, or did you keep that a secret from her too?"

He cleared his throat. "Let's start with the lesson."

"Why do you want me to learn to shoot?" she pressed. His expression sobered.

"Because your father has put out a reward for your return. That makes this journey even more dangerous. We could get separated. And if only one of us is spotted, the other must hide, so at least one of us can escape."

Her eyes softened. "By *one of us*, you really mean me, don't you?"

He didn't hesitate. "Yes. Nobody is hunting me. But they might see me as a threat... and kill me."

A sharp ache tightened her chest. That was the fear she could barely breathe through, the thought of him dying because of her choices. He saw it flicker across her face and shifted smoothly back to instruction.

"We'll start simple," he said, drawing a revolver from his belt. Hope blinked at it. It looked far heavier than she'd imagined. He placed it gently in her hands. "Careful. It's loaded. Let's go through the basics." His tone was patient, steady, unexpectedly gentle. He showed her where her thumbs should rest, how her fingers should curl, where her elbows should settle. She tried to mimic his stance.

"Your posture," he murmured, stepping closer. "It's off."

Before she could react, his hands slid to her hips, not indecently, but firmly, confidently, adjusting her alignment.

Hope went utterly still. A faint tremor ran up her spine. She prayed he hadn't noticed. He had. His breath hitched, barely, before his hands dropped away.

"Try lifting your arms," he said, his voice rougher than before. She obeyed. He stepped in behind her now, close enough that she could feel the warmth of him along her back. His arms reached around to guide her aim, his hand sliding along her forearm, slow, steady, deliberate. Her breath caught. Her pulse leapt. His scent, clean soap, leather, and the faintest trace of spice, wrapped around her. Her knees nearly buckled.

Startled by the rush of sensation, Hope jerked away, spinning out of his hold. Her face burned. Her voice came out sharper than she intended.

"What do you think you're doing?" she snapped. He blinked, then his lips curved into the slowest, most infuriatingly self-satisfied grin.

"I'm trying to teach you how to shoot," he replied calmly. The glint in his eyes made it painfully clear he found her fluster far too delightful.

"This is completely inappropriate."

"How?" he asked, all innocence.

"You're touching me and—"

He laughed. Actually laughed. "Hope, I have to correct your stance. And how you're holding the weapon."

"I can't concentrate when you're that close to me," she blurted before she could stop herself.

His brows lifted. Slowly. Deliberately. Her face went from pink to thoroughly scarlet.

"And why is that?" he asked softly, stepping half a pace closer. The daring spark in his eyes stole her breath. Her mouth opened.

Closed. Opened again. Nothing. He leaned in, his voice dropping to a deep whisper.

"You need to learn to shoot even with distractions. Your ability to focus could determine your fate."

Hope swallowed, unable to look away. He wasn't wrong. And yet... her heart was pounding hard enough to betray her entirely.

"Now," he said gently, "let's try again."

She drew in a steadying breath and prepared herself as best she could. But his nearness... his voice... his hands correcting her stance with warm, assured confidence, every touch sent butterflies skittering wildly through her. She lifted the gun. He guided her wrist. She steadied her breathing. And with every thudding heartbeat, Hope realized that learning to shoot was no longer her greatest challenge. It was surviving his closeness without the entire world catching fire around her.

They practiced for two full days, and Hope was genuinely surprised by how quickly she improved. Reverend Shaw complimented her more than once, especially when she struck the targets with impressive consistency. She found she enjoyed shooting, especially the sense of control it gave her, the steadiness it demanded. But when she stepped out of the house on the third morning, something felt different. There were no targets. No logs set up. No marks painted on trees. The revolver remained holstered at his side.

"No shooting lessons today?" she asked and was startled by how disappointed she sounded. He shook his head.

"Not today. Today, I'm teaching you how to fight off an attacker."

Her jaw dropped. "Fight off an attacker? Reverend Shaw, I'm a small woman. I can barely lift a heavy kettle, let alone—"

"You'd be surprised," he interrupted calmly. "You fought off Jared."

She stiffened. She hated even hearing the man's name.

"Only because I got hold of a knife. And because he angered me beyond sense. That was luck, not skill."

"Which is exactly why you need to learn," he replied. "Different techniques. How to use your size instead of fighting against it." His expression sharpened slightly. "Now, fair warning. I'm not going to hurt you, but I won't pretend you're made of glass either. You need to learn what it feels like to be trapped, so you can stay calm if it happens again."

"I already know what it feels like to be trapped," she whispered. Her voice trembled as she turned away. "Twice, in only a few days."

He saw the fear she tried to hide and stepped closer, softening his tone.

"Which is why you must practice. If fear controls you, you lose your advantage."

Hope swallowed. His sleeves were rolled up again, revealing strong, tanned forearms, and she hated the way her stomach fluttered at the sight. She could not afford distractions.

"I don't think this is a good idea," she insisted. "Let's just... continue with guns." She tried to walk past him. He stepped in front of her. She shifted the other way. He blocked her again. Irritated, more at herself than him, she spun on her heel and marched off. He followed. Before she even realized what was happening, strong arms wrapped around her from behind, trapping her. It felt too familiar. Too much like Jared. Hope's breath hitched painfully.

"Reverend Shaw," she choked out, "let me go. At once." Her voice shook. He heard it.

"How would you escape if someone held you like this?" he murmured near her ear. His tone wasn't cruel, just deliberate, controlled, steady. "Think, Hope."

"I can't—I can't do this," she whispered, chest tightening. "Please. Let me go."

"No attacker will release you because you cry," he said firmly, though not unkindly. "You must learn to push past fear. If you show it, they will use it to break you."

She knew he was right. He wasn't trying to hurt her. He was trying to give her power. She closed her eyes and forced herself to breathe.

"Now," he repeated softly, "what could you do?"

Hope focused on what her body could reach.

"Grab his gun. Or knife," she murmured.

He nodded. "Good. What else?"

"I could... kick his leg. Or stomp his foot."

"Likely not enough to make him release you," he said. "Think carefully. What's free?"

Her breath caught as realization dawned. "My head."

"Exactly."

She explained how she could slam her head backward, into an attacker's face, throat, or chest.

He released her immediately and stepped back, offering an approving smile.

"Well done." He crossed his arms. "Now, once he lets go, what do you do?"

"Run," she answered without hesitation. "As fast as possible. Call for help."

"Correct. But what if he comes after you?"

"If I have his weapon, I can shoot him in the leg to slow him."

"And if you don't?"

She hesitated.

"Show me," he said.

Her eyes widened. "What?"

"Show me. Run. Escape. I'll come after you, and you tell me how to get free."

"Reverend Shaw—"

"Hope." His voice dropped, firm and dangerous. "Show me. Or I tackle you right now."

She gasped, then spun and ran. He gave her just enough time to think she might succeed before she felt his hands at her waist. She slapped at them, but he was too quick, too strong. A heartbeat later, she was on the ground, his weight pinning her hips, her wrists held above her head. Heat flared through her cheeks. Anger mixed with something far more unsettling. His confident grin nearly made her furious. *Nearly.*

"How do you escape this?" he challenged.

"There is no way," she snapped. "You're sitting on me."

"There's always a way." He tilted his head slightly, watching her. "Think."

She inhaled deeply. Then, suddenly, she thrust her hips upward with every ounce of strength she had. He was completely caught off guard, and pitched forward, nearly planting his face in the dirt, and she yanked her arms free with startling speed.

She twisted toward his side, shoving at his arm to roll away, but he recovered just as fast, smoothly pinning her again. This time, both were breathless.

"That," he said through a grin, "was very, very good. Surprise is your greatest ally. If you can break free even for a second, that's enough time to grab a weapon, or run. We'll work on this." He rose and extended his hand. Hope hesitated... then took it.

His grip was warm, steady, far too comforting. Their eyes met and lingered a fraction too long. Then he pulled her to her feet with ease, and the lesson, dangerous, infuriating, exhilarating, continued. Despite the fear. Despite the memories. Despite the dizzying closeness of him... Hope knew she was finally learning how to survive.

They walked side by side for only a moment before Reverend Shaw seized her again, swift, deliberate, and shoved her back against a tree. Hope gasped. His left hand pinned both her wrists above her head. His right arm wrapped firmly around her waist, drawing her in. The rest of his body pressed into hers, unyielding, immovable. Her breath stuttered. His face was inches from hers, so close his lips nearly brushed her cheek.

"What would you do," he murmured, voice low, "if a man had you like this... and tried to kiss you?"

A tremor ran through her. She lowered her eyes.

"I—I don't know," she whispered.

"Don't look down," he said sharply. "Never look down. Keep your eyes on your attacker. It tells him you are watching. That you're thinking. That you haven't broken." His mouth drifted closer. She felt the warmth of his breath.

"Men who trap women like this will toy with them," he continued, his tone darker now, harder. "They might lean closer to your throat..." Before she could protest, he buried his face in her hair.

A whimper escaped her. Tears sprang instantly to her eyes. That was exactly what Jared had done.

Exactly.

"Reverend Shaw, don't," she breathed. "Please. You're scaring me."

"An attacker won't care," he said coldly. "And tears won't stop him."

She tried to push against him, but he didn't move, not an inch. His lips hovered near hers again.

It was too much. Too real. Too close to the nightmare she had barely survived.

"I don't want this," she cried, her voice breaking. "Let me go. Please."

Something flickered in his eyes, regret, perhaps, or recognition, but he forced it aside.

"This isn't a game, princess," he said, his voice low and frighteningly unfamiliar. "Either find a way to break free... or you're mine."

Hope froze. Her heart slammed against her ribs. Instinct screamed at her to twist toward the house, to cry out, but she didn't make it that far. His mouth crashed into hers. Not gentle. Not tender. Not a kiss meant to coax or seduce. It was a shock, bruising, forceful, meant to provoke, to overwhelm, to ignite something he believed she needed. And it did. Just not what he expected. It sparked rage. White-hot. Blistering.

Without hesitation, she dropped her weight, letting her body go slack like a stone. His arm slid downward instinctively, keeping her from scraping against the tree. The instant his grip loosened, just a whisper of slack, she shoved him. Hard. He stumbled backward, boots skidding in the dirt.

Hope didn't hesitate. She darted out of reach, chest heaving, eyes blazing.

"How dare you?" she cried, her voice ringing through the quiet grove. "I told you not to do that! You have no right to cross boundaries like that. You are completely out of control!" She spun toward the house, fury driving her forward, but his hand caught her wrist. Not rough. Not painful.

But firm. Unyielding.

"I'm teaching you to survive," he said fiercely. "Women don't get attacked gently. Men like Jared don't ask permission. They use their size, their strength, their mouths, their hands, anything they can, to frighten you and break you down!"

"You're insane," she snapped, wrenching against him. "Completely insane. I'm not doing any more lessons with you!"

He didn't release her.

"Hope," he said, his voice strained, "you need to know how to stay alive."

"Alive?" she cried, her chest aching, vision blurring. "You just made me relive everything he did! Why would you do that to me?"

"Because I saw the fear in your eyes when I reached for you," he shot back, something desperate threading through the anger. "When Jared attacked you the second time, I saw how fast terror overtook you. If that happens again, if you freeze, you lose. And I won't let that happen. Not to you."

Her hands shook violently at her sides.

"You don't know what it feels like!" she shouted, the words tearing out of her. "To be targeted like that. To think he's going to—" Her voice broke. She turned away, and the tears she'd fought so hard to contain finally spilled. He exhaled, a harsh, pained sound, and when he spoke again, his voice softened, just a fraction.

"I know what Jared wanted to do," he said, something fierce and protective burning in his eyes. "And I refuse, do you hear me? Refuse, to let any man take what isn't his to take."

She stared at the ground, shoulders shaking.

"Be brave, Hope," he urged, still intense but quieter now. "You were unstoppable when we left San Francisco. You had fire. Anger. Fight."

"That was before," she whispered. "Before I was attacked. Before I realized that I—women—can be hunted for reasons that have nothing to do with revenge or murder." She looked up, anguish hollowing her eyes. "I was naïve. I didn't think—"

"Hope—"

"No!" She stumbled backward, raising both hands. "Don't touch me."

He didn't. He stayed where he was, letting her breathe. Letting her fall apart. She didn't notice Sonny until the little boy burst out from behind the woodshed, fists clenched, tears streaming.

"Don't you hurt Hope!" he sobbed, pounding Reverend Shaw's legs with his tiny fists. "You made her cry! Let her go!"

Both adults froze. Hope swallowed her sobs and dropped to her knees, pulling Sonny into her arms.

"Sonny, darling," she whispered through choked breaths, "Reverend Shaw didn't hurt me. He's teaching me how to protect myself if someone wants to hurt me."

The boy blinked up at her, cheeks wet. "Really?"

"Yes," she whispered. "I promise."

Sonny turned slowly toward Reverend Shaw, his lip trembling. Reverend Shaw knelt, placing a gentle hand on the boy's shoulder.

"I would never hurt her," he said softly. Sonny sniffled, accepted the answer, and allowed Abigail, who had hurried over, to guide him back toward the house.

When they were gone, Hope lifted her gaze to him, her eyes still red and shimmering with tears.

"I can't do this," she whispered, her voice trembling. "I can't keep reliving it."

Reverend Shaw immediately wrapped his arms around her again, not restraining this time, but holding. Anchoring. Protective.

"Yes, you can," he said softly against her hair. "Not all at once. Not without fear. But you can. The beginning is always the hardest, Hope. You're learning to fight a battle you should have never been forced to face. We'll go slowly. We'll practice different scenarios every day. And each time, you'll gain more control... more confidence. You won't be powerless again. Not ever."

Her breath stuttered, and her fingers clutched at his shirt.

"Why do men do that?" she asked, her voice cracking with anguish. "Why do they attack women in such horrible ways? What kind of person does that to someone?"

He exhaled, a deep, heavy, grieving sigh. His jaw tightened. His hand curled instinctively into a fist at her back.

"Because it is power to them," he said quietly, simmering fury beneath each word. "Twisted, corrupt power. Domination for the sake of domination. Humiliation wrapped in violence. When a man forces himself on a woman, he isn't seeking companionship or affection. He is seeking control, the cruelest kind."

Hope swallowed, her voice barely more than breath.

"But why... why would anyone want that?"

"Because evil delights in destroying what God made sacred." His voice deepened, calm but burning with conviction. "Men like Jared," he continued, "they don't just want to hurt a woman's body. They want to crush her spirit. To tear away her dignity, her peace, her voice. They want to make her believe she is small and helpless so they can feel powerful."

He shook his head, his eyes dark with righteous anger.

"That kind of abuse, forcing a woman, stealing her right to choose, it's one of the purest forms of evil there is. It's not just sin, Hope. It's a deliberate attempt to break the precious agency God gave His daughters."

Her tears rose again. He brushed one from her cheek with the gentlest touch.

"Satan has always tried to force," Reverend Shaw said softly. "From the beginning, he sought to take away choice, to bend God's children to his will. Abuse, especially of women, is his reflection. It's the closest thing to his ideology there is."

Hope shivered, not from fear this time, but from the weight of truth.

"This is why I'm teaching you," he murmured. "Not to frighten you. Never to hurt you. But to give you back the power those men tried to steal. You deserve to feel strong again. You deserve to feel safe. You deserve to choose."

Slowly, Hope leaned into his chest, letting herself breathe, letting herself settle into the unspoken promise beneath his touch, a promise that he would guide her through this darkness, not drag her into it. A promise that she would not fight alone.

Hope hated these lessons, every single one. They dredged up memories she would rather bury and forced her to face fears she wished would disappear. But she also knew, deep down, that Reverend Shaw was right. Every new skill she learned gave her a little more control, a little more courage, and a little less terror. And that mattered.

When Reverend Shaw felt she was finally ready, he announced they were moving to *surprise attacks*, a phrase that made her stomach knot instantly. He had recruited Brother Jeremiah, Brother Jacob, and Sam to help, which meant she never knew who would jump out at her, or when. They promised not to hurt her, but the unpredictability alone was enough to spike her pulse. Even so, she learned. Slowly. Unevenly. But she learned.

One evening, she walked beside Esther along the lake, enjoying the calm water and the cooling breeze, when Reverend Shaw stepped out from behind a tree and seized her in a full hold, while Brother Jacob lunged for Esther, pressing a wooden knife to her throat. Esther had been warned. Hope had not.

The moment his arms wrapped around her, Hope reacted with instinct. She slammed her head back into Reverend Shaw's chest. The impact made him grunt and loosen his grip. She twisted free, grabbed his gun from the holster, and pointed it at his chest, steady hands, steady aim.

"That was good," Reverend Shaw said, breathless but clearly impressed. "Now your friend is still in danger. The attacker threatens to kill her if you don't put the weapon down. What do you do?"

Hope didn't look away from Esther. "I would lower the gun slowly, without losing sight of either of them."

"That is correct."

But the moment the gun touched the ground, Reverend Shaw grabbed her again, his arms locking around her like steel.

"What now?" His voice whispered close to her ear. Too close. Distracting. Infuriating. Hope swallowed and forced herself to think.

"If Esther doesn't know how to free herself, I would mouth to her what I did earlier. My priority is to get her loose." She and Esther locked eyes. Hope exaggerated the movement with her shoulders and head. Esther understood immediately. She jerked her head back. Brother Jacob released her with a dramatic groan.

"Shove him and run!" Hope shouted. Esther gave her father a surprisingly fierce push and darted away. Brother Jacob stumbled over a rock and nearly toppled backward, but Esther was already sprinting toward the trail.

"Well done," Reverend Shaw said. "Now you've got one problem, you're trapped again. Esther will get help, but you're on your own."

"I know he doesn't have a weapon anymore."

"Correct. But he could shove you toward his gun to reclaim it. How do you stop him?"

"I'd kick it away as soon as it's close, probably into the lake."

"Good."

"I can't use my head again. He'll expect it this time. But I could pinch his leg, hard."

"Pretend."

She reached down to pinch, and suddenly Reverend Shaw tightened his grip, yanked her backward, and flipped her to the ground. Her back hit the earth. His hands pinned hers above her head again. Hope gasped. He grinned, infuriatingly smug.

"Good thought. But it could land you right here."

Hope glared. She bucked her hips with full force. He pitched forward, momentarily off-balance. She tore her hands free, scrambled to the side, and felt around desperately until her fingers closed around a rock. She pretended to swing it. Reverend Shaw flopped sideways in mock collapse. Hope rolled, sprang to her feet, and bolted away.

"Well done, Hope!" he called. She flashed him a triumphant smile over her shoulder. "Now come back, we still have another scenario."

"Why would I?" she called. "I freed myself fair and square."

"Hope..." He raised an eyebrow that clearly meant *don't test me.* "You know I'll catch you."

She shook her head with a mischievous grin. "Let's call it a day."

His growl made her eyes widen. "Hope."

But she didn't budge. When he stepped toward her, she turned and sprinted away. She had a solid head start, but not enough. Reverend Shaw caught up quickly, wrapped an arm around her waist, and tackled her gently but firmly to the ground.

"See?" he said triumphantly. She rolled her eyes. "Now," he continued, "say you thought the attacker lost consciousness, but he grabs you when you're escaping. The wound on his head is bleeding."

Hope scanned her surroundings, breathing quickly. She spotted the lake just feet away.

"I'd do what I did before, but instead of reaching for a rock, I'd throw sand or dirt in his face. Then put all my weight into his elbow and try to shove him off."

"Alright." He hauled her up. She braced herself. The moment he grabbed her again, she threw her head back. When he staggered, she shoved him hard, harder than she expected, and he toppled straight into the lake. Unfortunately, he grabbed her wrist out of pure instinct, and she went down with him. Cold water swallowed them both. They surfaced coughing and sputtering. Reverend Shaw grinned when he saw her shock.

"You didn't expect that, did you? Nice try, Hope."

She shoved her soaked hair out of her face.

"If you want to use the water to escape an attacker," he continued, "you must be sure he can't pull you in. Otherwise, you'll drown."

Hope swallowed hard. That was exactly what Jared had tried to do. Panic threatened, but she forced it down. She would not let him take her strength again. Reverend Shaw climbed out first and pulled her up after him. Esther arrived at a run and immediately wrapped a blanket around Hope's shoulders.

"Thank you," Hope murmured.

"That was sneaky," Esther said, beaming. "But Reverend Shaw saw it coming."

Hope shot him a suspicious glance.

"How do you know so much about defending yourself?"

Reverend Shaw shrugged, droplets rolling off his sleeves.

"I've had some training with the U.S. Marshals."

# 14

# Too Close in the Hayloft

"Esther, Hope, can you bring lunch to the men in the fields?" Abigail handed each girl a basket filled with sandwiches, fruit, and a few jars of lemonade.

Hope and Esther stepped outside, chatting softly as they made their way along the dusty path toward the fields. They hadn't gone more than a hundred yards when the bushes ahead rustled violently. Two horses burst out onto the road, hooves skidding in the dirt. Hope gasped, stumbling back.

"Eric? Sheriff Craig? What in the world are you doing here?" Her voice trembled, and the color drained from her face. Eric smirked down at her from the saddle.

"What do you think, Hope? Before he was arrested, Jared told us exactly where you were hiding. So naturally, we came to retrieve you." His eyes gleamed with triumph. "You're going back to San Francisco."

"No." Hope took a step back, but Eric and Sheriff Craig were already dismounting. Both men lunged, grabbing her arms and trying to haul her toward Eric's horse.

"Let her go!" Esther cried. Then she spun around and bolted toward the fields as fast as she could run.

Hope twisted violently, managing to wrench one arm free. She broke into a sprint, but the men were stronger and faster. Eric caught her around the waist, lifting her clean off the ground. Before Sheriff Craig could grab her legs, Hope slammed her head backward, hard. It connected squarely with Eric's nose. He howled, stumbling away as blood poured down his face.

"You little—!"

Sheriff Craig grabbed her and dragged her closer, but Eric, still clutching his bleeding nose, closed in again.

"If you think you can run anywhere," Eric growled, "you're dreaming. We made sure the stagecoach won't be arriving in two days."

Hope froze, breath catching. "What did you do?"

Eric's grin was wicked. "Let's just say an explosion near the stagecoach sent it rolling into a canyon."

Her soul sank. "You killed the driver?"

"The driver jumped off. Should still be alive somewhere."

"Should be?" Hope shouted, horrified. "You didn't even check on him?"

"We didn't have time," Eric said dismissively. "Our priority was getting to you." He stepped closer, fingers digging painfully into her arm. "Now quit fighting. Let's get this over with."

"Let go of the girl." The deep command echoed across the meadow and path. Hope, Eric, and the sheriff turned to see several settlers emerging from the trees, Brother Jacob, Brother

Jeremiah, Sam, and others, each one armed. Behind them, a small unit of soldiers appeared as well. A young Army captain and a second sheriff stepped forward with purpose.

"Thank you for your confession," the unfamiliar sheriff said coldly, eyes fixed on Eric and Craig.

Eric gaped. "What are you doing out here? This is the middle of nowhere. Since when do settlements have sheriffs?"

"The stagecoach never reaching its destination raised alarm," the sheriff replied. "We found the injured driver, who told us which direction you fled." His expression hardened. "Next time, choose a route where you don't leave clear hoof prints behind."

Eric scoffed, blood still dripping onto the ground, but the sheriff seized his arm and snapped handcuffs around his wrists. Sheriff Craig received the same treatment.

"You are hereby arrested," the sheriff announced, "for the destruction of a public road and stagecoach, attempted murder of the driver, and the attempted kidnapping of this young lady."

Hope stood trembling, breath coming in shaky bursts, but she was safe. And this time, the men who hunted her were not riding away free.

Hope was unusually quiet that evening. She drifted into the sitting room without a word, wrapped in a dazed stillness that made everyone uneasy. Reverend Shaw exchanged a glance with Abigail and Brother Jacob before the three of them followed her. Hope stood near the window, arms wrapped tightly around herself, as if holding in the last remnants of her composure.

"How are we supposed to leave now?" she finally asked, her voice thin and strained. "We can't wait another month for the next stagecoach. That's too long. Whitmer could find me before then."

She turned to Reverend Shaw, fear glimmering in her eyes. He lifted one shoulder in a weary shrug, clearly hating that he had no simple answer for her. Brother Jacob cleared his throat.

"Brother Jeremiah and I have to take some of our harvest to Logan this weekend. Reverend Shaw can come with us. He can buy, or rent, a pair of horses there."

Hope straightened at once. "I should go with you too."

Brother Jacob shook his head immediately.

"That wouldn't be wise. If your father has truly put out a reward for your return, bounty hunters will be watching the more populated towns first. Logan is larger. It's safer for you to stay here until Reverend Shaw comes back."

Hope's jaw tightened, frustration rising beneath her fear.

"But I can't travel as myself anymore. I'll be recognized the moment someone looks at me. That's why I brought those clothes from my half-brothers."

Abigail blinked, stunned. "You want to travel... looking like a boy?"

Hope nodded, steady and resolute.

"I must. My face is too well known now. If Whitmer, or any bounty hunter, has my description, it won't take long for them to find me."

Reverend Shaw watched her carefully, seeing both her determination and the tremor beneath it. Brother Jacob rubbed his chin thoughtfully.

"She's right," he said at last. "If she's going to continue this journey, hiding in plain sight may be her safest option." He looked around at the others. "I don't believe anyone else knows she's here. Sheriff Craig and that fiancé of yours," he practically spat the word, "clearly kept that information to themselves because they wanted the reward. But we cannot assume that secrecy will last."

Hope exhaled shakily, her shoulders sagging. For the first time since the ambush, she looked as though the weight of everything might finally crush her.

"But she can't afford to risk being recognized," Brother Jacob finished quietly. "Not anymore."

Saying goodbye to the little settlement several days later was far harder than Hope had anticipated. The community had taken her in as though she had always belonged there, and leaving felt like tearing herself away from a warm, protective cocoon she had desperately needed. She hugged Abigail, Esther, Elizabeth, and the others one by one, promising, more than once, that she would keep in touch and write whenever she could.

Some of the settlers lifted their brows and exchanged curious smiles when they noticed her new attire. The oversized trousers, buttoned shirt, vest, and worn hat made her look more like a young cowboy than the refined young woman they had welcomed into their homes. But Brother Jacob had explained everything, and instead of judgment, the community offered nods of understanding and murmurs of encouragement.

The hardest farewell of all came from little Sonny. When the moment finally arrived, he clung to her leg, his small face scrunched and wet with tears.

"Don't go, Hope! Please don't go," he sobbed, his tiny arms refusing to let go.

Hope knelt and pulled him into the tightest embrace she could manage. The lump in her throat made it nearly impossible to breathe.

"I'll come visit someday," she whispered into his hair, stroking his back soothingly. "I promise. And I will never forget you."

"You better come back," he sniffled, wiping his cheeks with his sleeve. "Or I'll come find you."

Hope laughed softly despite the ache in her chest and kissed the top of his head.

"I'll make sure to stay put long enough for you to catch up."

With great reluctance, Sonny finally let her go. Esther brushed at her own tears and hugged Hope fiercely before she climbed onto the wagon beside Reverend Shaw and Brother Jeremiah.

It was far from a comfortable ride. With the wagon stacked high with crates of vegetables bound for market, Hope had to wedge herself between sacks of potatoes and a barrel of apples. Every jolt of the wheels sent her bumping into something, but she didn't complain. She was too grateful, grateful they had a way to leave, grateful she wasn't traveling alone, grateful she was moving forward again instead of hiding.

Still... beneath that gratitude simmered a sharp thread of worry. What if they were too late? What if Whitmer had already moved on, or worse, already harmed the woman mentioned in the letter? Hope adjusted the brim of her hat and glanced toward Reverend Shaw, who rode horseback beside the wagon. He caught her eyes briefly and offered a small, reassuring smile. It helped, just a little. But as the settlement disappeared behind her, Hope couldn't shake the hollow ache in her chest, or the quiet urgency pushing her onward.

After traveling through several towns and tiny settlements over the course of a few days, they finally reached Cheyenne. Hope stared at the bustling streets in surprise. It wasn't a city like San Francisco, but it was far larger than anything she had seen since leaving home, busier, louder, alive with people traveling on foot, horseback, and wagon. Train whistles sounded faintly from the station, and the distant clang of metal on metal hinted at the constant flow of arriving passengers. Cheyenne felt alive, and dangerous.

They rode into the center of town, passing a saloon that spilled laughter, piano music, and loud conversation into the street. A respectable-looking hotel stood across the way, though it was clearly crowded. Hope stepped toward it instinctively, eager to finally rest somewhere clean and warm. Before she could push the door open, Reverend Shaw caught her arm and tugged her gently but firmly back.

Hope blinked at him, confused. "What is it?"

His gaze swept the street, every face, every doorway, every pair of eyes that lingered too long. Then he stepped a little closer, lowering his voice.

"We need to be careful here," he murmured. "Cheyenne sees more travelers than anywhere we've passed through. Cowboys, railroad workers, bounty hunters... people you do not want to recognize you."

Hope swallowed hard. The reminder sent a fresh wave of unease through her.

"Do me a favor," he continued. "Go to the General Store. Stay inside until I come get you."

She frowned. "Why? Why can't we just stay at the hotel?"

He exhaled slowly, giving her a look that was half caution, half something else entirely. His voice dipped lower.

"Because you look very young for a boy. Anyone who takes even a moment to truly look at you will know you're not one."

Hope gasped softly, her cheeks flushing with heat. She tugged at the brim of her hat, suddenly acutely aware of how close he was standing. He noticed, of course he noticed. And to her absolute mortification, his lips twitched as though he were fighting a grin.

"And," he added, deliberately avoiding her eyes for a beat, "I doubt you would want to share a room with me."

Her breath caught. Her heart lurched violently, and she turned her face away so he wouldn't see the crimson spreading across her cheeks. The thought of sharing a room, of being that close to him, sent a confusing, dangerous shiver through her.

"I—I didn't think of that," she managed to whisper.

"No," he said softly, his voice warm now, "I figured you didn't."

Heat swept over her again. He looked away, the corner of his mouth lifting just enough for her to know he was definitely hiding a grin this time.

"Farmers and ranchers have more room," he continued more calmly. "And they won't ask questions if I tell them you're my younger brother. It's safer."

Hope nodded slowly. She didn't like being separated from him, not when every place felt more frightening than the last, but she trusted him more than she trusted her own instincts.

"All right," she murmured. "I'll stay in the General Store."

He stepped closer again, lowering his voice. His eyes dipped briefly to her lips before returning to her gaze.

"And, Hope?"

Her breath stilled.

"Don't wander. Not even a step outside. Understand?"

Her heart fluttered uncontrollably. She nodded, unable to find her voice.

"Good." He brushed a gloved hand over her shoulder, barely a touch, but enough to make her knees feel weak, before turning toward the street. "Stay put," he called over his shoulder. "I'll come back for you."

Hope exhaled shakily as she watched him walk away, her pulse racing faster than it had when she'd outrun wolves. And she wasn't entirely sure which danger was worse.

Hope watched Reverend Shaw ride off until he disappeared between two passing wagons. Her stomach twisted with nerves. She already missed the safety of having him nearby. Still, she forced herself to breathe and made her way toward the general store. Tugging her hat lower to hide most of her face, she slipped inside.

A small bell jingled above the door. The store smelled of spices, leather, and oiled wood. Hope drifted toward the back, away from prying eyes, pretending to study shelves of canned goods, flour sacks, tin lanterns, bolts of fabric, and lead-weighted scales. She traced her finger over a price tag, trying to steady her racing pulse.

"Do you need help with anything?"

Hope nearly leapt out of her skin. She whipped around to find a tall, broad-shouldered man watching her. His expression was friendly, but his eyes were sharp, too observant for her comfort.

She shook her head quickly.

"You're new here, aren't you?" he asked, tilting his head. Hope felt several other customers glance in her direction. Her throat tightened. When she nodded, the man extended a hand. "Welcome to Cheyenne. Name's Jonah Miller."

Hope forced herself to meet his gaze and accepted his handshake, deepening her voice as much as she dared. "Hunter Gabriel, sir."

"Well, good to meet you, Hunter." He smiled broadly. "You travel far?"

Hope nodded again.

"Mind if I ask where from?"

"Sacramento," she answered, praying her voice didn't break.

"Long trip." His brows lifted. "You traveling alone?"

Hope shook her head quickly. "No. My older brother is with me."

Mr. Miller nodded thoughtfully. "You boys aim to settle here?"

Hope shrugged, wishing desperately that he would stop. She could feel other eyes lingering, listening. Before he could ask more, a warm female voice called from behind him.

"Jonah, leave the boy alone." An older woman bustled over, nudging the general store owner back toward the front with practiced ease. "You don't have to interrogate every new face that walks through this door," she scolded lightly.

"I was being friendly," he grumbled.

"I know," she said, patting his arm, "but you overwhelm folks."

Hope nearly smiled behind her collar. She let out a shaky breath, relieved, if only for a moment.

She was about to slip away to find a quiet corner to wait when a young woman approached her. She looked close to Hope's own age, with bright green eyes, long auburn hair braided neatly down her back, and a sweet, curious smile.

"Welcome," the girl said warmly. "Sorry about Grandpa. He means well, just forgets that sometimes."

Hope blinked. "He's your grandfather?"

Lilly nodded proudly. "Oh yes. Jonah Miller is known for running this store and interrogating half the town. I'm Lilly."

Hope relaxed enough to smile genuinely.

"Pleased to meet you, Lilly."

Before the girl could say anything more, Hope's breath caught. Her entire body went rigid.

Someone familiar had walked past her. Several inches taller than she was. Dark coat. Purposeful stride. Anthony Whitmer. Hope's blood ran cold. He didn't look at her. Didn't notice her. But he was heading straight for the door.

"Excuse me," Hope blurted, stepping past Lilly. But Lilly caught her hand.

"Will you be back?" she asked softly, almost hopeful. "I—I'd like to talk more."

Hope forced a reassuring nod. "I'll be in town for a little while." She tugged her hat lower, slipped from Lilly's grasp, and hurried toward the door, her heart slamming against her ribs. She had finally found Whitmer. And now all she could think was—Where was Reverend Shaw? And what would happen if Whitmer saw her without him?

Outside, Hope paused on the boardwalk and scanned the bustling street. Wagons rattled past, horses snorted, and townsfolk hurried about their business, but she finally spotted Whitmer's unmistakable figure weaving through the crowd with determined purpose. Her pulse spiked.

She hurried after him, careful to keep her hat low and her steps quiet. Whitmer strode straight toward the saloon, pushed through the swinging doors, and climbed the stairs to the upper floor where the guest rooms were.

Hope slipped inside just far enough to watch without being seen. Men at poker tables barely glanced up, laughter and shouting drowning out her pounding heartbeat. Whitmer stopped at room fifteen. She repeated the number silently, once, twice, committing it to memory. Before anyone noticed her lingering, she turned on her heel and slipped back outside. The moment she stepped onto the boardwalk, she froze.

Reverend Shaw was striding down the street from the direction of the general store, and the intensity in his eyes sharpened the instant he spotted her. He quickened his pace. Hope tried to put distance between herself and the saloon, but he reached her in only a few long strides, grasped her arm firmly, and pulled her into the narrow space between two buildings.

"What," he said through gritted teeth, "were you doing in the saloon?" His voice wasn't loud, but it was sharp enough to make her wince. Fury and fear warred openly in his expression. "I told you to wait at the general store."

Hope nearly rolled her eyes. "I did. But then I saw Whitmer walk out. So, I followed him. I needed to know where his room was." Irritation slipped into her voice before she could stop it.

"You followed him?" His voice rose, too loud. Several people on the street turned to stare. "Have you lost your mind?"

Heat rushed to Hope's face. She dropped her gaze, mortified by the curious looks drifting their way.

"Do you have to make such a big deal about this?" she muttered. "You're causing a scene."

"You are in big trouble now, young man," he continued at full volume, still playing the part, but utterly ignoring her discomfort.

That did it. Hope jerked her arm free and marched toward her horse, fury bubbling over. She reached for the saddle horn, but Reverend Shaw caught up in three long strides and seized her arm again. She shook him off violently.

"Leave me alone," she snapped, her voice sharp enough to cut. "Why would you humiliate me like that?"

"Why would you leave the general store after I specifically told you not to?" His tone was a blend of frustration, fear, and something else she couldn't quite name.

"I already explained why," she bit out.

"Hope." His voice deepened, firm, unyielding. His brown eyes locked onto hers with an intensity that made her heart stumble. "Whitmer is a killer on the run. He is dangerous. He will not hesitate to kill you."

"I was careful," she insisted, though her voice trembled despite her resolve. "He didn't see me. I only wanted to know where he was staying."

Reverend Shaw exhaled slowly through his teeth, controlled frustration radiating off him. For a moment, he looked as though he wanted to shake sense into her or pull her into his arms. She couldn't tell which. Finally, he forced himself to relent.

"Let's go," he said, his voice low but still tight. "I found us a place for the night."

Hope looked away, her throat tight, her heart pounding with leftover fear, anger... and something warm and disorienting she refused to name. She mounted her horse in stubborn silence, fully aware that Reverend Shaw was watching her with a storm of emotions he wasn't voicing. And for the first time, Hope wasn't entirely sure whether she wanted the distance she'd demanded, or whether she wished he'd pull her back.

"The hayloft is up there," the rancher's wife said, nodding toward the wooden ladder. "You sure you and your brother will be all right?"

Reverend Shaw offered her a polite smile. "We'll be fine. Thank you kindly."

With a satisfied nod, she turned and left the barn, the heavy door closing behind her. Hope climbed the ladder first, her boots thunking softly against the rungs. When she reached the top, she took one look around, and gasped. A moment later, she spun on him, her glare sharp enough to cut.

"And where," she asked icily, "are we supposed to sleep?"

He pointed toward a large pile of fresh hay where someone had laid out two thick wool blankets and a pair of pillows.

"Right there," he said simply. Her eyes narrowed, bright with outrage.

"You told me we couldn't stay at the hotel because they would make us share a room. How," she demanded, gesturing wildly at the hayloft, "is this any different?"

"They think we're brothers," he replied, entirely too calm for her liking. "And this is a barn, Hope. Anyone could walk in at any time. Nothing inappropriate will happen here."

Hope let out a hard, disbelieving scoff.

"I'm not sleeping here. I'm going back into town to rent a proper room." She whirled around, but Reverend Shaw reached out and caught her hand just as her foot slipped on the loose hay. She lost her balance, and he instinctively tried to steady her. Instead, they toppled backward together into the hay pile with a muffled thump, sending dust motes floating up around them like flecks of gold.

When she looked up, he was braced above her, his face only inches from hers. Her heartbeat thundered in her chest. She broke eye contact at once, pushing at his shoulder until he moved.

"There is no room at the hotel," he said, dusting off his shirt. "I checked. They're preparing for some kind of celebration, and every bed is taken."

She shook her head in disbelief. "I don't know what to think anymore. You—your behavior—it puzzles me exceedingly."

A corner of his mouth twitched, but he suppressed the smile.

"There's a washroom beside the ranch house door," he said gently. "They've already warmed water for a bath. Go first. Take your time. I'll go after you. That way we both have privacy."

Hope fixed him with a long, measuring stare, searching his expression for some hidden meaning. Finding none, only steady patience, she huffed softly, grabbed her bundle of clothes, and climbed down the ladder.

The washroom was nicer than she had expected. The tub was deep and already filled with steaming water scented faintly with lavender. For the first time in days, she felt truly warm. As she soaked, the tension slowly unwound from her shoulders, and she allowed herself a quiet moment of peace.

Once she was dressed again, she hurried back to the barn, not wanting him to think she had run off. Reverend Shaw left for the washroom without a word, and Hope set about preparing her sleeping space. She smoothed the blanket, arranged the pillow, and tried, unsuccessfully, not to feel self-conscious about sharing a loft with him.

This was ridiculous. Completely improper. Entirely nerve-wracking. She was certain she would lie awake all night. But the hay was soft and warm beneath her, the blanket surprisingly comfortable. And as soon as her head touched the pillow, exhaustion claimed her. Despite her worries, she drifted into a deep, dream-heavy sleep.

Hope woke before dawn. The barn was still dark, the faintest gray light, only beginning to creep through the cracks in the wood. For a moment, she didn't understand why she had woken so suddenly, until an unfamiliar warmth brushed against her side. She blinked, confusion turning quickly to alarm when she realized just how close Reverend Shaw was.

They hadn't fallen asleep touching... but now there were only inches between them. Her breath caught. She lay stiff as a board, barely daring to inhale, her mind racing. How had this happened?

Very carefully, Hope shifted, just enough to put a sliver of space between them. But the movement roused him. Not fully... just enough for him to turn toward her in his sleep. His arm slid over her waist as naturally as though he had done so a thousand times, gathering her against the solid warmth of his chest. Hope nearly passed out on the spot.

Her heart launched into a frantic rhythm. Her cheeks burned. Every inch of her body went rigid. He was deeply asleep, she could tell from the slow, even rise and fall of his breathing, but that did nothing to ease her predicament.

*What am I supposed to do now?* If she moved too quickly, he might wake and think she had crept closer to him. The mere thought twisted her stomach in mortification. So, she stayed perfectly still, barely breathing, praying he would shift again. Minutes dragged by in agonizing slowness.

Finally, he rolled away, his arm sliding off her and returning to his own blanket. Hope exhaled shakily. Quiet as a mouse, she scooted as far to the opposite side of the hay as the loft would allow, placing a very deliberate gap between them.

Her heart still fluttered wildly, but exhaustion eventually reclaimed her. Wrapped tightly in her blanket and facing away from him, Hope closed her eyes and drifted back into an uneasy sleep, hoping fervently he would never discover how close they had been.

# 15

# Protection Built on Secrets

Reverend Shaw stirred at the sound of footsteps brushing across the barn floor. He opened his eyes, blinking away the last threads of sleep, and shifted just enough to see who had entered. A moment later, a young woman's face appeared at the top of the ladder, peeking over the edge of the hayloft. Her gaze landed on Hope, still curled in her blanket, and her entire expression brightened with curiosity and delight, as if she had stumbled upon a charming secret.

Reverend Shaw's brows lifted sharply. Before the girl could speak, or wake Hope, he fixed her with a firm look and motioned her back down the ladder. The girl's smile faltered, but she obeyed, disappearing as quietly as she had come. Reverend Shaw rose at once, shaking off the last remnants of sleep, and followed her down into the barn.

The soft creak of the ladder rungs pulled Hope fully from slumber. Her eyes fluttered open just as Reverend Shaw disappeared below, his boots sounding briefly against the wood before fading. For a moment, she lay still, disoriented, wrapped in the lingering warmth of sleep. She considered rolling onto her side and drifting back under, pretending she hadn't noticed his sudden departure at all.

But then she heard voices. Low. Urgent. Carefully hushed. Hope's drowsiness vanished at once. Her heart began to tick faster, a quiet, insistent rhythm in her chest. Slowly, she pushed herself upright, careful not to disturb the hay beneath her or let the blanket slip. She held perfectly still, scarcely daring to breathe, as the conversation drifted upward through the loft.

The words were indistinct at first, blurred by distance and the wooden walls, but the tension threaded through them was unmistakable. This was not idle morning chatter. Whatever was being said carried weight, concern, perhaps urgency, and the deliberate quiet told her one thing very clearly. It wasn't meant for her ears.

That realization alone sent a prickle of unease down her spine. Hope wrapped her arms around herself, listening harder, every sense alert, her curiosity sharpening into something closer to apprehension. Whatever awaited below, whatever had drawn him away so abruptly, she knew it would change the calm of the morning. Sleep, once so heavy and welcome, was gone entirely.

 

"Claire, why were you up there?" Reverend Shaw's voice carried a sharp edge of reprimand.

"I just wanted to see what she looked like." The girl sounded utterly unbothered. "She is gorgeous, Uncle Logan."

*Uncle... Logan?* Hope's breath hitched. Her heart picked up speed so suddenly she could hear the rush of blood in her ears. Logan? His name was William. Reverend William Shaw. So, who in the world was Logan?

"You need to leave," he murmured sternly. "Hope should not see you here."

Claire huffed lightly. "Grandma sent me to warn you. Harriet Silvers just arrived, and she is very eager to see you."

A heavy sigh followed, then a soft, unmistakably irritated groan. Hope could picture his expression without even peeking over the edge, the raised brow, the jaw set tight enough to crack stone. Whoever Harriet Silvers was, she was clearly unwelcome news.

Bootsteps shifted in the straw below. He was about to step out through the barn doors when they swung open again.

Hope flinched and went utterly still, her pulse thudding painfully against her ribs. Another voice, feminine, floated upward through the quiet barn. She strained to listen, every nerve pulled taut, breath shallow as she fought the urge to move. Curiosity clawed at her, nearly driving her to lean over the edge of the hayloft, but she stopped herself just in time. Even the smallest shift would stir the hay. Even the faintest sound might betray her wakefulness.

And if they realized she was listening, she knew she would never get answers. Her mind raced as she lay frozen, questions tumbling over one another in relentless succession. Why did he have another name? Who was this woman who was so *eager* to see him? And why did it suddenly feel as though Reverend William Shaw, the man she had come to trust, the man who had protected her, challenged her, steadied her, was hiding an entire life from her?

The thought sent a cold ripple through her chest. Whatever was unfolding below, whatever truth hovered just out of reach, Hope sensed it would change far more than she was ready to face.

"Does she know why you brought her here? Have you told her anything?"

Hope finally recognized the voice. It belonged to the woman from the night before. The words drifted up into the hayloft, quiet but urgent, threaded with worry. Hope went completely still. Her breath caught halfway in her chest. Footsteps shifted below. She heard him, *Logan*, not Reverend Shaw, release a slow, controlled breath.

"She doesn't know anything, Ma," he replied. His voice was low, firm... guarded in a way she had never heard before. "Let's talk outside."

Something scraped softly against straw, as if he were guiding them toward the door. Hope strained to hear every sound, every movement. Then came the faint creak of the barn hinges, followed by the muted hush of morning air as they stepped outside.

Hope didn't hesitate. Her heart hammering violently, she scrambled to her feet and crossed the hayloft in two quick, silent strides. She shoved open the small window tucked beneath the rafters, wincing at the faintest whisper of wood against wood.

Cool dawn air rushed in, carrying with it the low, indistinct murmur of voices just beyond the barn.

She leaned closer, careful not to disturb the hay beneath her boots, pulse roaring in her ears.

*Ma.* The word echoed in her thoughts, unsettling and sharp. Whatever they were hiding, whatever truth he hadn't told her, whatever reason he had brought her here instead of anywhere else, Hope knew one thing with chilling certainty. She was about to learn that Reverend William Shaw was not the man she thought she knew.

"You did not tell her?" Logan's mother sounded anxious, almost accusing. He shook his head, opening his mouth to answer, but a shrill, delighted squeal cut through the morning air. All three of them turned just as a young woman in a bright dress sprinted across the ranch yard.

"Logan!"

Before he could react, she launched herself into his arms and smashed her lips against his, in a dramatic, breathless kiss. Claire, standing nearby, made a gagging noise so loud that even the chickens looked offended. She spun on her heel and fled back into the house.

Logan immediately pulled the young woman, Harriet, off him, holding her firmly at arm's length. A frown pulled at her painted mouth as she tucked a curl of fiery red hair behind her ear.

"What are you doing here, Harriet?" Logan asked, his voice clipped.

"I heard you were back in town," she said, her lower lip trembling, "and that you'd finished your mission. I couldn't wait to see you."

"I am not finished with my mission," he corrected sharply. "And you need to leave. Now."

"But I missed you," she whispered, forcing tears into her green eyes.

Logan exhaled through his nose, a long, exhausted sigh.

"Harriet, we've been through this. I am not interested. You need to move on. I am not going to marry you."

Her eyes flashed with instant fury.

"You won't make a better match than me," she snapped loudly enough that several ranch hands slowed to stare. Logan's mother stiffened beside him, offering a tight, uncomfortable smile to the men passing by.

"Harriet, dear," she said gently but firmly, "it's best if you leave now."

But Harriet shook her head, red curls flying, her lips pressed into a thin, furious line. Claire reappeared in the doorway, creeping closer. Logan didn't like the look in her eyes, worried, guilty.

"You know there isn't a prettier girl in town than me," Harriet shrieked suddenly, pitching her voice high and dramatic. "I already told my parents we would marry!"

Claire muttered under her breath without thinking, "Prettiest girl in town? ... Maybe the most arrogant." She rolled her eyes. "And even if it were true, it wouldn't be anymore. Uncle Logan brought Hope here. She's gorgeous."

Logan and his mother both gasped and whipped their heads toward Claire in unison. Claire slapped her hand over her mouth, too late.

"I am so, so sorry."

Logan gave a faint shake of his head. He knew she hadn't meant harm. But the damage was done. Harriet spun like a wildcat scenting blood.

"He brought a girl here?" she screeched. "Where is she?!"

Claire flinched beneath the fury directed at her. Logan stepped forward at once.

"The girl is none of your concern," he said sharply. "Stop your tantrum. Keeping her safe is part of my mission."

"Tell me where she is!" Harriet shrilled, even louder now, drawing more unwanted attention. "You are no sheriff or U.S. Marshal, Logan Shaw! Who are you to protect anyone?!"

His mother's patience snapped.

"Harriet," she said in a voice that could freeze boiling water, "that is enough. Leave this property at once. Your behavior is shameful, and no decent man would want to court a woman who behaves like this."

"Oh?" Harriet asked sweetly, venom dripping from every syllable as she turned to Logan's mother. "And who are you to lecture me on decency? Everyone knows how you trapped Mr. Shaw, had his eldest son out of wedlock before he married you."

The entire yard fell silent. Even the wind seemed to stop. Logan watched his mother's face drain of color, her hand trembling as Claire rushed to her side and wrapped her arms around her. Harriet's triumphant, vicious smirk widened, just as Logan grabbed her around the waist, flung her over his shoulder like a sack of potatoes, and carried her straight to the water trough.

"Logan—!" she shrieked. He didn't slow. He dropped her in. Harriet splashed, sputtered, and surfaced with her hair plastered to her face, gasping in outrage. Logan leaned over the rim, his voice cold steel.

"I recommend you keep your filthy mouth shut."

Harriet froze.

"You've crossed boundaries before, but what you just said was beyond unacceptable," he growled. "Your father spread those lies years ago because my mother refused to court him. She never behaved improperly, and she did not have relations before marriage."

Several ranch hands murmured in agreement, they remembered that old scandal.

"My father and grandparents warned your father that if he ever repeated those lies, he would be sued for slander." Logan leaned closer, eyes blazing. "The fact that he told you means he hasn't learned his lesson."

Harriet's lips quivered, but she said nothing now. No shrieks. No arrogance. Just trembling shock.

"You will leave this ranch immediately," Logan finished. "And if you dare to set foot on our land again, I will have you arrested for trespassing."

The ranch yard remained silent as Harriet scrambled out of the trough, drenched and humiliated. Logan stood tall, shoulders rigid, jaw tense, watching her flee without a backward glance.

Hope stood hidden behind the wall beside the small hayloft window, watching the scene unfold below with wide, troubled eyes. Harriet scrambled out of the trough, drenched and sputtering, her once-perfect curls plastered flat against her furious face. Without a backward glance, she tore across the yard, climbed into a small buggy, snapped the reins, and sped away from the ranch as if a swarm of hornets chased her.

Only when the wheels disappeared into the dust did Hope release the breath she had been holding. The anger and hurt twisting in her chest didn't ease, if anything, they tightened. Logan Shaw. Logan, not Reverend Shaw. And clearly a man with secrets. The kind that changed everything she thought she knew.

Yet even through the confusion and the sting of betrayal, her heart tugged in another direction.

Her gaze drifted to Logan's mother. The poor woman stood stiffly in the yard. Her dress soaked at the hem where Harriet's splashing had reached her. Claire was still wrapped around her grandmother's waist, shielding her as though protecting her from further blows. The older woman's hand trembled in Claire's, and she pressed a shaking palm to her forehead, blinking back tears she clearly did not want anyone to witness. Her face looked stricken, not merely embarrassed, but wounded in a place far deeper. Hope's anger wavered.

Despite feeling betrayed, despite the dread knotting her stomach at the thought of what else she might discover... she could not ignore the sight of that gentle, dignified woman being publicly humiliated for something she had never done. Her heart softened with empathy, cracking through the hurt like a fragile beam of light.

*No woman deserves that,* Hope thought, her throat tightening. *No mother deserves to have such cruel lies flung at her in front of her family.* A wave of protectiveness rose inside her, a feeling she knew all too well. It was the same instinct that had driven her to stand up to her father, the same instinct that had pushed her into this dangerous journey in the first place.

Even in her confusion and uncertainty, Hope found herself praying quietly that Logan's mother would not carry shame for something so false, praying she would feel surrounded by the love of the family who had rushed to her defense. And yet... Hope's heart clenched again. Because she knew that as soon as Logan returned inside, she would finally have to demand answers. And she wasn't sure she was ready to hear them.

~

But Logan didn't come back into the barn. Instead, he turned to his mother.

"Ma, I am so sorry." Logan raked a hand through his damp hair, his jaw clenching until the muscles jumped. "I can't believe that vile woman spoke to you that way." His fists balled at his sides, knuckles whitening, but his mother stepped forward and gathered him into her arms before his temper could flare any further.

"She has always been cruel, darling," she murmured against his shoulder. "Her tantrums are practically legendary. I'm not surprised she lashed out at me, only that she waited this long."

"I should have thrown her into the dunghill instead of the water trough," Logan growled as he pulled back, anger still simmering in his dark eyes. "It would have suited her better."

His mother gave him a faint, weary smile.

"She isn't worth the effort. Let's put her behind us." Then her expression sobered. "You still haven't told me about Hope. How much does she know?"

Logan let out a slow breath and scrubbed his hand over his face.

"Her mother told her she'd find answers in her diary. Hope found a letter and a train ticket the killer lost. When she pieced things together, she insisted on going after him. William tried to talk her out of it, but..." His voice softened briefly. "When Hope decides something, there's no stopping her. And since Whitmer was heading in the direction Georgiana meant Hope to go anyway, we... allowed it."

"Does she know who you really are?" his mother pressed. He shook his head immediately.

"No. William and I switched places in Elko. He returned to San Francisco, and I continued the journey in his place."

"And she never noticed?" His mother's brows lifted. "You and your older brother could pass for twins, but there *are* differences. The age gap alone—"

"I made sure she never saw them," he said quickly. "I dressed like him, styled my hair the same, even added gray streaks. I think she has so much on her mind that she didn't pay close attention to the details. She's confused by a few things, but she still believes I am her reverend."

His mother exhaled slowly. "And her relatives? Have you told her they live here?"

Again, Logan shook his head. "Not yet. She's still chasing her mother's murderer, and until he's caught, or dead, I can't risk exposing them. And with her father after her now... if he learned where her mother's kin live, he'd use it against her."

His mother nodded grimly. "Georgiana would never have wanted that. She only wanted Hope safe." Her voice wavered with old grief. "It's heartbreaking that they killed Georgiana just as she was preparing to flee. Wasn't her brother supposed to escort them here?"

"Marshal Stewart," Logan confirmed with a slow nod. "Yes. He was meant to fetch them. But he received Georgiana's letter about what she'd uncovered just before he left and sent for me instead." His jaw tightened. "Her death wasn't random, Ma. They must have learned she planned to escape."

"Has anyone uncovered the rest of their scheme?" she asked quietly.

"Not yet." Logan shook his head. "Georgiana discovered that her father was involved in planning the murder of a government official's wife in San Francisco. Marshal Stewart never reached her in time to warn her. The killer escaped as well." He exhaled sharply. "Hope's father had no idea his wife even knew about the plot until months later. Georgiana suspected their butler of spying, since she caught him in her room twice. She sent her maid with the final letter to William, but the girl couldn't escape until after Georgiana was shot. William never had a chance to save them."

His mother pressed a hand to her heart, eyes shining with unshed tears.

"Poor Georgiana," she whispered. "Poor Hope."

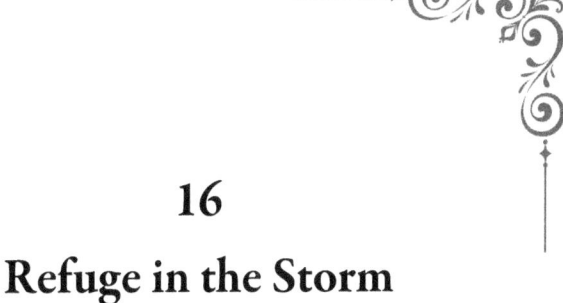

# 16

# Refuge in the Storm

Up in the hayloft, Hope slammed the window shut so hard the frame rattled. The sound echoed sharply in the still barn, but she barely noticed. Her breath hitched, coming too fast, too shallow. Her vision swam, the edges darkening as the world tilted beneath her feet. For several long seconds, she stood frozen, gripping the sill with white-knuckled hands, fighting the urge to collapse.

*They lied to me. All of them. Every single one.* Her entire body trembled as anger, betrayal, and grief collided inside her chest, twisting together into a violent storm she could barely contain. Logan Shaw. Not Reverend Shaw. Not the man she thought she knew. Not the man she had trusted with her safety, her fears, her heart. Every memory replayed itself now, warped and sharp, each kindness laced with deception.

Without giving herself time to think, or to talk herself out of it, Hope spun away from the window. She grabbed her satchel and began shoving her belongings inside with shaking hands, fabric snagging, buttons clattering, her movements frantic and unrestrained. She didn't care how much noise she made. She didn't care if they heard her. Let them hear. She needed out. She needed answers. And she needed to confront Logan, now, before the words burned their way out of her chest or shattered into silence she might never recover from.

With her bag slung over her shoulder and her heart pounding hard enough to hurt, Hope turned toward the ladder, fury propelling her forward. Whatever he thought he was protecting her from... he had just made himself the one thing she could no longer ignore.

They both flinched when the window above them slammed shut. The sound cracked through the early morning stillness like a gunshot. Logan and his mother exchanged a look, dread darkening his features, quiet resignation settling over hers.

"This isn't good," Logan muttered, rubbing the back of his neck. "I should never have talked to you out here. She heard us. She's going to explode."

His mother laid a gentle hand on his arm.

"Go talk to her, son. Try to make her understand."

Logan exhaled a long, heavy breath.

"Making her listen will be the real challenge. Getting her to understand? Even harder." He shook his head. "If everything you ever told me about Georgiana is true, then Hope has her mother's spine... and her temper." A tired, humorless smile tugged at his mouth. "She's already gotten furious with me more than once for 'overstepping boundaries'—things she thought William did, of course." He pinched the bridge of his nose. "This... this is going to get ugly."

His mother nodded, sympathy softening her gaze.

"She has every right to be upset. But she also needs the truth."

"I know," he said quietly. "And I'll give it to her." His voice dropped lower. "I'm just grateful we're finally where she was meant to end up. If she runs again..." He swallowed, a muscle ticking in his jaw. "I can't lose her. Not now. Not with Whitmer here in Cheyenne."

His mother's brows lifted sharply. "He's here?"

Logan nodded grimly. "She saw him. Followed him before I even realized he was in town." He dragged a hand through his hair, frustration and fear tangling together. "If she bolts before I explain everything, she'll walk straight into danger." His gaze shifted toward the barn, urgency tightening his chest. "I need to reach her, before she decides to do something reckless."

Hope had barely set foot on the ground before Logan stepped back into the barn. She stiffened the instant she saw him, her jaw locking, her eyes turning to ice. Without a word, she brushed past him as though he was nothing more than a shadow in her way.

"Hope, wait. We need to talk."

He reached after her, but she didn't slow, didn't even acknowledge his voice. She moved with fierce purpose until she reached her horse. The moment she swung a leg into the saddle, he caught her arm. That was a mistake.

"Don't touch me." Her voice cracked like a whip. She turned on him, eyes blazing with a mix of hurt and fury so sharp, it nearly winded him. "You are a liar," she spat. "Nothing, absolutely nothing, that came out of your mouth was the truth. And clearly your older brother was part of it." A cold, brittle laugh escaped her. "No wonder you crossed so many boundaries. This was all some kind of game to you, wasn't it?"

"Hope—"

She cut him off with a slicing wave of her hand.

"I don't want to hear any more lies, *Reverend Shaw*." Her voice carried across the yard, drawing the attention of several nearby cowhands. "Oh, wait," she sneered. "You're not a reverend at all, are you? You're Logan."

He opened his mouth, but she wasn't finished, not even close.

"Ever since you kissed me in Elko, I've been so confused I could hardly breathe," she cried. "I kept telling myself it wasn't real, that the man I looked up to as a fatherly friend would never... *could* never... do something like that." Her voice shook. "It felt wrong. And then you showed up in Halleck, looking younger, acting different, and everything inside my mind shattered." She began pacing, hands trembling as anger, betrayal, and heartbreak poured out unchecked.

"I questioned myself endlessly," she said, her voice rising. "Wondering if it was sinful, or disgusting, to feel drawn to you. Because you were old enough to be my father. And then suddenly you weren't. You changed everything, your face, your voice, who you were, and I thought I was losing my mind." She turned back to him, fury blazing.

"You took advantage of every moment. Every situation. You knew I was drawn to you, and you *used* it. You pushed it. You wanted to confuse me."

"That's not what happened—"

"You didn't want to teach me anything," she cut in sharply. "Not weapons. Not defense. You wanted to play with my head. And I fell for it. I'm such a fool." A trembling laugh tore free. "I should have questioned every odd thing instead of trusting you like an idiot." She grabbed the saddle horn again, but he caught her wrist.

"Hope, please. Just let me explain."

"No." Her voice dropped, quiet, final, far more devastating. "I don't believe you. And I don't trust you. Not anymore, Logan Shaw." She yanked her hand free. "Not once were you honest with me." With one furious, fluid motion, she swung fully into the saddle. When he reached for her again, she slapped his hand away so hard the sound echoed across the yard.

"Stay away from me," she choked. "I don't want anything to do with you ever again." She kicked her horse hard and bolted from the yard, disappearing down the road in a cloud of dust.

Logan didn't move until she was completely gone. Then a guttural sound ripped from somewhere deep inside him as he turned and slammed his fist into the barn door. The wood shuddered beneath the blow. His mother stepped quietly from the house, her expression soft but weary, and laid a gentle hand on his back.

"She'll come around," she murmured. "She has a good heart. And beneath all that anger... she cares for you far more than she wants to admit."

Logan stared at the fading trail Hope had left behind, pain tightening every muscle in his face.

"Just don't give up on her," his mother whispered. He swallowed hard, fists still trembling.

"I won't," he said. "Even if she hates me right now... I'm not letting her face any of this alone."

---

Tears of pure, blinding, anger stung Hope's eyes as she urged her horse faster, the wind ripping at her hat and her breath catching in furious gasps. She was so done, so sick and exhausted, with people lying to her. Every time she dared to trust someone, another hidden truth came crashing down around her. And worst of all... even her mother, the one person she had worshipped, had kept secrets from her.

Hope understood why. Her mother had been trying to protect her, trying to keep her safe from dangers she hadn't understood yet, but that didn't take the sting out of the betrayal. It didn't heal the ache in her chest or the feeling of being utterly alone in the world.

She rode without a destination, her heart pounding as hard as her horse's hooves. The road blurred beneath them until the trees parted and a shimmering lake came into view, breathtaking, still, untouched. Hope slowed, chest heaving. She needed to think. She needed space. She needed the world to stop spinning for one blessed minute.

She couldn't go back to the Shaw ranch, not after what she'd overheard, not after the lies, not after feeling so foolish. But she also couldn't stay in town with Whitmer dangerously close. He was her mother's killer. And there was still so much she didn't know, why he was in Cheyenne, what his connection to her father truly was, and what murderous plan he might be carrying out next.

Hope scanned the lake, her eyes catching on a small cabin tucked between the trees. Smoke was absent from the chimney, and the yard was quiet. A refuge. A hiding place. Maybe even, if she were lucky, time to breathe and think.

She guided her horse around the shoreline until she reached the cabin. It looked welcoming enough, more cared for than the rundown shacks she'd been forced to hide in before. A small barn sat behind it, half-hidden by a pine tree. Hope led her horse inside and filled a small wooden trough with water.

"Good girl," she whispered, brushing her fingers over the mare's neck as she drank. She grabbed her things and walked over to the cabin, pushing open the door. Warmth washed over her instantly, not from heat, but from the startling sight before her. It was clean. Organized. Safe-looking. Nothing like the filthy, broken-down shelters she'd suffered in. The main room had a cozy simplicity, and an alcove near the back divided the space into two small sleeping areas with sturdy wooden bunk beds.

Someone lived here. Someone who clearly cared about keeping things in order. But she couldn't stay outside, not with her emotions spiraling and danger still nearby. Drawing a steady breath, Hope slipped inside fully and set her things on a small table near one of the bunks.

"I hope you don't mind," she murmured to the empty cabin, her voice trembling despite her efforts. For now, this place would have to be her refuge, until she figured out her next move. And whether she was strong enough to face the lies, or the truth waiting just beyond them.

Hope sat at the edge of the lake, knees pulled to her chest, trying, truly trying, to force her thoughts into something resembling calm. But her agitation clung to her like a second skin. No matter how long she stared across the still water, her mind refused to settle. Every breath felt tight, every memory from the past hours burned behind her ribs. Eventually, she gave up.

Her eyes lifted toward the sky. Heavy, bruised-looking clouds rolled over the mountains, swallowing the remaining patches of blue. A storm was coming—fast. She drew in a shaky breath and pushed herself to her feet. If she was about to be trapped inside the cabin, she needed to prepare.

Inside, she slipped off her hat and hung it on a nail by the door, the gesture feeling strangely domestic, almost as if she belonged there. The silence of the cabin pressed around her, making her painfully aware of how alone she truly was. *Well... alone was safer than lied to.*

She drifted to the small kitchen area and opened the cupboards, not expecting much. A surprised breath left her when she found several canned goods, mostly beans, and a small tin of peppermint tea. Relief softened her shoulders. She still had some of Abigail's bread tucked in her satchel, but warm food sounded heavenly. And warm tea... something comforting, something steadying... she needed that more than she wanted to admit.

The wind outside gusted hard against the walls, rattling the windows. A cold draft slipped across the floor, making Hope shiver. Right. Fire. She crossed to the stone fireplace and dropped to her knees, but her heart sank. No wood. Not a single piece. But she had seen the little woodshed tucked beside the cabin.

Grabbing a bucket, she stepped outside. The air had grown even colder, the wind sharp enough to nip through her borrowed shirt. She hurried to the shed, scooped up as much firewood as she could carry, and rushed it inside before returning again, and again. She wasn't going to risk running out in the middle of the night, not with a storm coming and not in an unfamiliar place.

The clouds had turned nearly black by the time Hope returned with another heavy bucket of firewood. She barely made it inside before the sky opened and rain came pelting down in cold, slanting sheets. Grateful for her timing, she knelt at the hearth, struck a match, and coaxed a small flame into a proper fire. Once it was burning steadily, she set a pot of water to boil for tea.

While she waited, she drifted toward the window, arms folded tightly against the sudden chill. The wind howled across the lake, and then the door burst open. Hope gasped, spinning around. A young man stood in the doorway, broad-shouldered, dripping wet, and clearly startled.

"Who are you?" he asked, his voice a deep, pleasant rumble. His eyes widened slightly as he took her in.

"I—I'm sorry," she stammered. "Is this your cabin? I didn't mean to intrude. I saw the storm coming, and I had nowhere else to go. I'll gather my things and leave—"

He lifted a hand and gave her a warm, disarming smile. "You won't be going out in that, young lady. Not unless you want to drown. I was just surprised to find someone here."

Before Hope could respond, the door opened again and another man stepped inside, shaking rain from his coat.

"You won't believe this," he said with a grin, tugging off his soaked hat, "but there's already a horse in the barn." He noticed Hope and blinked. "Ah. That explains it."

Hope flushed. "I was only looking for refuge."

"No need to look uneasy," the second man replied cheerfully. "You picked the right spot. It's turning nasty out there." His gaze drifted curiously over her trousers and shirt. "Though I gotta ask, what brings such a pretty girl out here wearing men's clothes?"

Hope turned back to the boiling water at once. She poured it into a coffee pot and added the tea leaves, grateful for the distraction. The first man retrieved a few tin cups and set them out.

"You're making tea?" he said. "Perfect. We could use something warm."

Hope filled the cups, then eased into the armchair by the fire. The two men hung up their wet coats and settled nearby, both radiating easy friendliness. Still, Hope sat stiffly, uncertain whether she should trust them.

"Let's try this again," the first man said with a wink. "You're new around here. What brings you to this area? I don't think I've ever seen you in town."

"I'm not from here," she said carefully. "I arrived yesterday."

"And you're alone?" the second man asked.

Hope shook her head. "Not exactly."

"And the clothes?" he pressed, his tone more curious than judgmental.

"It's... a long story," she admitted. They exchanged a glance, immediately sensing her discomfort.

"Sorry," the first man said at once. "We're being rude. Should've introduced ourselves before asking questions." He extended his hand. "My name's Brent Stewart. This is my brother, Sawyer."

Hope offered a shy smile, and then a thought struck her like a spark.

"Are you... by any chance related to Georgiana Faith Spencer? Her maiden name was Stewart."

Both men straightened. Before they could answer, Hope hurried on, heat climbing up her neck.

"I know it's far-fetched. Stewart's a common name. It just... crossed my mind."

Brent's grin widened. "Georgiana was our aunt. We just learned she passed away recently. A shame, really. We haven't seen her since we were little." His expression softened. "How do you know her?"

Hope's throat tightened. "She was my mother. I'm Hope Spencer."

Sawyer nearly leapt out of his chair.

"Well, would you look at that, Brent?" he exclaimed. "We hide out from a storm and run straight into our little cousin." Without hesitation, he pulled her into a tight hug. Hope froze, then Brent wrapped her in an embrace as well. When they finally settled again, Sawyer leaned forward, studying her face.

"Now I'm even more curious why you're out here alone."

Knowing she could trust them, her mother's family, Hope told them everything. Whitmer. The disguise. Her arrival the day before. They listened without interrupting. When she finished, Brent raised an eyebrow.

"And you traveled here without a protector?"

Hope shook her head. "Logan Shaw traveled with me."

Both brothers visibly relaxed.

"Well, good," Brent said. "You had me worried. Logan's a good man."

Hope scoffed before she could stop herself.

"You disagree?" Sawyer asked, puzzled. She sighed and relayed what she'd overheard at the ranch.

"Ouch," Brent muttered. "No wonder you came looking for refuge." He leaned back, exhaling. "But, for what it's worth, despite how things look, Logan *is* a good one. We grew up with him. He's my age, twenty-eight. Sawyer's two years younger."

Hope blinked in surprise. "He said he trained with the marshals. Was that true?"

Brent nodded. "Yep. Uncle Jeff's a U.S. Marshal. He trained all of us. We're ranchers, but we figured some extra skills wouldn't hurt if trouble ever came knocking."

Hope grew quiet, absorbing that. Relief mingled with confusion. So... he hadn't lied about everything.

"Does he know where you are?" Sawyer asked gently.

"No," she admitted. "I... blew up at him. And I left."

"Blew up?" Brent repeated with a chuckle. "Sounds like our little cousin's got some fire."

Her cheeks warmed.

"Just like your mom," Sawyer added with a grin. "Sweetest woman alive, but Dad always said making Georgiana angry was like waking a volcano. Lava and rocks everywhere."

"I should have gone after her." Logan stood rigidly in front of the large sitting-room window, his broad shoulders tense as he watched rain lash against the glass in steady, punishing sheets. The storm mirrored the turmoil inside him, dark, relentless, and heavy with regret. His mother stepped up beside him, her expression soft with understanding.

"She needed space, son. Finding out so much all at once, especially the lies, it must have felt like the ground dropped out from under her."

Logan exhaled sharply, his jaw tightening.

"I just can't bear the thought of something happening to her. She doesn't know this area. She could get lost, or—" His voice faltered. "She could run straight into Whitmer."

"She's clever," his mother said gently. "And from what I've seen, she's resourceful. I doubt she'd put herself in danger on purpose. She strikes me as a young woman who has learned how to survive."

"Oh, she's determined all right," Logan muttered, dragging a hand over his face. "Determined. Stubborn. Hard-headed. And impossible to reason with once she's made up her mind." Frustration edged his words, but beneath it pulsed something far deeper, fear. His mother slipped an arm around him and rested her head briefly against his shoulder.

"That stubbornness probably kept her alive all these years, especially these past few weeks. Losing her mother the way she did... Hope had to learn how to stand on her own. That kind of pain shapes a person."

Logan swallowed hard. "She deserves more than this. More than running. More than danger at every turn. She deserves the truth. And justice. And a life where she doesn't have to be afraid."

His mother nodded. "She will have it, Logan. But she needs her own way of reaching it. Let her breathe. When she's ready, she'll listen."

Logan's gaze swept the rain-darkened landscape once more.

"I hope you're right," he whispered. "Because if anything happens to her... I'll never forgive myself."

"That doesn't sound like Mama at all," Hope said quietly, her expression shifting into something deeply troubled. "She was as meek and submissive as they come. At least... that's what I thought."

Brent poured himself more tea before settling back in his chair.

"Why don't you tell us a little about yourself, what it was like growing up?" he suggested gently. Sawyer was already warming a pan of beans over the fire. Hope let out a long, weary sigh.

"I never really questioned it until after Mama died... but no, I didn't grow up in a loving home. Mama was the only person who showed affection, and she poured it on so thick, maybe that's why I didn't realize how cold everything else was." Her gaze drifted toward the window, watching the trees bend beneath the force of the storm.

"My grandmother moved in shortly after my grandfather passed away. That was when I was a baby, so... she was always there. But she wasn't loving. Not at all. Father had been married before he met my mother, and he already had children. They were grown and gone by the time I was born, but they were the ones he cared about. Not me." Her voice softened, but a sharp ache lingered beneath the words.

"And you never saw your mother raise her voice? Not even once?" Sawyer asked, his brows furrowing with concern. Hope shook her head.

"Never. Mama taught me from the time I could walk that I had to be quiet, pliable, and obedient, especially when Father was around. But I..." She hesitated, a wry breath escaping her.

"I always had these big feelings. When something felt unfair, I couldn't keep it in. I lost my temper a few times, and every time I did, I was scolded harshly, first by Grandmother and then by Father." Her fists clenched at the memory, but she closed her eyes and forced herself to relax.

"Each time I snapped, I was sent to my room. I didn't see Mama for days afterward, which I always thought was strange, but... I think—" Her eyes widened as realization struck like a blow. Brent and Sawyer exchanged a tense glance.

"I think he punished her," Hope whispered. "He kept her away from me to force her obedience. I thought that only happened when she tried talking about her family, or when I asked questions about them."

"Your mother never talked about her family?" Brent asked carefully.

"She wasn't allowed to." Hope's voice hardened. "Father forbade it entirely. He told me once that her family had abandoned her, and after that, any mention of them was forbidden. But now... it all makes sense. He controlled her by isolating her from the people she loved."

"And your grandmother never intervened?" Brent asked. "Is she submissive too?"

Hope scoffed. "No. She's exactly like my father, cold, strict, and quick to scold. She wanted me sent away to a boarding school, but Father refused. I think he recognized my mother's spirit in me and wanted to stamp it out. So instead, he hired a governess."

Sawyer leaned forward. "Did your mom ever try to run away with you?"

Hope frowned, searching her memory. Then it surfaced.

"Once," she said softly. "I was eight. Mama never said we were running away, but everything was packed. Father caught us at the train station." Her jaw tightened. "I didn't see Mama for a month afterward. She must've been terrified of trying again. He would've taken me from her permanently, I know he would have."

Brent let out a low whistle. "So, you didn't grow up with fatherly hugs or someone protecting you?"

Hope shook her head. "No. Father never hugged me. Grandmother neither. The only warmth I received, came from Mama, and from Reverend Shaw and Doc Baker back home. They were friends of hers. They looked out for me when they could, but Father restricted that too. Mom disobeyed him only in that. She still saw them whenever she could manage it."

Sawyer offered her a gentle smile.

"Well, you won't experience that with our family. Grandma and Grandpa? They'll hug you until you can't breathe. And the rest of us aren't much better."

Hope's lips curved into a small, hopeful smile.

"I can't wait to meet them."

"We should take you there first thing tomorrow morning," Brent said, then paused when Hope's expression shifted.

"No," she said quickly. "Please... don't tell anyone you've met me. Not yet. As long as we don't know the truth about my mother's murder, and what my father is involved in, nobody can know I'm here. He'd use you to control me. I won't let what happened to my mother happen again."

Brent nodded slowly. "Makes sense now why we left San Francisco. I always wondered. I guess she begged our grandparents to leave, so your father couldn't touch them."

"Mom and Dad never talked about the details," Sawyer added. "We were young when we moved, but we knew something was wrong. Your father... he has money and influence. Your mom must've wanted her family far out of his reach."

Hope looked puzzled. "But how come the Shaw family is here, when Reverend Shaw is in San Francisco?"

Brent cleared his throat. "William was twenty when the old pastor asked him to take over the church. Logan and I were eight when we moved here. Our families were close, so Logan's parents came too. His father had always dreamed of owning a ranch."

Hope nodded slowly, absorbing every new truth. It was late by the time the last cup of tea went cold. The storm raged outside, but inside the cabin, warmth, and a strange, unfamiliar sense of belonging, wrapped around her. Hope had come seeking refuge. Instead, she had found family.

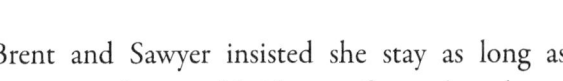

Brent and Sawyer insisted she stay as long as she needed, promising they would ride out often to keep her company. Their warmth soothed some of the ache inside her, but it did nothing to quiet her determination. As soon as the storm let up, Hope saddled her horse and headed toward town. She needed answers. She needed to know why Whitmer had come to Cheyenne... and what he planned to do next.

When she reached the bustling main street, she dismounted, tied her horse, and stepped into the saloon. The room buzzed with early-morning chatter, clinking glasses, and the heavy scent of whiskey and fried eggs. Her gaze swept the tables until it found him. Anthony Whitmer. He sat near the window with two other men, eating breakfast casually, as if he weren't a murderer. As if he hadn't destroyed lives.

Hope pulled her hat lower, ordered food from the barkeep, and slipped into a table just behind them, close enough to catch every word but far enough not to draw attention. Her heart pounded hard against her ribs, but she forced herself to breathe evenly, to appear calm. This time, she wasn't running. This time, she was listening.

"So," one of Whitmer's men said around a mouthful of biscuit, "Jared, Eric, an' Sheriff Craig're behind bars now? Spencer couldn't weasel 'em out?"

Hope stiffened. Her father had tried to free them?

Whitmer shook his head. "No. Seems his girl talked some U.S. Army boys into believin' her tale." His tone soured like old milk. "That sure muddies the waters. We don't know where she's holed up, but once she shows her face here, we'll be ready."

Hope's pulse hammered in her ears.

"Are we fixin' to kill her?" the second man asked casually, as if discussing cattle prices. Hope held her breath, cold fear rippling up her spine.

"Not yet," Whitmer grunted. "Spencer wants her dragged back first. He's madder'n a hornet she ran, even after he forbade it. Sounds like the girl's a spitfire."

All three chuckled, and Hope swallowed a wave of disgust. She leaned in slightly as their conversation shifted.

"So, what're we doin' today?" one of the men asked.

"We're ridin' for the Archer place," Whitmer muttered, his voice dropping low. "Need to see if Mrs. Archer's returned... so we can finish our business with her."

Hope froze.

"Why're we out in Wyoming after her? I thought they was from San Francisco," one of the men said, brow furrowing.

"They are," Anthony replied impatiently. "Archer's a senator outta California, but his missus inherited her folks' ranch up here, an' she's fond of comin' back. Word is she ain't too happy livin' in San Francisco."

"And what's got folks so eager to be rid of her?" the second man asked. Whitmer scoffed.

"Her husband's gettin' twitchy," Whitmer said quietly. "She knows 'bout the President business, and she knows he's been steppin' out on her. He wants her dealt with. She slipped the leash back in Washington, and ain't a soul found her yet."

"She can't hide for good," the other man said. "Woman'll get tired and head home."

Hope held her breath, her pulse thundering in her ears. Mrs. Archer. Senator Archer's wife. So that was the woman marked for death. No wonder her mother had been terrified. No wonder so many people were involved. The senator's influence stretched far beyond San Francisco. If he wanted his wife silenced, he had the money and the connections to make it happen. But not if Hope reached her first.

*Over my dead body will I let them kill her.* Keeping her head low, Hope watched from the corner of her eye as Whitmer and his men stood, tossed a few coins onto the table, and strode out of the saloon. She waited for a full count of ten before rising. The moment she stepped outside, she spotted them mounting their horses and riding out of town at a swift pace. Only when they disappeared around the bend did she move, and she moved fast.

Hope crossed the street, hurried back into the saloon, and climbed the stairs to the aging wooden hallway. Room fifteen. She checked both ends of the corridor. Empty. Perfect. She slipped a hairpin from beneath her hat and knelt by the lock. Her hands trembled at first, but she forced herself to breathe steadily. This wasn't the first lock she'd picked. Reverend Shaw's—*Logan's*—lessons had covered almost everything.

After a few tense seconds, a soft click sounded. Hope eased the door open and slipped inside, locking it behind her. The smell hit her immediately, whiskey, sweat, dirt, and something sour beneath it all. She pressed her sleeve over her nose and mouth. The room was a wreck. Empty bottles littered the floor, muddy boots lay abandoned near the bed, clothes strewn everywhere. Whitmer lived like a pig.

She didn't waste time. Hope searched the drawers, rifled through the filthy wardrobe, shoved her hands beneath the mattress. Nothing. Frustration twisted in her gut until she spotted a heavy wool coat crumpled over a chair. She slid her hand into the inside pocket—and froze. Papers. A thick bundle. She pulled them free and sat at the small table, spreading the sheets across its scarred surface. Names. Dates. Locations. Code phrases. Schedules. Riders. Watchmen. Money transfers.

And a crude sketch of a woman who could only be Mrs. Archer. Hope's blood ran cold.

She pulled loose pages from her jacket and began copying everything she could, her hand flying across the paper. She didn't dare take the originals. If Whitmer noticed anything missing, she'd be dead before sundown. Somewhere downstairs, a bottle shattered, followed by rough laughter. Hope worked, faster. Line after line. Map after map. Name after name. She had never known this much before, never understood the full scope of the plot. But now she did. And it was far worse than she had imagined.

When she finished, she tucked her copies safely inside her jacket, folded the original papers with care, and placed them exactly where she had found them. Then she stood, heart pounding, knowing she had just crossed a line she could never uncross, and that everything depended on what she did next.

***

"I didn't find her." Logan took a deep breath, frustration tightening his jaw. "I searched the entire town. I even went into the saloon, checked every corner, but she wasn't there."

His father leaned back in his chair, thoughtful.

"She might be hiding in one of the hotel rooms."

Logan nodded grimly. "That's what I'm thinking, too. But I can't very well knock on every door and hope I run into her. If she's avoiding me, she won't answer anyway."

His mother folded her hands, worry etched into her features.

"No matter how angry she is, she can't hide forever. Eventually, she'll need food, or rest... or help."

Logan exhaled heavily, pacing once before stopping at the window again. Rain streaked the glass, turning the yard outside into a blurred wash of gray.

"She is so determined to catch the man who killed her mother," he murmured, his voice tight with worry he could barely contain. "So desperate for justice... or closure... that I'm terrified she'll do something reckless. She could walk straight into Whitmer's path and not even realize it until it's too late."

His father rose and clapped a steadying hand on Logan's shoulder.

"You'll find her."

Logan didn't look convinced. "I'll head back to town after lunch. I'll watch the hotel... the saloon... every alley if I must." His eyes hardened with resolve. "She thinks she can do this alone, but she has no idea what she's up against."

His mother met his gaze with a soft, knowing look.

"Be patient with her, Logan. She's hurt more deeply than any of us can fully understand. But she's also young... and afraid. Anger is easier than trust."

Logan nodded, though the tension in his shoulders didn't ease.

"I just don't want to lose her. Not like this." He stared out at the rain, jaw clenched. *Where are you, Hope?*

# 17

# A Marshal Turned Traitor

Hope glanced out the window after tucking the last of Whitmer's papers back into the filthy coat pocket. Her pulse was still racing from the fear of being caught, but another jolt struck when she saw Logan stride out of the saloon. He scanned the street with sharp, searching eyes before mounting his horse and riding hard out of town.

Hope's heart sank. *He must have come into the saloon right after I went upstairs... he was probably looking for me.* She let out a shaky sigh. For a moment, guilt flickered through her, then anger rushed back like flame catching dry brush. He could search all he wanted. She wasn't ready to face him, not after everything she had overheard.

She slipped quietly down the stairs, eased out of the saloon, and forced herself to refocus. She didn't have time for emotional turmoil. She had a killer to catch, and now a senator's wife to protect. Hope headed toward the train station at a brisk pace, keeping her hat low and her stride confident. She studied the posted schedules and felt both relief and pressure coil inside her.

*The next train arrives in the morning.* If Mrs. Archer truly was returning, that would be Hope's only chance to find her before Whitmer and his men did. She swallowed hard. She didn't know what the woman looked like, but surely someone in town would, someone would greet her. Or worse, Whitmer or one of his men might notice her arrival. Either way, Hope needed to be there.

After committing the arrival time to memory, she turned toward the general store. Inside, she kept her voice low, buying only what she needed, food, matches, a few items for her disguise, and tucked everything carefully into her saddlebags. Her nerves jumped at every creak of the wooden floor, every passing customer, every glance that lingered a moment too long.

When she finally stepped outside into the fading afternoon light, she released another breath she hadn't realized she'd been holding. Time was slipping away. Whitmer was plotting. Mrs. Archer was in danger. And Logan—

Hope pushed that thought aside before it could claw deeper. She mounted her horse and rode back toward the cabin by the lake, keeping to the trees, her mind racing with plans, dread, and burning determination. By the time she reached the quiet clearing, her heart had steadied again. She fed her horse, stepped inside the cabin, and stored her new supplies.

Tomorrow, everything could change. Either she would save Mrs. Archer... or she would become Whitmer's next target.

It was nearly dusk when a firm knock sounded at the cabin door. Before Hope could even rise from her chair, the door swung open and Brent stepped inside, brushing droplets of rain from his hat. His face lit up the moment he saw her.

"There she is!" he announced with a broad smile, striding over and pulling her into a warm, cousinly hug. "How was your day, Cousin?"

Hope exhaled, slowly. "Pretty informative," she murmured, handing him the stack of copied notes she had collected from Whitmer's room. Brent scanned the first few pages and let out a long, low whistle.

"My word... Hope, this is a pile of dynamite."

"They intend to kill Mrs. Archer," she said, folding her arms tightly. "And that's only part of it. They're planning to assassinate the president when he arrives here for the town's celebration."

Brent's head shot up. "The president?"

Hope nodded grimly. "I don't know why. Killing him won't end the government, the vice president would take his place. My guess is they're aiming for chaos. Maybe they want something bigger... more deaths, more panic." Her voice tightened. "Mrs. Archer must have discovered too much. That's why they're hunting her."

Brent dragged a hand through his hair.

"Hope... this is dangerous. This isn't just tracking down a murderer anymore. This is a conspiracy."

"I know," she said quietly. "But if I can stop innocent people from being killed, if I can do anything, then I have to try."

Brent studied her for a moment, his expression torn between admiration and worry. Then he nodded.

"All right. Do you want me to come into town tomorrow? I can point out Mrs. Archer if she gets off the train."

Relief softened Hope's face. "That would help. If she doesn't show up tomorrow, I'll keep going back every day. It's not as if I have anything else to do." She gave him a teasing grin and a wink.

Brent chuckled. "Only you could joke about hunting down assassins."

Her smile faded, replaced by determination.

"If Mrs. Archer knows more, I need to speak with her. She could be the key to understanding the whole thing."

Brent tapped the papers thoughtfully.

"If Whitmer's after her, then as soon as we find her, she'll need a safe place. Somewhere they wouldn't think to look."

Hope nodded. "Is there such a place around here?"

"Oh, definitely." Brent's grin returned. "Mrs. Archer is close friends with Marjorie Shaw."

Hope's breath hitched. "Logan's mother?"

"The very one. Their ranch house is big, with plenty of room, and plenty of hiding spots. And trust me, no outlaw in his right mind would try sneaking past their cowboys. She'd be safe there."

Hope's pulse fluttered with mixed emotions, hope, worry, and that persistent ache at the mention of Logan. She wrapped her arms around herself and stared into the firelight.

"Good," she said softly. "Because if these men get to her first... I don't even want to imagine it."

Hope was already waiting at the train station when Brent arrived the next morning. He pulled up in the family buggy, reins in hand, greeting her with an encouraging nod. The plan was simple: Brent would offer Mrs. Archer a ride to the ranch, ensuring her safety and giving him the chance to quietly introduce Hope. Since Whitmer had never met Brent, there was no risk of him recognizing him.

Hope wished her stomach weren't tied in knots. Every creak of the arriving train made her shoulders tense. Every stranger who stepped onto the platform made her heart jump. She scanned each face carefully, searching for someone who looked frightened, exhausted, or out of place.

Passengers began to spill out, families, businessmen, a pair of ranchers carrying saddlebags. Hope shifted on her feet, trying not to look as anxious as she felt. Only when the last passengers stepped down did Brent subtly nod to her. *That's her.*

Hope followed his gaze. A refined woman in her mid-fifties stood at the end of the platform, dressed modestly but with unmistakable grace. Her hair was pinned neatly beneath a traveling hat, but her eyes, sharp, alert, and shadowed with strain, constantly swept the area as if searching for danger.

Hope's pulse quickened. *Mrs. Archer.* Brent walked toward her with a warm, familiar smile, while Hope veered in the opposite direction, straight toward Whitmer and his men. They lingered near the freight crates, pretending to be uninterested, but Hope could feel their tension from across the platform.

Brent reached the older woman.

"Mrs. Archer, welcome home," he greeted, tipping his hat with a beaming smile. The woman startled slightly, but when she recognized him, her guarded expression softened into genuine relief.

"Brent Stewart. Well, isn't that a sweet way to greet me."

Brent offered a respectful bow of his head.

"It's mighty good to see you again, ma'am. I brought the buggy today, in case you need someone to drive you home."

A gentle smile touched her lips. "Now, that would be mighty nice of you."

"Let me help you with your luggage," Brent said, reaching for her bags. She allowed it, gratitude clear in her eyes, but her gaze drifted nervously over her shoulder, scanning the station just as Hope had moments before.

Hope swallowed hard. Whitmer's eyes followed Mrs. Archer too. Hope positioned herself near the outlaw's group, staying far enough to avoid suspicion but close enough to overhear. Brent guided Mrs. Archer toward the buggy, his demeanor calm, and natural, as if he weren't discreetly shielding her with his body. Hope clenched her jaw. Stay focused. Stay calm. Stay ready. Today, everything would change.

"We takin' her out right now?" one of the men whispered harshly, edging closer to Anthony as the last of the passengers cleared the platform. Whitmer didn't even look at him. His jaw worked slowly as his eyes tracked Mrs. Archer's every movement, calculating, cold. He shook his head once.

"No," he muttered. "That'd be dumb as dirt. Half the damn town's standin' here gawkin' at the train, and she's got herself an escort." His lip curled in faint irritation. "Too many eyes. Too many chances for things to go sideways."

Hope felt her stomach twist, bile rising in her throat.

Anthony shifted his weight, lowering his voice further.

"We wait till dark. Folks'll be settled in by then. Ranch hands'll be eatin' supper, doors shut, minds elsewhere." His gaze sharpened. "That's when we move."

"And the woman?" the second man asked quietly.

Whitmer's mouth pulled into a thin, humorless smile.

"She won't even know we're there. We slip in, finish what we started, and slip out again." His eyes flicked briefly toward Brent and Mrs. Archer, now nearing the buggy. "No witnesses. No loose ends."

Hope's pulse thundered in her ears. Darkness. That was their plan. Silence. Surprise. Death wrapped in shadow. She forced herself to remain still, head bowed, hat brim low, even as every instinct inside her screamed to move, to act, to warn someone, anyone. They weren't just hunting anymore. They were planning an execution. And now she knew exactly when it would happen.

"Now, Brent," Mrs. Archer said as they moved toward the buggy, her tone warm but unmistakably sharp, "why were you in town? I refuse to believe for a single second that you simply happened to show up to fetch me, especially since you couldn't have known I was returning today!" She cast him a sideways glance, the kind that suggested she had known him since he was in diapers and could still see through him like clear glass.

"I know you too well. You're holding something back. And unless age has dulled my senses, you clearly have something you need to tell me."

Brent exhaled and offered a sheepish smile.

"You're not wrong, Mrs. Archer. But I'm afraid I'm not the one who needs to talk to you." He paused, glancing subtly over his shoulder as if ensuring no one suspicious lingered nearby. "It's my cousin," he said quietly.

"Oh?" Her brows lifted with both interest and a flicker of concern. "And who might that be?"

Brent hesitated, clearly weighing how much to say, and how quickly to say it.

"Someone who's... been hoping to speak with you. Someone who's gotten tangled up in matters involving your husband, and the danger you're in."

Mrs. Archer stopped walking for a heartbeat, her gloved fingers tightening around the handle of her satchel.

"Danger?" she repeated softly. "Brent Stewart, what on earth have I walked into?"

Brent offered her his arm again, guiding her toward the buggy with steady, reassuring gentleness.

"Nothing we can't handle, ma'am. But you'll want to hear what my cousin has to say." His voice lowered. "And sooner rather than later."

———

Brent stopped the buggy in front of the large ranch house just as Hope rode into the yard. Gravel crunched beneath her horse's hooves, and Mrs. Archer turned at the sound. Her brows lifted with curiosity as she watched the disguised 'boy' approach.

Hope slid from the saddle with more grace than she intended, nerves tightening her stomach. Out of habit, she tugged her hat lower, though one glance at Mrs. Archer's keen, knowing eyes told her the disguise was useless to someone so observant. The older woman's gaze moved over her slowly, gently, as if piecing together a story she already half understood. Then her expression softened into a warm, welcoming smile.

"Well," she murmured, "aren't you a surprise."

Hope swallowed, offered the most respectful nod her churning nerves would allow, and stepped closer. Brent joined them, but Mrs. Archer's focus remained keenly, intently, on Hope. Without hesitation, without even a flicker of judgment, Mrs. Archer reached for the young woman's arm.

"Come inside, both of you," she said kindly, her voice low but steady. "It seems we have quite a bit to talk about."

Hope's shoulders loosened by a precious inch at the unexpected warmth. She followed Mrs. Archer up the steps toward the house, feeling, for the first time in days, as though she might finally be walking toward answers, not away from them.

"What is it you have to tell me, young lady?" Mrs. Archer asked once they had all settled in the sitting room. Her tone was gentle but braced, as though she already sensed the storm coming.

Hope drew a deep breath. Her hands trembled in her lap, but her voice remained steady as she recounted everything she had discovered, Whitmer's involvement, the plans whispered in the saloon, the documents she had found in his room, and the list of intended targets. She spoke until there was nothing left but silence and a racing heartbeat.

Mrs. Archer's warm smile faded by degrees, replaced by a look of grim understanding. When Hope finished, the older woman pressed a hand over her chest and released a long, sorrowful sigh.

"First," she said softly, "I am terribly sorry that your dear mother was murdered. I cannot imagine the weight you've had to carry these past weeks... nor the bravery it took to come warn me." Her voice wavered. "I had prayed that by staying away long enough, they would lose interest. Clearly, I was wrong."

Hope nodded, her throat tight. Mrs. Archer continued in a hushed tone.

"I, too, learned pieces of their plan. They intend to kill the president, and from what I gathered, they plan to strike the government in Washington on the very same day."

Hope gasped. Even though she had suspected it, hearing the confirmation from someone directly involved jolted her like a blow. Brent stiffened beside her, alarm flashing in his eyes.

"I know my husband is involved," Mrs. Archer said bitterly, "but he is not alone. At least two senators whispered warnings to me, men I once trusted. But I do not know the full scope. I wish I did."

"They're trying to take over the government," Hope said, outrage igniting in her gaze. "Whoever is part of this... they're committing treason against the entire country."

"But they can't do that without help," Brent added. "Is the U.S. Army involved? Or part of it?"

Mrs. Archer shook her head firmly. "I saw no unusual movement of troops in any city I passed through. If soldiers are involved, it is not openly."

Hope leaned forward, her brows drawn tight. "Then they're recruiting. Buying loyalty. Or trying to build their own force."

Both Brent and Mrs. Archer stared at her, horrified. Hope didn't flinch.

"We need to get this information to someone who can act," Mrs. Archer said urgently. "Brent, you must contact your uncle."

Brent nodded. "Uncle Jeff will be here when the president arrives for the festivities. But sending a telegram is dangerous. We don't know who's been bought off, or how far this reaches."

"Then we wait for him," Hope said quietly. "And warn him the moment he sets foot in Cheyenne. The president needs to know too... or he's walking straight into a trap."

Mrs. Archer rose suddenly, resolve tightening her posture.

"I should not remain here another hour. Brent, take me to the Shaw ranch. At least there I'll be surrounded by people I trust."

He stood instantly. "Of course."

"I'll pack a few essentials," Mrs. Archer said, turning toward the hallway. But before she stepped away, she paused and reached for Hope. Her hands were warm and trembling as she pulled the young woman into a tight, motherly embrace.

"Thank you," she whispered into Hope's hair. "You are brave, braver than you know. And I am grateful to you with all my heart. But promise me, darling... promise me you won't take unnecessary risks."

Hope swallowed hard, blinking back sudden tears.

"I'll try," she murmured.

"Promise," Mrs. Archer insisted.

Hope hesitated, then nodded. "I promise to be careful."

Mrs. Archer cupped her cheek briefly, eyes filled with gratitude and fear, before turning away to gather her things.

Hope watched her go, her heart pounding. The stakes had never been higher, and she knew this was only the beginning.

⁂

"It's good to see you again, Caroline," Marjorie Shaw said warmly as she drew her friend inside. Brent followed with Mrs. Archer's bags, disappearing down the hall toward the guest room. "And of course you may stay with us as long as you need. Come, sit. We'll have some tea first, and then you can explain everything."

They settled into the sitting room just as one of the maids entered with a tray of steaming cups and a plate of shortbread. Logan stepped in quietly, but the tension in his shoulders betrayed his worry. The moment the tea was poured, Mrs. Archer finally spoke, sharing what she had discovered, and that Brent and Hope Spencer had warned her.

Logan's head snapped up. "You saw her?" he asked, his voice tight. "Is she all right? Was she safe?"

Mrs. Archer smiled softly. "She seemed quite well."

Hope's name alone eased a fraction of Logan's stiffness, but his jaw remained tense.

"Do you know where she is?"

Mrs. Archer shook her head. "I do not. She didn't tell me. Only that she is determined to keep an eye on Mr. Whitmer and learn everything she can before acting." A hint of admiration touched her voice. "She is quite the detective, Logan. Hope even snuck into Whitmer's hotel room two days ago while he was away at my ranch. That's how she gathered the information she has now."

Logan gasped, sprang to his feet, and began pacing so quickly that even the thick carpet could not muffle the force of his steps.

"I want to strangle that girl," he burst out, raking a hand through his hair. "She's putting herself in incredible danger, alone, and she's still hiding from me."

Mrs. Archer smiled knowingly. "Well, if I knew a man wanted to strangle me, I'd stay clear of him too."

Marjorie chuckled into her teacup, her eyes sparkling with amused sympathy. Mrs. Archer leaned forward.

"Logan, I can see how deeply you care for her, anyone would. But she is a clever young woman. Don't underestimate her courage or her judgment. Hope wants justice for her mother, yes, but she also wants to ensure that every guilty man pays for his crimes. She won't play recklessly with fire. Every move she makes is careful... calculated... purposeful."

Logan halted his pacing. His breath came unevenly, his eyes shadowed with fear and fierce protectiveness.

"I know she's intelligent," he muttered, sinking into a chair, "but intelligence doesn't stop bullets or protect her from a man like Whitmer."

Mrs. Archer reached out and touched his hand gently.

"No," she agreed softly. "But determination can be stronger than fear. And Hope has plenty of both." Her voice warmed. "And from what I've seen, she also has someone very determined to protect her."

Logan swallowed, unable to deny it. Marjorie stood and placed a quiet, reassuring hand on her son's shoulder, her expression tender yet firm.

"Keep looking for her," she said. "But trust her, too. She has her mother's fire, and that fire is what has kept her alive this long."

Logan nodded, though worry still stormed behind his eyes. Because fire could guide Hope... or burn her if she drew too close to danger.

"How the hell did she manage to escape?" the man beside Anthony Whitmer hissed through his teeth.

Hope couldn't see his face from where she crouched behind a stack of supplies, but the voice, sharp, ice-cold, merciless, hit her like a blow. She knew it. She was certain she had heard it before... she just couldn't place where.

"We watched her climb off that train," Whitmer muttered under his breath. "Checked the barn. The carriage ain't moved an inch. Somebody 'round here must've helped her make herself scarce."

"But why in blazes would anyone help her?" the cold voice snapped, his fist slamming down so hard Whitmer's cup jumped.

"Maybe she caught on we were after her," the third man said nervously. "Or maybe someone recognized her and whisked her off, took her down a side trail or through the woods."

A chair scraped violently against the floor.

"I want you idiots ridin' out to every settlement, ranch, and dusty town within thirty miles," the man barked. "Her husband's dead set on killin' her, same as the rest. If she slips away from us one more time, it'll be your necks in the noose." With that, he strode out of the saloon, boots pounding against the wooden floor. One of Whitmer's men muttered a curse under his breath.

"I can't stand that fella," he growled.

Whitmer snorted. "Man walks around actin' like he owns the whole territory just 'cause he's wearin' a marshal's star, and 'cause his daddy's knee-deep in this business."

"We still best tread careful," the third man warned quietly. "Spencer won't blink before puttin' a bullet in us if we foul this up. He does whatever his pa snaps his fingers for... and he's the one holdin' all the money."

Anthony slammed a few coins onto the table and stood. The three men turned and headed for the door, disappearing into the street beyond.

Hope stayed frozen behind the crates until the door shut behind them. Her breath slipped out in a shaky exhale as her mind reeled.

*Spencer. Her husband wants her dead. Marshal. Money. Obedient to his father.* Her stomach dropped like a stone. Gregory Spencer. Her oldest half-brother. The man she barely remembered was working with her father, with Whitmer, with corrupt senators. A marshal sworn to uphold the law, now breaking every vow, he'd ever made. Her jaw clenched. A hot, fierce determination flared inside her chest.

*A marshal?* No. Not anymore. Her brother wasn't merely part of this conspiracy. He wasn't just aiding her father. He was hunting her. Hope's hands curled into fists at her sides, nails biting into her palms. If Gregory Spencer believed he could terrify her into silence. If he thought fear would make her disappear quietly, then he had no idea who he was dealing with now. Not anymore.

# 18

# Found by Love,
# Hunted by Blood

Hope made a fire the moment she returned to the cabin. The temperature had been slipping day by day, autumn crawling down from the mountains with sharp teeth. Tonight felt colder still, an early whisper of winter. She was grateful Brent and Sawyer had stacked the shed full of firewood and packed the cabinets inside. At least she wouldn't have to venture out into the darkness, where hungry mountain lions and wolves prowled closer to town this time of year.

She was just about to make herself some tea when a knock sounded at the door. Sawyer had promised to bring coal and more wood, so she expected him, until she opened the door. Her heart stalled.

"What are you doing here, Logan?" she breathed, her eyes slicing at him with icy fury.

"I guess I finally found you," he shot back, an edge of relief hiding behind his stern tone. Hope immediately stepped into the doorway, barring him from entering.

"Please leave. I told you—I don't want to see you anymore."

He studied her for barely a heartbeat before bending, sweeping her legs from under her, and tossing her over his shoulder. Hope gasped, fists pounding against his back in outrage as he stepped inside, kicked the door shut behind him, and only then set her back on her feet.

"What are you doing?" she demanded, cheeks flaming, her rage rising like a storm inside her.

He almost smiled at the fire in her.

"I've been looking for you for days. You had me worried sick." His eyes locked onto hers, unblinking, earnest, but she tore her gaze away and turned toward the window.

"Why?" she snapped. "Did you forget to tell me a few more lies?"

He exhaled slowly. "Hope... I tried to apologize."

She said nothing, arms crossed tightly over her chest, staring out at the falling dusk. Logan stepped closer.

"We tried to protect you. Your mother wanted nothing more than to get you away from your father. She didn't care what happened to herself, only that you were safe." His voice softened. "She trusted my family. And she trusted William."

Still, Hope didn't look at him.

"I couldn't tell you about your relatives because they are still at risk. And I couldn't tell you about myself because you thought I was William. You weren't ready to hear the truth. Not then."

"Why didn't your brother travel with me?" Hope whirled around, fury sparking. "He was supposed to. That was the plan. So why send you? To play games? To twist my feelings? To use me because you knew I had no one else?" Her voice cracked. "At least your brother didn't treat me like a little girl."

"I never saw you as a little girl, Hope."

"Then explain why you did all of it. Explain why you confused me. Why you ignored my feelings. Why you pushed boundaries you had no right to push."

He swallowed, searching her face.

"I liked you from the moment I first saw you, two years ago, when I visited William in San Francisco. I noticed you immediately. And when he told me who you were... I wanted to know you more."

Hope blinked once, then dropped her gaze again.

"When I visited a year later and found out you were engaged, I was... heartbroken. And angry. I saw that man beside you and knew he didn't deserve you, didn't even see you. When William told me I was needed to help bring you to safety, I hoped... maybe... if we spent enough time together, you would notice me too."

Her breath caught. She didn't want it to, but it did.

"I kissed you both times for the reasons I told you," he admitted, stepping closer. "But also, because I needed to know if I even had a chance. After each kiss, you were furious, so I didn't know what to think. It wasn't until I saw your reaction when I touched you, the way you trembled, the way your breath caught, that I realized you felt something too. And yes, you admitted you were attracted to me."

"Attraction doesn't mean love," she said softly.

"I know. But attraction can grow into love, and it often does." His hands slid gently onto her shoulders, warming her skin through her shirt. "And I am in love with you, Hope." His breath brushed her ear. Goosebumps rippled down her spine despite her attempt to resist him.

"How can I trust anything you say now?" Her voice trembled. "You lied about so many things."

Logan gently turned her around and tilted her chin up. His thumb brushed her cheek, a touch that made her knees weaken.

"Do you think everyone who saw us together was lying? Brother Jacob? Abigail? Esther? Elizabeth? They all saw how I looked at you, long before you accepted it yourself."

She stared into his brown eyes. Eyes that didn't look like the Reverend's anymore. Eyes that burned with something raw and honest. Something that terrified her even as it pulled her in. His lips hovered just above hers.

"I want to kiss you, Hope," he murmured. "As me. Not as William. Not as some confusion in your mind. Just... me. Logan. Will you let me?"

Her breath hitched. Her heart kicked. Part of her wanted to run, but a greater part wanted him. Had wanted him from the moment she realized the truth. He saw that war in her eyes. And then he kissed her.

His lips claimed hers with a hunger that stole her breath, a passion that nearly buckled her legs. His arms wrapped around her, powerful and protective, pulling her flush against him. The world melted, the cold, the anger, the betrayal, everything but him. The kiss deepened, slowed, then deepened again. His mouth was warm and sure, hers yielding with growing urgency. She flung her arms around his neck, kissing him back with all the longing she'd tried so desperately to deny.

He kissed her until her lungs demanded air. They parted, breathless, his forehead resting against hers. His smile, warm and devastating, made her tremble all over again.

"I daresay the attraction between us is rather strong," he whispered. Hope's lips twitched before she sobered.

"Physical attraction isn't enough," she whispered. "I've seen where that leads. The beginning can be beautiful... but I've watched marriages crumble when the beauty fades. I watched men trade their aging wives for mistresses. My mother..." Her voice cracked. "She was young and beautiful once. And my father, he never loved her. I don't want that life."

Logan's expression softened with fierce tenderness. He pulled her into a warm, protective embrace.

"Is that why you fought your feelings for me?" he murmured. "Because of the age difference between your parents?"

Hope nodded against his chest.

"I've known three marriages like that," she whispered. "Two ended in death. One in divorce. I don't want to be replaced when I get older."

He lifted her chin again, eyes blazing with sincerity.

"Hope, listen to me." He took her hand and pressed it to his heart. "I don't love you because you're beautiful, though you are. I love you because you're brilliant. Fierce. Loyal. Stubborn to the point of madness." A soft smile touched his lips. "And because you look at the world with a fire that could light up an entire valley."

Her eyes shimmered.

"My parents still kiss, flirt, argue, and adore each other like newlyweds," he continued. "They're proof that love doesn't fade unless people choose to let it. I would never be like your father. Ever. I want to love you with my whole heart, and my whole life. I want to protect you with every breath I take." His thumb brushed her lower lip, making her pulse race. "My heart is yours, Hope," he whispered. "I'm yours."

Her tears slipped free, but she smiled, radiant and trembling. Logan kissed her again, slow and intoxicating, until she melted fully into his arms. And for the first time, Hope let herself fall.

"How did you find me?" Hope asked once they had settled into the two armchairs before the fireplace. The flames cast warm flickers across Logan's face, softening the hard lines of worry that had etched themselves there over the last few days. Logan leaned back slightly, a slow grin tugging at the corner of his mouth.

"Mrs. Archer told me you were keeping an eye on Whitmer, so I went into town at dawn. I hid near the saloon, close enough to watch who went in and out, but far enough not to be seen. When you slipped away and headed for the cabin, I followed you."

Hope's brows lifted. "Sneaky," she said, though the corner of her lips curved upward in reluctant amusement. He chuckled, but the sound faded quickly.

"I just wish you wouldn't put yourself in so much danger." His voice dipped, lower and rawer than before. "It drives me insane knowing you're shadowing a man who murdered your mother, one who wouldn't hesitate to kill you if he realized you were tracking him."

She softened, just a fraction. "I'm careful, Logan. I make sure he doesn't notice me. I stay hidden. I stay quiet. And I only went into his room because I knew he'd be gone for a while. I'm not being reckless. I promise I'm not risking anything."

He leaned forward, elbows braced on his knees, eyes locked on hers with an intensity that sent a shiver skittering across her skin.

"You think you aren't risking anything," he murmured, "but to me, the moment you're anywhere near that man, the risk is already too great. Losing sight of you for days... not knowing if you were safe..." He exhaled sharply, dragging a hand through his hair. "Hope, I can't go through that again."

Her breath caught at the vulnerability in his voice, so unguarded it tugged painfully at something deep inside her.

"I won't let him catch me," she said softly.

"That's not the point," he countered gently. "I don't want you anywhere near someone like him. I want you safe." His gaze softened, turning warm and achingly tender. "I want you alive. With me."

Hope swallowed, startled by how deeply those words pierced her. But she didn't look away. Not this time.

"And I intend to stay that way," she whispered. "I'm not as reckless as you think."

Logan gave a slow, rueful smile and shook his head.

"No," he said quietly. "You're far braver than you think. And far more frightening than you realize, at least to any man who loves you."

Her pulse fluttered wildly at that word. *Loves.* He didn't take it back. Didn't soften it. Didn't apologize. He simply held her gaze, steady and unwavering, as if the truth had been sitting on his tongue for far too long. And Hope felt her heart both tremble, and steady, at once.

"Spencer's ridin' back in tomorrow, and we still ain't laid eyes on Mrs. Archer," Anthony hissed through his teeth, his voice tight as rawhide soaked in rain. His fingers drummed a jittery rhythm against the saloon table. "He's gonna kill us, sure as sunrise." He leaned closer, panic sharpening every word.

"The president's due in just a few days. If that woman gets to anybody with real pull, anybody who'll believe her, we're done for. They'll hunt us down like coyotes after a gut-shot calf. We gotta make damn sure she don't get within a mile of that president."

The man beside him muttered something dark under his breath, but Anthony barreled on, desperation bleeding through his scowl.

"Spencer don't stomach failure, and his pa's twice as mean about it. If we don't track that woman down soon, we might as well start diggin' our own graves."

# 19

# The Bullet She Took

Hope pressed herself flat against the wall just beyond their table, her breath locked tight in her lungs. A chilly draft from the open doorway brushed her shoulder, but she didn't dare move. The shadows cloaked her, yet she could practically feel her heart pounding against the wooden boards beneath her ribs.

Mrs. Archer was safe, for now. But the danger was far greater than Hope had imagined. These men weren't merely running from the law. They were plotting something vast, something treasonous. And even as that realization sent a cold whisper down her spine, another thought burned just as fiercely.

Her mother's diary. It was still out there. Somewhere. Maybe discarded. Maybe stolen. Maybe hidden exactly where her mother had hoped Hope would one day find it. Whatever secrets it held, about the conspiracy, about her past, about her mother's final days, Hope needed them. Even if the diary contained nothing about this murderous scheme, it was still the last piece of her mother that remained. Her voice. Her hopes. Her fears. Her wisdom, pressed into those pages.

Hope swallowed hard, her fingers curling into the wood beside her. No matter how dangerous these men were. No matter how close they came to discovering she was alive. No matter how much Logan begged her to stay away, she would find that diary. And when she did, she would finally have the truth. About her mother. About her father. And perhaps... about herself.

She returned to the saloon the following day, slipping into the same shadowed corner table near Whitmer and his men. She had barely settled into her chair when the door swung open again and two more men strode inside. Hope's breath hitched. Her father.

Winston Spencer moved with the cold precision of a man accustomed to obedience. Beside him, her half-brother, Marshal Gregory Spencer, wore the same icy, unyielding expression. Hope's pulse thundered in her ears as she shrank deeper into her seat, praying neither of them glanced her way.

"Any word on Mrs. Archer?" Gregory demanded the moment they reached Whitmer's table. "You found her trail?"

All three men shook their heads. Hope could see the anger simmering beneath her half-brother's rigid posture, but her father's fury was something else entirely. His jaw pulsed, nostrils flaring with every measured breath.

"What about my daughter?" Winston snapped. "Has she arrived yet? She was last seen in Saint Charles. It does not take this long to travel from there to Cheyenne."

"Maybe the gal changed her mind," one of Whitmer's men muttered. Winston's stare cut through him like a blade.

"She ran," he spat. "She disobeyed me. Took advantage of my absence and fled." His voice dropped into something poisonous. "I should never have allowed her out of my sight after you took care of her mother."

Hope's nails dug into her palms, rage burning hot behind her ribs. *He thought he had us both broken.*

"I thought we'd made her as meek and obedient as Georgiana," Winston continued, lips curling. "She said foolish things after her mother's death, grief, I assumed. But clearly..." His eyes narrowed. "She is more tempered, more defiant, than I expected."

Anthony Whitmer cleared his throat carefully, shifting the conversation before Winston's temper fully ignited.

"So... when's all this supposed to go down?"

Winston exhaled slowly, visibly reining himself in.

"The men are ready," he said coldly. "Once the president is dead, the senators and their forces in Washington will seize control of the government and eliminate anyone who stands in their way." A thin smile curved his mouth. "The ships will officially arrive shortly, though," he added, almost smugly, "they've already reached the Washington coast and are nearing San Francisco."

"How many men per ship?" someone asked.

"Two hundred," Winston replied. "The East Coast forces will keep the army occupied, preventing them from reclaiming the capital. Meanwhile, those arriving in San Francisco will board trains, gather recruits as they move east, and build a force strong enough to secure the entire country."

Hope nearly passed out. The room tilted, her vision narrowing to a tunnel as the weight of what she'd overheard slammed into her like a physical blow. This wasn't merely corruption. It wasn't simple murder or political scheming. This was treason of the highest order, a plan to overthrow governments, assassinate presidents, unleash foreign armies, and drown two nations in blood. And her father, her own father, sat at the center of it.

Her heart hammered wildly, each beat sharp and painful, as though it were trying to break free from her chest. The blood drained from her face and down her spine, leaving her cold, lightheaded, trembling. Her legs gave out, and she sank into the nearest chair before she could collapse outright.

They must be stopped. The ships. The soldiers. The assassinations. The uprising. All of it had to be stopped before the country tore itself apart under the weight of their violence.

Hope pressed a hand over her mouth to keep from gasping aloud, fighting the panic clawing at her throat. Her mind raced. Her mother's diary. The secrets it held. The truths she still hadn't uncovered. That diary suddenly felt as vital as breath itself.

*Where is your diary, Mama?* she thought desperately. *What did you discover? What did you leave behind for me to find?* Because whatever answers her mother had hidden might be the last chance they had.

Hope, weak, shaking, disguised in men's clothes, had stumbled into the heart of a conspiracy capable of destroying nations. She swallowed hard and forced her spine straight, drawing on every ounce of resolve she had left. She couldn't faint. She couldn't freeze. She couldn't run. She had work to do.

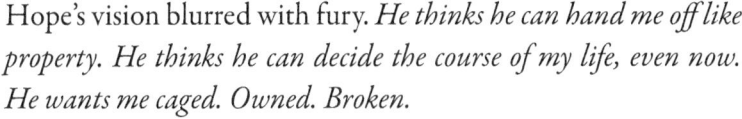

"I also want you men to find Hope," Winston Spencer growled, his voice low and venomous. "If she shows her face at the festivities, we need to reach her before she has a chance to warn the president."

Hope's stomach twisted violently. Her father's voice, so cold, so absolute, sent a chill racing down her spine.

"And I want her alive," he continued, each word dripping with ownership and cruelty. "I will be the one to punish her for her disobedience."

Hope bit hard into the inside of her cheek to keep herself silent, even as rage flared hot and sharp in her chest.

"With Eric out of the picture now," her father went on, "I've already secured a new husband for her. A man who will not tolerate even a hint of rebellion. He will keep her under control, properly this time."

The men around the table exchanged looks. Some shifted uneasily. Others smirked, clearly entertained by the notion. Hope's hands curled into fists in her lap.

*Over my dead body.*

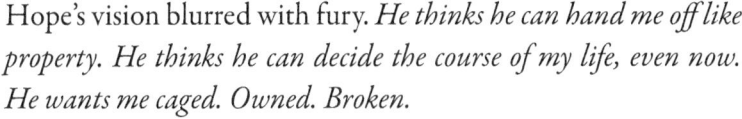

Hope's vision blurred with fury. *He thinks he can hand me off like property. He thinks he can decide the course of my life, even now. He wants me caged. Owned. Broken.*

But she wasn't eight years old anymore. She wasn't meek, as her mother had been forced to become. And she wasn't alone. Her hands trembled slightly where they rested beneath the table, but the fire inside her only burned hotter.

If her father thought he could drag her back under his control, he had no idea who she had become.

*Never again,* she promised silently. *No man will ever own me. Not him. Not any of them.* Not while she still had breath in her lungs.

Hope rode hard toward the cabin, her breath catching in her throat as panic and purpose warred inside her. If they didn't stop this conspiracy in time, countless lives would be lost, families torn apart, the entire country overturned, freedom smothered beneath tyranny. The thought alone made her chest tighten.

*I will not let that happen,* she vowed fiercely. As she approached the clearing, she spotted several horses tied near the cabin. Good. Brent, Sawyer, and Logan were already here. Relief flickered through her, but it was quickly chased away by dread. Logan looked too much like William. If her father or Gregory saw him, they would kill him on sight. He could not risk setting foot in town until this nightmare was over.

Hope swung off her horse, her mind racing with everything she'd overheard in the saloon. She hurried toward the cabin door, reaching for the latch. A hand clamped around her arm. Another slapped over her mouth. She was yanked sideways, dragged away from the door and behind the cabin.

Hope screamed, but the sound was smothered beneath the man's palm. She kicked and twisted, fighting with everything she had, but he was too strong, his grip iron, his body a wall behind her.

When he spun her to face him, recognition slammed into her. One of Whitmer's men. Her heart lurched painfully.

"Well, well," he snarled, leaning so close she could smell the hot, rancid stink of his breath. "Yer pa's gonna be mighty pleased when I drag you back to him." His lips curled into a cruel, self-satisfied smirk. "Knew somethin' was off 'bout you, showin' up at that saloon day after day. Anthony's a damn fool, couldn't see past his own nose. But I did."

Hope jerked her face away, fury overtaking fear.

"Unhand me at once," she hissed, shoving both hands against his chest. He only pressed himself harder against her.

"Did ya truly think a hat an' a pair o' trousers was gonna fool anybody?" he drawled, his gaze crawling over her in a way that made her stomach heave. "You're too little to pass for a man. Too soft." His hand drifted toward her jaw, slow and ugly. "Even now... I can tell exactly what you are." His lips brushed her cheek, wet, unwanted, revolting.

Hope's stomach churned. Her skin crawled. He was just like Jared. Another man who believed he could dominate her simply because he was stronger. No. Not again.

"Help!" she screamed, forcing every ounce of strength into her voice. "Somebody, help me!"

The man cursed and slammed her back against the cabin wall, his hand clamping over her mouth again. Pain shot through her shoulder.

"You ain't slippin' away from me, Hope Spencer," he growled. "I'm haulin' you straight to yer pa, and then—"

His mistake was talking. While his mouth moved, Hope's hand moved faster. She reached for his holster, fingers closing around the grip of his gun. In one fluid motion, born of pure instinct and survival, she ripped it free and slammed the heavy metal hard against his skull. His eyes rolled back. He crumpled to the ground like a sack of flour.

Hope staggered away, her entire body shaking. She didn't wait to see if he would stir. She ran, nearly tripping over a tree root, straight for her horse. She grabbed the saddle, ready to haul herself up and flee before another attacker appeared, when a hand closed around her arm again. Hope whirled, a strangled gasp tearing from her throat, her heart plummeting.

"Hope."

It was Logan. His brown eyes were wild with concern as they searched her face.

"What happened?" he demanded. "We heard you call for help."

The sound of his voice, familiar, steady, fiercely protective, nearly buckled her knees. She opened her mouth, but no words came. Not yet. Not with fear still gripping her like a vice.

She swallowed her tears and forced herself to speak, her voice breaking as she explained what had just happened behind the cabin. Logan's jaw tightened with every word, his eyes darkening, his body bristling with fury he was barely containing.

Only when he turned did she notice Brent, Sawyer, and an older man standing a few yards away, having heard everything. Hope stiffened. The older man wore a badge, *U.S. Marshal*, engraved in metal that glinted under the moonlight. Her breath caught, her eyes widening in shock.

Before she could say a word, the three men rushed to the unconscious attacker, who was beginning to stir. They grabbed him roughly under the arms and dragged him toward the barn. Logan gently touched Hope's cheek, his thumb brushing away a tear she hadn't realized had fallen, then guided her inside. Her legs trembled beneath her, and he didn't let go until she was seated. Moments later, he pressed a warm cup of tea into her shaking hands.

Sawyer and the marshal stepped into the cabin shortly after, shutting out the cold night air.

"Where is Brent?" Hope asked, trying to steady her breath. Her voice trembled despite her efforts, tears still clinging to her lashes. Sawyer gave her a reassuring smile.

"He's keeping watch on the man we tied up. And Hope," he added, gesturing toward the older man beside him, "this is our Uncle Jeff. We sent him an urgent telegram. He dropped everything and came as fast as he could."

Hope turned to face the marshal fully. The moment their eyes met, something inside her jolted. The shape of his jaw. The warm brown of his eyes. There was no mistaking it, he bore her mother's features. Tears blurred her vision, and before she could gather herself, Marshal Jeff Stewart crossed the room in three long strides.

He took her hand, studying her face with something between wonder and heartbreak, then pulled her into a firm, protective embrace. Hope's composure shattered. She clung to him as sobs wracked her small frame.

"It is so good to finally see and hold you, Hope," he murmured into her hair. "Ever since we received Georgiana's letters, ever since she begged us to get you away from your father, I've prayed for your safety every day." He held her until her sobs quieted, then gently tipped her chin up so she met his eyes.

"You look just like your mother," he whispered with a trembling smile. "Georgiana was one of the loveliest souls I have ever known."

Hope smiled through her tears, her heart swelling.

"Thank you, Uncle Jeff. It's good to finally meet my mom's family. I... I can't wait to meet everyone." She drew a shaky breath. "What's going to happen to the man who attacked me? He said neither Anthony Whitmer nor my father knows I'm here yet. Can we keep him away from them? I don't want him warning anyone."

Jeff nodded. "We'll take him back to our ranch tonight. I'll send for my deputies from there so he can be taken into custody quietly. No one will know he's been captured."

Hope released a slow, relieved breath, then quickly recounted everything she had overheard earlier in the saloon, the conspiracy, the planned attacks, the timeline. By the time she finished, her uncle's expression had hardened into pure alarm.

"That doesn't give us much time," he said grimly. "Tonight, I'll contact marshal headquarters in Washington and San Francisco. We'll alert the army as well, but we must do it covertly. If they suspect we're onto them, they'll strike early."

Hope frowned. "But will telegraphing be safe? We don't know who they've bribed or coerced. They could intercept everything."

Jeff squeezed her hand reassuringly.

"There are emergency channels for situations exactly like this, underground Morse stations, private relays, trusted operators scattered across the territory and country. We'll reach the right people without tipping off the wrong ones. I promise you that."

Hope nodded slowly, comforted but still anxious.

"Will you prevent the president from stopping here?" she asked. Her uncle shook his head.

"No. Keeping the visit as planned will draw every conspirator out of hiding. It gives us the best chance to capture them all at once. And we will take every measure possible to safeguard the president."

Hope inhaled sharply as understanding settled over her. They weren't just fighting for her mother anymore. They were fighting for the country. And time was running out.

The morning of the festivities dawned crisp and bright, as though the sky itself had no idea the nation hung on a knife's edge. Hope had barely slept, but she rose before the sun, saddled her horse, and headed into Cheyenne long before most of the town had stirred. She hadn't seen Uncle Jeff since their meeting at the cabin, but she trusted him. Trusted he and his deputies were already in place, hidden somewhere amid the rising excitement. Today would determine everything.

By the time she reached Cheyenne, the town was already alive with anticipation. People poured into the streets dressed in their finest, lace-trimmed bonnets, polished boots, pressed suits. Families clustered together, children perched on railings for a better view, vendors shouting over one another as they sold flags, ribbons, and warm bread to the swelling crowd.

Hope slipped into the background, choosing a shadowed spot along the side of the railroad station where she could see everything without being seen. Her pulse thundered. Every breath felt tight as she scanned the crowd.

There, her father, Winston Spencer, standing tall in his immaculate coat, his expression carved from stone. She had never seen him look so alert, so predatory. Two gunmen lingered close to him, pretending to be ordinary townsfolk, but she recognized them from the saloon. Gregory, her half-brother, was nowhere in sight. Hope's stomach tightened. *Where was he? Had he already boarded the presidential train? Was he part of the escort?* Or worse, was he positioning himself somewhere she couldn't see?

A whistle pierced the air. The crowd surged forward as the train approached, steam billowing around it like a curtain of fog. Hope pressed herself harder against the wall, her eyes darting across windows, rooftops, alleys. Then she saw him. Anthony Whitmer crouched on the roof of the feed store across from the station. His rifle rested on the ledge, angled directly toward the platform where the president would step out. Hope's breath caught in her throat.

One shot. One moment of distraction. That was all it would take. Her heart hammered so violently it felt as though it might break through her ribs. She had to move. She had to warn someone. She had to stop him. But one wrong move could expose her, and if her father or any of Whitmer's men spotted her before she reached help, they would silence her before she could speak a word. For a split second, panic clawed up her spine. Then she inhaled sharply, steadying herself.

*No matter what happens, she vowed, I will not let him kill the president.*

When the train finally hissed to a halt, steam curling through the air like fog, the first person to step onto the platform was an older, distinguished-looking gentleman, followed closely by a young red-haired woman whose smile could have lit half the town. Hope's heart sank the instant she recognized her. Harriet Silvers. Of course. The mayor's daughter.

No wonder she strutted through life as though she owned the entire Wyoming Territory. Hope watched as Harriet clung proudly to her father's arm, then turned toward the crowd, practically preening as her gaze swept eagerly over the platform. She was looking for Logan.

A sharp spark of jealousy pricked Hope's chest, hot, irrational, unwelcome. She tightened her jaw and forced it aside.

*Focus, Hope. You're not here to compete with anyone. You're here to save lives.* Keeping her head low, she slipped along the length of the train, scanning faces and uniforms as passengers disembarked. Marshals. Deputy marshals. Soldiers. More deputies. She recognized many by their badges and the rigid alertness in their posture. But she wasn't looking for them.

She was looking for her uncle. Then she saw someone else, the person she most wished she hadn't. Gregory Spencer. Her half-brother stepped down from one of the passenger cars and immediately strode across the platform with sharp, purposeful determination. Hope froze behind a stack of trunks, watching him until he disappeared into the crowd. Only then did she slip from her hiding place and hurry toward the train.

She had to find her uncle. Had to warn someone before Whitmer made his move from the rooftop. She mounted the steps of the first-class compartment and slipped inside, hurrying down the corridor, when a hand clamped around her arm.

"Where do you think you're going, boy?" a deputy barked. Hope kept her head down, praying her voice wouldn't tremble. Before she could answer, a second deputy reached up and yanked the hat from her head. Both men froze. A girl. And not just any girl, a girl dressed as a boy, sneaking aboard the presidential train.

"Please," Hope said breathlessly. "I'm trying to warn the president of a planned attack." She tried to move past them, but both deputies seized her arms again.

"You're not going anywhere, young lady," one snapped. "A disguise like that means you're hiding something."

"I'm hiding from my father because he's trying to kill me!" she shot back, panic sharpening her voice. She struggled against their grip as they dragged her toward the door. "Please, listen to me! The president is in grave danger! If you won't let me go, then at least call my uncle, Marshal Jeff Stewart!"

The name stopped them cold. They exchanged a startled glance. Then the doorway filled with a broad-shouldered figure.

"Hope?"

Relief crashed through her. "Uncle Jeff."

The deputies released her instantly. Jeff Stewart crossed the compartment in three long strides and wrapped her in a fierce, protective embrace.

"What in heaven's name are you doing here?" he murmured, pulling back just enough to see her face. Hope grabbed his arm and pointed through the window.

"Whitmer is on the roof of that building. He has a rifle. He's waiting for the president."

Jeff's expression hardened. "What about the others?"

"My father is in the crowd. Gregory got off the train, but I lost track of him."

One of the deputies frowned. "What's wrong with Marshal Spencer?"

Jeff turned on him sharply. "He is involved in this conspiracy and the murder plot. Both he and his father."

The deputies blanched. Jeff turned back to Hope.

"You need to get somewhere safe. Now."

Hope shook her head, stubborn resolve blazing in her eyes.

"No. If I run, my father or his men might see me. And Mrs. Archer is with the Shaw family, she's a witness. We can't risk leading anyone to her."

Jeff studied her for a heartbeat, then nodded grimly.

"All right. Stay hidden. And stay quiet." He turned to the deputies. "You two, move. If you hurry, you can reach Whitmer before he pulls that trigger."

They bolted from the compartment. Hope barely had time to breathe before another presence filled the doorway. The president himself stepped inside. Hope's breath caught. She straightened instinctively.

"Young lady," he said warmly, his voice rich with sincerity, "your courage in coming here today, and delivering this warning, has undoubtedly saved lives. I am deeply grateful."

Hope curtsied, her heart pounding.

"It is my honor, Mr. President. These men must be stopped. They already murdered my mother."

A shadow crossed his eyes, anger, sympathy, and iron resolve.

"Then justice," he said quietly, "will be served."

When Hope stepped off the train and onto the platform, she pulled her hat low over her face, blending into the shadows beside the railcar. Her boots hit the ground softly, but her pulse thundered in her ears. She forced herself to breathe slowly as she glanced around. Where was Gregory?

She scanned the crowd again, her heart thudding harder with each passing second. Her father stood exactly where she had seen him earlier, rigid, expectant, his eyes sweeping the station as if he owned every person present. But her half-brother was nowhere to be seen. That was not good.

If Gregory wasn't here, he had to be somewhere close. Somewhere hidden. Somewhere dangerous. Her gaze lifted to the rooftops, to windows, to every vantage point a trained killer might use. Then it returned to the man she feared nearly as much as her father, Anthony Whitmer. Where are the marshals? Why hasn't he been arrested yet?

Hope watched him nervously. He was already in position, rifle raised, body angled forward with deadly intent. The sight of him sent a cold bolt of horror straight through her. He was seconds from firing. A roar surged across the station. The president had stepped onto the platform. He walked into the sunlight with a warm, confident smile, lifting a hand in greeting. The citizens of Cheyenne erupted in cheers, pressing forward for a better glimpse. Flags waved. Hats lifted. Children squealed. The train's brass gleamed behind him like a stage.

Hope remained tucked into the cool shadow of the railcar, but her hands curled into fists. Her entire body vibrated with tension. She still couldn't see Gregory. He could strike from anywhere.

But Whitmer—Whitmer was right there.

Hope's breath hitched. Then she saw movement. Subtle at first. Then unmistakable. Two marshal deputies appeared at the base of the building Whitmer occupied. Then two more. They climbed swiftly, efficiently, men who had received clear, urgent orders. Hope's heart pounded so violently she thought it might burst. Whitmer adjusted his aim.

At that exact moment, a deputy lunged over the roof's edge and seized him. The rifle clattered across the rooftop. Whitmer swung an elbow, but another deputy tackled him from behind. The struggle was brief, furious, desperate, but within moments he was overpowered, pinned, and disarmed. Hope sagged against the train, nearly weak with relief. A breath escaped her, a long, trembling exhale she hadn't realized she'd been holding.

One threat neutralized. But the other, the half-brother she still hadn't seen, her muscles tightened again. The danger wasn't over. Not even close. But for this one moment, she allowed herself a single thought, warm and fierce: *Mama... we stopped him.*

All of it unfolded so quickly, and so quietly, that the crowd remained blissfully unaware. Cheers and chatter drowned out the scuffle on the rooftop. No one noticed that Anthony Whitmer was now handcuffed, dragged away by federal marshals like a venomous snake finally subdued.

No one... except Hope.

Her uncle caught her eye across the platform. A single, grave nod passed between them, confirming that Whitmer was no longer a threat. Hope released a shaky breath. Then the president stepped forward to address the town, lifting his hand for silence. The crowd hushed at once, a ripple of stillness spreading outward from the platform. Excitement and pride filled the air, hats pressed over hearts, children perched on shoulders, every face turned expectantly toward the man about to speak.

That was when she saw him. Gregory Spencer. Her half-brother stood on the saloon porch, half-hidden behind a thick wooden beam that cast his body in shadow. The sun blazed behind him, obscuring his features, but Hope recognized the rigid line of his jaw, the coiled tension in his stance. A chill slid down her spine.

She tried to catch someone's attention, anyone. She lifted her hand. Motioned. Took a step forward. Whispered hoarsely to the nearest deputy. But every marshal and soldier was scanning the dense crowd in front of them, never once looking back toward the saloon. They were watching the wrong direction. Gregory was behind them.

Hope's pulse hammered. Her throat tightened. She kept her gaze locked on him, unwilling to blink. One moment of distraction, it felt like it could cost the president his life. And then a horrifying realization struck her. Father.

She tore her eyes away from Gregory just long enough to find Winston Spencer in the crowd. He stood near the front, hands folded neatly behind his back like a dignified spectator. But his expression... Hope's stomach twisted. His smile was wrong. Thin. Icy. Expectant. Deliberately, Winston inclined his head toward his son. A signal.

"No," Hope breathed, dread freezing her from the inside out. Her gaze snapped back to Gregory just as he stepped out of the shadows and into full sunlight. His hand slid inside his coat. When it emerged, he held a gun, already cocked, already raised, already aimed straight at the president's heart.

Hope's breath seized. Time slowed. The world narrowed to a single, horrifying image: Gregory Spencer, son of her father, brother by blood, assassin by choice, ready to murder the leader of the nation. And no one else had seen him. Not yet. But Hope had. And she knew she had only seconds to stop him.

Without a single thought for her own safety, Hope sprinted forward. Harriet, standing closest to the president, whirled just as Hope lunged past her. Instead of moving aside, she lifted a trembling hand and shrieked, her voice slicing through the air like a blade.

"He is going to attack the president!" Her words rang across the platform, sharp, panicked. But her finger was pointed at

Hope. Every soldier and marshal on the platform instinctively turned toward the commotion, toward Hope, and not toward the real danger behind them.

"No!" Hope cried, but the sound was swallowed by the roar of the crowd. A hand shot out, trying to grab her arm. Hope twisted away, leaping out of reach with every ounce of strength she possessed. She knew she had only one breath, one heartbeat, before Gregory pulled the trigger. She hurled herself at the president just as a shot cracked through the air.

The bullet tore through her shoulder an instant before she collided with him. She wrapped her arms around the older man, twisting so that her body took the brunt of the attack as they crashed brutally to the ground. Screams erupted. Panic swept the platform like wildfire. Marshals and soldiers surged forward, forming a shield around the president so quickly it was impossible to tell where one man ended, and another began. Some aimed their rifles toward the saloon. Others scanned the rooftops. A few grabbed for Hope, trying to pull her away from the president's fallen form.

"Stop!" the president barked, his voice fierce. "Do not touch him, he saved my life!"

The deputies froze. Harriet, still shrieking, stumbled backward until her father seized her arm and hissed for her to be silent. The entire crowd had turned toward the platform now, eyes wide, faces pale, trying to understand what had just happened.

# 20

# Into the Fire

Jeff reached Hope in seconds, dropping to his knees beside her. He pulled her gently into his arms, horror etched into every line of his face.

"Why did you do that?" His voice cracked. "Hope, why did you jump in front of the president?"

Hope opened her eyes, their brightness dulled by pain, and coughed weakly.

"I had to... nobody saw Gregory but me."

Her uncle sucked in a sharp breath.

"Doctor!" he shouted. "We need a doctor here, now!"

Hope winced as she breathed. Fire radiated from her shoulder with every small movement.

"Stay with me," Jeff urged. She swallowed hard.

"Please... don't let my father see me," she whispered, her voice barely audible. "And... don't tell Logan what happened." She tried to draw another breath, but the pain was too sharp. She coughed again, and her vision blurred. Shadows crept into the edges of her sight.

"Hope. Hope!" her uncle called, his voice breaking as he held her. But the world was already slipping away. The noise, the shouts, the president calling for help, everything faded into a hollow, distant echo. Hope exhaled one last trembling breath. Then darkness overtook her completely.

"Jeff," a voice called sharply behind the marshal. Jeff turned just as the town doctor dropped to his knees beside him. The man's breath caught when he saw the blood soaking Hope's shirt, and then his eyes widened further as a few loose strands of her long hair slipped free from beneath her hat.

"My word..." he whispered. "She's a woman. And she—she took the bullet for the president?"

Jeff could barely speak. His voice tightened with fear as he nodded, one trembling hand brushing a strand of hair from Hope's pale face. The doctor pressed a hand to her shoulder, quickly assessing the wound.

"We're losing time. Jeff, can you carry her to my clinic?"

Jeff nodded again, more firmly this time. Without hesitation, he slid one arm beneath Hope's back and the other beneath her knees and lifted her gently but swiftly into his arms. Her head rested against his shoulder, limp and frighteningly still.

"Easy, Hope... I've got you," he murmured, his voice breaking. Sawyer and Brent sprang forward at once, their expressions fierce and protective. They stepped in close, forming a human shield around their cousin as Jeff carried her across the platform.

"Stay close," the doctor ordered as he rose and led the way through the chaotic crowd. Sawyer nodded sharply, positioning himself at Jeff's right, while Brent moved to his left. Their broad shoulders and determined strides created a wall of protection, shielding Hope from the public's stunned, curious, and prying glances.

Behind them, townspeople murmured in disbelief. Soldiers shouted orders. Marshals scrambled to secure the scene. But Jeff saw none of it. His entire world had narrowed to the fragile weight in his arms.

"Hold on, Hope," he whispered as they hurried toward the clinic. "Hold on, sweetheart... don't leave us now."

Sawyer swallowed hard at the words. Brent clenched his jaw, his eyes fixed straight ahead. And together, the three men rushed her toward safety, praying they were not already too late.

---

"Did you see that, Pa? That was a girl, not a boy." Harriet's voice trembled with a volatile mix of excitement and spite as she watched Jeff Stewart disappear into the crowd, Hope limp in his arms. Mayor Silvers narrowed his eyes.

"It appears so," he murmured. "Doesn't look like anyone we know, though."

"Oh, I wouldn't be so sure," Harriet replied, her lips curving into a knowing smirk. "I bet that's the girl Logan brought back with him. His niece told me her name was Hope."

"Hope?" Her father's eyebrow shot up. "Spencer?" His tone sharpened. "Wait... I've seen a Wanted Poster for a Hope Spencer. Her father offered a thousand-dollar reward for her return." He scanned the scattering crowd again, calculation flickering behind his gaze, before a slow, greedy grin spread across his face.

But Harriet was no longer watching the marshal, or Hope. Her attention had shifted to the fringes of the platform. Something tugged at her awareness. A movement where there shouldn't have been one. Her gaze locked onto Gregory Spencer just as he slipped behind the saloon, vanishing into the shadows. Her breath hitched. So that's the man who shot her... Logan's precious Hope.

The realization ignited something ugly inside her, envy, humiliation, resentment, all twisting together into bitter resolve. She straightened her shoulders, lifted her chin, and smoothed her curls with a sharp, deliberate flick of her fingers.

"I know exactly what I have to do," she whispered to herself, eyes glittering with vindictive purpose. And without another moment's hesitation, Harriet Silvers turned toward her father, her expression alight with eager determination.

⁂

They followed the doctor into the clinic, boots thudding urgently against the wooden floor. Bright lamplight flooded the small surgery as Jeff carried Hope inside and gently lowered her onto the examination table. Her face was pale, far too pale, and her breathing shallow.

The doctor moved immediately, barking orders to the nurse who hurried in behind them. Before Jeff could steal even one more look at his niece, the nurse ushered him out and shut the door firmly. The click of the latch echoed like a gunshot.

Sawyer and Brent leaned against the wall nearby, their expressions tight with worry, and fear. Jeff exhaled shakily and pressed his hand to the wall, as if to steady himself. Then he began to pace, long, restless strides back and forth across the narrow hallway. His jaw was clenched, his fists opening and closing at his sides. He had expected danger. He had not expected *this*.

Hope, sweet, fierce, stubborn Hope, had thrown herself between the president and a bullet. She hadn't hesitated. She hadn't faltered. She had acted before the soldiers, before the marshals... before him. The realization sent a tremor through his chest. She saved the president's life.

*My sister's daughter saved the president.* And now she lay behind that closed door, bleeding because she had done the bravest, and most reckless, thing he had ever witnessed. Jeff dragged a hand through his hair, swallowing the tight ache building in his throat. He had promised Georgiana he would protect Hope. Keep her safe. Give her the life she deserved. He had sworn it over the trembling ink of her final letter, prayed it over her memory. And now he felt as though he had failed her.

He stopped pacing and stared at the closed door, his expression carved from anguish and fierce resolve.

"Hold on, Hope," he whispered. "Please... just hold on."

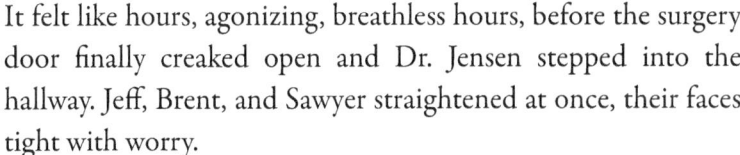

It felt like hours, agonizing, breathless hours, before the surgery door finally creaked open and Dr. Jensen stepped into the hallway. Jeff, Brent, and Sawyer straightened at once, their faces tight with worry.

"She should be all right," the doctor said, wiping his hands on a cloth. "We removed the bullet. As long as the wound doesn't become infected, she's strong enough to make a full recovery."

Three deep, shaky breaths filled the corridor at once. Brent ran a hand through his hair and leaned back against the wall in visible relief.

"Is she awake, Dr. Jensen?" he asked quickly.

The doctor shook his head. "Not yet. She's still unconscious from blood loss and shock." His expression shifted, curiosity flickering across his features. "Do you know who she is?"

The cousins exchanged glances before turning to Jeff. The marshal exhaled slowly and cleared his throat.

"She's my niece," he said quietly. "My sister Georgiana's daughter."

The doctor's eyes widened. "Good grief... How did she get all the way here?"

"Logan brought her," Jeff replied. "Under the belief she'd be safer away from San Francisco. But she was determined to follow her mother's murderer and tracked him to Cheyenne. We caught Whitmer before the shooting occurred." His jaw tightened. "But her father and half-brother are here as well. They're involved in this conspiracy to overthrow the government, and they want her back. Badly."

Dr. Jensen paled. "Do you believe one of them fired at the president?"

Jeff nodded grimly. "Yes. Harriet Silvers caused a commotion that distracted everyone, so most didn't see the shooter. But Hope must have. That's why she ran forward." His voice dropped. "That's why she took the bullet."

The doctor let out a long, shaken breath.

"Do your parents know she's here?"

Jeff shook his head. "No. Georgiana contacted me in secret before her death, begging me to get Hope out before her husband discovered what she knew. Only Logan and his brother William were aware of the plan. Brent and Sawyer met her by chance when she took shelter at one of our cabins."

Jeff took a step toward the front door.

"I need to check on the president."

But the door opened before he could reach it, and the president himself stepped inside.

"I'm well," he announced, lifting a hand before Jeff could speak. "And I have ample security for the moment, Marshal Stewart. Please, stay with your niece. It is the least we owe her after she saved my life."

Jeff bowed his head respectfully, but the president wasn't finished.

"When she wakes," he added, his tone warming, "ask her if she'd like to join the federal marshal service. A young woman with instincts like that would be invaluable."

The men exchanged brief, startled smiles at the dry humor, but the president's expression soon sobered.

"She has risked a great deal to warn us of today's events," he said quietly. "And the fact that she not only spotted a second threat but acted without hesitation... that takes rare courage." He placed a hand on Jeff's shoulder. "Give her my sincerest thanks. And if she chooses not to be a marshal," he added with a faint smile, "I would be honored to have her in my cabinet." With that, the president turned and left the clinic, leaving the three men stunned, humbled, and more determined than ever to see Hope wake safely.

It was another long, breath-holding hour before Hope finally stirred. Her eyelashes fluttered, then her eyes opened, hazy and confused. The moment she woke, her uncle and cousins were leaning over her, relief flooding their faces.

"Uncle Jeff... Brent... Sawyer..." Her voice was small and strained, and she struggled to keep her eyes open. A sharp, stabbing pain radiated through her shoulder, and she released a soft groan. Jeff immediately cupped her cheek with a trembling hand.

"Oh, Hope," he breathed, his voice thick with emotion. "I still can't believe you threw yourself in front of the president like that."

She winced and swallowed. "Gregory would have killed him," she whispered. "The sun was blinding everyone else. He blended right into the glare. I only saw him because... I was standing at a different angle. I noticed movement."

Jeff's jaw tightened. "So, it was Marshal Spencer who fired the shot?" His tone was low, dangerous. Hope nodded weakly. Sawyer exchanged a stunned look with Brent.

"What's going to happen now?" Brent asked, turning toward their uncle. Jeff exhaled slowly.

"The marshals are hunting Gregory and Winston Spencer. Headquarters in Washington and San Francisco have already received the emergency alerts. We've ordered mass arrests for everyone connected to the conspiracy. Once Winston, Gregory, and their hired men are caught, Mrs. Archer will give her testimony."

Sawyer moved closer and took Hope's hand gently between both of his.

"Hope, are you in pain?" His face was etched with worry.

She nodded. "A little... but it's bearable." Her gaze drifted back to her uncle. "Do you think Father and Gregory already left Cheyenne?"

Jeff shook his head grimly. "No. They know every marshal across three territories will be hunting them, and if they aren't caught soon, it'll turn into a full-country manhunt. My guess? They're holed up somewhere close, waiting for the crowds to thin out."

Before Hope could respond, a quiet voice interrupted them.

"Gentlemen," Dr. Jensen said as he stepped into the room, "I'm afraid I must ask you all to leave. This young lady has had enough excitement for one day and needs rest." He gave Hope a warm, reassuring smile.

Her uncle bent down, pressed a gentle kiss to her forehead, and whispered, "You're safe now, sweetheart."

Brent and Sawyer each hugged her carefully, though Sawyer muttered something about wrapping her in cotton, so she'd never scare them like this again. Hope offered them a tired but grateful smile as they filed out of the room. Jeff hesitated at the doorway, looking back at her with fierce tenderness.

"I'll be meeting with the president now," he said softly. "Rest. When you wake, we'll have a plan."

Then he was gone, leaving Hope to the doctor's care, and to the growing ache of exhaustion finally overtaking her.

"Did you find out who that young man was, the one who threw himself in front of the president?" Winston Spencer growled, pacing like a caged bull. "Someone here must have known about our plan. They arrested Whitmer before he could fire a single shot." He slammed his fist against the doorframe just as Gregory entered the hotel room, a young woman slipping in behind him. Winston's eyes narrowed at the sight of her.

"What is this, Gregory?" he snapped. "Why is she here?"

His son scoffed, folding his arms.

"Because she saw what happened. She saw who took the bullet meant for the president." He jerked his chin toward Harriet. Winston raised an eyebrow.

"Well then? Who was he?"

Harriet inhaled sharply. She didn't like being here, every instinct warned her these men were dangerous, but greed and pride had lodged themselves too deeply to back out now.

"It wasn't a young man," she said, her voice wavering only slightly. "It was your daughter. She took the bullet for the president."

"What?" Winston roared, his face flushing a violent shade of red. He stepped forward as if he might strike her. "Are you absolutely sure?"

Harriet nodded. "She's not from here. She was disguised as a boy. And Logan Shaw returned from a mission recently. Everyone knows he's the one protecting her."

"Curse that girl," Winston spat, smashing his fist against the wooden frame again before forcing himself to breathe. He dragged a hand down his face. "Thank you for the information." He flicked his fingers toward the door. "You may go."

But Harriet didn't move.

"What now?" Winston snapped.

"The reward money," she said, lifting her chin. "You know, the money you promised to whoever returned your daughter."

"What money?" Winston growled.

Harriet didn't flinch. "The one thousand dollars you offered for Hope Spencer. I just delivered her location to you. Unless you want me to tell the sheriff and the marshals that you're behind all this, you'd better honor your end of the bargain."

Gregory snorted, amused, and a few of the other men chuckled darkly. But Winston's glare could have cut stone.

"You've got quite the mouth, girl," he hissed. "Threatening me won't go well for you. Leave before we lose our patience."

Harriet gave him a cold smile. "I'm not afraid of you, Mr. Spencer. My father, the mayor, knows exactly where I am and why I'm here. He told me I had thirty minutes to meet with you. If I don't return on time, he'll hand you straight over to the marshals." Her eyes glittered with arrogance.

Winston unleashed a string of curses under his breath. Finally, with a vicious snap of his fingers, he motioned to Gregory. Gregory retrieved a small leather pouch and shoved it into Harriet's waiting hand. She opened it, counted just enough bills to feel satisfied, then flashed them a triumphant smile.

"Pleasure doing business with you, gentlemen," she said sweetly before slipping out of the room. The moment the door shut, Winston began pacing again, seething.

"We have to get out of this town immediately," he snarled. "I don't trust that woman or her father. They'll blackmail us for more money if we stay another hour." He stopped abruptly, his voice dropping to a low, venomous growl.

"Let's go get Hope. That little beast will pay for crossing me. I knew her mother was ill-tempered, but our daughter, she hid her true nature well." His lip curled with contempt as he turned sharply toward his men. "Keep eyes on the marshals and the soldiers. Move quietly. Meet us at the cabin."

The men nodded, checking their weapons before slipping out of the hotel room and blending into the bustling streets of Cheyenne, shadows melting into shadows, closing in on their prey.

"Is there anything I can get for you, Miss Spencer?" the nurse asked gently. Hope nodded, her throat painfully dry.

"I'm really thirsty. Could you fetch me some water, please?"

"Of course. I'll be right back." The nurse hurried out, and Hope exhaled slowly. Her shoulder throbbed, and despite the pain medicine, her body felt weak and unsteady. She shifted, trying to sit up a little straighter, when she heard the door open again.

"That was quick," she murmured, starting to turn her head toward the sound. Before she could finish the movement, a large hand clamped over her nose and mouth, pressing a damp cloth against her face. The smell hit her instantly, sharp, chemical, suffocating.

Hope gasped instinctively, but the breath she drew was thick and numbing. Panic shot through her veins. She clawed weakly at the hand, trying to push it away, but her injured shoulder screamed in protest. Her heartbeat thundered in her ears. The room tilted.

The figure leaning over her was nothing but a shadow, cold, determined hands and merciless strength. She fought once... twice... her fingers curling around air. But the drug worked fast.

Her limbs grew heavy, her vision wavering. The ceiling blurred into a gray haze. The last thing she registered, was the helpless sinking of her body back into the pillow. Then darkness swallowed her whole.

Claire jumped from her chair the moment the knock sounded at the front door. Before her grandparents even had the chance to rise, she was already darting into the hallway.

"I'll get it," she called, breathless with urgency. She swung the door open. "Mayor Silvers, come on in," she said politely, though his stiff posture and icy expression immediately unsettled her. She led him into the sitting room, where Marjorie and Robert Shaw stood to greet him. Logan entered from the adjoining room just as Claire stepped aside.

"Thomas, what brings you here?" Robert asked, offering his hand. The mayor shook it, but the gesture was cold, almost hostile.

"I've come to have a discussion with Logan, and how he treated my daughter the last time she was here," he said sharply. The words hit the room like a spark to gunpowder. Marjorie stiffened. Robert's jaw tightened. Logan's entire posture went rigid.

"How I treated your daughter?" Logan shot back, fury flashing in his eyes. Claire slipped quietly from the room, instinctively avoiding what she knew was about to explode. "Harriet came here to manipulate me into marrying her—and insulted my mother in the most disgraceful ways."

"What did she say that was so insulting?" Thomas challenged, his voice dripping with sarcasm.

Logan scoffed. "Your same old lies about my parents having a relationship before marriage. I visited your wife that same day and told her everything. Did she not inform you?"

"No, she didn't. And frankly," the mayor added with a vicious smirk, "I don't recall that being a lie."

Logan's fists curled. Robert looked ready to strike him. But Marjorie stepped forward, her voice steady and sharp as glass.

"You are a disgraceful, selfish man, Thomas. It is time you let the past go. I chose Robert for a reason, and your behavior made that decision very easy. I never cared for you. Your attempts to manipulate me and my parents only repulsed me."

Thomas's expression curdled into contempt, his eyes turning dark and ugly.

"Well," he sneered, "too bad your parents are no longer alive. I imagine they'd be devastated to hear how much you entertained men whenever they traveled for your father's work. The fact that you didn't run a brothel—"

Robert lunged before he could finish, his fist cracking against the mayor's jaw and sending him stumbling. Logan grabbed him next, slamming him back against the wall. Thomas struggled, but Logan held him pinned with unyielding fury. Before the situation could escalate further, another voice cut sharply through the tension.

"Mayor Silvers, you are a disgrace to your family name and to this town." Mrs. Archer stepped into the room like a storm, her presence commanding instant silence. "I have seen men behave poorly when they are rejected," she continued coolly, "but you are the perfect example of an ego rotted beyond repair. And

I trust you are aware of the many connections I have across this country, including several very influential people in San Francisco."

Thomas froze.

"I am also a close friend of the governor and first lady of Wyoming," she went on crisply. "Your time as mayor is finished. I will call a special council meeting. You will not be reelected."

"Mrs. Archer—" Thomas sputtered, paling.

"Enough," she snapped, silencing him with a glare. "I know about your money laundering and corrupt railroad dealings, just like my husband's. And I know about your infidelities, just like his. We have tolerated your dishonesty for far too long. And now, you will pay for it."

Thomas jerked toward the door, but Logan slammed him back against the wall, harder this time.

"I'll send one of the cowboys to fetch the sheriff," Robert said through gritted teeth. "We're locking this scumbag away."

"I don't think you'll find the sheriff in town," Thomas said suddenly, his voice filled with near-gleeful malice. "He's currently looking for a missing young lady who pretended to be a man to protect the president."

Everyone in the room froze. Logan's eyes went wild.

"What did you do to Hope?" he roared, his hand tightening around Thomas's throat. "Where is she?"

"I did nothing to her," Thomas wheezed. "We simply let her father know where she'd be."

"You evil piece of prairie coal," Logan growled, shaking him violently. "If anything happens to Hope, I swear I will end you. You deserve to rot—"

"Rot where, Logan boy?" Thomas sneered once Logan loosened his grip. "Hope ratted out her father. Something is bound to happen to her. Best accept you won't see her again." He chuckled.

Logan didn't hesitate. His fist connected with the mayor's jaw, dropping him to the floor, unconscious.

Hope gasped as consciousness slammed back into her. Her head throbbed. Her shoulder burned. And she couldn't see. A blindfold. She instinctively tried to move, but her wrists and ankles were bound tightly to a chair. Panic seized her chest, and a pained moan slipped from her lips before she could stop it.

Footsteps creaked across the floorboards. Someone yanked the neckerchief from her eyes. The sudden light, dim as it was, stabbed at her vision. She blinked hard until the shapes before her sharpened. Her father leaned casually against an old table, arms crossed. Her half-brother stood beside him, his expression cold and triumphant.

"You didn't expect us, did you, Hope?" Winston growled, his voice a venom-laced snarl. His eyes burned into her. "Your disobedience and treacherous behavior ends now. You will return to San Francisco with me, and you will marry whom I choose."

Hope lifted her chin, meeting his gaze without flinching.

"Treacherous behavior?" she spat. "You are the one committing high treason. You are the one who had my mother murdered. You're a monster, nothing more." She barely finished before his hand whipped across her face. Once. Twice. A third time.

Her head snapped to the side with every brutal strike. Heat exploded across her cheek. Her nose began to bleed instantly, a warm trail sliding toward her lip. Pain roared through her, but she bit it down, refusing him even a flicker of weakness.

"You will regret everything," he hissed.

"I regret nothing," Hope rasped, tasting blood. "I only regret that Mother wasn't able to escape your torture."

His face twisted with rage. The next blow wasn't a slap. It was a beating. A full minute of punishing strikes rained down on her face. Her vision blurred. Her lip split, bleeding freely. Tears sprang to her eyes, but she forced them back, swallowing them like fire. Her father finally withdrew his hand, breathing hard.

"You will return with me and marry the man I've chosen," he said coldly. "He will ensure you learn perfect obedience and never defy a man again."

"No." The word trembled with pain but landed with steel. "I will not—"

He struck her again, this time with his riding crop. The impact was sharp, hot, blinding. Tears spilled before she could stop them, sliding down her cheeks as she fought to choke back the sob clawing at her throat.

"I swear, Hope," Winston snarled, leaning close, "say one more word of back talk and I will beat you until you beg for mercy. I should have begun this discipline when you were young, as my mother urged." He inhaled, regaining his composure with chilling ease. "But it no longer matters. You are back in my hands. You will not escape again. And your future husband will see to it that you never challenge a man for as long as you live."

Hope closed her eyes, forcing herself to breathe past the pain. He was stronger, crueler, and fully willing to torture her. For now, survival mattered more than defiance. She opened her eyes slowly.

"Who," she whispered hoarsely, "am I supposed to marry?"

Winston's lips curled. He lifted his hand and pointed at Gregory. Hope's blood turned to ice. She stared at him, first Gregory, then her father, unable to speak for several long, horrified seconds.

"He is my half-brother," she finally choked out. "Even you must understand how vile that is."

A wicked grin spread across Winston's face. He stepped forward, grabbed her chin, and squeezed until she gasped.

"That's what everyone thought," he murmured. "But Gregory isn't related to you at all. My first wife's parents died shortly after our marriage. Gregory was their youngest child. We took him in. Raised him as ours." His grip tightened. "He is no kin to you."

Hope's stomach lurched. Her pulse thundered. Her entire body trembled, not from fear, but from the unbearable wrongness of it all. Winston released her with a shove.

"Looks like we finally have you where we want you," he said smoothly. "You thought you had the upper hand? Foolish girl. You may have slowed our plans, but you won't stop us." He turned to Gregory. "Do whatever you wish with her. If she refuses to cooperate... you know what to do."

Gregory smiled, slow, cold, hungry. Hope's breath caught. Winston nodded to the other men in the room. One by one, they filed out of the cabin, leaving her alone with Gregory and the shadows closing in around her. And for the first time since waking, Hope felt real fear claw its way into her chest.

Gregory stepped behind her, yanking the knots loose with rough, impatient movements. The instant her wrists were free, Hope tried to scramble away, but he was faster. He seized her arm, hauled her upright, and hurled her onto the narrow bed so hard the breath was punched from her lungs.

"I will gladly make you mine now," he snarled, climbing over her. "We don't need marriage for what I want from you."

His mouth crushed against hers, brutal, possessive. Hope's stomach revolted. Rage flared white-hot. She opened her mouth wider, and bit him. Hard. Gregory screamed and jerked back, blood instantly welling along his lip. That split second of shock was all she needed. Her hand shot down, tore his gun from his holster, and she swung with every ounce of strength she had left. The butt of the weapon cracked against his skull. He swore violently, staggered, then lunged for her, murder blazing in his eyes.

Hope fired. The gunshot thundered through the cabin. Gregory dropped to one knee with a howl, clutching his thigh as blood soaked through his trousers.

"You..." he gasped, breathless with pain and fury. "You little—"

He launched himself at her with a savagery she had never seen. He ripped the gun from her hands and slammed her head against the bedpost. Pain exploded behind her eyes. Stars burst across her vision.

"You are not worth saving, Hope Spencer!" he roared inches from her face, spittle striking her cheek. "Say goodbye to everything you love, because you will die tonight." He fisted her hair, yanking her so hard she cried out, and dragged her across the floor. She clawed at him, fought to twist free, but he shoved her down again with brutal force and stormed toward the door. Hope scrambled after him, but the door slammed shut in her face. A heartbeat later, she heard the lock slide home.

Hope froze. Then her blood ran cold. Because the next sound was unmistakable, the scrape of tinder, followed by the soft *whoosh* of flame catching. Gregory's voice drifted through the door, gleeful and unhinged.

"You'll never get out, Hope. The window's boarded shut, and the fire will reach the front before you can even stand." His laughter echoed, warped and inhuman. "Burn well."

His footsteps faded. Silence followed. Then the crackling roar of flames began to rise, hungry, spreading, devouring everything in their path. Smoke seeped into the room. Heat pressed in from all sides. Hope's pulse thundered in her ears. She was trapped. Alone. And the fire was growing.

# 21

# Bruised, Not Broken

H ope drew a sharp, trembling breath. Every part of her wanted to collapse, to finally let the tears she had been holding back for hours fall freely, but there was no time for that. No room for weakness. No space for grief.

It didn't matter what she had done or what she might have done. Her father had planned her death either way. If she had submitted, she would have been handed to a husband who would beat her into obedience. And because she resisted, she would die by fire. But she refused to accept either fate.

Smoke was already creeping beneath the door, thick and suffocating. The flames crackled and roared like a living beast, devouring everything in their path. Hope stumbled to the window and yanked the curtains aside. The glass was shattered, shards scattered across the sill, but several heavy wooden boards had been nailed across the frame from the outside. No light seeped through the cracks. No escape.

She coughed violently, tasting ash. *Move. Think. Fight.* Hope rushed to the bed and shoved it with all her strength until it scraped across the floor and wedged against the door, hoping to slow the fire's advance. Then she dragged the small table beneath the window, climbed onto it, and pressed her shoulder against the boards.

Warm blood trickled down her face from the blow Gregory had dealt her earlier. More seeped down her back where the reopened bullet wound pulsed with every movement. Dizzy. Lightheaded. Weak. But not defeated.

Hope braced herself, lifted her leg, and kicked with everything she had. Pain exploded through her body. The board rattled but held. She kicked again. And again. Each blow was weaker than the last as her strength drained away. Sweat mingled with blood. Her lungs screamed for clean air.

Nothing budged.

Flames suddenly licked through a crack beneath the door. Heat slammed into her like a wall. Smoke swirled thickly around her, blurring her vision. Panic clawed at her throat, but she forced herself to breathe shallowly and think. *Find something. Anything.*

She jumped down from the table, coughing so hard, her ribs ached. Her gaze swept the room, sparse furniture, bare walls, until she caught a faint glint beneath the lowest shelf. Hope dropped to her knees and reached beneath it. Her fingers brushed cold steel. An ax.

A wild, breathless prayer of relief tore from her chest. She seized the tool and scrambled back onto the table. Above her, the roof groaned ominously, timbers cracking, embers drifting down like deadly fireflies. Hope raised the ax and swung. Wood splintered. She swung again. CRACK.

A third swing—the roof gave way. A thunderous crash erupted overhead. Hope screamed as a section of the burning roof collapsed. She hurled herself forward, ramming her shoulder against the boards with pure, primal desperation. Nails tore free. The boards snapped. And the world tipped sideways.

Hope tumbled through the opening, falling several feet into thorny bushes outside. The impact knocked the breath from her lungs, but she scrambled upright, staggering backward as flames consumed the cabin behind her. The heat was overwhelming. The roar deafening. She tried to run, but her knees buckled.

Smoke burned her eyes, forcing tears free. She coughed violently, each breath shallower than the last. Her hands shook uncontrollably as she pressed them to the dirt, trying to steady herself.

*Move... get up... keep going...* But her body was done. Her vision blurred. A ringing filled her ears. Darkness crept in from the edges of her sight. Hope collapsed onto the ground, sobbing, coughing, choking, until everything went black.

When Hope opened her eyes again, the world around her was blurred and trembling. Cold raindrops struck her face like needles. It was pouring, so heavily that the sheets of water looked almost silver in the faint glow cast by the burning cabin. Everything else was swallowed by darkness.

The flames hissed angrily as rain struck them, sending up clouds of thick gray smoke that curled low to the ground. Each breath Hope drew tasted bitter and harsh, scraping down her throat. She coughed weakly, her body shuddering with the effort. When she tried to lift herself, her limbs felt filled with lead. Every muscle protested.

Her shoulder throbbed mercilessly, the reopened wound warm and wet beneath her torn clothing. She was freezing, cold to the bone, and utterly disoriented. The forest around her was a wall of shadow and indistinguishable shapes. She had no idea which direction led to safety or how far she had crawled from the blaze before collapsing. The thought of stumbling blindly through the darkness, injured and alone, made her stomach twist. She couldn't do it. Not tonight.

Hope dug her fingers into the wet earth and dragged herself inch by inch closer to the collapsed structure. The fire, still burning, still dangerous, offered the only warmth in this black, merciless night. When she reached a safe distance, she curled onto her side, trembling uncontrollably. Heat brushed her skin in uneven waves, enough to ease the bite of the cold, but not close enough to scorch her. Rain pattered against her face. Smoke drifted past in thick, swirling tendrils.

She whispered a shaky, silent prayer into the darkness, half plea, half gratitude, for having made it out alive at all. At last, her body went limp as exhaustion claimed its victory. Moments later, Hope drifted into a heavy, dreamless sleep, rain falling softly over her as the cabin smoldered beside her.

The sun had barely crested the horizon when Hope stirred at the faint sound of hoofbeats. Her eyes flew open. Panic surged through her, but when she tried to scramble away, her legs refused to cooperate. Her body was stiff, trembling from exhaustion, smoke inhalation, and blood loss.

# CHASING THE KILLER

The cabin was no more, just a smoldering heap of blackened ruins, hissing quietly beneath the morning drizzle. A graveyard of charred beams and collapsed timbers. Hope swallowed hard. If her father and Gregory had returned, they would find her helpless and finish what they had begun.

She braced herself, watching through blurred vision as the rider came closer. But instead of the nightmare she expected, she saw a familiar figure, a young woman with braided brown hair and anxious eyes. The same girl from the general store. Lilly.

Hope tried to call out, but her battered face throbbed painfully, and her shoulder felt as though it were on fire. The only sound she made was a sharp, broken gasp.

Lilly's eyes widened. She slid off her horse, skirts swishing around her boots as she hurried to Hope's side.

"Thank goodness I found you," she breathed, her voice shaking. "Everyone in town is looking for you. What have those devils done to you?" Tears sprang to her eyes as she gently took Hope's hand.

Hope struggled to focus. "How... how did you find me?" she rasped, wincing as even speaking tugged at the bruises along her cheek and jaw.

"My parents' farm isn't far from here," Lilly explained quickly. "I saw the fire and smoke last night, but I was alone, I couldn't risk riding through the forest in the dark. I waited until morning. I prayed all night that whoever was inside had escaped."

She stood and hurried to her horse, retrieving a canteen. Kneeling again, she tipped it to Hope's lips. Hope drank greedily, the cool water easing her parched throat. When she stopped, Lilly pulled a folded handkerchief from her pocket, dampened it with the remaining water, and gently dabbed the blood and soot from Hope's face.

Hope clenched her teeth, breathing through the sharp stabs of pain. Tears burned behind her lashes, but she forced them back. There was no time to break.

"You need to leave, Lilly," she whispered urgently. "My father and his men... they could come back any moment."

"Why did they burn the cabin?" Lilly asked, horror tightening her voice.

"They trapped me inside," Hope said, swallowing hard. "They meant for me to die in the fire."

Lilly's hand flew to her mouth. "How did you get out?"

Hope recounted it in short, gasping phrases, breaking through the boards, the collapsing roof, the jump through the window. Lilly looked sick.

"You should be dead," she whispered. "Hope, I am not leaving you here."

"Lilly, please," Hope begged softly. "They won't hesitate to kill anyone in their way. If they find you—"

But Lilly cut her off with a fierce shake of her head.

"I'm not running while you're lying here bleeding. Your shoulder is soaked through." She glanced at the crimson stain spreading across Hope's shirt. "If I don't get you help soon, you won't make it."

Their argument was cut short by the unmistakable sound of horses. Several. Close. Hope's breath hitched. Her heart hammered with terror.

Lilly's eyes widened, but she leaned in, whispering urgently, "Do you remember where you dropped the ax?"

Hope nodded weakly and pointed toward the collapsed wall where the window had been. Lilly rushed to the ruins, kicking aside damp ash with frantic urgency until something metallic glinted beneath the charcoal remains. The ax head—blackened but intact. The wooden handle had burned away completely. She snatched it up, hurried back, and hid the heavy metal blade beneath the folds of her skirt.

Hope stared at her, fear tightening her chest, not just for herself now, but for the girl who refused to abandon her. Lilly positioned herself beside Hope, crouching low behind a fallen tree trunk. She took a steadying breath. Eyes fixed on the tree line. The hoofbeats grew louder. The men would crest the hill any second, and when they did, they would find them. Unless hope, courage, and timing worked in their favor. Hope's pulse thundered in her ears as the first shadowed figures emerged through the smoke.

"Looks like the fire finished her off." Winston Spencer kicked at a charred beam, his voice cold as slate. Gregory, limping heavily, gave a satisfied nod.

"There was no way for her to escape," he said, though a flicker of uncertainty crossed his face as he surveyed the collapsed structure. Their men followed behind them, boots crunching over wet ash and debris. Then one of them stopped abruptly.

"Boss! Footprints!"

Winston spun on his heel. "Footprints?" he barked. "How is that possible?"

Gregory froze, staring down at the trail, fresh prints, small, unmistakably feminine, leading away from the wreckage. His already pale face drained further. Winston's head snapped up. His gaze swept the tree line, and then he saw them. Two figures huddled in the thick ferns: Lilly, half-hidden behind a fallen tree trunk, and Hope slumped beside her like a broken doll.

With a furious snarl, Winston stormed forward, seized Hope by the arm, and yanked her upright. Her legs barely held beneath her.

"How did you get out of there?" he roared into her face, spittle striking her cheek. "How did you escape?"

Hope's swollen lips parted, her voice barely audible.

"It doesn't matter how, Father..." Her breath trembled. "You only care that I'm still alive."

His grip tightened, bruising her arm.

"Who is that?" he demanded, stabbing a finger toward Lilly. Gregory, panting heavily, limped toward the other girl. He reached out, and Lilly struck without hesitation. The ax blade flashed from beneath her skirt, slicing into Gregory's already wounded leg.

He screamed, a raw, primal sound, and collapsed into the dirt. Blood poured from the reopened wound. His hand scrabbled helplessly for support as he swayed, close to fainting.

"You little—!" Winston shouted, whipping out his gun and aiming it straight at Lilly's chest. But before he could fire, Hope threw herself over the girl, shielding her with her own battered body.

"Move, Hope!" he thundered, grabbing her shoulder and trying to drag her away. She clung tighter, planting her feet, refusing to budge. Her entire body trembled, yet her voice remained steady.

"No," she snapped. "I will not move. And I will not let you kill an innocent person."

"I can put you both in the ground," he hissed. "And I ain't bothered by the thought." He lifted the gun, finger curling around the trigger—

Gunshots shattered the quiet. Several sharp, deafening cracks ripped through the forest. A bullet tore clean through Winston's wrist, forcing him to drop his gun. Another punched into his shoulder. He screamed, stumbling backward, shock and fury twisting his face. His men scrambled, returning fire wildly toward the trees as more gunshots rang out from the approaching rescuers.

Clutching his bleeding arm, Winston staggered toward the remaining horses. In desperation, he mounted Lilly's mare, kicked hard, and vanished into the forest canopy.

Hope collapsed onto her side, her breath coming in shallow, agonized gasps. Her face was ghostly pale now, tinged almost blue around the lips. Her body shook uncontrollably from pain, smoke inhalation, and blood loss.

"Hope!" Lilly cried, dropping beside her. She lifted Hope's head into her lap, tears spilling freely. "Hope, look at me. Please, stay awake."

Hope's eyelids fluttered. She tried to breathe, but the air rattled harshly in her throat.

"You have to hold on," Lilly sobbed, shaking her gently. "Please, Hope. Don't leave me."

But Hope's strength was gone. Her vision dimmed. Sound drifted farther and farther away. And then the world slipped into total, suffocating blackness.

Jeff Stewart, Sawyer, and Brent burst through the trees only seconds later, rifles raised and eyes sharp. They froze when they saw the two girls on the ground, Hope lying motionless, Lilly kneeling beside her, trembling. Lilly's father barreled into the clearing right behind them, wild-eyed and breathless. Several other armed townsmen thundered past, fanning out to chase Winston Spencer and the remaining criminals as they fled deeper into the forest.

Two marshal deputies skidded to a stop near Gregory Spencer, who was still writhing in agony from the reopened bullet wound. Without hesitation, they forced him onto his stomach, wrenched his arms behind his back, and snapped iron cuffs around his wrists. Gregory cursed them, but the deputies ignored him entirely. They had seen the carnage, the fire, and now Hope's condition. Any sympathy for him was long gone.

Jeff Stewart reached Hope first. The marshal dropped to one knee, his face draining of all color as he hovered a shaking hand above her blood-streaked cheek.

"Oh, Hope..." he whispered, his voice cracking with panic he rarely allowed himself to feel. He slid his arms beneath her limp form with heartbreaking gentleness, lifting her against his chest as though she were made of fragile glass. Her head lolled against his shoulder, her skin cold and clammy beneath his touch.

Behind him, Lilly finally broke. Her sobs tore through the clearing, raw, helpless, devastating. Lilly's father rushed to her, gathering his daughter into his arms as she clung to him, shaking.

"She tried to save me," Lilly cried into his coat. "She saved me, Pa."

Even Brent and Sawyer, hardened cowboys who had weathered their share of grief, felt their throats tighten. Sawyer wiped at his eyes, while Brent turned away, jaw clenched, fighting the sting of tears.

Jeff lifted his gaze to the men around him, his expression sharpening into fierce determination.

"Get the doctor ready," he ordered, his voice low but commanding. "Hope doesn't have much time." With Hope cradled securely against him, he strode toward the horses, every step purposeful, every heartbeat echoing with one silent, desperate plea: *Hold on, Hope... please, hold on.*

"Will she be okay, Alan?" Jeff's voice was steady, but only just. He stepped toward the physician the moment the examining room door closed behind him. The doctor exhaled slowly, shoulders heavy with what he had seen.

"Hope lost a significant amount of blood," he began, eyes shadowed with concern. "Her shoulder wound reopened, and whoever struck her... did so with brutal force. Her face is badly swollen and severely bruised. This wasn't just violence, this was rage."

A sharp hiss escaped Logan through gritted teeth. His hands balled into fists so tight his knuckles blanched, but he said nothing, he couldn't, not without losing control. Beside him, Brent and Sawyer went rigid, their faces dark with fury and grief. Across the room, Lilly pressed herself against her father's side, trembling as tears spilled down her cheeks. Her father wrapped an arm around her shoulders, though even he looked shaken by the doctor's words.

Jeff swallowed hard, the muscles in his jaw working.

"Can we see her?"

Dr. Jensen hesitated only a moment before nodding.

"Yes... but she hasn't woken yet."

Jeff took a step toward the door, but the doctor reached out and caught his arm, stopping him. The simple gesture made Jeff's heart plummet.

"Prepare yourself, Jeff," Dr. Jensen warned quietly. "Her face... it looks horrifying. What was done to her wasn't meant to scare or restrain her. It was meant to break her."

A ripple of cold fury swept through the men. Logan's entire body coiled as if ready for war. Brent's eyes burned. Sawyer's jaw flexed in silent agony. Jeff drew a long breath, bracing himself, for Hope, for Georgiana, for everything that had been stolen from their family.

"Let us in," he said. And together, they stepped toward the room, toward the girl who had risked her life for the president, survived a burning cabin, and fought enemies who should never have been hers to face.

No matter how much the four men had braced themselves, no matter how vividly they had imagined what might have been done to her, nothing prepared them for the sight that met them when they stepped into the room. All four gasped aloud.

Hope lay motionless on the bed, her face barely recognizable beneath layers of black, blue, yellow, and angry purple bruising. Both eyes were swollen shut, the delicate skin around them mottled and dark. Her lower lip was split open, no longer bleeding, but raw and painful. Worst of all was the long, deep-red welt slashing across her right cheek, precise and linear, unmistakable. A riding crop.

Someone hadn't merely struck her. They had punished her. Near her temple, a small, stitched gash marked where her head had been slammed against something hard with force. Sawyer inhaled sharply and turned away, overwhelmed. Brent pressed his hand to his mouth, eyes burning with fury he couldn't voice. Even Jeff, who had seen more than most men ever should, who had carried her from fire and blood, stood frozen, horror tightening every line of his face.

But Logan went still in a different way. His fists clenched so tightly his nails cut into his palms. His jaw locked. His chest rose and fell with slow, deliberate breaths, each one barely containing a storm. He stared at Hope as if carving a vow into his very soul.

*Never again. No one would ever harm her again. No one would ever lay a hand on her.* No one would break her body or spirit as long as he lived. If it came to it, he would protect her with his life.

Slowly, almost reverently, he stepped closer to her bedside and brushed a gentle hand over the only uninjured part of her face.

"I'm here, Hope," he whispered, his voice thick with restrained emotion. "And I'll never let anyone hurt you again."

Hope didn't wake until two days later. Dr. Jensen and a nurse rushed into the room the moment she stirred, but Logan was already there, leaning forward, gripping the side of the bed as if he'd willed her back to life through sheer force of devotion. He had barely left her side since she'd been brought in, stepping away only when absolutely necessary.

Hope turned her head slowly. Her face ached, but she managed a faint smile for the young man beside her.

"Logan..."

He inhaled sharply, relief flooding through him, and reached for her hand.

"You're awake," he breathed, his voice rough with emotion. She tried to speak, but her lips cracked painfully. Still, when the words finally emerged, thin, fragile, they were steady.

"What happened after the fire? Did anyone hurt Lilly?" Worry flooded her eyes, pushing past her own pain. Logan immediately leaned down and pressed a soft kiss to her forehead, the gentlest touch imaginable, full of gratitude and aching relief. He offered her a small, reassuring smile.

"She's perfectly fine. Not a scratch on her. She told us you protected her."

Hope exhaled shakily, a tremor of relief mingling with the lingering fear still lodged in her chest. Logan watched her with a look that held both admiration and exasperation, deeply moved, yet half-ready to scold her for risking herself again.

"I wish," he murmured, brushing a thumb across the back of her hand, "that you would think of your own safety sometimes."

"Lilly came to help me," Hope insisted, pain flickering across her expression. "I begged her to leave, but she wouldn't. I couldn't let my father shoot her."

Logan's handsome smile softened, warm and full of something tender, something that made her stomach flutter despite the pain. She could never grow tired of looking at him. Never. But the thought of her father sent a chill back into her bones.

"Was everyone arrested," she whispered, "or did they get away?"

Before Logan could answer, the door swung open and her uncle strode in. Jeff didn't hesitate. He hurried to her side and gathered her carefully into his arms, giving her a fatherly embrace so full of love that her eyes stung.

"Everyone was captured and arrested," Jeff said once he released her, smoothing her hair back gently. "Except for your father. He got away."

Hope stiffened. For a heartbeat, her breath caught in her throat. If her father was alive and free, then nothing was over. He would come for her, to finish what he had started.

"He won't stop," she whispered, her voice trembling. "He'll come back. He won't rest until—"

Jeff guided her chin up with gentle fingers, forcing her to meet his steady gaze.

"Hope," he said firmly, "we will find him. Every man who worked for him is in custody. He has no army now, no allies, no power. He cannot hide forever. And he will not get another chance at you."

"But he already escaped..." she argued weakly.

"And we will track him," Jeff replied. "You are not alone anymore. Not ever again."

Her gaze drifted to Logan, whose expression was fierce and unyielding. He stepped closer, taking her hand again.

"I meant what I said," he murmured, as if making an oath before heaven itself. "I will not allow anyone to ever hurt you again. I'll protect you with my life, Hope."

Her heart fluttered, painfully and beautifully all at once. She believed him. She felt the depth of his vow, and for the first time in weeks, she let herself breathe.

# 22

# Belonging at Last

Hope stood in front of the mirror in her hospital room, brushing her hair with slow, deliberate strokes. The swelling had faded enough that she finally recognized her own reflection again, though faint yellow and purple shadows still clung stubbornly to her cheekbones. Lilly sat perched on a chair nearby, swinging her feet lightly as she watched her.

"I am so glad these bruises are almost gone," Hope muttered, tilting her face left and right. "How Logan didn't run away the moment he saw me is a miracle." She rolled her eyes dramatically.

Lilly snorted. "Please. Logan saw, from the beginning, what a beautiful woman you are. Bruises don't change that. And they certainly don't scare men like him away."

Hope gave her a skeptical look, and Lilly softened.

"You *are* beautiful, Hope. Anyone can see that. But what really makes you shine is your heart. Some men notice that more than anything else."

Hope's lips curled into a shy smile, and she turned from the mirror to face her new friend.

"Did you know I was a girl when we first met at the general store?"

Lilly nodded immediately. "Right away. You might've fooled my grandfather and half the men in town, but not me. A gorgeous girl like you can't hide behind a pair of trousers and a hat."

Hope blinked. "Then why didn't you say anything?"

Lilly shrugged with a gentle smile. "Because I figured you had your reasons. And I wasn't about to put you on the spot, or in danger."

Gratitude warmed Hope's chest. "Thank you."

A sudden, confident knock sounded at the door. Both girls turned just as Logan stepped in, sunlight at his back, a slow grin spreading across his face the instant he saw Hope. His eyes softened, lingered on her. Hope felt her cheeks flame instantly, as if someone had pressed a hot iron on them.

Lilly nearly giggled. She stood, leaned toward Hope, and whispered teasingly, "A handsome man walks in, and you turn prettier already."

Hope swatted weakly at her arm, flustered, which only made Lilly grin wider.

"I'll leave you two," Lilly declared brightly, giving Hope a knowing wink. She slipped past Logan, who tipped his hat politely to her, before closing the door with a soft click. The room suddenly felt warmer. And quieter. Logan took a step forward, his expression softening even further as his gaze settled fully on Hope.

Seeing Logan stride toward her, so purposefully, sent Hope's blush all the way to her ears. There was nothing hesitant in his approach, no pause, no doubt. He reached her in three long steps, slipped an arm around her waist, and pulled her against him with a tenderness that still carried unmistakable strength.

Before she could say a word, his mouth was on hers. It wasn't a careful kiss this time. It was longing, hungry, urgent, filled with relief, pent-up fear, and everything he hadn't said aloud. Hope inhaled sharply, her knees weakening as his lips moved against hers. Her hands slid instinctively up his chest, clutching the fabric of his shirt as her heart hammered wildly.

The kiss deepened for a moment, slow and intoxicating, and Hope melted into him helplessly, the world tilting until there was nothing but his warmth, his breath, his arms caging her protectively. When Logan finally pulled back, he rested his forehead lightly against hers, his breath uneven. Hope was breathless too.

"Are you ready to meet your relatives?" he asked softly, brushing a stray wisp of hair away from her cheek. Hope nodded, though her pulse raced with a different kind of anticipation now.

"I think so... but are you certain it's safe? My father is still out there." Her voice wavered despite her best attempts to sound brave. Logan cupped her chin gently and tilted her face up toward him. His brown eyes held hers with fierce, unwavering devotion.

"Hope," he murmured, his thumb sweeping tenderly across her cheek, "your family is safe. You are safe. Cheyenne is locked down tighter than a bank vault. Every marshal, deputy, and soldier is searching for Winston Spencer. The second he shows his face, anywhere, he's finished."

Hope tried to smile, but the tremor of worry hadn't fully left her expression. Logan noticed. His hand slid down her arm until his fingers found hers, threading them together in a warm, grounding hold.

"Your uncle will meet us right outside your grandparents' house," he continued in a low, reassuring tone. "Brent and Sawyer are already there, and they'll make sure nobody leaves or gets in without us knowing." He leaned down, his lips brushing her temple in a soft, lingering kiss that made her heart flutter wildly. "I won't let anything happen to you," he whispered. "Not now. Not ever."

Hope exhaled shakily, her nerves still fluttering like delicate wings, but beneath it all, a growing warmth bloomed. A warmth that came from knowing she wouldn't have to face her family, or her fears, alone. Not ever again.

"You look beautiful, Hope," Jeff said with a beaming smile, his eyes softening as he took in his niece's appearance. He pulled her into a warm, fatherly embrace. "How are you feeling?"

Hope swallowed, her fingers tightening nervously around the small reticule she carried.

"I'm so nervous," she admitted in a breath. "I can't even picture what Mama's parents look like... but I'm excited. Scared, but excited."

Jeff squeezed her shoulder reassuringly.

"They've been waiting a very long time to meet you."

Together they walked to the front door. Jeff opened it gently, as if the moment itself were fragile.

"Ma, Pa," he called out, his voice filled with restrained emotion, "I have a surprise for you."

Logan entered first, and the older couple smiled warmly at him, prepared to greet him, until another figure stepped into the doorway. Hope's grandmother's hand flew to her mouth, her eyes filling instantly with tears. Even her grandfather, a man whose stern countenance suggested he didn't show emotion easily, looked utterly undone. Hope froze.

"Hope..." her grandmother breathed, her voice breaking. Then she rushed forward. Hope barely had time to exhale before she was enveloped in a tight, trembling embrace. The feel of her grandmother's arms, soft, warm, familiar despite the years lost, broke the last of Hope's composure. Tears flooded her eyes, spilling freely as she clung to the older woman with all the pent-up longing of a lifetime.

"Oh, my sweet girl," her grandmother whispered, stroking her hair. "My precious Hope."

Her grandfather stepped forward next, clearing his throat gruffly, but his voice betrayed him as he leaned in and wrapped her in a strong, protective hug.

"Welcome home, child," he murmured into her hair. "Welcome home."

Across the room, Sawyer and Brent exchanged wide, boyish grins. Both blinked more often than usual, fighting their own swell of emotion. It was a rare thing, watching a family knit itself back together, thread by fragile thread.

Logan stood quietly off to the side, his hands tucked into his belt, watching Hope with a look so full of pride and tenderness, it softened even the shadows in his eyes. This was what she deserved: love, belonging, family. And now, finally, she had it.

The older couple didn't let her go for several long minutes, each heartbreak and missed year melting away in the others' arms. They asked no questions, offered no explanations, only unconditional acceptance.

Sawyer leaned close to Brent and whispered, "She's going to fit right in."

Brent nodded, his grin stretching even wider.

"Just you wait until tonight. The rest of the family's going to adopt her faster than we did."

But for now, they all remained at a respectful distance, giving Hope and her grandparents the precious quiet they needed, this moment of reunion that had been denied to them for far too long.

"You look just like your mom when she was your age," her grandmother whispered, her voice thick with awe and grief. Tears still glistened in her eyes, trembling at the edges of her lashes. Hope's throat tightened, and she had to swallow hard to steady herself.

"I am so sorry you didn't get to see your daughter again," Hope said, her voice breaking. "I should have been home earlier. My maid tried to fetch the doctor in time, but it was too late." Her next breath shuddered out of her, and quiet sobs spilled free. Guilt weighed heavily on her chest, guilt for her grandparents, for that final moment they never had.

Everyone in the room froze, stunned by the depth of her sorrow. Jeff reached for her at once, pulling her into a strong, protective embrace. His arms wrapped around her with fierce tenderness, holding her tight as if he could shield her from her own heartbreak. Her grandmother shook her head, wiping her cheeks.

"Oh no, sweet girl. Don't you dare blame yourself. This was beyond anyone's control." Her voice wavered, but her eyes remained steady, filled with pure, unfiltered love.

When Hope's sobbing finally softened, Jeff gently lifted her chin, so their eyes met.

"We are grateful you weren't there," he murmured, his voice low but firm. "They would have murdered you as well. Your mother was relieved you were away that day, I know it. All she wanted was for you to be safe. And she would never have wanted you to witness her death. It was horrible that you found her afterward... that alone was too much for you to bear."

Her grandparents gasped in unison.

"You found her?" her grandfather asked, his voice tight with grief and disbelief. Hope nodded, leaning into her uncle for strength.

"I... I think it was a blessing for Mama," she whispered. "She didn't have to die alone." Her voice cracked on the final word, sharp as a splinter. She drew a shaky breath and blinked rapidly, determined not to cry again. Jeff's arm tightened around her, grounding her.

Hope looked up at him, studying the warmth and pride in his eyes. Then she turned toward her grandparents and cousins. A faint, fragile smile broke through the sorrow.

"I miss her," she said softly. "But I'm grateful I'm here now. Grateful to have all of you in my life."

Jeff pressed a gentle kiss to the top of her head. In the next heartbeat, everyone gathered around her, arms wrapping around shoulders, hands brushing her back, heads leaning in. A full, encompassing embrace. A family circle closing around her, filling every hollow left by fear, loneliness, and loss. And Hope felt it fully. She belonged.

That evening, the Stewart ranch was livelier than it had been in years. Lamps glowed warmly in every window, laughter drifted through the halls, and the savory scent of roasted chicken and fresh bread filled the air. Hope stood near the parlor doorway, watching as more people arrived, faces she had never seen, yet who looked at her as though they had known her all her life.

She hadn't realized her mother's siblings still lived so close, scattered throughout the nearby towns and settlements. One by one, aunts and uncles stepped inside, their expressions softening the moment they laid eyes on her. Cousins she hadn't known existed rushed forward with wide smiles, eager to embrace her, as if welcoming back a long-lost piece of their family.

It was overwhelming... but in the gentlest, most beautiful way. At first, Hope felt rooted to the spot, unsure how to respond to so much affection. But the joy on everyone's face slowly melted the hesitation from her heart. Her great-uncle Thomas lifted her into a brief but hearty hug, as if she were still a little girl. Aunt Clara, who had her mother's eyes, cried openly as she cupped Hope's face between her palms.

Even the youngest cousins circled her shyly, tugging at her skirt and whispering, "Is it true you saved the president?"

Hope couldn't help laughing softly. "Something like that," she murmured. As the evening stretched on, the house buzzed with excited conversation. Stories about Georgiana, her laughter, her strength, her stubborn streak, filled the room, and Hope soaked in every word like someone starved for water. For the first time, she heard the happy parts of her mother's past. Her childhood mischief. Her secret love for building forts in the woods. Her habit of giving away desserts to anyone who looked sad.

Hope listened with glistening eyes, feeling the ache of loss blend with a profound sense of peace. Everyone was glad, truly glad, to finally meet their youngest sister's only child. And Hope, surrounded by arms, voices, smiles, and warmth she had never known before, finally understood what it meant to belong to a real family.

Hope settled into ranch life quickly, perhaps more quickly than she had expected. She adored her grandparents from the moment she met them, and Brent and Sawyer's parents, Parker and Shirley, welcomed her as though another daughter had simply come home. Her older cousins teased her endlessly, but Hope was quick-witted and unafraid to toss their jabs right back. Before long, their playful arguments sounded exactly like those of siblings who had grown up together.

Lilly visited whenever she could, and the two young women became inseparable. Hope soon noticed a different kind of tension whenever Brent entered the room. He suddenly stood a little straighter, spoke a little deeper, and watched Lilly as though someone had lit a lantern inside his chest. Lilly, for her part, blushed every time Brent so much as glanced her way. Hope hid a knowing smile. Brent might have ignored Lilly, back when she was younger, but now? Now, he couldn't look away.

A few days after Hope moved to the Stewart ranch, Logan arrived and asked if she would join him and his family for supper. His mother wanted to meet Hope officially, and Logan seemed unusually eager, almost boyishly nervous, to introduce her to his sister and father.

When they reached the small cabin, the same one Hope had fled to the day the truth unraveled, she looked at Logan in utter confusion.

"Why are we stopping here?" she asked, brows knitting. Logan's slow, secretive grin made her heartbeat stumble.

"There is something I want to show you." He lifted her down from the buggy with gentle hands, keeping hold of her fingers as he led her inside. Hope expected... well, she wasn't sure what she expected. But certainly not what she found.

At first glance, the cabin looked unchanged. But when she turned toward the window, her breath vanished. A heart. A heart made entirely of red roses, meticulously arranged on the floor beneath the window, with more roses gathered in vases along the sill, their fragrance filling every corner of the small room. It felt like stepping into someone's soul.

# 23

# Vinegar Kisses and Vows

Hope walked toward it slowly, shyly, her fingers trembling. She knelt, brushed the velvet-soft petals, and felt tears burn in her eyes. She nearly jumped when Logan stepped behind her, slipping his strong arms around her waist. His breath brushed her ear, sending a rush of heat straight through her.

"Hope..." His voice was low, reverent, tender. "Will you make me the happiest man alive and marry me?"

Her throat tightened. Tears shimmered. She turned in his arms, her voice barely above a whisper, though there was a teasing sparkle in her eyes.

"Are you sure that's what you want? You know I have a temper, and I overreact, and—"

She didn't get to finish. Logan's mouth claimed hers with fierce, passionate certainty, stealing every thought from her head. His kiss was everything, heat, longing, and promise woven together. Her knees nearly buckled, but his arms held her close, steady, safe. When he finally lifted his head, she was breathless. He wore a grin that made her knees weak all over again.

"Now," he murmured, brushing his thumb across her flushed cheek, "let's try this again. Will you marry me?"

Still catching her breath, Hope nodded, small, shaky, overflowing with emotion. Logan's face lit up, radiant and boyishly triumphant. He pulled her tightly against his chest and kissed her again, another heated, possessive kiss that left her dizzy, before resting his forehead against hers.

"My parents will be so happy," he whispered.

Hope swallowed. "But your father doesn't even know me... and your mother might wish for someone better suited—"

Logan silenced her with a slow, tender kiss that contrasted beautifully with the passionate ones before.

"There is nobody better for me," he said firmly. "My mother knew from the moment I brought you home that I'd already lost my heart to you. And my father can't wait to meet you. He remembers your mother from childhood, he and Parker Stewart always hoped our families might one day become one."

Hope's breath hitched. Her heart fluttered painfully and beautifully as she looked at the man who had not only protected her, but loved her, completely, fiercely, and without hesitation. And in that little cabin full of roses, with Logan's arms around her and his future in his eyes, Hope felt, for the first time in her life, what it meant to be truly cherished.

When Logan helped Hope down from the buggy after they reached the ranch, he didn't release her hand. Instead, he pulled her straight into his arms, holding her close enough that her breath caught. His eyes, warm, teasing, entirely focused on her, sent a pleasant shiver through her.

"Just remember," he murmured, brushing a loose curl from her cheek, "Dad is essentially an older version of William. More gray hair these days, but the same stubborn beard."

Hope arched a brow, giving him a sassy side-eye.

"So, tell me... did you only wear a full beard when you were pretending to be your brother, or is that actually your usual look?"

Logan smirked, that dangerously charming, slow spread of lips that made her insides go soft, and leaned in to press a quick, mischievous kiss to her mouth.

"Would you prefer it if I looked like William?" he asked, his voice pitched low and playful. Hope blushed furiously and shook her head so fast her bonnet nearly slipped.

"Absolutely not," she muttered, flustered. "It wasn't Reverend Shaw's looks that... that attracted me."

Logan lifted a brow, amused. "No?" he prompted. Her cheeks burned hotter.

"My feelings changed when you showed up as you," she whispered, the last word barely audible. "I mean, your scruffy beard is... well..." She stared at his chin as though it might leap up and speak. "It's very manly. And handsome. Extremely handsome. But I have no desire to see you turn into your brother's twin again."

When she finally dared to meet his eyes, she found them dancing with laughter, which only deepened her blush. Logan slid one arm more firmly around her waist and tugged her closer, so closely she let out a soft gasp. His grin was pure male satisfaction.

"I'm very glad you find me handsome and manly," he said, brushing his lips lightly along her jaw in a way that made her knees go weak, "because I have no intention of becoming William's lookalike ever again."

Hope tried to glare at him, but she couldn't help the breathless smile tugging at her mouth.

"Good," she murmured. "Because I like you exactly as you are."

Logan's answering look nearly melted her.

"Careful, darlin'," he whispered, lowering his forehead to hers. "If you keep saying things like that, I might forget there are people inside waiting to meet you."

Her blush returned full force. "Logan!"

He chuckled, kissed her once more, slow and lingering this time, and finally released her hand... only to take it again immediately, threading their fingers together as though he never meant to let her go.

***

"Hope, it is so good to finally meet you as myself," Logan's mother exclaimed the moment they stepped into the house. She didn't hesitate. She pulled Hope into a warm, motherly embrace that smelled faintly of lavender and hearth smoke. "And I am so sorry I had to lie to you when you first arrived in Cheyenne. I hated every second of it."

Hope shook her head quickly. "Please don't worry about that, Mrs. Shaw. I was only upset with your boys."

Marjorie shot Logan a pointed look.

"And who could blame you?" came a deep, rumbling voice behind Hope. She turned, and gasped. Standing before her was an older, broader, silver-haired version of Reverend William Shaw. The same strong jaw. The same steady eyes. The same quiet authority. Even the beard was nearly identical, save for a bit more gray.

"You... you really do look like Reverend Shaw," she breathed, stunned. The man chuckled, rubbing a hand over his chin.

"So, I've been told once or twice."

Logan slipped his arm around her waist, pulling her warmly to his side.

"Dad, I want you to meet my fiancée. Hope Spencer."

Marjorie let out a sound that could only be described as an excited squeal.

"She said yes?"

Logan nodded, wearing a grin that could have lit the entire house.

"She sure did."

Before Hope could blink, Marjorie swept the two of them into another embrace, one arm around Logan, one around Hope, squeezing them both with joyful vigor that made Hope laugh breathlessly.

Robert Shaw stepped forward then, pride softening his rugged features. He hugged his son firmly, then turned to Hope and clasped her hand with surprising gentleness.

"Will you allow me to hug you as well?" he asked, his tone warm, respectful... and hopeful.

Hope's heart softened. She nodded.

Robert pulled her into his arms, strong, but careful, as though he feared she might break. Hope felt a knot form in her throat. *This* was what a father's embrace should have felt like. Safe. Steady. Loved.

Before she could gather herself, footsteps echoed in the entryway, and another couple entered, followed by three teenagers, all curious-eyed and eager. The youngest was the girl who had peeked into the barn the day Hope arrived in Cheyenne.

Claire crossed her arms triumphantly and cast a smug glance at her older siblings.

"See?" she declared proudly. "I told you she was pretty."

Hope's blush flared instantly, and Logan pulled her a little closer, unable to hide his grin. The eyes of his entire family, warm, welcoming, and full of budding affection, settled on her, and Hope finally understood what it meant to be embraced not out of obligation... but out of genuine love.

"Hope?" Lilly called, glancing around the ranch yard.

"I'm here, by the creek."

Lilly rounded the house and followed the narrow path through the trees until she reached the water's edge. Hope sat on a fallen tree trunk, her hair stirred by the cold breeze, and offered her friend a soft smile.

"What brings you out here today?" Lilly asked. "It's freezing."

Hope exhaled slowly. "I just... needed a place to think."

Lilly settled beside her, nudging her shoulder gently.

"Are you worried about something? Is it your upcoming wedding?"

Hope shook her head. "I'm not worried. I'm just... having trouble deciding."

"Does it have anything to do with the wedding?" Lilly pressed. This time, Hope nodded. "What decision are you struggling with?" Lilly asked, brows lifting. Hope stared at the rushing creek for a long moment before answering.

"Who will walk me down the aisle."

Lilly blinked. "Isn't your grandfather going to do that?"

Hope nodded again.

"You... don't want him to?" Lilly asked carefully.

"It's not that," Hope sighed. "I would love for Grandpa to walk me down the aisle. But I'm torn." She hesitated before continuing quietly. "Do you think he'd be disappointed, or offended, if I wanted Uncle Jeff to do it instead?"

Lilly tilted her head. "Why would you want your uncle to give you away instead of your grandfather?"

Hope took a long breath, choosing her words carefully.

"I thought... since Grandpa has three daughters and he walked two of them down the aisle, maybe it would mean something for Uncle Jeff to walk his niece. He only has sons." She paused. "But that isn't the real reason."

Lilly smiled knowingly. "I didn't think so."

Hope swallowed hard. "I love my grandfather. Truly. And I'm grateful for all of them. But there's something about Uncle Jeff... from the moment I met him, I felt close to him. Safe." Her voice softened. "Maybe it's because he was close with my mother, they were only three years apart. Maybe some part of me feels connected to her through him." She hesitated, vulnerability creeping into her voice. "But I don't even know if he'd want to do it."

"Why wouldn't he?" Lilly asked gently.

"I'm just a niece," Hope murmured. "And he has many of those. Just because he's special to me doesn't mean I'm special to him." Her eyes glistened as emotion rose. "When he hugged me for the first time... it made me realize what I'd never had. I wish..." Her voice cracked. "I wish he could have been my father. He's everything I ever wished for in one."

Lilly's expression softened deeply.

"Hope, I may not know your uncle well, but I know what I saw. That man loves you. And not in the casual, distant way some uncles treat nieces. When you took that bullet, and when you were taken afterward, he looked ready to tear the world apart to find you." She squeezed Hope's hand. "That wasn't duty. That was love."

Hope's breath trembled.

"And your grandfather won't be hurt," Lilly continued. "He'll understand. And Jeff?" She smiled. "He'll be honored."

"You think so?" Hope whispered.

"I know so."

Hope's face relaxed into a grateful smile, and she leaned in to hug her friend, when a deep voice behind them made both girls jump.

"You have no idea how happy it made me to hear that," Jeff said. Hope spun around, cheeks flushing, joy lighting her eyes. She hurried to him, and he swept her into his arms, holding her tight.

"I love you, Hope," he murmured into her hair. "You are like a daughter to me. Having you here... it brought a piece of Georgiana back to us."

Hope's tears spilled as she buried her face in his shirt. Footsteps sounded, and Parker joined them with a fond smile.

"And your feelings did not mislead you," Parker added. "Jeff and Georgiana were inseparable when they were young, best friends as well as siblings."

Hope lifted her head, looking between them. "Really?"

Jeff nodded, emotion shining in his eyes. Parker squeezed her hand.

"Pa won't be disappointed, you wanting Jeff to walk you down the aisle," he said. "Quite the opposite. We all know it's what your mother would have wanted."

Hope's lips trembled into a smile, and Jeff's embrace tightened around her, steady and protective.

"You'd better get down from there this very moment," Logan growled, though the playful edge in his voice and the massive grin on his face made it anything but threatening. From above, Hope didn't even bother showing her face.

"I don't think so," she called back, all prim and sassy. "You threatened me with punishment, and for what? You asked for a cold drink, and I brought you one."

"Ha! You know perfectly well, I meant cold water. What I got was definitely not that."

"It was an honest mistake," she insisted, though Logan could practically hear her smirk.

"Are you coming down now," he warned, "or do I have to come up there? Pulling up the ladder isn't going to stop me from getting to you."

She went quiet at that, too quiet, which only confirmed she was plotting something. Footsteps sounded, and someone entered the barn.

"Hey, Logan. What are you doing?" Brent asked, stopping beside him. Sawyer trailed behind, already wearing the expression of someone who recognized mischief when he saw it.

"I'm trying to get my hands on your cousin," Logan announced. Brent's eyebrows shot up. Sawyer burst out laughing.

"Uh oh. What did she do this time?"

"I asked her to bring me a cold drink, clearly meaning water," Logan said through gritted, amused teeth, glaring up at the loft. "And she came back with vinegar. Vinegar. And like a fool, I drank it. A big sip. By the time I spat it out, she'd vanished."

Brent winced sympathetically. "Oof. Rough."

Sawyer shielded his eyes dramatically and called up, "Hope, you little terror! You're going to get yourself murdered one of these days."

Logan ignored them both, narrowing his eyes at the hayloft. She was up there somewhere, crouched in the shadows, probably holding in her laughter.

"All right then," he muttered. He crouched slightly, then in one swift movement jumped, grabbed the edge of the loft with both hands, and hauled himself upward. Muscles flexed. Boots scraped wood. Both Brent and Sawyer let out low whistles.

"He's serious," Brent murmured. Hope squeaked, actually squeaked, somewhere above him.

"Oh no," she whispered frantically.

Logan grinned wider. "Ah. There you are."

Hope waited until Logan swung one leg over the edge of the hayloft. The instant his weight shifted, she darted toward the ladder, dropped it back into place, climbed down faster than she ever had in her life, and bolted across the barn floor. She was inches from freedom when—

*Thud.* Logan dropped from the loft like a mountain lion pouncing on its prey, landing directly in front of her. Hope skidded to a halt, her heart leaping into her throat as a startled gasp tore from her.

"Going somewhere?" he drawled. Before she could answer, he grabbed her around the waist and tossed her over his shoulder as if she weighed nothing. Hope shrieked and immediately started wiggling.

"Logan Shaw! Put me down!"

He didn't even flinch. Strong arms locked around her legs as he carried her straight toward the creek with long, determined strides.

"No, please don't throw me in!" she begged. "It's freezing! Logan, it's cruel, inhumane, even!"

"You should've thought of that before poisoning me with vinegar," he said far too cheerfully.

"Please, Logan." She tried changing tactics, softening her voice. "You can't be that heartless. Don't you love me anymore?"

He stopped walking. Hope froze. Then, in one smooth motion, he slid her from his shoulder and pulled her flush against his chest, his hands firm at her back.

"That isn't going to work on me, Hope," he murmured. Before she could deny the accusation or attempt another plea, his mouth claimed hers.

The kiss wasn't gentle. It was hungry, fierce, the kind that made her toes curl and her knees go weak beneath her. She melted completely, clutching his shirt as her heart thundered. When he finally drew back, Hope was breathless, her cheeks a fiery shade of red.

"That... that wasn't fair," she gasped.

Logan's smirk was sinful. "I'm only showing you how I intend to kiss you after we say, '*I do*' in a week."

Hope's eyes flew wide. "Logan Shaw! We will be inside a church. You cannot kiss me like that during the ceremony, that is inappropriate!"

He lifted an eyebrow, wholly unbothered.

"It is? You asked me if I still loved you, and I simply demonstrated my devotion. Quite thoroughly, I might add."

Hope opened and closed her mouth, gaping at him like a flustered fish. Then she spun around and marched away with an indignant huff.

"Where are you going?" he called after her, amusement dripping from his voice.

"I'm getting you another glass of vinegar! Clearly the sip you had wasn't enough!" She burst into laughter as she sprinted toward the house, but she'd forgotten one very important thing. Logan was much faster.

He caught her mid-step. Arms wrapped around her waist as he spun her into him. Hope squealed, then went instantly still when she realized how close they were, his chest against hers, his breath warm on her cheek, his smile softening into something achingly tender. Hope rose on her tiptoes and pressed a gentle kiss to his lips.

"I love you, Logan," she whispered. His hands tightened at her waist, drawing her even closer.

"I love you too, Hope. More than you'll ever know."

"Are you ready to meet with Reverend Fisher at the church?" Logan asked as he stepped closer, brushing a stray curl behind her ear. Hope nodded, though her brows pinched together.

"Tell me again why we're meeting with a reverend we don't even know? It still makes no sense."

"Reverend Matthews had an urgent family matter," Logan explained gently. "He asked a friend to handle our final premarital discussion. I met with him this morning, he seems like a good man. I'll join you when it's time for the couple's meeting."

Hope wrinkled her nose adorably.

"I don't like the idea of meeting him alone. It feels... awkward."

A warm, reassuring smile softened Logan's feature.

"He's friendly. You'll like him, I promise. But if it eases your mind, I'll try to get there as early as I can. I just need to stop by and speak with my father. He wants to go over something about the ranch."

Hope relaxed a little, though her fingers still fidgeted with the reins.

"When will your brother get here?"

"He should arrive sometime the afternoon before our wedding," Logan replied, a quiet excitement in his voice that made Hope's stomach flutter. He helped her mount her horse, his hands lingering just a second longer than necessary. She blushed at the tenderness in his eyes. Logan swung into his own saddle a moment later.

"He's looking forward to seeing you again. And yes," he added with a grin, "he'll be the one marrying us."

Hope felt warmth bloom in her cheeks.

"Good. I... I'd like that."

They rode together for a while, the crisp air brushing against them, the horses' hooves thudding rhythmically beneath the bright sky. As they neared the fork in the road, Logan slowed his horse.

"I'll see you soon," he said softly.

Hope nodded, releasing a breath she hadn't realized she'd been holding. She watched Logan turn his horse toward the Shaw ranch, urging it into a gallop. Something tight in her chest eased as she followed the opposite path toward town, toward the church, the reverend, and the next step toward becoming Mrs. Logan Shaw.

When Hope arrived at the church, she dismounted her horse, took a steadying breath, and walked toward the entrance. A young red-haired woman stood rigidly by the doors, her posture stiff, her green eyes fixed on Hope with an unblinking, territorial intensity.

Though they had never been formally introduced, Hope recognized her instantly. And from the way Harriet Silvers tracked her every step, it was clear the mayor's daughter had been waiting, specifically, for her.

"Hope Spencer," Harriet called sharply as Hope neared. "We meet at last."

"It seems that way," Hope replied coolly. She hadn't forgotten Harriet's shameless attempt to manipulate Logan into marriage, nor her theatrics at the president's arrival. A sharp, unwelcome jealousy tightened in Hope's chest, fierce and unexpected. She almost wanted to claw the smug expression off Harriet's pretty face.

"Do you know who I am?" Harriet asked, chin lifted arrogantly, as if the world existed solely to admire her.

"I do," Hope answered evenly, though irritation prickled beneath her calm.

"It seems you've caused nothing but trouble for me and my family since the day you arrived."

"Is that so?" Hope replied dryly. "An interesting accusation, considering we've never actually spoken until now."

Harriet's cheeks flushed.

"I was supposed to marry Logan Shaw. And you—" She jabbed a finger at Hope as though she were filth. "You little temptress stole him from me."

Hope's expression hardened. "That isn't what I heard. From what I understand, Logan was never interested in you. It seems you were attempting to manipulate him into a marriage he clearly didn't want."

Harriet scoffed loudly. "What would you know? You weren't here. Logan and I grew up together."

"And yet," Hope countered with a cool, triumphant smirk, "he chose me. Odd how childhood closeness didn't help your case."

Harriet's eyes flashed with humiliation and fury.

"My father is in prison now, thanks to you."

Hope folded her arms. "Your father is in prison because of his own crimes. Don't try to place that burden on me."

"He's in prison because of you," Harriet insisted.

"No," Hope snapped. "And if we're pointing fingers, perhaps you should be the one behind bars. You ran to my father and half-brother after I was shot. You nearly got the president killed because you couldn't control your jealousy."

Harriet gasped. "How do you know that?"

"It wasn't difficult to deduce," Hope replied coldly. "Your outburst distracted the marshals long enough for Gregory to take his shot." She leaned closer. "I know you saw me lying there, bleeding. And instead of helping, you ran to your father."

Harriet's lips pressed into a thin, offended line. Hope turned toward the church doors.

"Now, if you'll excuse me, delightful as this conversation has been, I have a meeting with the reverend."

She reached for the handle when arms seized her from behind. She was shoved forward so abruptly she stumbled. Her first instinct was that Harriet had attacked her, but no. These arms were far too strong. She twisted in horror. A man held her in a crushing grip. And standing inside the church was her father's butler.

# 24

# The Day the Lies Died

"Mr. Pratt," Hope gasped. "What is the meaning of this—?"

Before she could finish, her captor, spun her around. She stared into the cold, familiar eyes of a nightmare she believed, she had escaped.

"You and I will be married at once," Gregory hissed. "Nothing will stop it this time."

Hope's blood froze. "How... how did you get out of prison?"

"That wasn't difficult," another voice answered darkly.

Her father stepped into view. Hope's stomach dropped. She fought, but Pratt and Gregory overpowered her easily, forcing her into a chair and binding her wrists tightly. Winston Spencer stepped in front of her, his expression a blend of fury and triumph.

"Why can't you leave me alone?" Hope cried. "You murdered my mother, isn't that enough? Why force me to marry a traitor? He tried to kill me!"

Her father's icy gaze never wavered.

"Yes, killing you was part of the plan. But we need you after all."

Hope scoffed. "For what? And why is Harriet here?"

Winston glanced toward the girl, who stood smugly near the front pew.

"Since you ruined everything, I need money so Gregory and I can leave the country. My former in-laws will pay handsomely if my offspring marries one of their heirs. Harriet is conveniently unencumbered now. Once you are married, Logan will finally be free to take her."

Hope laughed bitterly. "He'd sooner choose a cactus over her. And what nonsense is this about Gregory's parents? You told me they died."

"I lied," Winston said flatly.

Hope's fury ignited. "Do they know you're a murderer? Did you kill your first wife when she stopped being useful? Did your father teach you how to be a monster, or did you kill him too?"

"Silence!" Winston roared, raising his hand. Before he could strike, Reverend Fisher stepped between them.

"If you touch her," the reverend warned, "I'll see you locked away for the rest of your life."

Winston shoved him aside. "Get on with it!"

Hope's heart sank. "You're working with them?"

The reverend's eyes glistened with shame.

"They threatened my family. And Miss Silvers exploited it."

Harriet merely shrugged, smug and unrepentant. Gregory gagged Hope, and the rushed ceremony began. Minutes later, Reverend Fisher declared them husband and wife. Gregory yanked the gag away and leaned in. Hope jerked back in revulsion.

"This isn't legal! I never consented!"

"My consent was all that mattered," Winston sneered. "Everything is exactly as it should be."

The world tilted. Hope's knees buckled, but Gregory hauled her upright and crushed his mouth against hers. Nausea surged. Then, the church doors slammed open. Logan and his father stormed inside, guns raised.

"Let her go!" Logan thundered. Winston only grinned.

"Too late. She's Gregory's wife now. But don't worry, Harriet Silvers is eager to take her place at your side."

Harriet attempted a radiant smile. Logan didn't even glance at her. Winston turned to his son.

"Kill him."

Gregory clamped a hand over Hope's mouth, drew his gun, and aimed at Logan. Hope screamed, muffled, desperate. Gunshots exploded. Her vision blurred. Strength drained from her limbs. Gregory dragged her backward toward the rear exit as men flooded the church. Someone shouted. Someone fell. Then the world tilted. Hope collapsed. And everything went black.

Hope opened her eyes, though at first, she couldn't place where she was. A low groan slipped past her lips as she blinked, trying to bring the room into focus. Wooden beams. Tall windows. Pews. She was in the church, lying across one of the benches.

Around her stood several U.S. marshals and deputies, along with the sheriff and his deputy. Across the room, the three criminals were bound and handcuffed. Dr. Jensen had just finished tending Winston Spencer's shoulder wound. Hope's gaze darted frantically around, searching for one person.

Logan reached her side instantly.

She threw her arms around his neck and dissolved into tears, trembling so hard he instinctively swept her up, holding her firmly against his chest while gently stroking her hair.

"It's over, Hope," he murmured against her temple. "You're safe now."

"I—I don't care about that," she sobbed into his shoulder. "I thought they had killed you."

He sat down on the bench with her still clinging to him, refusing to loosen his hold. It took several minutes before her crying eased into shaky breaths. When her body finally stilled, Jeff Stewart stepped forward and gently eased her into his own arms.

"I'm sorry we couldn't intervene sooner," he said softly. Hope blinked up at him through puffy eyes.

"You... you knew this would happen today?"

Jeff nodded. "We suspected they would attempt something, so we enlisted several men in town to play along should your father or Gregory reach out to them."

Hope tried to absorb that, but her thoughts tangled.

"Harriet Silvers..." she whispered. Jeff nodded grimly.

"She kept in touch with your father and informed him of the meeting with Reverend Matthews. She knew when it would take place. She'll be placed under house arrest for her involvement. Reverend Matthews has already arranged a place for her."

"But Reverend Matthews wasn't even here."

"No," Jeff replied. "He asked his friend Curt Fisher to pose as the clergyman."

Hope looked at the unfamiliar man stepping closer, and then the meaning hit her all at once.

"So... I'm not married to Gregory?" Her voice came out small, thin, almost childlike. Her face had gone pale again. Jeff shook his head firmly.

"No, Hope. You're not."

She sagged with relief. "Thank goodness..."

Another man, one she didn't recognize, spoke up.

"Even if Curt were an ordained clergyman, the marriage would not have been valid without your father's consent."

Hope swallowed hard. "But my father gave his consent," she murmured, unable to meet their eyes. Curt Fisher stepped closer and offered a gentle squeeze of her hand.

"I wish I could have prevented what happened. But when Reverend Matthews asked for help, I knew this was the only way to stop them once and for all."

Hope's gaze drifted toward the front of the church. Toward the enemy she still needed answers from. Gregory and Mr. Pratt had already been taken away by the marshals, but her father sat chained to a bench, hateful and silent. Hope pushed herself shakily to her feet and walked toward him.

"I want answers," she said sharply, leveling him with a glare. Winston scoffed. "Come on, Father," she pressed. "It's over. You may as well tell me when you sold your soul, and why." She shook her head in bitter disbelief. "Was Grandfather so terrible that it turned you into this as well?"

"My father?" Winston spat. "Your grandfather was a weak coward. It was my mother who taught my brothers and me to be real men."

"Real men?" Hope echoed, her voice slicing the air. "Real men don't torture people. Real men protect those in their care. If Grandmother thinks cruelty is a measure of manhood, then I pity her. There is nothing manly about making people afraid of you."

His jaw tightened, but she pressed on.

"So, did you kill Grandfather? And your first wife? And your youngest brother?" Her voice wavered with disgust. "Since I never even met them, I must assume you disposed of your brother too."

Winston's laugh was chilling. "You don't have to kill everyone to get them out of your life. But yes, I made sure my first wife and father would never return. They were worthless anyway."

Hope's stomach turned.

Winston sneered. "Tell me, Hope, how did you hide who you truly are? How did you keep your temper at bay?"

Her expression darkened. "Just because you can't control yourself doesn't mean others can't. Mama taught me everything about controlling anger, not to please you, but to protect herself... and me." Her voice softened, but her eyes blazed. "She kept in contact with Reverend Shaw behind your back. And with Dr. Baker. You might have thought you controlled her, but she carved out whatever small freedoms she could."

A visible crack appeared in Winston's confidence. Hope pressed harder.

"You hired Governess Brighton to watch me? Did you ever question who she was loyal to?"

Her father stiffened.

"She applied for that job because Reverend Shaw sent her," Hope said, savoring the shock on his face. "She only pretended to be strict so you wouldn't suspect anything."

Winston shook with rage.

"When I got older," Hope continued, "my governess and I had a silent understanding. She taught me exactly how to appear obedient when it mattered. Mama taught me how to hold my temper, how to choose my battles. And it's because of her that I survived you."

Winston scoffed. "I should have known you're more like your father than your mother."

The remark hit Hope like a whip.

"I am nothing like you," she hissed. "I have my mother's strength and stubbornness, and her will to survive—"

Winston cut in with venom. "Her will didn't last very long, did it? In case you forgot, your mother is dead."

Hope's face crumpled, anguish ripping through her. Logan stepped in instantly, pulling her into his arms. Several marshals moved forward, tension thick enough to choke on. Before Hope could steady her breathing, two of the unfamiliar men stepped aside, and a third entered the church, marching straight toward Winston Spencer. He seized Winston by the throat and yanked him forward with enough force to make every marshal flinch.

"I suggest you keep your mouth shut, Winston," the man growled. "You are the most demonic man I've ever encountered."

Hope stared in confusion. Winston's eyes widened in horror.

"Charles?" he choked, struggling for air. "What are you doing here? I was told you were dead."

Charles scoffed, a low, bitter sound rumbling from deep in his chest.

"It seems there were plenty of secrets you didn't know, Winston." He nodded once toward the two strangers who had remained at the back of the church, hats low, faces hidden. They stepped forward now, removing their hats in unison. Winston Spencer's face drained of all color.

"This... this is impossible!"

The two men stood tall despite their age, weathered, strong, and steady. Hope guessed they had to be close to eighty, perhaps even older. Their posture was proud, their eyes sharp with decades of unspoken truth. One of them stepped closer, his voice deep and trembling with restrained emotion.

"Are you surprised to see me... son?"

The word *son* cracked through the church like lightning. Gasps echoed. Hope went white as chalk, and Logan tightened his arm around her waist, steadying her as her knees threatened to buckle. Winston staggered back, staring at the man who should have been long dead.

"You can't be alive," he rasped. "We—you—we poisoned you!"

The older man smiled sadly.

"No, Winston. You thought you poisoned me. Georgiana discovered your plan and warned me. She saved my life. With the help of Dr. Baker, we staged my death, and I left California for Colorado, where my younger brother lived."

Winston's face twisted in rage. "So, you hid like a coward all these years?"

"You may call it cowardice," the man replied, his eyes blazing, "but I chose survival. The Lord wasn't ready to call me home, not while my sons fell deeper into darkness."

Winston barked out a cruel laugh.

"So that's why you left us nothing? Not even Mother? Everything went to your brother instead!"

"That is correct," the man said with chilling finality. "Your mother married me for my wealth. She raised you boys to be greedy, selfish, and merciless. All of you, except Charles." He rested a hand on Charles's shoulder. "I refused to leave my fortune to people who had no intention of doing good with it." He drew a slow breath, trying to steady the fury trembling through his hands.

"When Georgiana died, I contacted Charles. That's when I learned what you'd done, keeping him a prisoner under his own roof."

Winston scoffed.

"He deserved it."

"No one deserved what you did," Charles cut in sharply. "But that doesn't matter now. You won't win this."

Winston's lip curled into a sneer. "I already won, Charles."

Charles stepped forward, his eyes burning.

"You may have won some battles... but the war ends today."

He glanced toward Hope, his expression softening for the briefest moment.

"After I ensured my own family was safe, I staged my death as well. I've been working quietly with the marshals ever since. I wasn't going to let you win this, not while Georgiana's daughter was still in danger."

Winston snarled, "Go to—"

"I have no desire to go where you will be headed," Charles cut him off coldly. "I'm here for one reason, to tell Hope the truth you've hidden all her life."

"She won't believe you," Winston spat. His expression twisted further when he saw Hope trembling with shock, her hand clinging tightly to Logan's. Another voice spoke then, calm, steady.

"I think she will believe us."

Hope looked over sharply as the second older man stepped forward. He met her gaze with gentle, grief-lined eyes.

"After all," he said quietly, "I am a living witness to everything your father has done."

Hope's gaze moved from one man to the next, her pulse thundering in her ears. She had followed everything that had been said, yet her mind struggled to keep pace with the implications. Her grandfather, alive. Her uncle, alive. Her entire childhood, built on lies. But one man remained a mystery. The third stranger.

"Who are you?" she asked, her voice taut with exhaustion and suspicion. The older man stepped forward with a gentle, almost apologetic smile, his eyes warm despite the weight of grief etched into them.

"My name is Walter Jessop. My daughter... she was Winston's first wife."

Hope's expression hardened instantly.

"So you are behind this twisted scheme," she snapped. "Behind forcing me into a marriage with your youngest son?"

Walter raised both hands, shaking his head quickly.

"Gregory isn't my son," he said. "He's my grandson. My daughter married once before she ever met Winston." His voice tightened. "I came because I wanted justice for her death. Winston murdered her, I never doubted it. I knew he could be manipulated with money, but when your mother died, I realized something far worse was happening. I believed that if I cornered him, he might confess." His gaze softened as it returned to Hope.

"You," he added gently, "brought the truth out of him far better than any plan I ever devised."

Hope's breath hitched. Confusion pressed down on her chest like a suffocating fog.

"I don't understand," she whispered. "Why are you here now? What does any of this have to do with me?"

Walter exchanged a weighted glance with Hope's grandfather. Her stomach dropped.

"There is no simple way to say this," Walter said quietly. "But Winston... is not your father."

Gasps rippled through the church. Hope's own escaped before she could stop it. Her shock lasted only a heartbeat before anger surged, fierce and protective.

"This isn't the time for cruel jokes," she snapped. "My mother was only ever married once, to Winston Spencer. I sincerely hope you're not suggesting she was unfaithful—"

"I'm not," Walter said gently.

"... or that I was born out of wedlock," Hope continued sharply. "Because I will not stand here and listen to anyone tarnish her honor."

Walter lifted a calming hand.

"Your mother's honor is not in question. She was a good woman. A loyal wife."

Hope shook her head firmly. "Then what are you saying? I was born ten months after my parents' wedding."

"No," Walter corrected softly. "You were born four months after their wedding."

The world tilted beneath Hope's feet. Her eyes blazed.

"You contradict yourself with every sentence," she shot back. "You claim she was faithful, then imply she wasn't. You say she wasn't unwed yet insist the dates don't align. So, which is it? Are you accusing her of improper relations before marriage? Or are you suggesting I'm illegitimate, and Winston married her because she was with child and another man abandoned her?" Her voice shook with restrained fury. "Because I've seen their wedding record. And nothing you're saying is possible."

"The wedding record," Walter said sadly, "was falsified."

Silence crashed down upon the church. Hope stared at him as though he had claimed the sky was green. Her pulse hammered. Her breath came fast and shallow. Every instinct inside her screamed to reject it, but something in Walter's expression, something in her grandfather's grief-shadowed eyes...

*No*, she thought fiercely. *Absolutely not.*

# 25

# Home at Last

"You know what?" Hope snapped, her voice trembling with outrage. "I'm done listening to this nonsense. Yes, my father is a vile man who murdered my mother, but for you to stand here and spread lies about her—"

She spun toward the church doors, but Charles caught her arm.

"Unhand me at once," she barked, jerking free, her eyes blazing.

"Hope, listen," Walter urged, stepping forward. "We know how unbelievable this sounds. But please, please, hear us out."

Every face in the church turned toward her, watching the storm raging behind her eyes. She stood rigid, trembling, breath uneven. Part of her wanted to flee, to leave them all drowning in their madness. But something else, something buried deep, urged her to stay. Slowly, she turned back. Walter exhaled softly in relief and continued.

"When your mother met Winston, she was charmed at first. He knew how to manipulate, how to appear kind and generous. But she soon discovered the truth, how dark he truly was." He paused, weighing his next words. "Not long after that... she met someone else. Someone she fell deeply in love with. And because Winston only wanted to possess her, she ran. They ran. They eloped."

Hope's jaw tightened. Her eyes burned, but she said nothing.

"They married in a small church in Montana," Walter went on. "They lived quietly for several months, happily, secretly. I didn't know any of this at the time. I believed Winston was courting your mother. That's what he told everyone. My own daughter had died only weeks earlier, and Winston played the grieving widower well. I believed him." His eyes darkened. "But one day, I overheard him speaking with Mr. Pratt, and it became clear my daughter's death had not been an accident."

Hope's breath hitched. Logan's arm tightened around her shoulders.

"I approached Winston," Walter continued, voice heavy with regret, "pretending I wanted an alliance. I suggested our families might someday unite through marriage. I spoke of influence, wealth, and heirs." He swallowed hard. "I didn't know he had suffered an accident years earlier, one that left him unable to father children. If I had known... I would never have said those words. But it gave him a reason, a sick reason, to hunt Georgiana down. When he finally found her five months later, she was expecting a child."

Hope's knees wobbled. Logan steadied her instantly. Jeff Stewart stepped forward, voice firm.

"Taking Georgiana from her husband and raising Hope as his daughter doesn't make her his heir."

Walter shook his head. "It does, if she is blood-related."

Jeff frowned. "But she isn't."

Walter's gaze shifted to Hope. "Actually... she is."

Hope's heart stopped. The world tilted violently beneath her feet.

"The man your mother married before Winston forced himself into her life," Walter said quietly, "was Winston's brother. Charles."

Hope gasped, air rushing from her lungs as if she'd been struck. She looked at Winston, then at Charles, then back again, her body numb. Logan held her upright. Jeff's voice was tight.

"Do you have proof of this?"

"Of course he doesn't!" Winston snarled. "It's all lies—"

"We do have proof," Walter cut in sharply, turning a murderous glare on Winston. "Winston arrived at the church in Montana, dragged Georgiana away, threatened the clergyman, and forced him to renounce the marriage. He burned the wedding record. Then he marched her to a doctor and forced him to certify that the unborn child was his." His voice hardened. "He threatened everyone who stood in his way."

Charles stepped closer, pain etched deep into his face.

"It was torture, for years. Not only losing Georgiana but being unable to free her. Winston told the world you were his daughter. He kept constant watch over me, wouldn't allow me to leave. He convinced everyone he had married Georgiana long before, and that her family wanted her back because they were abusive."

Hope stared at the man she had believed was her father and saw something she had never seen before. Fear.

"How do you even know all this?" Winston barked. "You weren't anywhere near us. Everyone who worked for me followed my orders."

"You only believed they obeyed," Charles replied coldly. "You controlled Georgiana through fear. But I remained in quiet contact with Dr. Baker. My current wife carried letters through trusted friends. Reverend Shaw passed along what little he could. And after Georgiana's death, the clergyman who married us and the doctor who treated her both came to me. They kept duplicate records. They offered to testify."

Winston's face drained of color.

"Walter and I joined forces," Charles continued. "We wanted to rescue Hope, for different reasons, but we wanted her free. Walter is an attorney. He understood the legal dangers. When we learned Georgiana's family had settled in Wyoming, we planned to meet Hope here and tell her the truth. But then one of my daughters fell desperately ill, and I had to delay our travel."

Hope swayed again, but Logan wouldn't let her fall.

"When Winston escaped," Charles finished quietly, "we had to wait again. If he discovered I was alive, he would have tried to kill me. So, we came as soon as it was safe."

Hope's breath trembled. Her head spun. Her pulse thundered in her ears as she stared at Charles, the man who might be her true father, and felt something stir in her chest. Something uncertain. Something aching.

*Was this why Mama wanted me to find the diary? Was this the truth she died protecting?*

As if he had read the very question trembling in her mind, Hope's grandfather reached slowly into his coat pocket. His weathered hand emerged holding a small, leather-bound book.

"It is time for you to have this," he said gently. Hope's breath caught. She accepted the book with trembling fingers, the weight of it somehow heavier than its size should allow.

"Where... where did you find it?" she whispered.

Her grandfather smiled sadly. "Your mother gave it to me before I faked my death and left for Colorado. She confided in me not long after she was forced to marry Winston. She told me everything, her elopement with Charles, Winston's threats, the annulment he forced upon her. Neither of us knew the truth until she told it. I was devastated... but nothing could be done. She asked me to keep this safe and to give it to her child when it was finally safe to do so."

Hope swallowed hard as her vision blurred.

"But Mama always had a diary. When she told me I'd find answers in it... I thought Whitmer stole it."

Her grandfather shook his head. "Your mother was far too clever to trust Winston or Pratt with the truth. The diary you knew was a decoy, nothing but harmless entries meant to keep suspicion away. This one," he said, gesturing to the small book in her hands, "holds the truth. Her past. Her fears. Her love for you. She wanted you to know everything, if she never had the chance to tell you yourself."

Hope's fingers trembled as she opened the diary. The moment she saw her mother's familiar looping handwriting, emotion slammed into her so hard, her knees nearly buckled. A soft sob escaped her. Logan stepped closer, pulling her gently against his chest, one hand cradling the back of her head. She clung to him, the diary pressed between them, like a fragile heartbeat.

Charles approached slowly, his expression full of grief, love, and years of unspoken sorrow.

"Hope," he murmured, "I am so sorry you had to learn all this without your mother here to guide you. You were forced to grow up under the roof of a man who claimed to be your father yet never offered you love." His voice wavered.

"I am grateful you now have your grandfather. He will show you, truly show you, that not every Spencer is a monster. Winston, my brothers... even my own mother, they were consumed by greed, pride, and cruelty. But not all of us are like that."

Hope lifted her head. Cheeks streaked with tears. Logan kept his arm around her, grounding her. She met Charles's gaze fully and saw something she had longed for her entire life. Fatherly love. Real fatherly love. Gentle. Patient. Aching.

Charles continued softly, "I loved your mother more deeply than words can express. I wanted to protect her, Heaven knows I tried but following her would have put her in grave danger. Winston had power, influence... and malice. He threatened me more than once. He said if I ever pursued her again, he would have her killed the moment the baby was born." His voice broke.

"I could not risk her life. Or yours. He did not love her. He only wanted to possess her. And he wanted you for reasons darker still."

Hope's throat constricted. She turned toward him fully now. Tears shimmered in her eyes, but beneath them, something new glowed, recognition, longing, an aching possibility.

"I've waited for this moment my whole life," Charles whispered. His voice trembled as if the words themselves might shatter. "Hope... will you allow me to hold you?"

Silence filled the church. Everyone watched her, but no one dared to speak. Hope hesitated, only a heartbeat, just long enough to steady her breath, before she nodded. Charles exhaled shakily, relief and love flooded his face. He stepped forward, took her hand with profound gentleness, and drew her into his arms.

Hope melted against him, her forehead pressing into his shoulder. His arms wrapped around her with careful strength, protection and reverence, as though she were something precious he had long believed lost. Her tears soaked into his shirt, but he only held her closer.

And in those arms, in the warmth of a man who should have held her from the moment she came into the world, Hope felt something she had never known from Winston. The embrace of a father. The embrace of someone who loved her. The embrace of someone who would protect her, not break her.

Logan watched them with quiet reverence, his hand resting over his heart. Jeff brushed a tear from his cheek. Even the marshals lowered their eyes, granting them a moment of sacred privacy.

And for the first time in her life, Hope felt whole.

The days leading up to the wedding passed in a blur, sweet, busy, and filled with more joy than Hope had ever dared imagine for herself. Every spare moment she could steal, she spent with her true father and her grandfather, learning everything she could about them and allowing them, at long last, to learn about her. There was so much time to make up for. Years stolen. Memories they had never been given the chance to build. But none of them intended to lose another second. Both men made one thing abundantly clear: they were staying. Permanently.

After decades of living under threats, secrets, and distance, they wanted their lives rooted where Hope was. They had missed every milestone of her childhood, her first steps, her first words, her laughter, her tears, and they would not miss another moment if it was within their power.

Charles, eager to reclaim the life that had once been stolen from him, approached Dr. Jensen about the future of the clinic. The two physicians spoke for hours, and by the end of their discussion, Charles had agreed to work alongside him until the older man retired, after which Charles would take over the practice entirely. Hope could hardly contain her excitement at the thought of her father becoming one of Cheyenne's trusted doctors.

Her grandfather, Loren Spencer, made similar plans to settle in town. Hope found herself quietly delighted by his presence. His steady strength, gentle humor, and warm affection soothed parts of her heart she hadn't even realized were wounded. He took great pleasure in accompanying her on afternoon walks, sharing stories of her mother, and watching Hope rediscover the laughter she had been forced to bury for so many years.

Jeff, too, began to see Cheyenne through new eyes. With his sons grown, married, and managing lives of their own, the pull of his childhood home grew stronger with each passing day. He announced his intention to retire there, a decision that brought nothing but joy to his parents.

But the town had plans of its own. Within days, word spread about Jeff Stewart, the man who had helped save the president, who had brought down Winston Spencer's gang, who had protected Hope with unwavering devotion. The townspeople banded together, and before Jeff fully understood what was happening, they approached him with a unanimous request: they wanted him to be the new mayor of Cheyenne.

At first, Jeff laughed, certain they were joking. But they weren't. They admired his integrity, his leadership, and his calm, steady presence. They trusted him. And for the first time in a very long while, Jeff found himself considering a role that wasn't about chasing outlaws or moving from town to town, but about putting down roots. About coming home.

Hope could hardly believe how much her world had changed. In the span of only a few days, her family had grown, truly grown, branching outward in ways she had never dared to imagine. The two men she had feared, resented, and wondered about for most of her life were suddenly here, alive, choosing her. Choosing to stay. Choosing to build a future that revolved not around control or obligation, but around her happiness and safety.

For the first time, Hope felt anchored. Rooted. Surrounded by people who wanted her not for what she could provide, but simply because she belonged to them. It felt like the beginning of something beautiful.

And as that truth settled warmly into her heart, another realization followed close behind. Her wedding day was drawing near.

The evening before the wedding, Hope was invited to supper with Logan and his family, a gesture that warmed her heart while making her stomach flutter with nerves all at once. This would be her first time meeting Logan's two older sisters, and her first time seeing Reverend Shaw again since the day she had left San Francisco behind.

When she stepped into the Shaws' cozy sitting room, lanternlight spilled amber warmth across the walls. Reverend Shaw rose at once and took a few steps toward her, wearing a soft, almost hesitant smile, one she had never seen from him before.

"Hope," he greeted gently, emotion threading his voice. "It's good to see you again. Have you forgiven me yet?" His sheepish grin made several of the women in the room exchange amused glances.

Hope inhaled deeply. She was grateful for everything the Shaws had done, the risks they had taken, the protection they had offered, the family she had found because of them, but the sting of being lied to still lingered somewhere tender and raw in her heart.

"For the most part," she said honestly.

"Enough," William ventured, hope flickering in his eyes, "to allow me to hug you?"

The room seemed to hold its breath. Hope resisted the urge to roll her eyes, but only barely. Instead, she sighed and gave a small nod. William didn't hesitate. He wrapped her in a warm, heartfelt, brotherly embrace. When he stepped back, she noticed the relief and affection etched across his face.

"That doesn't mean I've forgotten about it, Reverend Shaw," she warned lightly.

"It's William now," he corrected gently, reminding her that tomorrow she would become his sister-in-law. "And I understand more than you know. None of us took any of this lightly. If your mother had lived, you would have traveled with her, and she would have been the one to tell you the truth, step by step. But with her gone… everything became far more complicated than any of us were prepared for."

Hope nodded slowly, letting his words settle.

"I suppose I understand that much. But what I don't understand is why you and Logan pretended to be the same person."

William chuckled softly. "That idea came from your uncle. We needed to avoid suspicion at all costs. If I had accompanied you, Winston would have noticed my absence immediately and accused me of kidnapping you. Logan and I look similar enough, our voices are nearly identical, and, well," he shrugged, "Logan was willing to grow the beard."

Logan stepped forward, sliding his hand into Hope's.

"And some of that trouble was your doing too," he teased. "You were so determined to chase Whitmer yourself that we had to keep adjusting our plans on the fly."

Hope widened her eyes at him, but he only grinned, utterly unrepentant.

"And," Logan added, turning to his brother with a smirk, "that's why I kissed her at the hotel in Elko when Sheriff Craig walked in. He'd seen you in San Francisco. If he'd recognized me as you, everything would've unraveled."

William's brows shot up. "You kissed Hope while you were still pretending to be me?"

Logan puffed up proudly. "I did. Only way to distract the sheriff long enough to get him out of the room. And it worked, but it set her off like a firecracker."

Hope's cheeks flamed. She lowered her gaze, feeling Logan's arm slide securely around her waist. William laughed.

"I cannot fault her one bit. That must have felt outrageously inappropriate."

"Oh, it did," Hope said dryly. "And I told Logan so, with those exact words."

The room erupted in warm, affectionate laughter, the kind that made Hope feel like she truly belonged here, deeply, genuinely. Logan kissed her temple, unable to hide his pride and adoration.

From there, he introduced her to his sisters, their husbands, and their children. They welcomed her with excited chatter, bright eyes, and open arms. Hope found herself instantly drawn in by their warmth and teasing familiarity. Within minutes, she felt less like a guest and more like someone the family had always been waiting to claim. Tomorrow, they would become her family officially.

But tonight, they made sure she knew she already was.

They were just about to take their seats at the long dinner table when a maid entered quietly, stepped close to Marjorie Shaw, and whispered something in her ear. Marjorie's eyes brightened at once. She nodded, and the maid slipped out again. Then Marjorie turned toward her son with a knowing smile.

Logan immediately reached for Hope's hand, threading his fingers through hers. The tender, excited squeeze he gave her made her look up at him in surprise.

"We have a surprise for you," he announced, his grin stretching boyishly wide. Before Hope could ask what he meant, the patter of small, rapid footsteps thundered down the hallway. A heartbeat later, a little boy burst into the room like a joyful whirlwind.

"Sonny!" Hope gasped, tears filling her eyes instantly. She dropped to her knees just in time to catch him as he flung himself into her arms. She held him tight, burying her face in his hair, overwhelmed with joy.

Behind him came the rest of the Middleton family, Abigail, Brother Jacob, Esther, and Elizabeth, all smiling warmly.

"Abigail... Brother Jacob... Esther... Elizabeth... what are you doing here?" Hope exclaimed, rising to her feet with Sonny still clinging to her neck. They gathered around her in an embrace so full of affection it nearly knocked the air from her lungs. Abigail held her the longest, rocking her gently, as though Hope were a daughter returned home at last.

"Logan invited us to your wedding," Abigail explained once she finally released her. "Sam and my parents are watching the little ones. We only planned to bring Lizzie and Esther, but once Sonny overheard where we were going, well, there was no keeping him behind." Her smile softened. "He missed you terribly."

Hope blushed as she wiped at her eyes.

"Did you... did you know who Logan really was? Did he tell you the truth?"

Abigail shook her head. "Not until his letter arrived. But honestly?" She tilted her head, giving Hope a knowing look. "It didn't surprise me. The way he watched you when he thought no one noticed, I knew he cared deeply. And I suspected you felt something too, though I wasn't entirely sure."

Hope laughed softly, embarrassment and nostalgia mingling in her chest.

"At the time, I didn't know what to feel. I was drawn to him but believing he was his brother... everything in me said it was wrong."

Elizabeth stepped forward, eyes bright with curiosity.

"How did you react when you learned the truth, Hope?"

Hope winced playfully. "I was furious. And hurt. Finding out he, and everyone else, had lied to me wasn't easy."

Logan slipped an arm firmly around her waist, drawing her close as he addressed the Middletons.

"She was ready to rip my head clean off," he said with a teasing grin. "This woman has a temper no sane man should ever provoke."

Hope let out a mortified groan, hiding her face against his shoulder as her cheeks ignited. Logan only chuckled and pressed a kiss to the top of her head. Esther clasped Hope's hand gently.

"But you forgave him," she said with a radiant smile. "That's what matters."

Abigail nodded, her eyes misting.

"And look at you both now. You're such a beautiful couple. It's clear how happy you make each other."

Hope lifted her gaze to Logan just then, his warm, steady eyes already fixed on her, and her heart fluttered. Tomorrow, she would become his wife. Tonight, she realized, she already belonged to him.

The big day had arrived. The back room of the church was strictly off-limits to every man involved in the wedding. Esther and Elizabeth were Hope's bridesmaids, while Lilly, steadfast, loyal Lilly, served proudly as her maid of honor. Brent stood as Logan's best man, with Sawyer and Logan's oldest nephew beside him as groomsmen.

Hope was surrounded by the women who had become her family: her grandmother, Aunt Shirley, Marjorie Shaw, and Abigail. Yet she was unusually quiet. Anyone else might have assumed it was the typical nervousness of a bride about to walk down the aisle, but Lilly knew better. Something deeper troubled her, and Lilly suspected exactly what it was.

Slipping out quietly, she returned only a minute later, her eyes confirming her suspicion. Once Hope was fully dressed, the other women filtered out of the room, leaving only Lilly beside the bride. She stepped forward and wrapped Hope in a warm, steadying hug.

"You look stunning, Hope," she whispered. "Logan is going to fall in love with you all over again."

Hope's gown fit as though it had been crafted from heaven itself, graceful, modest, perfectly suited to her figure. Abigail and Shirley had pinned her hair beautifully, two delicate curls framing her face, and the veil draped softly behind her completed the image of a bride ready to meet her future.

"Are you ready?" Lilly asked gently. Hope gave a small nod.

"I think so." But her feet stayed planted. "I mean... I'm not sure." Her voice trembled. Her hands trembled. The color drained from her face, and her breath began to come too fast.

"Hope?" Lilly's brow furrowed with worry. "What's wrong?"

"Nothing. I'm fine," Hope insisted, but it was unconvincing.

"You're not fine," Lilly said softly. "Sit down before you faint."

Hope shook her head. "I can't. Everyone's waiting for us." She tried to draw in a slow breath, but it only came out as a gasp. Suddenly, tears spilled free and her knees buckled. Lilly barely caught her in time.

"Jeff!" Lilly cried. The door swung open immediately, and Hope's uncle and father rushed in. They reached her side at once. Jeff lifted Hope gently into his arms and laid her onto the nearby settee. Lilly hovered nearby, wide-eyed with worry.

Hope turned her face away, ashamed, but her father clasped her hand and drew her into his arms. She sobbed against his chest until the tears slowly eased. When she finally leaned back, both men remained close, flanking her protectively. Jeff slipped an arm around her shoulders.

"What's wrong, sweetheart?" he asked softly. "Are you having doubts about Logan?"

Hope shook her head at once. "No. Not at all." Fresh tears welled despite her effort to stop them. "I just... I miss Mama. It hit me all at once. I'm about to get married, and she isn't here. She should be here."

Jeff gently lifted her chin. "Hope... your mother is here. She's never left your side. She loved you fiercely, more than I've ever seen a mother love a child. You kept her going. And every time she looked at you, she saw the man she loved. You were her joy. Her strength. Her heart."

"Uncle Jeff..." Hope sniffed, offering him a watery smile. "You're going to make me cry again."

He kissed the top of her head. Charles brushed away her tears with fatherly tenderness.

"Jeff speaks the truth, my darling girl. Brian Baker wrote to me whenever he could. Even under Winston's watch, he found ways to tell me how deeply your mother adored you. You were her pride. Her treasure. Her world."

Lilly dabbed her own eyes with a handkerchief. Hope managed a trembling smile and hugged Jeff, then Charles, holding both tightly. When they straightened, Jeff spoke gently.

"Now... are you ready to get married?"

Hope opened her mouth, to answer or protest, she wasn't sure but froze. Lilly stepped closer, understanding instantly. Before she could speak, Charles extended his arm.

"Would you do us the honor," he asked softly, "of letting us walk you down the aisle?"

Hope stared at him, speechless, then turned to Jeff. He, too, offered his arm, smiling with such love that her eyes filled again.

"You mean... both of you?" she whispered. Both men nodded.

"I remember how torn you were," Jeff said softly, "when you wanted me to walk you down the aisle instead of your grandfather. And I suspected today might feel even harder. Lilly confirmed it."

Hope shot her maid of honor a tearful, grateful look. Lilly only shrugged with a gentle smile.

"I told Charles he should have the honor," Jeff continued, "because he's your father. But he insisted we do it together."

Overwhelmed, Hope hugged them again.

"Thank you," she whispered.

A knock sounded, and Sawyer peeked in, grinning broadly.

"Everyone's ready for the bride," he announced. "And you'd better come quick, your groom is five minutes away from barging in here to carry you to the altar himself."

Hope blushed a deep crimson. Lilly ushered the men out, adjusted Hope's veil one final time, then squeezed her hand.

"Ready?"

Hope nodded, her breath shaky but steadying. Knowing Logan was waiting eased her nerves more than anything else. Lilly stepped out first. Hope followed, taking her father's arm on one side and her uncle's on the other. The sanctuary fell silent as they entered.

Logan stood at the altar, devastatingly handsome. The moment his eyes found Hope, every muscle in his body softened. He never looked away, not until she stood beside him. She trembled, but Logan stepped closer, steadying her with a warm, reassuring presence.

William stood beside Reverend Matthews as an additional witness, smiling proudly at his brother and future sister-in-law. The ceremony passed in a beautiful, breathless haze. And when it was over, Logan wrapped his arms around her, dipped his head, and kissed his wife, firmly, fully, lovingly, while the entire church erupted in joyful applause.

As the time came for the young couple to depart, Logan effortlessly lifted his bride onto her horse before mounting his own. Hope blinked in confusion.

"Are we not taking the buggy?"

Logan only shook his head, a mischievous glint lighting his eyes. Without offering an explanation, he nudged his horse forward. Hope followed, still puzzled but trusting him completely.

They rode in comfortable silence for several miles beneath a sky streaked with the warm hues of early evening. When they reached the turnoff that led toward the Shaw ranch, Hope instinctively guided her horse in that direction. Logan, however, continued straight ahead. Hope slowed, staring at him in bewilderment.

"Wait, where are we going?"

He glanced over at her, the corner of his mouth lifting into a smile that sent butterflies whirling through her stomach.

"It's a surprise."

Before she could press him further, he leaned over and kissed her, quick, warm, intoxicating. Breathless and blushing, she barely registered him urging his horse into a light gallop again before she followed.

Not long after, they arrived at a small cabin nestled between towering pines. Logan swung down from his horse, helped Hope dismount, and led the animals toward the small barn out back.

Hope took a moment to look around. Twilight softened the edges of everything, turning the clearing into something out of a dream. The air was crisp, but the quiet, wrapped around her like a warm blanket. Somewhere nearby, she heard the gentle splashing of water. Drawn by the sound, she stepped closer and discovered a narrow creek winding behind the barn, fed by a small waterfall tumbling over smooth stones. The sound was soothing, alive, yet peaceful. Her heart swelled in her chest. Everything felt still. Intimate. Theirs.

She nearly jumped out of her skin when Logan suddenly appeared behind her, slipping his fingers through hers. His hands were warm, steady, grounding.

"I didn't mean to startle you," he murmured with a grin. "Come here." He drew her toward him, and Hope melted into his embrace even before his lips captured hers. The kiss was fierce and full of promises, everything she had dreamed of, everything she had imagined, when she pictured being his wife.

Then, without breaking eye contact, Logan swept her into his arms and carried her toward the cabin. Hope clung to him, her heart pounding for more reasons than one, her breath catching as the doorway came closer. Whatever surprise Logan had planned for her tonight... she was ready for it.

***

It was just as beautiful inside as it had been outside. Hope's breath caught the moment Logan carried her over the threshold. Warm lamplight glowed softly against the log walls, casting a golden hue across the cozy furnishings. A small stone fireplace crackled invitingly, and a quilted blanket, clearly handmade by someone in Logan's family, was draped neatly across the bed. Hope turned in his arms, her eyes wide with wonder.

"What is this place?"

Logan slowly lowered her to the floor, though his arms never left her. Instead, they slid securely around her waist, holding her close as if he had no intention of letting her go.

"This," he murmured, his voice deep and warm near her ear, "is my family's honeymoon cabin. Every newly married couple stays here when they first wed."

The heat of his breath against her skin sent a shiver dancing down her spine. Hope swallowed hard.

"I thought we would be staying at your father's ranch," she managed, glancing around as she tried to steady her wildly fluttering heart. The cabin was intimate, secluded... perfect for a pair of newlyweds in love. Logan gently turned her to face him fully, his hands sliding to the small, of her back. Their lips hovered a breath apart. Hope's lungs forgot how to work.

"So..." he began, one eyebrow lifting as his eyes filled with wicked amusement, "you'd rather stay with my family instead?"

Her cheeks flamed. "That's not what I meant."

"Oh?" he teased, leaning in just enough for his nose to brush hers. "Then what is it, Mrs. Shaw? You just don't want to be alone with me?"

Hope gasped, scandalized, yet her pulse leapt all the same.

"Logan Shaw," she protested breathlessly, "will you stop putting words in my mouth? What I meant was—"

She never finished. Logan closed the distance in an instant, his mouth claiming hers in a heated, hungry kiss that stole the rest of her breath and every coherent thought. One hand rose to cradle the back of her head, guiding her deeper into him, while the other splayed firmly against the small of her back, pulling her flush against his strong frame.

Hope's knees wobbled. She clung to him, heat rushing through every inch of her. As his lips moved over hers with growing intensity, Logan nudged the door closed behind them with a quiet thud, sealing them inside the warm glow of the cabin, alone together for the very first time as husband and wife. And Hope, heart racing and cheeks flushed, could think of nothing except how impossible it would be to ever pull herself away from his embrace.

Hope opened her eyes to darkness, the soft kind that lingered just before dawn. The cabin was quiet, warmed only by the faint embers still glowing in the fireplace. Beside her, Logan's arms were wrapped securely around her, his breath warm against the back of her shoulder. She exhaled a contented sigh. This sense of safety... she had never known anything like it.

The man beside her stirred, tightening his hold as though even in sleep he feared she might slip away. A moment later, he shifted, brushing a slow, sleepy kiss against her cheek.

"Are you okay, Hope?" he murmured, his voice rough with drowsiness. Hope smiled and turned in his arms until she faced him. She pressed a brief kiss on his lips, soft, warm, already familiar. Logan deepened it for a heartbeat before pulling back just enough to meet her gaze. Even in the dim light, his eyes held a sincerity that made her chest swell.

"I love you, Hope."

"I love you more," she whispered, snuggling into his chest. He kissed the top of her head, and she felt his smile against her hair. A quiet moment passed before Hope lifted her gaze again. "Did you notice how Sawyer and Byron looked at Esther and Elizabeth during the ceremony?" she asked, her voice full of teasing warmth. "I'm almost certain it won't be long before they start courting."

Logan's chest shook with a low laugh. "It'll certainly keep the Middletons traveling back and forth. Or..." He paused, mischief flickering in his tone. "It may just convince them to move closer."

Hope smiled. "Either way, we'll see them often."

Their conversation faded into the gentle hush of the cabin. Within moments, Logan's breathing evened out, steady and deep. He had fallen back asleep. Hope lifted her head slightly, studying his face with quiet wonder. His strong jaw softened by sleep. His dark lashes resting against his cheeks. The faint shadow of stubble that always made her fingers itch to trace it. Just looking at him set her heart racing. She knew, deep down, certain as the sunrise, that she had finally come home.

Wealth had surrounded her growing up, but love had been scarce, save for her mother's unwavering devotion. For a fleeting moment, she allowed herself to imagine what her life might have been if not for her mother's strength... or if she had never met Logan... or if she hadn't found her relatives, her true family.

Gratitude washed over her so fiercely she had to close her eyes. The Middletons came to mind first, kind, gentle, steadfast. They had taken her in when she was lost and terrified, cared for her as if she had belonged to them forever. They had been God's mercy in human form, guiding her toward safety, friendship, and eventually, love. They were the family she hadn't known she needed.

Her thoughts darkened as Winston's shadow crept back into her memory. If he had succeeded in forcing her to marry

Gregory... Hope swallowed hard. She would have become a prisoner, just as her mother had been. Miserable. Unprotected. Alone. The thought chilled her blood.

Her mother had intended to escape. She had tried, more than once, perhaps, and failed. Hope imagined the heartbreak of the moment when Winston tore her mother away from Charles, from the man she truly loved. And all because of greed. Because of power.

Would he have left her mother alone if she hadn't been expecting a child? Would he have allowed her and Charles to remain together if there had been no heir to claim? Had Gregory always been cruel, or had Winston twisted him into what he became?

There were so many questions, painful, tangled questions, and she knew she would never receive the answers. And she didn't want them anymore. Winston and Gregory were imprisoned, and she would never set eyes on either man again.

A shudder passed through her, but she forced her thoughts away from the past and back to the man sleeping peacefully beside her. Warmth spread through her chest. Logan. Her husband. Her partner. Her safe place.

She would never love anyone the way she loved him. He was everything Winston had never been, protective rather than possessive, strong without cruelty, gentle without weakness. Logan never demanded her obedience, only her honesty. Her heart. Her laughter. Herself. He respected her fiercely, cherished her deeply, loved her openly.

Hope rested her palm lightly over his heart and closed her eyes as a line from Charles Dickens rose softly in her mind: *"Think now and then that there is a man who would give his life to keep a life you love beside you."* Her heart fluttered. Logan was that man. And nothing, no past, no darkness, could ever change that.

She nestled closer, letting his heartbeat lull her as the first faint streaks of dawn whispered against the horizon. She was safe. She was loved. She was home.

**The End**

# Epilogue

"Where is Hope?" Marjorie Shaw turned in a slow circle, scanning the crowded reception hall with a mother's anxious precision. When she failed to spot her newest daughter-in-law, a small frown creased her brow. Logan stepped beside her and gently slipped an arm around her shoulders.

"She'll be back shortly," he assured her. "She finally agreed to see Dr. Jensen, and he said he could see her once the ceremony was over."

Jeff and Parker Stewart approached at once, both wearing matching expressions of concern. Having already lost too many years with their niece, any hint that something might be wrong immediately put them on edge.

"What's wrong with her?" Jeff asked quietly. "Is she sick?"

Logan exhaled slowly, rubbing the back of his neck.

"She hasn't been feeling well these past few weeks. Upset stomach, lightheadedness... and she hasn't been eating much either. I've been trying to convince her to see the doctor for days. She finally agreed, but it took some persuading."

Marjorie's expression softened with worry as she moved toward Abigail, Hope's grandmother, and Shirley Stewart, who stood chatting nearby. Before she could say a word, music drifted through the hall, and the newlyweds, Esther and Sawyer on one side, Elizabeth and Byron on the other, stepped onto the dance floor for their first dances as husbands and wives. As the crowd shifted to watch them, the back doors opened. Hope entered.

She paused for half a heartbeat, scanning the room, and the soft lanternlight seemed to catch her from every angle.

"She's glowing," Abigail whispered, a knowing smile tugging at her lips. The other women followed her gaze. Hope did look different, radiant, breathless, as though something wonderful were lighting her from within. Marjorie instinctively took a step forward, ready to claim her daughter-in-law and fuss over her, but Abigail gently lifted a hand.

"Wait," she murmured. "Look, she's walking toward Logan. Let her tell him first."

They turned just in time to see Hope weave her way across the dance floor, slipping between onlookers and swaying couples as if drawn by an invisible thread. When Logan spotted her, he broke away from his conversation and met her halfway. A moment later, Hope flew into his arms, smiling brightly, eyes shining, her relief and excitement impossible to miss.

Marjorie, Abigail, Shirley, and Hope's grandmother exchanged grins that were equal parts joy, and *I think we all know what this means.*

---

Logan caught Hope as she launched herself into his arms, her embrace fierce and trembling with excitement. He steadied her, brushing a thumb along her cheek before tilting her chin up. The smile she gave him, soft, luminous, overflowing with something she was barely containing, made his breath hitch.

"What did Dr. Jensen say?" he asked gently. "Is everything okay?"

Hope heard the worry beneath his calm tone, but her smile only widened. Delight shimmered in her eyes, and for a moment she looked as though she might tease him by drawing out the suspense. Instead, she released one shaky, joyous breath and blurted, "Everything is perfectly fine... we're going to have a baby."

For three full seconds, Logan simply stared at her, blinking, lips parted, as though his mind had completely short-circuited. Then the meaning struck him like sunlight bursting through heavy cloud cover. His entire face lit up, raw emotion blazing through his expression.

"Hope," he whispered, before pulling her close, his hands cradling her face. "Is Dr. Jensen sure? It isn't something else?"

Hope laughed softly and nodded. "Yes. He's sure. You're going to be a father, in just a few months."

Whatever restraint Logan possessed vanished. He kissed her hard, full of wonder, then swept her off her feet and spun her in a joyful circle. Hope let out an astonished squeak, laughing breathlessly when he finally set her down.

Charles and Robert Shaw hurried over, alarm flickering across their faces.

"Is everything all right?" Charles asked, stepping closer. Before Hope could respond, Logan grabbed her hand, his chest rising and falling with exhilaration. He looked from his father to hers, practically vibrating with emotion.

"We're going to have a baby!" he proclaimed, loudly enough that half the room turned. Hope froze. Her face flamed scarlet.

"Logan!" she hissed, clapping a mortified hand over his mouth. "You didn't need to shout it."

But the damage was already done. The music faltered. Conversations halted. People turned and then rushed toward them. Laughter bubbled through the hall, joyful and warm, and Logan merely beamed down at her from behind her hand, utterly unrepentant.

Charles and Robert broke into grins of their own, both men pulling them into hearty embraces, congratulations spilling freely. Sawyer, Byron, Esther, and Elizabeth abandoned the dance floor to hurry over as well. Hope wanted the floor to swallow her whole.

"This isn't our special day," she whispered urgently to her husband, who only raised a teasing eyebrow. Esther looped her arm through Hope's and pulled her into a gentle hug.

"Oh hush," she said with a grin. "There's room for more than one celebration tonight."

Elizabeth nodded enthusiastically. "And we couldn't be happier for you."

Relief washed through Hope as she realized there wasn't a single frown among them, only joy, laughter, and an outpouring of love. She and Logan were hugged, kissed, congratulated, and passed from relative to friend to marshal to ranch hand.

By the time Hope finally caught her breath, Logan squeezed her hand and leaned down to whisper in her ear, "I'd shout it across Wyoming if I could."

Her blush returned, but this time, she didn't try to hide it.

It took some time before Hope finally managed to slip away unnoticed. The joyful chaos of congratulations, hugs, kisses, and excited chatter had warmed her heart, but she needed a moment of quiet, to let reality settle inside her, to breathe, to feel. She wandered down the familiar path toward the small wooden bridge that arched across the river beside the church.

The air was crisp, touched with the cooling breath of evening, and the last rays of the sun dipped low, turning the water to shimmering gold. Hope leaned on the railing, breathing in the peace around her as her heart brimmed so full it felt as though it might overflow. She rested both hands on the smooth wood and let the breeze cool her flushed cheeks.

Then, unexpectedly, something fluttered deep within her belly, a whisper of movement so faint she almost wondered if she had imagined it. Hope froze, eyes widening, before a radiant smile slowly spread across her face. Tears welled as she pressed a trembling hand to the place where she'd felt the delicate nudge.

"You will be so loved, little one," she whispered, her voice thick with emotion. "More than you can possibly imagine." Her words flowed like a prayer. "You won't just have a mama who adores you. You'll have a father who will lay down his life for you. Grandparents who will spoil you rotten. Great-grandparents who will treasure you. Aunts and uncles who will protect you. Friends who will love you like their own." Her breath trembled, and another tear slipped down her cheek.

"I didn't have everything a child should growing up... but God gave me a mother whose love made up for every broken thing. And when He took her home..." Hope swallowed hard. "...He filled my life with new people, good people, who became my family. You, my sweet baby, are already blessed beyond measure. God loves you. And so do all of us."

Warmth enveloped her as two strong arms slid around her waist from behind. Hope leaned back instinctively, tears still glistening as she tilted her head up. Logan stood there, the sunset catching the edges of his dark hair, his expression tender enough to steal her breath.

"I've been looking everywhere for you," he murmured, brushing a tear from her cheek with his thumb. "But now I understand why you needed a moment." He pressed a gentle kiss to the side of her head before resting his hands over hers, his palms warm against her stomach.

"Our baby," he whispered, awe filling his voice. "Hope, our baby will never endure the pain you went through. I'll move heaven and earth before I allow it." He drew her closer, his breath stirring her hair. "The man who pretended to be your father never deserved you or your mother. But this child, our child, will grow up surrounded by love from their very first breath."

Hope turned fully in his arms, cupping his face as more tears spilled, this time from gratitude rather than grief. Logan kissed them away, slowly, reverently, before his lips found hers in a kiss so gentle, so full of unwavering devotion, that her heart melted entirely.

She clung to him, feeling his strength, his promise, his love surrounding her like a shelter. In that moment, Hope knew with absolute certainty that she had been given a gift greater than anything she had ever dared to dream, a husband who loved her fiercely, a life built on faith and healing, and now... a child who would grow up safe in the arms of a family who cherished them.

Hope pressed her forehead to Logan's and whispered, "I don't know how I deserve you... but I thank God every day that He brought you into my life."

Logan's answering smile was soft and sure. "And I thank Him for bringing you into mine."

Did you love *Chasing the Killer*? Then you should read *Flames of the Fire*[1] by Rebecca Lange!

[2]

**She was a fierce spitfire and would protect her family with her life.**

Her heart raced and she kept staring at the burning building before her. Pure Panic caused her heart to beat faster and Joy ran closer, yelling her sister's name. She heard a toddler crying somewhere and after what seemed like forever, her sister's voice. Joy's heart sank. Alice was still in the house. Where was her sister's husband? Why had the house caught fire? One look was

---

1. https://books2read.com/u/b6Jgzy

2. https://books2read.com/u/b6Jgzy

enough. It wouldn't take long before the entire building collapsed.

# About the Author

**Rebecca Lange** is a devoted romantic at heart. Though she has explored a variety of genres throughout her writing journey, her deepest passion lies in historical fiction—particularly stories set in the 1800s American West and the Regency era.

A passionate advocate, Rebecca uses her stories to raise awareness of abuse, human trafficking, and the devastating impact of drug and alcohol addiction. These themes are not woven in for suspense alone, but as a reminder that such struggles are tragically real—and that victims are never to blame.

She is also a firm believer in women's rights, inspired by the courageous women of the 1800s who fought to prove they were not the property of their husbands but their partners and equals. Rebecca upholds the conviction that violence has no place in relationships or marriage.

Originally from Germany, she was born and raised there before moving abroad in 2002 to serve a mission for her church in Scotland. A member of The Church of Jesus Christ of Latter-day Saints, she now lives in Utah with her husband, their two sons (ages 18 and 20), and two lively Yorkie puppies.

Her writing motto is: *Never Smut, Always Sizzling Kisses, Consistently Closed Door.* Rebecca delights in weaving passion and tenderness into her stories, offering what she calls "sweet and diet spice" romance. Diet spice—what is that, you ask? It's the thrill of longing gazes, passionate kisses, and close embraces that build anticipation without ever crossing into explicit territory. For her, the most powerful love stories are those that remain tasteful and teasing, proving that romance can be both heart-stirring and wholesome.

Read more at https://authorrebeccalange.wixsite.com/bookstolove.